REVELATION

MAKAH ISLAND MYSTERIES
BOOK ONE

BY

AMY DRAYER

Revelation: Makah Island Mysteries Book One
Copyright © 2020 Amy Drayer
www.MakahIslandMysteries.com

ISBN 978-1-7345865-0-3

Everything, always,
for Erin

THE MAJOR PLAYERS

Joanna Ford
Investigative Journalist
Laura Tanaka
Retired Investigative Journalist
Vi Mitchell
Publisher, Makah Quartermaster
Frank Tanaka
Owner, Tanaka Antiques
Brittany Roebuck
Student, Makah High School
Randy Fuller
Janitor, Kibo Outerwear
Elijah Hill
Captain, King County Sheriff's Office
Brian Stewart
Entrepreneur
Jered Brasier
Wannabe
Tyler Sealth
Artist
Luke Sorensen
Artist
Ashley Sorensen
Student, Makah High School
Beth Berge
Managing Editor, Seattle P.I.
Valerie Larson
Veterinarian
Tolliver Larson
Student, Makah High School
Brenda Locke
Captain, King County Sheriff's Office

THE ORDER OF THINGS

MAKAH ISLAND

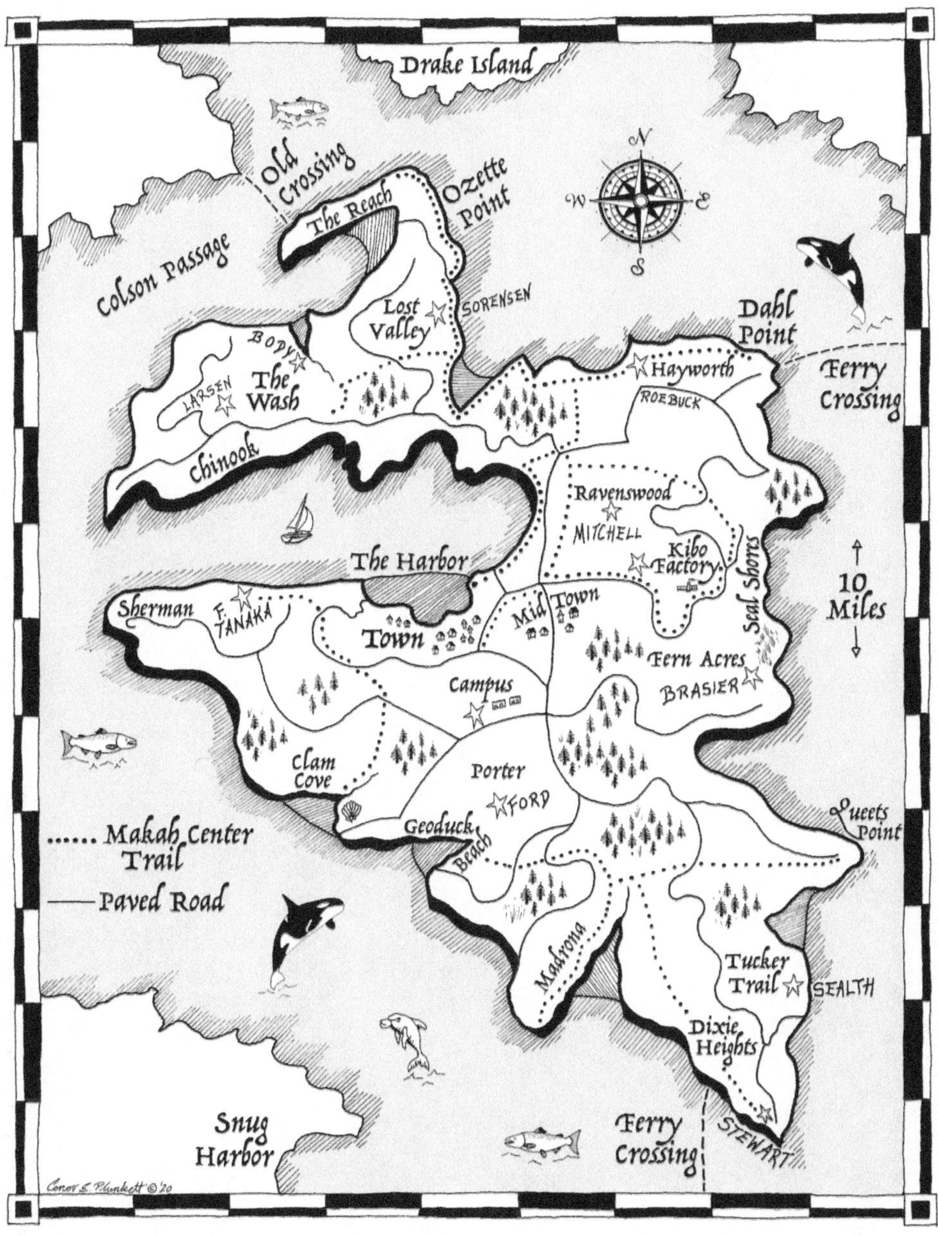

PROLOGUE: VI MITCHELL OPINES

It's hard to tell when something breaks. Not hard to tell when it's broken, of course, but when it breaks. The whole damn universe tends to entropy and so following the fault line back is quite a trick. Take my grandmother, for example, and her young friend Angus Miller.

She talked about him in a certain way. In her mind he was a tall, blustery boy. Just her own tender age of twelve when he stopped aging. Angus had gone with bucket and shovel one day out near the Hook to harvest clams. A fine day for a fine boy looking to take in the air and gentle sun, he had skipped school. As summer came on, children skipping and wandering the world was not an uncommon nor unwelcome occurrence on Makah Island.

His absence that day had, however, been noticed by my grandmother. Twenty children and one room could not conceal much when it came time to call attendance. So, as they had on occasion held hands, and even kissed once, and knowing Angus's predilection for early morning outings wherein he would fill his belly and then nap away the mild afternoons, she resolved herself to skip after lunch and rendezvous on their favored beach.

There, high up on the sandy shore, under the bright sun glittering off the sparkling cobalt Sound, just shy of tender blackberry shoots and fragrant blossoms, she had certainly found blond Angus in quiet repose. She found him silent, covered in tacky vomit, eyes frozen, glassy, and bloodshot, hands clawed in rictus and clutching at nothing. Angus had not known better. Or, had disregarded the warnings of old people, the way younger ones do. Disregarded that the crimson tide brings toxin and death, long after the stain of it disappears.

Right here in this tale you can come to the right conclusion that this was the moment Angus broke. His family too. His father started drinking and didn't stop and the wet-brained bastard went and shot himself and his grieving wife within the year.

The boy ate the bad clams and the little toxic microbes ate his gray matter and that's that. But where did the bad clams come from? Do you see the trouble in that question? Because the red tide that year came from somewhere. As it turns out, the rendering plant down south, overtown in Commencement Bay, hadn't been minding what it should've been minding.

The waters of our Western passage run swift and every time the tide went out the mighty Pacific sucked the shit and rot of the runoff from the slaughterhouse through our little Hook. When the sun shyly appeared in May, a deep scarlet bloom of deadly algae found a home tucked into the loving shores of Makah Island, and the red death was duly taken in by our innocent bivalves.

Now you think you've got the answer, don't you? It was the bosses at the rendering plant, the boys responsible for braining the cattle and pigs and some-times horses and gutting and bleeding them into what used to be sacred waters that killed our favorite son. It was at that. It was one boss in particular. A man named Len Olsen who had broad shoulders. His boy had also died, the year before. Blood cancer was all the words they had for it then. Broad as they were, Len's shoulders had stooped and kept his eyes on the ground, not minding what he ought to be.

Have we finally come to it, then? The moment when Angus broke, the rea-son? But see, don't you want to know now why Len's boy had broken? Was it God that gave him the leukemia? Maybe. Perhaps, though, it was the fact that Len and his wife and his pride and joy lived downwind of the arsenic smelter. Seems the likelier truth to me. But it can't be that we're all to blame for Angus's death.

So, it takes some work to get to how a thing, a person – or even a place, ends up broken. Most people aren't all that interested in work. But I am. That's all I'm interested in right now because I'm running out of time to understand how Makah broke, and to figure my way out of what I've done.

I've been editor of the Makah *Quartermaster* for almost two decades, so it won't be hard to tell a story, even this one. I'll get the worst of it out of the way first. For Makah Island, the worst would be when I hired Joanna Ford because it was the right thing to do, and she and Brian Stewart got into a twister over what he did to Brittany Roebuck; when I lost our Randy and we all lost what made this place home.

WHAT HAPPENED TO RANDY

The battered aluminum skiff cut the flat black water of Puget Sound. Mist clung to the surface of the murky passage, trapped at either side by the jutting outline of evergreen trees against a low sky. The thrum of the outboard was lonely, but not out of place. Any Islander up early enough to miss the stars but catch the sunrise would find it as ubiquitous as a barking dog, a running chainsaw, or a jet passing overhead. Small boats skimming the shores of Makah Island were as familiar to the ear as damp loam and low tide were to the nose.

Distant orange and white lights from Tacoma and Seattle covered the matte underside of the clouds with only enough glow for Randy Fuller to guess at his destination. It was still too early even for the gulls, heron, and buffleheads to be hunting breakfast in the shallows and the tide pools. He coughed and hud-dled against the chill. His passenger took no notice. He twisted the throttle and slowed the vessel to a crawl as he scanned for the right place to put in, scowled at the white shell beach of the hooked inlet before him. The tide was high and that was simply luck, the first he'd had this morning. If it were out, he would have stuck on the sandbar hidden a hundred feet from shore. His passenger would not notice that, either.

He cut the motor and its dull hum was replaced by the slap of wake along the shoreline. He beached where the rocky sand met a thick stand of crimson madrona trees. Sharp smoke from a hardwood fire caught his nose. The Island was waking. He climbed over the bow, swearing, slipping, and struggling in the deep gravel as he wrestled the boat further ashore, breaking the still with his unwelcome sounds, huffing great freezing clouds into the air. He heaved again. This would be slow, awkward work; the tide was in but had already turned. It wouldn't do at all if it took the skiff along with it before he finished his hike through the dense thicket of blackberry and salal.

He stood over the boat and stared at the body wrapped in black plastic contractor bags, duct-taped together; ran a hand back and forth at the base of his neck, then strapped the hiking headlamp over his knit beanie. With another huff he lifted the burden over his shoulder. Under his breath he muttered, "Sorry Brittany," then began the slow climb into the ravine.

By the time he returned dawn was breaking. With the heat of day, the wind and current would pick up and the skiff couldn't handle that. It wasn't made for this kind of work. Randy ripped hard on the starter and tore off into the weak morning light. The bow pounded up and down on the dark surface of the water. The lifting and the landing drummed away at his hurt. The hum of the motor cleared away all errant thoughts. In the clarity only one thing mattered, what he had just done. He'd disobeyed a direct order from Brian Stewart because he couldn't stand the thought of Brittney Roebuck just disappearing into the Sound, turning into bloated, rotten food for scavengers. But why he'd done it didn't matter. There wouldn't be any living with it.

As he cleared the southern point of Makah, Randy's gaze stayed fixed on the Tacoma Narrows bridge. It hadn't been built the right way. The massive concrete piers had solid footing, all the way down into bedrock. It was what was *above* that wasn't right. Because of those engineering flaws, the bridge deck had vibrated so much once that it finally tore itself apart. But it had been fixed. Randy was the opposite. It was the below inside him that had crumbled — and you can't fix that.

Ahead of him the first ferry of the morning glided toward the dock at the south end. It blasted its horn. The sound rang in Randy's chest. He was called home. He twisted the throttle half-way, and then, finally, wide open. The little vessel was sent airborne with every ripple on the surface of the passage. The Evinrude strained at its mounts. He held his thick black-rimmed glasses covered in spray to his face. His jaw clacked at every impact as he hurtled through the sweet, chill, morning air toward absolution. The clouds above parted, the red sun cleared the jagged horizon. Crimson fingers of light poured into the world through the silhouettes of black trees and down over the water.

When the bow of the skiff collided with the broadside of the ferry, Randy Fuller caught air. He slammed head-first into the MV Olympic, leaving not even a dent; leaving nothing behind but a stain and a smear as his fractured mind, broken spirit, and useless body sank to the silent fathoms below.

IT HITS THE FAN

The green can of Western Family creamed corn flew past Joanna Ford's head. It crashed through a display rack behind her, smashing a dozen glass canning jars. Shoppers from all four checkout lanes at the front of Olsen's grocery, even those who had not already been surreptitiously observing her confrontation with the rabid woman, turned to stare.

"Holy shit." A tall man wearing a tie-die bandanna over volumes of long, wavy gray hair decided he had something to say, and laughed out loud.

"You're not helping." Joanna glared at him. He stopped laughing. She turned her attention back to the enraged Happy McElroy.

The woman waved a rolled-up copy of this week's *Quartermaster*, her ruddy complexion flushed and volume pegged at eleven as she continued to rant. "King County's going to shut Ruth down now. She only hired that girl, the one who talked to you, because she felt bad for her – she had a couple kids who needed a roof. Now she's out of a job, my sister's out of her business and her house, and folks have to pay twenty-bucks to go overtown and use a laundromat. You think people without a washer got that kinda extra, bitch?"

"Happy, listen – your sister's place is a toxic mess," Joanna replied. "What about the environmental damage she caused? What happens to her now isn't my fault." She crossed her arms, almost shrugged. She simply reported the sins – it wasn't up to her to suffer the consequences.

Happy took a step forward, grabbed another can from the shelf. "It's damn well your fault, and you're going to pay for that – "

Joanna gasped as a bottle of olive oil hurtled over her shoulder, this a shot from behind. Poorly thrown, it missed Happy and crashed into an endcap displaying the latest Makah Island-themed swag. It cracked against the shelf, splattering a dozen or so t-shirts and hoodies with Italy's finest extra virgin. She closed her eyes. Now, she was actually upset. She glared at Happy; the woman's shoulder's slumped as guilt bled onto her face.

Immediate tension diffused, Joanna turned to this new culprit, her wife, who stood next to their shopping cart with her shoulders back and frustrated tears burgeoning.

"Sorry, Jo," she whispered.

"Laura, babe. It's going to be okay." The situation had gone from tenuous to terrible. It would get worse if she couldn't get this settled. Frustration would yield quickly to anger. Laura squirmed, her face strained and tight as she struggled with emotions her frontal lobe was no longer equipped to deal with. She pointed at Jo's assailant; a lonely finger suspended in midair substituting for words she didn't have. Jo took her gently by the shoulders, looked her right in her dark, watery eyes. "Everything's fine, alright. She didn't mean to hurt me."

Happy piped up – "I definitely meant –"

She was abruptly silenced. Whipping around from the next aisle over, Vi Mitchell flowed to a stop directly in front of Happy. "Honey, what you're meant to do is start minding your own business, and yesterday. Shut your mouth now, and let's all move along with our day."

"This is just as much your fault as hers, Vi," the other woman whined. "How could you let her write this – and put it in your paper?"

Happy was not placated, nor apparently intimidated, by the appearance of Jo's boss, *The Quartermaster's* publisher. Or the fact that Vi's cart contained nothing but cat food – and her prized Siamese, Paula, in the fur.

"How is this my fault?" Vi asked. "Jo's right. Ruth's been playing fast and loose and cheap. Only thing she's dry-cleaning these days are whatever little micro-boogers live in the ground near that cracked tank under her shop –" Vi continued, yowling Paula-cat staring up at her with loving, languid eyes; but Jo stopped paying attention.

Because she, Laura, Happy, and Vi were no longer the most interesting thing happening in Olsen's grocery store. The olive oil that had ruined hundreds of dollars of tourist-bait t-shirts hadn't stopped its reign of chaos there. A pool of golden liquid had spread over the beige floor tiles and across the aisle. Kenny Olsen, owner and manager, who had presumably rushed to address the commotion, discovered that too late. He lay sprawled and covered in viscous fat.

He struggled to sit up, hands planted in the impromptu slip and slide. His white short-sleeved button down was soaked through the back. Oil shone on the remaining wisps of sand-colored hair, and an ominous line of red blood dribbled through the stubble under his nose. "Anyone want to tell me what happened here?" He grimaced and gestured to the ruined merchandise, the glass at Jo's feet.

"The Mason jars you can blame on her – " Jo cocked a thumb at Happy. "And the rest of it is my fault."

Several members of the peanut gallery cast glances toward Laura, but no one spoke up.

"Then both of you can leave your carts where they are and join me in the manager's office." Kenny surveyed the two middle-aged women who'd started a food fight in the middle of his store on a Monday afternoon. Then, he turned to Vi. "What do you have to do with this?"

"I'm just trying to keep a lid on, that's what." Vi offered him help up. Planted on dry ground and with ample leverage, she managed to get him standing. "And go easy on Jo, son. It wasn't exactly her fault."

Jo took her wife's hand. Laura held fast, her lips smashed together and white as she silently surveyed her would-be accusers.

Kenny huffed, dripping oil on the floor. He wiped the blood from his nose with the back of his hand. He seemed to be choosing between anger and laughter as he studied his slick, hairy arms. Finally, he grabbed a t-shirt from the shelf. Bright red, there was a cartoon decal across the front, a smiling green and white ferry boat with the caption, "You're on Island time now!"

He wiped his hands on the shirt. The crown of his head glistened in the fluorescent lights. He glowered at Jo, then Happy, thrust his chin toward the back of the store. "Now is a good time for me."

Happy set down the can of green beans she'd grabbed to reload and stalked down the aisle. The check stands beeped back to life. A teenage boy in a black apron appeared with a bucket and a mop and orange caution-cones. The shitty muzak hadn't stopped, but it was only now Jo noticed it again. She turned to Vi. "Thanks, I guess?"

"You're welcome, I guess." Vi sniffed and placed her fists at her hips. She shifted her weight to one side, squinted one eye. "You know this whole thing is your fault. Told you you'd catch hell over that article, didn't I?"

"You did. But you printed it anyway." Jo glared back at her boss.

"Yes. Because I can't tell you anything, Jo Ford. You're stubborn."

"I'm stubborn?"

Kenny cleared his throat.

Jo held up a finger toward him, then asked Vi, "Can you stay up here with Laura while I go deal with – all this?"

"Course. Want me to do your groceries too while you go face the consequences of your actions?" The older woman considered Jo's meager basket. There were several frozen meals and boxes of dinner ready to make, as well as a dozen cartons of yogurt. To Jo, easy to deal with for her picky eater. To residents of Makah, lazy, artificial, and environmentally irresponsible. As she surveyed, Paula swished back and forth in the upper rack of Vi's cart. Finally, she let out a demanding cry and hopped lithely into Jo's basket. She turned her slightly crossed blue eyes on Laura and complained until Laura put a hand on her head.

"I'd appreciate the help. Thank you." Jo grinned at Vi. She reached out to the cat and tried to join in the love fest, but Paula swiped at her and flicked her black tail. "Anyway. With Frank gone last week on that fishing trip, it's been a tough." No way Laura was going to make it much longer this afternoon without completely losing her shit, and their cupboards were bare. She turned her attention back to her wife. She hugged her before she started her apology. "I need to go and deal with – everything. Stay with Vi. I'm really sorry about all this. But you need to chill out, right?"

"Right." Laura took a shuddering post-cry breath.

"I'm sorry about this. But it's okay. And we need to work on that arm. Your aim was terrible." Jo smiled and forced calm on her wife, waiting for the good to take over again – pushed back everything and everyone around them with the force of her will until their world had space to balance out. Jo kissed her cheek.

She thanked Vi and headed to the manager's office to take her licks. She'd had more than one ass-tearing after publishing an investigative piece. Six years ago, in D.C., it had been a bullet screaming past her head. Creamed corn was a preferable alternative.

Jo started toward the back of the store. Her boot slipped on the oil-soaked copy of Monday morning's *Quartermaster* that Happy had dropped in the muck. The headlining article that detailed the multiple code violations levied against Ruth's Cleaners. Next to that, copy she'd thrown together covering law enforcement's lack of progress on a low-stakes string of thefts involving, of all things, heirloom copper pots.

She bent over to pick up the paper and clear littering from the litany of her sins this morning. She stood, and was startled by Vi, who had suddenly reappeared, waving her cell in her hand, flushed and bearing the look that every journalist – anyone who'd ever even thought about being a journalist – would recognize in an instant. There was a story breaking, and it was a big one.

Jo heard three different versions of what was happening at the south end ferry by the time she pulled out of the grocery store parking lot. All of them sounding like real news and each account more spectacular than the last.

Before heading out herself, Vi read her a text from known gossip and exag-gerator Connie Wilcox – screen awash in exclamation points, digitally shouting that the ferry had collided with a cargo ship and had sunk in the middle of the Puget Sound. Another Olsen's patron within earshot received an actual phone call from someone on the ferry boat, quarantined at the dock, which certainly contradicted the sinking account. Last, on their way out the door a random woman with eyes only for her phone almost knocked Laura down with an inadvertent shoulder-check.

The hefty shopper who looked like her last name had to be Eastern European fumbled out apologies to Laura, then realized who she'd clocked – at which point she started to make apologies to Jo. Her excuses included being completely absorbed by the fact that her sister in law was reporting that the Olympic was now on fire.

But lookout rumors, Jo thought to herself; she was on the case and headed straight for the truth. Pulitzer-winning investigative journalist for the Washing-ton Post blowing the doors off graft and corruption, to has-been, middle-aged, middle of nowhere rural reporter dog paddling through the small-town grapevine. Still, today's turn of events carried the hefty potential of real news. Probably not an investigation, but Jo had learned well that you can't have it all.

More than once on their way south she checked the King County Sheriff's Twitter feed and was disappointed by radio silence. Which meant @JoannaJFord had even more opportunity to become the turn-to source for every other local news outlet – if she could get down there in time. Jo leaned on the Volvo's accelerator, trying to suppress the hope that she was speeding her way toward relevance.

Squashing that hope was made easier by the fact that they were now stuck on the main road right at morning rush hour – also known as school drop-off time at the central campus. In perfect Makah form her late-model red Volvo station wagon was sandwiched between a rusted Kubota front loader and a first-generation Prius covered in glitter paint. It also had a bumper sticker plastered in the middle of the back window, "Makah Island – we're all here, because we're not all there."

There were no real alternate routes to the southern tip of the Island. Only plenty of long gravel driveways as they crawled along. Occasionally, greening mailbox posts were accompanied by lonely, leftover Halloween pumpkins. The chill air preserved them well but some were sagging. They idled now across from a particularly gruesome remnant. It had started with a broad, merry, mouthful of pointed, carved teeth. A month later most had caved in.

They cleared the flashing red four-way stop and finally picked up speed. As they made their way deeper inland, the dense forest hugged the road tightly at every turn. To Jo the trees seemed eager to take the real estate back, as though the cars were cutting through their dark green bodies and leaving scars behind yearned to heal. Sometimes it were as though the Island itself had closed up a passageway and the route she'd taken last week was gone. She often got turned around. Her father-in-law assured her that even Makah's long-term residents missed a fork occasionally, or found themselves headed down the wrong unstriped black-top if they weren't paying attention.

Lucky for Jo and her growing anxiety the road to the south-end dock at Queets Point was a straight shot. Laura made a decent co-pilot on her native soil, if you caught her at the right time of day. Mornings were most likely to be the right time of day.

"What do you think the real story is, babe?" Jo snuck a glance at her wife. Laura nodded her head rapidly and smiled. She had something to say, just needed to work up to the right words. Finally, "A good one."

"Can we cross our fingers for lots of fi reworks and no fatalities?"

Laura held up two fingers, index and middle barely touching.

Jo answered back with hers fully crossed raised in the air – snagged her wife's attempt at the gesture and they shook on it.

JO FORD TAKES THE CASE

The MV Olympic had not caught fire; nor had it sunk. Engines cut, she rolled gently against the dock at Queets Point, an innocent hunk of white and green steel wondering at its possible offense.

Fifty yards out from the ferry the channel between Makah and Tacoma was clogged with official boats from myriad agencies. Jo studied harder as she took in the scene top to bottom; black heads of divers bobbing like shiny seals next to a rescue vessel that popped bright red against the clouds, Coast Guard insignia on the side and a small crane tower at the stern. Shouts and naval horns punctu-ated gusts of wind. Shipping tankers to the east and west idled noisily off shore waiting for the well-used commercial passage to clear.

There were surprisingly few gawkers. She chalked it up to the nasty winter weather. Jo made her way through the small handful of eyewitnesses with noth-ing to say, mostly volunteer emergency personnel milling around who'd been called to the scene and had nothing to do. She squinted against flecks of rain drifting out of the sky. A gunmetal squall was moving down from the north. The impatient misery of all involved was about to get cold company.

Her phone buzzed – a text from Vi Mitchell, full of her signature charm. *"Cal My oR find. Dock. Val. Some BullShit story Rndy Fuller."*

As she scrolled another poorly typed text came in from Vi. *"Did U gat my teSt."*

"Yep. Will look for you. Thanks." She hit send and a new alert rolled down from the top of her screen.

"Are we still on for Monday?"

Jo turned quickly from Laura. Monday was just going to be lunch. Jo wouldn't see Beth Berge and feel the way she did right now. Wouldn't get short of breath and short of willpower. Long on anticipation and need. She closed her eyes and gave in to denial, typed and sent her answer.

"Yes."

She didn't wait for a response, shoved her phone in her pocket, scanned the handful of people on site. She didn't see the frizzy black and white head of her boss anywhere. But she did spot her original primary target at the yellow police line – Elijah Hill.

As though working to fulfill each stereotype possible of small towns, the consensus on Makah about the Sheriff from Seattle wasn't one of confidence or competence. On the plus side, he wasn't a red-faced hay-chomping bigot. Jo liked him just fine and found him good at his job; it didn't hurt their vibe that they shared a little main-lander status. She had a sneaking suspicion that a black guy law-enforcer on the lily-white libertarian Island added a layer to his outsider ranking. They'd hit it off nicely when she'd done a profile on him six months ago, a little get to know you she hoped might smooth over his relationship with Makah, and hers. So far so good.

"Good morning Elijah – what can you tell me?"

He nodded at her, then Laura. "Well, approximately one hour ago a small personal craft collided with the Olympic. Right now, it appears there was one person aboard. We're looking for the pilot. No injuries reported on the ferry. We're questioning folks, then letting them off-load."

"ID?"

"Not until we find the pilot. We've got divers out, but with the currents – better chance of finding the skiff than her captain." Hill glanced out at the churning Sound. Whitecaps were beginning to peak as the impending squall arrived. "Weather gets worse, we'll have to hold the investigation. Coast Guard's equipped to do this out on the Pacific – this far south in the Sound, not as much call for it."

"Any idea what the pilot was up to?"

"Now how would we know any kind of why when we don't even know who was onboard?" Hill looked down at her, wide brim of his hat shielding Jo a little from the rain as she looked up, his kind brown eyes shielding her from the worst of his obvious disdain for the question.

She chased a new angle, partially – mostly – true based on what she'd pieced together already. "Three people here have told me they've heard from passengers on the port side it was Randy Fuller. They said they'd recognize him anywhere, even at speed. Also said they couldn't imagine what he was doing."

Randy was local legend. He walked the two-lane main highway of Makah day in and day out. It was more like a constant, fluid, stomping swagger. He had a dark shaved head, typically dressed in an army-green coat and combat boots, wore seventies-style thick, black-rimmed sunglasses, and his black eyes were slightly crossed. On his walks, he often carried either a machete or a chainsaw. Occasionally he would shout and flip-off passing cars if they were too loud or too fast. Mostly he was simply about his own business. Most of all, he was unmistakable, even flying across the water.

"Come on Jo. You know I can't comment on what you heard second hand."

"Can you clear me to talk to the captain of the Olympic?"

"I can give you the PIO at Washington State Ferries. I'm sure she's got a statement ready."

"Come on, Elijah."

"This isn't the sinking of the Titanic, Ms. Ford. Take some pictures, get some statements. Keep it in the lines –"

"Captain Hill –" Deputy Brenda Locke had been hovering, finally stepped in and cut Hill off . "Can you talk to Frank Tanaka now?" She ducked her head at Jo, then at Laura standing quietly at her side. "Morning ladies."

"Your dad's here?" Jo looked at her wife, reflexively expecting an answer.

Laura fumbled at the pocket of her red parka. Jo breathed in and out steadily as the rain pattered down. Hill and Locke waited respectfully as she struggled to produce her phone. The screen was blank. No calls, no texts. No word from Frank on his part in all this.

Locke resumed her explanation. "No, Frank's not here. Had to get into the store. But I was with him this morning. Says his boat was stolen off the dock at the Hook, maybe five am? I was taking his report when I got the call about what was going on here." Brenda had to take off her own hat to get her head back far enough to address Hill.

Jo floated a theory to see how hard Hill would work to knock it down. "Any idea why Randy Fuller would steal a boat just to commit suicide?"

She got only a sideways glance from the sheriff . Vi Mitchell might think differently, but the man was good at his job. He did a double take on Jo, then addressed Locke.

"Tell Frank I'll call within the hour. Best I can do. Tag me out here. I want to talk to a few more folks on the boat."

"Yessir." Brenda ducked under the tape.

Hill nodded at Jo and walked off.

"Alright then." Jo took a minute to send a final tweet. She was getting fair traction and a satisfying number of retweets from the Seattle and Tacoma papers, television, and radio news. Finally, she turned to Laura, ready to pack her up and get out of the cold. The wind had whipped her wife's shining black hair out from under her hood and she kept swiping at her face.

"Hold on." Jo took a tie from her own wrist. She delicately gathered the fine, flying strands and tied them at the nape of Laura's scarred neck. The angry ropes were losing their red flare, softening to wider pink lines up the base of her skull and down over her collar bone.

"Thanks."

"Yep." Jo smiled. Laura's black eyes weren't as sharp anymore, but still crystal clear. She took a minute to hunt through her pockets and produce another tie, quickly taking care of her own dirty-blonde hair whipping all over the place. "Did you know your dad was going out this morning? I thought he had to get back to the store."

"Nope." Laura shook her head.

Jo crossed her arms over her navy peacoat. Up the shoreline the wind was rushing through the tops of the fi rs, sending the last of the dying leaves from the maples swirling to the ground. She was wet, cold, and miserable, but Laura didn't even seem to notice the damp. "Let's get out of here. I need hot coff ee, and I need it now."

Before they could make their escape, Jo spotted Vi Mitchell steaming down the hill toward the dock, trailed by Valerie Larsen – Vi's good friend and Makah's favorite veterinarian.

"There's no way on God's green earth it was Randy out there," Vi shouted the second she was within earshot. "To start with, that boy didn't *have* a boat."

"Good morning Jo – Laura." Good-natured Valerie took another tack.

"Morning Valerie." Jo almost went for a hug, then awkwardly reached out a hand. Valerie Larsen vexed Jo. The woman's lips twitched with persistent mirth, but she never brought you in on the joke, delightfully transparent and inscrutably private. Whether she was laughing at herself or at you, Jo never knew. She had an upsetting feeling it was the former.

Valerie shook Jo's hand, then went ahead and put her arms around Laura, gave her a once-over. "Looking good today. OT going well?"

Laura gave a thumbs-up.

"Good." Valerie smiled. "Wendy's the best. She had me right back in the saddle after I took that spill on Aggie last year."

Surviving a roadside IED in Pakistan and falling off the family horse didn't quite zero-out in Jo's mind, but Valerie was so genuine it was hard to do anything but smile at the woman.

Vi shoved her way into the middle of the little circle. "If we're done having tea, can I talk to Jo?"

"Vi, I know you're upset about Randy – but come on." Valerie shook her head, dark curls bouncing, then laid an arm over Laura's shoulder and strolled off.

Jo watched them for a second. Laura and her stilted gait, Valerie animated and pointing at anything that could possibly be of visual interest. Jo turned her attention back to Vi, who was also watching the two women – and now crying.

"Whoa. Hey – Vi." Jo looked back at Laura and Valerie, searching for an assist; the two were far out of range. "Is there something –"

"I'm being stupid, aren't I? About it being Randy. I've called him, texted him. Nothing."

"Well." Jo grimaced. "You were close?"

"Yes." Vi grabbed a tissue out of her coat pocket. "I was close to his mother, anyway. I did what I could for Randy, which wasn't much, but it was for Ilse –" she tapered off.

Don't be an asshole, Joey. The voice of Jo's father and the Ford family motto rang in her ears and left her with no alternatives. "Is there anything I can do?"

"Find out why he did this. Damn Sheriff won't do fuck-all. Just say Randy got shit faced and went off the rails." Vi started to walk off.

Jo followed. Vi was headed toward her truck. As they got closer, she saw Paula-cat sitting inside the rain-smattered dash and staring at her owner, who was probably right about the angle Hill would take on the case. Jo couldn't see many alternatives herself.

Randy's origin stories abounded. Based on his combat attire most assumed him to be a returned veteran who didn't get things back on track. But Jo had sussed out the truth of the matter. He'd spent most of his teen years in the ceiling rafters above the auxiliary buildings at the high school smoking or snorting what she'd heard locals refer to as 'hard core' drugs. He'd been to rehab more than once. If that hadn't stuck again, well, the dots connected themselves.

Twenty yards up the hill, just past where the dented guard rail suggesting a boundary between where the ferry waiting lane ended and the rugged cliff tumbled to the shore, she noticed a long-haired guy leaning against a tree and trying to look like he was casually lighting a cigarette. While he certainly looked like he wanted to seem nonchalant, the kid wasn't pulling it off ; his head scanned the scene far too frequently, and his greasy gaze lingered far too long on the faces of the various agency representatives milling on the dock.

He was focusing quite a bit of his inattention on Vi and Jo.

She put a hand on Vi's elbow as the other woman pulled open the creaking door of her Datsun. Paula stretched up from the driver's seat toward Vi. The cat glared at Jo with slivered crossed eyes, then yawned.

"You know him?" Jo sort of tilted her head at the guy.

"A-huh. Jered Brasier."

"He seems out of place," Jo said.

"Little shit is out of place anywhere decent humans are drawing breath." Vi got in and slammed her door. She waved Jo around to the passenger side and she ducked in.

"Can you think of any reason he's being out of place here, at this moment?"
"Sure can. Brian Stewart sent him." Vi looked in her side mirror, her eyeline angled up the hill. Finally, she stared at Jo.

It was a hard look to take in such close quarters. "What does Brian Stewart –" Jo started to ask her follow up but was drowned out as Vi cranked the engine until it turned.

"I can't leave –" Jo looked around, searched through the fogging windows for Laura and Valerie. She saw only the shape and color of Laura's red parka, sitting on a massive, bleached driftwood log. She looked content watching the ships troll back and forth in the choppy Sound. It was a thing she could tell about her wife that far away and this far into things, even now. "Are we going some-where?"

"Nope. Just warming it up. Will you help me?"

"Vi –"

"Listen for a minute. Let me tell you about Ilse – Randy's mom – and me. We were like sisters since we were kids. She was more than a sister." Vi shifted deeper into her seat, started to grin. "My fi rst day knowing her was watching our fathers raise that old white barn on their property fi fty years ago. She and I were sat in the middle of the straw on a sunny October afternoon. Everything was prickly and dry already because it was a damn hot summer. We'd picked sour early apples from one of her family's trees. Her apple had a wormhole in it. So, I let her have the rest of mine, because God put us here to give more than we take. She took a bite of mine, handed it back. Then she said we were best friends."

Vi paused. Paula kneaded her owner's soft lap as Vi absently stroked her golden fur. The rain pattered on the thin metal roof above them.

"Fifty years," Jo nudged her, quietly.

"Yeah," Vi muttered. Her body was there, but everything else about her was trapped in the past. "Maybe it's all those sins she ate for me that finally caught up with her. The cancer just burned out her guts. Like the broiler was stuck on inside. Knob broke off on high, just cooking her from the inside out.

Anyway, before she died, Ilse asked me to look out for Randy. Her husband was long gone, bad ticker, and she wasn't about to go anywhere on the earthly plane or otherwise without one last say-so that her boy was going to be fine. And I owed her, you know.

Vi chuckled. "Well, I told her she *still* owed me for that apple, and that was really piling on favors." And then Ilse said, 'That's a fair point. I tell you what. You go pick two apples off that tree,' Ilse had raised her hand, gestured off to the orchard, fingers skinny as a green switch, 'And we're even.'

So off I went. It was deep down in the fall. Air sharp and crisp as the good apples still left for last harvest. I found two nice ones. No worms. I brought em' back to the porch, intending to give one to Ilse and square us. And you know what, she was dead by the time I got back. Never really felt like we were settled up." Vi rapped her knuckles on the steering wheel. "That's how Ilse was for me. For a lot of people. How she was for Makah, and why her boy means something. So –"

Jo sighed. It came from down deep. "I'm sorry, Vi. I am. I know how that feels to lose –"

Both women jumped and yipped at a sharp rap on the glass at Vi's window. Valerie and Laura had apparently decided they'd had enough rocky beach and cold rain.

Jo pulled up the handle of her door, turned to get out - Vi clutched Jo's fore-arm, liver-spotted fingers desperate in their grasp. "I need to do something for Ilse. And Randy. I need you to help me. You don't quit on a story until it's done, Jo Ford – and this story isn't done. I'm telling you that hand to God."

Jo had had enough of doing things for other people in the past two years. Still, if there were more to Randy's story, it'd probably have some meat on the bones.

Valerie opened Vi's door, poked her head in the cab. "We're cold. And I'm late on my rounds. Jeez it's been a morning. Tolliver's cross-country partner didn't show, and he waited way too long for her, so I had to take him to school, then I heard the siren and called in on this. Thought they'd need us down here, but they don't, so I'm headed home." She put her brown eyes on Jo, and for the second time that morning Jo found herself disarmed. "You two have a good talk?"

"Yep." Jo climbed out of the truck. She considered Laura, smiling from un-der her hood. Behind her the Olympic pitched again and again against the splin-tering pilings of the dock. Later today, probably tomorrow, the boat would go back into service. Return to normal, all systems go. Some things never are made right though, even when you want them to be. Even when that's what you want more than anything in the world. Who was she to deny hope to anyone? She turned back to her boss, the woman who had been and was the friend – the only friend – Jo desperately needed right now. "I'll look into it, Vi."

"Well good. Thank you. Just don't be late with your other work."

"Right." Jo took Laura's arm and led her off , but not before she cast a final glance up the hill. The lanky stranger was gone, replaced by a shining gray mist circling the evergreens as it rolled up from the shore.

Jo sat for a second before heading out, defroster in the Volvo on full blast. Fingers of frost slowly disappeared only to reveal an increasingly fogged mari-time landscape beyond as the heart of the storm rolled over them. She considered this new assignment. Vi wasn't secretive about how she felt about police on Makah. She'd explained several times to Jo why they were completely unnec-essary. Her grudge had been turned up to ten last year when Hill had ticketed several locals for driving without headlights during the annual luminary festival. Every December Islanders celebrated winter solstice in the depths of Lost Val-ley by placing hundreds of luminaries along the road at dusk. Jo could see how headlights might kind of kill the effect. The older woman had taken the whole thing as a personal affront.

Today, as most days when a new story landed on her lap, Jo thought of her father. Big Jack Ford. His frequent opinings every night at the dinner table during the summer of '86, his take on the Iran-Contra aff air. It had been the scan-dal that had started it all for a curious young girl.

She'd spent summer days lying on her stomach on his office floor at the Naval Academy in Annapolis, chin in her hands, watching the hearings. Then over dinner she'd ask him about it, trying to make sense of what she'd seen. Dad would give her his version of the answers. Most included additional lectures about military geopolitics.

One night, he'd paused mid-monologue. Set down his steak knife, picked up what was left of his Cutty Sark, shaking the golden ice at Jo. "We'd be to the truth a damn site faster if you were the one asking those old boys questions. Took 'em too long to get to Ollie in the first place." He leaned in toward her over the vinyl tablecloth, his breath spicy, and she leaned in toward him. "Listen to me. It's never the lie, Joey. No sir. It's always the cover-up." Young and impres-sionable as the mashed potatoes on her plate, she still took that investigatory angle right to heart – hard targets to apparent suicides to – copper pots.

Before the boat drama this morning, Jo had been moonlighting investigating that odd string of petty thefts; Makah collectors and seniors were up in arms after three break-ins involving the theft of nothing but heirloom copper pots. Crime on the Island wasn't unheard of, but it wasn't common. Unlocked doors were *de rigueur*, a nod to the supremacy of the rule of law here. *The Quartermaster* blotter occasionally reported smash and grabs, neighbor disputes and vandalism. Most of the cases were solved by the Makah grapevine before the cops even got out of the gate with an investigation.

The copper was conspicuous, unresolved; an outlier. Turning the pots into cash wasn't going to make anyone a fortune. But money was tight on Makah. Even a few hundred bucks could go awfully far, depending on what you were buying. Most people looking for scores like that were buying drugs.

Circumstance and drugs led her right back to Randy Fuller. Following the original sin, chasing physical evidence, or the lack of it, hadn't yet paid off for the cops when it came to the copper. Maybe she could satisfy Vi and her own curiosity here. It was time for Jo to start the hunt for those ever-telling secondary misdeeds. And she knew right where to start. With her father-in-law.

THAT'S ODD

Jo made her own parking spot in the gravel at the side of the road in front of the old Victorian that housed Tanaka Antiques in Midtown, a cluster of four business at an intersection a mile down the main road from Uptown. Makah's five-thousand residents clung tightly to their little neighborhoods. She'd covered a history exhibit at the library a few months ago profiling the unlikely rise and falls of clusters of community in a place that already seemed very small.

She pushed through the creaking wood door, held it open for Laura. Frank answered the ring of the bell and came through from the back holding a cup of coff ee and wearing a smile that he aimed mostly toward his daughter.

He leaned across a scratched-up glass case to kiss Laura's cheek. It was packed full of dusty trinkets ranging from turquoise bolo ties to golden cigar clippers, tarnished silver hand mirrors and ivory combs and barrettes, to vintage comics in cellophane and pocketknives of any shape and size you could want. The case was a micro world of the musty relics adorning burgundy velvet walls and encroaching on Jo from all sides. Dented tin samovars, rayon kimonos to rusted wood working tools, the shop reminded her of the worst of anything on off er on the Portobello road in London. The dim place and the proprietor both smelled of dust, mice, and moss – more so in the winter.

Jo pulled out two stools and they took a seat across the counter from the man in charge. Their empty spots were often occupied by any number of self-described old farts who stopped in to shoot the breeze on days too cold or too rainy to do anything but swap gossip and glory days.

Laura's dad reminded her of the beaches here. Rocky at first glance, and foreboding. On the other hand, there was a worn smoothness to him when you looked closely. Per Island custom for men over fifty – and several who were un-der – he wore his gray hair and his gray beard long. Also per custom he typically wore a plaid flannel shirt of indefinite age; Frank's spin was loose and open over a faded black Led Zeppelin or Grateful Dead t-shirt. Laura had caught some of his height, most of his stubbornness, but all of her mother's looks – thank god.

"Morning girls. How's things at the south end," Frank asked.

"Busier down there than it is here," Jo answered.

"Fair enough. You in a sharing mood?"

"Here's what I know so far," Jo replied. "Your boat was stolen this morning. Randy Fuller didn't own a boat but managed to crash one into the side of the Olympic."

"I did the same math. I haven't heard anyone else making noise about missing boats and Brenda didn't mention it, so –"

"Any idea why he took yours? Doesn't Randy live somewhere in the middle of the island?"

Frank shrugged at the first half, nodded his head at the second. "Yeah. Fullers have always been over in Fern Acres. They've got those apple orchards."

"Isn't that a neat little mystery," Jo said. "But you know, I thought you weren't going out this morning – you'd said you needed to catch up here." Catch up on what she wasn't sure, as she surveyed the visual chaos.

Frank's eyes slid sideways at her. He drained his coffee mug, inclined it at Jo. "Cup?"

"Love it."

Laura tapped her index finger loudly on the glass countertop. All three family members exchanged glances.

"We'll share." Jo narrowed her eyes at her wife, who narrowed hers back, then tilted her chin in the air.

From a peg on the wall next to her, Frank retrieved a beige mug sporting a worn decal of a bridge with a thick black line through it, then disappeared through a bead curtain to the back of the otherwise empty two-room store.

He attracted plenty of tourists to the antique shop in the summer, when the population on the Island nearly doubled. But a lot like Makah, the place was quiet and empty the rest of the year. The high-season dollars kept small shops like this and the rest of the struggling economy afloat. What kept Frank's head a little farther above water were the paintings Laura's mom had left behind. Before her heart attack, she'd been an oil painter of some local renown and quite prolific. There were always a few on rotation at the store, usually seasonal scenes. Next week a retrospective of her work was up in a gallery for the First Friday art walk.

This month one of Hannah Tanaka's larger pieces dominated the north wall at the shop. Delicate, seamless strokes captured a rare snowy day in winter. Ringing a barren, white field were sticks of elm trees with fluff ed branches. At the center of it stood a sagging blue cabin, the land already reclaiming it from the owner's abandon.

Frank reemerged. He pulled up his own stool and set the steaming hot coffee on the counter. "I wasn't planning on going out this morning. Just that I realized last night I'd left my good thermos on the boat after I put in. Rolled under one of the benches, I suppose, and I popped down first thing to get it. Rest is history."

"Makes sense." Jo sipped her coffee and slid it over to Laura. Decided to put the brakes on putting the full-court-press on her father-in-law. Randy's story, whether Vi liked it or not, was looking pretty open and shut. Next angle. "You have anything new for me on those copper pot thefts?"

"I haven't had anyone come through," Frank said. "Be the stupidest move you could make, coming here selling something you stole on the Island. Connie Wilcox would of sniffed out the bugger in less than a day on her routine bargain circuit."

"Fine," Jo conceded. "But maybe not everything that comes to you is sold here. Maybe some of it ends up overtown, in Seattle or Tacoma." Smart move, accusing her father-in-law of being a fence? Shading the truth on his stolen boat? Nope. But easy questions got easy answers - and stories nowhere.

"I might keep a secret here or there for a loyal customer. But not about this. Moving stolen goods is different than helping someone pawn the ugly as sin pair of earrings your mother-in-law gave you for Christmas. It's a small Island. I don't want that kind of reputation."

"Thanks. So, if I'm assuming your hands are sparkling clean, just spitball with me for a minute. What the hell?"

"Well this copper thing isn't as hare-brained as it seems. Quite as hare-brained anyway, if you're set-up right." He tapped the case with his middle finger. The last knuckle on from his index finger was missing. Jo was starting to get used to grizzled old men and missing digits. It seemed a table saw and a story were rolled into the closing costs of Island homes.

She followed the direction of his tap and he continued. "Few of these coins here are copper, and they'll get more melted into bullion than for their age. Not worth much, but worth something."

"So who's set up around here to melt down those pots?"

"Swing a cat. More metal-workers and artists per square foot on this rock than anywhere I ever been," he answered.

"That's why I'm here drinking bad coffee with you. Help me narrow the field?"

"Not with you hurling insults like that," Frank replied. "Roast my own beans and it's better than anything commercial. Beats the burnt mermaid any day."

"I apologize." She took another sip. Frank's assertion wasn't the truth. Starbucks had it all over his chicory-based mud. But coffee chat – or bar chat – was the fastest way to any information on Makah. Jo slid her cup back over to Laura, who this time wrapped her hands around it possessively.

"I guess you can't help being from back East," Frank continued. "You never had a chance to learn better."

"Insults aside," Jo came back, "Who's set up to turn those pots into cash?"

"You put it like that, doesn't make me feel right about saying anything else." He set his cup down, pulled out his pocketknife, and started cleaning under his nails.

"I'm just looking for a place to start. Be a good guy and save me hours of driving down rutted roads and tromping through private property looking for hot-smelter furnaces?"

Frank smiled when he looked up. "You always know a little more than you let on, huh?"

"That makes two of us."

He still didn't seem moved by her pleas. This was the best shot at a real story she was going to get anytime soon. And there was just no way these copper shenanigans dead-ended without at least getting a byline in one of the Seattle papers. Even if it were a color piece next to a feature on a homeless puppy. She was willing to throw a little capital behind it.

"Are you up for making a deal?"

"What do you think?" He leaned toward her with a smile full of crooked ivory teeth and gestured around the shop.

"I saw Art Matsumoto dumped a cord of fir at your house last week," Jo said. "I'll stack the whole thing for you."

"Be a little richer offer if it was madrone and I didn't have to watch and make sure you stack it right."

Jo stayed quiet. She looked over to Laura and winked.

Frank shoved his hands into his pockets and swayed toward the counter.

"Yeah, sure, okay then. Only a couple guys with a melting furnace big enough to handle this kind of a job. Terrance White, and Luke Sorensen who lives up near the Hook. Terry's near you, in Porter, but he's locked up tight. Been down in Mexico all month."

"Luke Sorensen – lives near the Hook? Where your boat was stolen this morning?"

"Uh-huh." Frank replied slowly, then glanced at Laura. "You probably want to go talk to him. Want Laura to stay with me the rest of the day?" He swiped his empty mug from the counter, turned his back and disappeared through the bead curtain again.

Jo stared down into the dregs of her remaining coffee. An ornate wood clock on the wall chimed the quarter-hour. She smiled over at her wife. Two years ago, she wouldn't have had to ask this next question. Two years ago, Laura Tanaka would have been one step ahead of Jo on any and every investigation. "You want to come with, babe, or stay with your Dad?"

Laura awkwardly patted Jo's hand. "Stay."

Relief punched Jo right in the face. But she smiled when Frank came back.

"Laura's going to stay," Jo said. "You want me to pick her up later, or you want to bring her down and we'll have dinner at our house?"

"Don't turn down free dinner." He paused to run a hand down his grizzled beard. "Just, if you're going to be late, you'll let me know?"

Jo stood, grabbed her keys out of her pea coat, ignored Frank's insinuation.

"Could you at least stay until you finish your coffee?"

"Yep. I was just going to grab my laptop from the car." Jo made a face like she wasn't pissed about his assumption. "If you don't mind, I'll stay with you and Laura while I do a little background research on Sorensen."

"Oh. Right. Sounds good."

"Very good." Laura corrected her father's sentiment.

Jo kissed the top of her head. "Love you." She threw a thank-you to Frank over her shoulder on her way out for the laptop.

SOMEONE'S LYING

Jo's cherry-red Volvo station wagon jumped and bumped down the half-mud half-gravel road leading out to the Sorensen property that afternoon. She flipped on her headlights. It wasn't even three p.m., but the daylight was fading quickly; almost gone where the evergreens pressed in, even with an hour before the sun sank below the horizon.

She passed an open green pasture, a llama, a cow, and two goats on the quarter mile trip down the driveway from the main road. The Sorensens were tucked far back into the trees of Lost Valley on the north end of the Island. Aptly named because of the dewy, deceptive mist she'd seen perpetually cling to the evergreens and maples like a patchwork of thick cobwebs, even on clear summer mornings.

It had taken a while to get out of Frank's. She'd just about finished with her background work on Sorensen when one of Frank's buddies had come sniffing in to see what Island news might be on offer. She'd been wise enough to stick around and learn that not only was it suspected that the Chinese restaurant was changing hands, but that the county and the school district were brewing a fight over whether the decrepit bus barn could be turned into auxiliary classrooms.

From her quality time on the laptop, Jo had found Luke Sorensen's work selling for almost ten years. But it was only in the last year that he'd started having pretty serious success commercially as a metal sculptor. His public bio was easily available and mundane. Graduate of Makah High School, undergrad at the University of Washington, then art teacher for a while at Makah High School. Married, with a teenage daughter. The only thing out of the ordinary she'd been able to find was that he'd been arrested during the '99 World Trade Organization protests in Seattle. Here that was hardly mentionable. On liberal Makah, you might as well sport a WTO arrest bumper sticker to angle for faster service at the Dairy Queen.

She'd seen several so very artistic black and whites of the bearded man on Luke's homepage, gallery sites, and in reviews. By her third cup of coffee, she'd pretty well put together an interview strategy and headed out.

Besides the scoop on who knew what, when it came to copper, at Frank's she'd also gotten a weak set of directions for getting out here, with precision hints like, "Turn right at the old Danaavich place," and, "If you get to Fox Holler you've gone too far." She winced and pitched against the seatbelt as her front right tire crashed into a puddle that hadn't seemed all that deep. Driveway maintenance had long fallen off the Sorensen radar.

It was still enough to hear her own breathing when she got out of the car. The sound of her door closing was deafening in comparison, dull and muffled by the close forest and loitering fog, which smelled like an amalgam of cedar and mud puddles.

She walked past a burgundy compact sedan that was literally being held together with duct tape, the bumper hanging half-way off and one of the windows covered by cardboard. Next to it was a ubiquitous Island pickup of indiscriminate age, make, model and color. The bed was littered with building supplies. It looked newer than the sedan. Perhaps the hardened layer of grime smattering it like a Jackson Pollock was a virtual clear coat protecting the paint. Next sat a rusted Subaru station wagon with a black and gold MHS bumper sticker, the only thing about it that reflected pride in anything.

Jo hitched her jeans and evaluated the two starkly different buildings in front of her. The two-story house sported a shake roof as green with mold as the winter bark on the nearby trees. The once-white siding was in similar shape. Two dogs announced her arrival from inside - one that sounded large, and one that sounded larger.

The garage workshop, clearly newer, was a high-roofed and well-maintained metal structure almost as large as the house. The only light she could see came from the big building. She started toward it, listening to the gravel crunching under the thick soles of her boots. Reporting deer population crises versus covering corporate and political graft did occasionally come with its perks. Including swapping three-inch Ferragamos for broad-toed Carhartts.

Standing under the shop light she wiped her boots on the black rubber mat, diamond webbed and thinning in the middle, and knocked on the door. A white light buzzed and shone down from above and bounced off a murky puddle. As she stared at the puddle, a drop of rain broke the surface and rippled out. She turned her gaze up to the dense ceiling of clouds, the ebb and flow of the shifting silver shadows. She startled when the door in front of her swung open.

"Help you?"

The young guy in front of her wasn't Luke Sorensen. A head taller than Jo's five-foot seven inches, the black-haired boy on the other side of the threshold wore a dark zipped-up hoodie and jeans, all wrapped in a leather apron. In his gloved hands he held a welding helmet and torch.

"Hi. I'm Joanna Ford. I'm looking for Luke Sorensen."
"He's busy. We're welding." The young man didn't make eye contact with her, instead gazing in the direction of the puddle at her feet, reflecting the rain.

"I don't mind waiting." Jo glanced over his shoulder, saw an arc of blue-white sparks flying from a sculpture towering over the man working at the base. She stared at the kid's charcoal eyes until he met hers, shoved her hands into her jeans in a serious willing-to-wait kind of way.

"You cops or something?"

"I'm not. Why do you ask?"

"No reason. Okay. Stay here. Don't touch stuff." The sulky doorman stalked off.

"Thanks. I won't touch stuff." Jo stumbled as she crossed the threshold to the concrete floor of the shop. There wasn't a significant change in temperature between inside and out. She unbuttoned her navy pea coat anyway to give a more settled-in impression.

The sculpture Sorensen was currently working on was massive in scope compared to the rest of the finished pieces and the waiting scrap metal that cluttered the walls and floors. She recognized some of the work from Island art shows and installations. He was most well-known for creating chunky but contrastingly lithe representations of soaring birds, in the style of those hanging over her. They were often assembled from recognizable scrap – I-beams, chrome fenders, rebar – but not always. Some were smooth and consistent, fluid and dynamic shapes that would have been right at home rippling over the blue Puget Sound on a sunny day next to their organic feathered avatars.

She wondered if one style or the other was more critically acclaimed or more valuable, and if either were selling well. She didn't disguise her curiosity as she glanced around for anything that resembled what she thought copper pots might look like in a new shape. Hands still in her pockets she started strolling the perimeter of the shop. Old maps of Makah, faded fishing and navigation charts, filled in any blank spaces on the unfinished drywall. A row of logo stickers for Kibo Outerwear, Makah's big claim to fame, stretched almost the length of the place. It was a historical tour of every iteration of the logo. It wasn't difficult to judge the era by the font. This collection went back probably three decades.

Luke spoke from behind and startled her. "My wife worked at the Kibo factory for almost ten years, before Brian shut it down." When he flipped up the visor on the bulky welder's mask he wore, she was set back on her figurative heels by beautiful light blue eyes the color of the clear winter sky. They were all the paler for the black smudges at his brow and stubbled cheeks.

She held out her hand. "Hi. Joanna Ford, with *The Quartermaster.*" Much like the *Washington Post, The Quartermaster* needed no further introduction. At least on Makah.

"Oh." He blinked, but then smiled, and stripped off a work glove to shake. His hands were calloused and scarred, smudged with the same grime that covered the rest of him. "Luke Sorensen. What can I do for you?"

"I suppose you might have heard that folks' copper pots have started to go missing?"

"I haven't heard about it. That's kind of a weird crime."

"Surprised you haven't heard. Over the last month. Three houses have been hit. Someone just waltzes in," Jo accompanied the narrative with a horrified, disbelieving face, a shake of her head, and an overly-dramatic sweeping hand gesture, "and walks right out with an armful of heirlooms."

Luke nodded. "That's a bummer. Sorry to hear it."

"You know it's not supposed to be like that here. No one had locked their doors, of course, and someone just took advantage of that."

"Yeah, yeah. Bummer," he said. "That's some overtown style stuff. It's not like that here. But what's that got to do with me?" He pulled off his welding mask and tucked it under his arm, glanced over his shoulder. "You here looking for something on Tyler? Because if you are you can leave."

The charming pale blue eyes lost their twinkle. Luke was probably forty, though he looked younger, and more than probably handsome. Jo wasn't always the best judge, but she could recognize the broad strokes of what made men attractive. Those unsettling eyes started it off. But it wasn't hard to catch his easy-does-it vibe softening square features and a sturdy build. She pictured him in an outdoor catalog. Maybe modeling the Carhartt boots she was wearing.

"I didn't come here to talk to Tyler," she replied. Luke hadn't waited long to try and throw her off course. "Didn't even know him until right now. I could just use your help. I was wondering if you – you know, someone who works with copper – might have a thought on it. Like why someone might steal it in the first place. Is it hard to come by?"

"Oh." He scratched at what looked like an L-shaped razor burn under the dirty-blond stubble on his neck. "I mean it's not hard to come by for anyone who knows what they're doing. Not the cheapest stuff to work with, that's for sure. I don't do much solid copper." He pointed at one of the delicately styled gulls hanging twenty feet down the way. It was shallow-pond green with oxidation. "That guy right there set me back a hundred bucks just for the metal, wholesale."

"I see. Mind if I take notes?"

"Nah. Go ahead." Luke crossed his arms.

Contrary to her conditioning, Jo had come to learn this meant the men of Makah had taken an interest in what you were saying. "You said 'people who know what they're doing.' Like you then. I mean, do you just order your material over the internet, or do you have a 'metal dealer' or something that you work with? You're so prolific – I know you're in demand. So, you must need a reliable source." She'd met an artist once who hadn't responded well to compliments. Once.

Sorensen smiled. "I don't know about that. But yeah. It's great to have reli-able supply. You know, if you get a vision and you need to go with it."

"Yep. You have someone overtown, in Seattle, I'm guessing?"

"Shop out of Harbor Island in West Seattle. They've got whatever I need. Know a few guys on Makah who use them."

Jo scribbled on the pad she'd pulled out of her back pocket. She didn't look up, didn't respond, but kept the pen over the paper.

Luke continued. "Called PNW Metalworks."

She stared around and studied the pieces hanging in the sterile white glow started to get the back and forth of Luke's style and lingo. "It's so cool to see all your stuff. How long have you been sculpting?"

"Full-time? Ten years now. I bailed out of a U Dub grad program early when my wife was pregnant with our girl Ashley. Taught at Makah High School for a few years to pay bills until I got established, could do what I love for real. Still miss working with the kids, but, you know, I couldn't say no to passion."

"Absolutely. That's the only way to fly." Joanna bobbed her head up and down. Here was the rapport. Islanders loved nothing so much as talking about the passions of their soul and living a life filled with deeper meaning. Their particular small-town identity was rooted in the artist-enclave mentality, a blend of communism and libertarianism she'd not encountered in many places.

"That's what you're doing at *The Quartermaster*? Chasing the dream?"

"You know it," she replied. "I spent decades in the wide world working for someone else. Surrounded by a lot of noise. Just woke up one morning and I was so over it all. Family had a place out here. Visited once and thought, what have I been doing?" None of that was true. But promised land was a tale that Makah residents loved to hear as much as they loved to tell. She wondered how many of them were lying to others or to themselves as convincingly as she was right now.

"Yeah, that's the Makah story, isn't it," he replied.
"Speaking of – how about what happened down at the south end this morning," Jo hinted.

"Yeah. Saw a video someone posted on the Makah Facebook group. Sure sorry to lose Randy like that."

"Looked a lot like him, didn't it?" Jo had seen the video that afternoon – there was little doubt in her mind Randy was the guy in the boat. Then again, doubt had always served her well. "Did you know him?"

"Not much. I mean, I did when we were kids. He was a couple years behind me. Until he flamed out. Wasn't the same after the first OD." Luke clattered his nails on a nearby drum of sheet metal. The flat ping blended with the patter of rain on the roof and she drifted for a second. It was the kind of sound that reminded you of good things past.

"Brown heroin was all over the goddamn island, for a while," Luke continued. "Total shame. What they got now, though – kill you just as easy, won't it?"

Jo was shocked to see tears in the man's eyes when she snapped back to the job at hand. "I'm sorry, Luke. Did –"

A cold draft blew past Jo. She turned to see the door of the shop open and a petite and apparently very angry teenage girl charging through.

THE KIDS AREN'T ALRIGHT

"Dad I'm not just going to fucking keep sitting around and fucking pretend-ing –" The girl clocked Jo and abruptly stopped her verbal and physical charge at Luke - presumably her father. Jo willed herself into invisibility. It had never worked before, but –

"Ashley." Luke relaxed his posture. He didn't seem fazed by the tantrum. "I'll be in soon. We'll talk." He gazed evenly at the girl; sort of silently assessing her, sizing things up like a zoo keeper who punched in one morning to come face to face with a lion on the loose wandering toward the zebra enclosure.

"Hi. I'm Jo Ford." Jo held out a hand to the teen.

"Yeah. I'm Ashley." Her grasp was as limp as the mouse-brown hair strung over her shoulders. It partially covered a faded black t-shirt with MHS XC stamped across her small chest.

"Now's not the time for this, is it?" Luke asked his daughter.

She'd been surreptitiously observing Jo. She threw a wide-open look at Jo, then sneered at her father. "Maybe it is."

"Okay. Let's talk. Gimme a minute."

"Fine." Ashley said, but didn't move.

"Hey Tyler," Luke called out. "You want to hang with Ash for a while? I'm cashed for today anyway."

Tyler had already been quietly approaching the awkward cluster at the front of the shop. "Sure." He shrugged at Ashley, who shrugged back, and they started for the door. Ashley kept her blank brown eyes pasted on her father, still disregarding Jo.

Luke stepped into Jo's line of sight. "Sorry about that. Teenagers, you know. You have kids?"

"No, we don't," she said. And now – they never would. "So, is it just you here and it's – Tyler, I think you said?"

"Yeah. Tyler's kind of apprenticing." Luke uncrossed his arms, started rear-ranging tools on his work bench.

"That's great. Is he at the high school?"

"Nah. Graduated a while back. Does what he can for money. He's good. Promising."

"Love to ask him what he thinks about what's going on," Jo hinted.

"You sure you're just wanting to get a little back story?"

Jo leaned into her feigned incompetence. "Kids just know more than we give them credit for."

Sorensen's eyes flitted in the direction of the house, back to Jo. His heel began to jimmy on the concrete floor. "Tyler's had enough trouble."

"I'm sorry to hear that."

Luke took a step forward. He grabbed his welding helmet from the table, and a massive pair of iron tongs.

She took a step back. "Okay. Well, thanks for your time, Mr. Sorensen. Still pretty amazing that I got to check out an Island artist in residence. I ought to do a feature someday. What's the sculpture you're working on now? It's incredible."

It was, particularly in comparison to the rest of the works around them. Large, heavy cross beams fell like a bad run of Tetris pieces.

"Just felt like doing something different."

"Well, good luck with your work. Can't wait to see what happens with this – " She nodded over toward the behemoth steel skeleton.

"Yeah. Thanks."

"Thanks for your time."

"Sure." Luke stood motionless as Jo showed herself out.

Outside, the early twilight gloom was deep and cold enough to sting her nose. She didn't look back until she got to the car. She took her time to button up her coat as she faced the workshop.

From the house, a yellow light shone on the bottom floor. Two figures crossed back and forth what looked to be the kitchen. She lingered and checked her phone. Her inbox was quiet again today. She had a text from Frank remind-ing her to pick up toilet paper on her way home. And she had that waiting text message from Beth, the one she knew would be there – a smart little winking icon. Jo deleted the text chain, threw herself into the car, and slammed the door.

The mist in Lost Valley was building along with the dark of the evening. She turned on the Volvo and cranked up the heat, pulled out her notebook and scratched out any lingering impressions and details from the afternoon. She kept one eye out as she did so. Despite the new arrivals on the scene and the rapid approach of the dinner hour, no one went back and forth from shop to house.

Jo considered knocking, seeing what she could get out of Ashley. Before she had a chance to think anything out, Tyler appeared in the doorway of the house. He lit a cigarette, a silhouette and a flare of orange in the dark twilight, and stared right at her. She threw the Volvo into reverse and drove off .

Jo headed to the office instead of home after her visit to Sorensen's. Tyler was pinging her radar, and it was too hard to focus and keep her eye on Laura at the same time. She disregarded the clock on the wall as she plunged into research, later and later past the time she was supposed to meet Frank.

A little digging had gotten her a last name on Tyler – Sealth. She'd found more than one link to click on the kid in the archives of *The Quartermaster* and on the King County Sheriff's blotter. He'd made the sports coverage frequently when he was younger.

According to a feature story on the baseball team from *The Quartermaster*, Tyler had been raised by his grandparents. She'd researched her way to figuring out that both his parents were still alive, living off the fat of the land in the King County Jail on fentanyl possession convictions.

By the time he was a sophomore in high school he was already on the varsity baseball squad. Then nothing at all, sports or otherwise. Finally, he reappeared on the police blotter two years ago for helping himself to whatever he could find in unlocked cars at the Park and Ride by the north end ferry dock.

Then, another whole lot of nothing. For two years Tyler Sealth had kept his nose squeaky clean. She called Vi for any color commentary and was answered by a series of grunts. "Got a place on the south end. Way down on Tucker Trail. Seems like it ought to be a recipe for trouble, away from prying eyes, but so far just the opposite." Vi's mood had gone from bad to worse that day and the conversation had been short.

So Tyler had gone to ground.

The thick forests and spider web of back roads here hid all the sins you could name in the Bible, and some that hadn't even crossed your mind until you heard about them. Not many bad actors lasted though.

Through her time in the archives, she'd learned that Makah had a way of organically excising the misfits as smoothly as soaking out a splinter. Tyler seemed to be sticking – and improving. He had the means to convert the copper. But why revert to his old ways now?

Jo reluctantly turned her attention to an overdue article on the local art cen-ter's "Fly Festival." Three days of film shorts, all centered around fishing. Her pun skills waned as the night wore on. She called it after she dared type the sentence, "These fintastic films will reel in afishionadoes of all ages."

She shut down her computer, glanced at the clock on the wall of the tiny wood-paneled *Quartermaster* office.

"Shit." It was past dinner. Well past. Time to head home and apologize for being late, getting carried away in her work again. She'd get a little closer to Tyler Sealth, Luke and Ashley Sorensen, tomorrow.

LIKE RIDING A BICYCLE

There were still plenty of unmarked lanes on Makah Jo hadn't wandered, despite the Sunday drives she took with Laura. Tucker Trail, leading down to Tyler's place, was one of them. It was steep and rugged and what there was of a road washed out with even an inch of rain. She wasn't sure how much more her axles or suspension could take of Makah. Maybe she'd drop the Volvo at Danno's garage and have them put on a lift kit. She chuckled to herself as she crawled along, picturing her car, the definition of suburbia, on monster truck tires.

She lurched through one more pothole and parked. It had taken almost thirty minutes from her house to get to this isolated south shore of the Island. The nearby cabin looked exactly as though a twenty-something misfit oversaw maintenance. The color had likely once been dark navy, washed by sun and storms to match the gray blue of the water lapping at the bulkhead holding it up. A blue tarp covered the ridge of the roof front to back. Tattered and faded Tibetan prayer flags swagged the front. Beneath them a collection of scrap metal, car parts, and beer cans created a rusted display decorating the porch the way some people set out planters of geraniums in the spring.

Jo heard a distant rumble. A massive Hanjin tanker cut slowly across the vista, blue and white dividing the horizon. The view the crumbling shack enjoyed was breathtaking. There was nothing between her and Mount Rainier except a mile of the Puget Sound and the silent cityscape beyond the water. The water swished and slapped on the rocky shoreline and chatted back at the circling gulls and crows, diving in and out of the drafts. It was hard to believe there wasn't a million-dollar bungalow tucked down here.

Jo took a deep breath of cold, wet, air, turned up the collar of her pea coat, and examined the parking lot of junkers sprinkled in between blackberry brambles behind the cabin, including the burgundy and duct-tape Nissan sedan.

Tyler Sealth appeared from around the far corner of the house, cigarette hung from his lips. Sleek hair stuck out at every angle under a black hoodie, his outfit a carbon copy of yesterday's grungy homage to Goth. The young man had already counted up the sins of the world and declared the total ironic.

"Hey Tyler. I'm Jo – you remember me from Luke's workshop? I wanted to follow up with you, since we didn't have a chance to talk really."

"I don't know anything about anything, lady. Mountain's worth seeing today, but you wasted a trip." He inclined his head at the rich man's view, ashed his cigarette, and shrugged.

She caught wind of the smoke and realized it wasn't a cigarette. The marijuana in the Pacific Northwest grew wet and it grew pungent. If Tyler was high, she might get something out of him. Then again anyone who smoked a joint the way James Dean smoked a Pall Mall probably didn't get high unless he tried pretty hard.

She took her classic angle of approach on tough guys who weren't all that tough. When he wasn't holding a blowtorch, this skinny boy whose eyes kept flitting toward the vista didn't even ping at the edges of her watch-your-six radar. "Maybe you don't know anything, but I didn't want to just write you off. I could really use your help. Need to keep my job, so I thought I'd try."
He sucked on the joint, pinched it out with his fingers as he exhaled, then pocketed it. "Reporters don't have jobs. They're just paid to be nosy."

"Everyone needs a paycheck. I've got a couple friends who are artists. Sometimes people don't think much of them getting paid either."

"Artists make things that are original. Things that last. They work, they should get paid."

"I agree." Jo nodded. "And artists also notice things. It's important that they get the details. So, I was wondering if maybe you noticed any details related to this whole copper business?" She couldn't help pulling her shoulders together against a gust of brackish sea air.

Tyler snorted. "I'm not an artist." He looked down at the sandy dirt and pulled his own arms close. "It's cold. Come inside if you want. Still don't know anything, though."

She followed him up on to the creaking porch and into the cabin that smelled like dirty socks, old beer, and fresh weed. She was wrong about being warm. The stove in the corner squatted black and empty.

She remembered the mound of wood rounds piled outside, next to the truck. Splitting and hauling firewood probably wasn't best done when drunk, and maybe wasn't any fun high.

She paused at the window, pointed to a small, asymmetrical sculpture that looked a lot like the larger version in Luke's workshop. "Did you make this?"

"Yeah." He stared at the passing curtains of rain, apparently uninspired by his own work.

"It's compelling. Looks like what Luke was working on the other day when I came by." Jo kept pushing.

"It's kind of a collaboration. He's been interested in my stuff lately. He says I've got a good 'voice.'"

"I can certainly see that. But doesn't apprenticeship usually go the other way around?"

"He's getting bored with his stuff. He's blocked." Tyler sparked, then took another hit of his joint, and turned his head away, out the side window facing east to Tacoma. Winter white light filled the cabin. He crossed the blistering beige linoleum toward the kitchen, pulled open a small fridge and helped himself to a can of Rainier beer. He didn't offer her one but did incline his head toward a decrepit orange sofa.

She focused on her next round of questions and didn't think about what old stains she might be sitting on as the couch sagged under her weight. Evidence of an unsupervised boy abounded. An open cereal box on the counter, three different stereos of dubious function, and bare walls with bubbled, peeling paint and a tattered map of Makah tacked up on one side of a large flat screen TV. On the other side, a poster of Marshawn Lynch mid-grind through the Bronco's offensive line. Island boys loved their Seahawks.

He flipped a metal folding chair at the kitchen table and sat facing her, rest-ing his arms on the back. "Ask away – uh" he paused and put up his chin. A strip of stubble told her that he was perhaps he was making a very bad life choice and working on a soul-patch.

"It's Jo – Joanna Ford."

"Right." He took a swig from the red and white can.

"How did you end up working with Luke?"

"I don't work with Luke. He works, I learn."

"How did you know you wanted to learn from him? Why sculpture?"

"Because sculpture is everywhere." He pulled on the beer again. This time though, he met her eyes. "Look around outside if you don't believe me. At the woods and the mountains."

"And the birds." Like those striking, serene metalworks floating in Luke workshop.

"Right." Tyler looked again toward the Sound and the mountain, and the black eyebrows that seemed glued together parted.

Steady on, Joey, Big Jack and Jo agreed on the warming status of the rapport with the kid. "Did you take many art classes at Makah High School?"

"Shit no. They don't have money for it. None of the stuff I want to do, anyway."

"So, you got lucky. Luke took you under his wing, so to speak?"

"Kinda." Just a flicker in his black eyes at her joke. "Luke's got plenty of kids who want to work with him. But I used to date his daughter's best friend."

"His daughter is Ashley, right? She okay? She seemed off yesterday."

Tyler considered his beer, then Jo. "Ash is pretty much always off, one way or the other."

"Why is that?"

"Couldn't say." With a third long pull, Tyler finished his beer. A rivulet of white trickled down his chin, which he wiped with his   sleeve. He hurled the empty toward an overflowing blue recycle bin and it clattered down a hill of brown bottles and white cans.

"But you're sort of close, I'm guessing, since you dated her best friend?"

"Maybe. Yeah. But we broke up like two years ago. It started to feel weird after I graduated. But Brittany was great. Really great."

"Was? Did she move away?"

"No. Just, like, was – she was great as a girlfriend, is what I meant."

"I see." Jo saw her window, threw the change up, and leaned back on the sofa to settle in with a hurt boy and an interview that had broken wide open. "You probably guessed I was going to ask, but did you know Randy Fuller?"

Tyler started to shake his head, when a shout from outside the cabin broke the silence between them.

"Hey! Fuck face! What I tell you about staying out of the Alibi?"

Tyler's thunderous brows came back together. He stood. He looked down at Jo as he towered over her. "Leave," he muttered, as he disappeared through the door.

She followed him on to the porch, where he replied to the less than friendly greeting from the newcomer.

"Look Jered. My ride home last night ditched me. I had to hang around for another one."

"Do I *look* like I give a flying fuck about your dying Jap-box car? I said stay the hell out of that bar." Jered – Brasier, she remembered. The boy from the south end dock with the pale skin, foul mouth and brown greasy hair hanging limp at his shoulders finally noticed Jo. He scraped a look up and down her sturdy frame. He leered. "What the hell you doing here, lady?"

"What are you doing here? I'm Jo Ford, by the way." Who let this bastard off his leash? She instantly agreed with Vi about this kid and where he belonged versus the decent half of humanity. She also wondered exactly what Brian Stewart and his Kibo fortune were doing with him. She put her hands in her pockets and strolled toward him, past Tyler and off the porch. Jo had one angle on bullies. She raised her pitch to match his. "Who are you?"

"Jered Fucking Brasier."

"Is that with an F or a Ph?"

"What? I don't know. And like I asked, why are you here?

"Same question back at you – why are you here? I'll add another one, if you can keep track. Why were you watching me and Vi at the dock the other day?"

"Bitch none of your business." Jered dipped his shoulder to the side and rolled his head at her. Under his unzipped hoodie, a baggy black Primus t-shirt told Jo that he had bad, angry white boy taste in music. His faded Kibo beanie told her he was old-school Makah.

He stepped toward her. He had to be six-foot-one at least, and he was lanky. He looked up at Tyler and the whine in his voice grew. "Seriously, man. Why's the blonde snatch taking up my time?"

Jo took another step toward the guy, and now there were only a couple feet between her and his skinny, crooked teeth and smelly jeans. If nothing else, these two boys loved their pot. "I said my name is Jo. Not snatch." It crossed her mind to be scared, and she decided against it.

"Bitch I don't have time to learn your name. Be on your way." His sharp Adam's apple bobbed as he rolled his long neck again and waved toward the driveway.

She turned to Tyler, scrambled around to give him an out. He and Luke were still her best leads. "Luke just told me you might do some welding for cash, on the side. But if you don't want the job, Tyler —"

Tyler's upper lip curled. He pulled the joint from his pocket, cupped a hand, and relit it. "Not from you."

"Fine." She shrugged, bumped Jered's shoulder as she started toward her car. The boys were still at each other with raised voices.

The rise in the seawall looked like it might provide decent cover. Jo decided to stick around, ducked into the woods, and doubled back.

The incoming tide lapped at the tip of her boots. The mist from the churning Sound had become a steady drizzle from black clouds that promised more, and her back was uncomfortably plastered to the jagged, crumbling bulkhead just down from Tyler's cabin. She'd had to circle back through the forest to get here. She was wet from her knees down and already shivering.

"What you got to drink, Ty," she heard Jered ask. "Ash gave me something that has me wound up. And who the hell was that old bitch? She wasn't looking for any welding job."

"Half a rack of Rainier left inside," Tyler answered. "Help yourself. Just some lady from the paper. She was asking me about the copper thing."

"What you say to her? I hope absolutely nothing, because the ass-kicking Brian sent me here to hand you can get turned up."

"It's no big deal. She doesn't know anything."

Anything about what, Jo asked herself.

"Damn right she doesn't," Jered said. "That stuck-up snatch wouldn't know a dog if it bit her in the ass. She going to be trouble, though?"

"No, dude. She's not. This isn't like *Game of Thrones* or something. And if it were, Brian's Littlefinger. You're just a henchman. Relax."

"I'm like the fucking dragons in that show, okay?" Jered's voice rose almost to a squeal at the end. "Now let's talk for real. Because you were at the Alibi, and we told you to stay out."

Jo heard shuffling and grunting. Now awkwardly crouched, she risked peering over the bulkhead to see Jered with his boot on Tyler's chest, the younger boy prone on the patchy scrub grass.

"Damn it, Jered. Get off me." Tyler grabbed Jered's ankle and squirmed. He crawled out from under him and stood.

"See, I'm thinking *no* on getting off you," Jered explained. "I'm thinking we gotta be tight on you like that old bitch who just peaced out gets tight on your mom. Because this isn't about you in the wrong place. It's about people looking into you. They look hard at you, maybe they start looking at me. And on and on it goes, man, until they're looking in places neither one of us wants, right?"

"Jesus, man. I didn't say shit to her or anyone. And you know I'm out. Anything anyone wants, goes through you guys. That's loud and clear." Tyler brushed by him and stalked toward to the porch.

Jered followed and gave him a little shove that sent him stumbling before he could get to the stairs. "Loud and clear. I like you knowing your place. Keep knowing it. You want a beer, no Alibi. You go to Hunters. You should thank me, man. Their plasma is sick. Russell Wilson looks like a god on that big screen."

Tyler reached into his pocket with shaking hands, relit his joint.

"Gimme that." Jered snagged it and took a hit. "Brian and me got something we need you to do. You do it, I'll have Danno's get your rolling shit-box rolling again." He ground the roach under his boot and thumbed toward the Nissan.

"No," Tyler whined. "I mean it. I don't need to be getting anyone's attention right now. I have some other business to handle."

"This isn't about your business. I do what I'm told, and so do you. Sorry man. But 'no' isn't an option here."

"Fuck." Tyler kicked at the dirt.

"Getting right with your place in the world ain't easy. I get it. See, your problem is you think some gay-ass art is going to move you up and out. And that just ain't how it is. You're Makah redneck through and through. It's a good life though, right? Just embrace it, man."

"Like you did?"

"Don't come at me like that. We go back, but there's still an order to things."

Tyler looked down again. "What do you want?"

"Minus dumbass Randy Fuller, we've got a distro problem. So let's go inside and discuss this like we're civilized." Jered hooked an arm around Tyler's shoulder.

"We both know it's not long before shit hits the fan over pretty little Brittany Roebuck. So let's just touch base about all that. Because we all want to stay guano-free, you know?"

"Yeah." Tyler muttered. "I know."

Jo stood, rubbed her aching back after the boys went inside. She'd heard plenty and she was frozen – and late to get home. She stayed right up on the bulkhead and inched her way back to where the trees met the shoreline, scram-bled awkwardly on all fours up the embankment. Her car stood out in the gloom, a red beacon a hundred or so yards away. Jo picked her way through the dark-ening woods. Every step, every breath bounced off the tree trunks and echoed in the quiet. Only a few yards into the forest, the sound of the waves had muffled dramatically.

Jo kept it slow and steady as long as she could bear it, then trotted the last few yards, piled into the Volvo, and locked the doors. As soon as she turned the engine, she cranked the heat. The windshield, everything glass, frosted up imme-diately - she'd have to wait for it to clear. Jo clicked down the driver window to scan the vicinity. No Jered or Tyler in the woods or coming up the trail.

Tyler Sealth was up to his neck in guano and needed money. He might not be friends with Jered, but the smarmy jerk had something over him. Randy Fuller was one-hundred percent complicit. And who the hell was Brittany Roebuck?

She whipped out her phone – damnit. She was going to be later than she thought to pick up Laura. Damnit. She hauled the car around in the small clearing and shattered the turtle rule for gravel driveways. She called Frank's cell, then his house, then the antique store. No answer on any line. *Damnit.* She wasn't going to be that late – but, still. Maybe Frank would understand that she'd gone the extra mile, taken the extra time to get the story. Laura certainly would, and that's what counted. Hell, she probably would have told Jo to go back and confront Jered and Tyler right now. She tapped the brakes – then back on the gas. She couldn't. Jo's clock was running on someone else's time now.

She dialed the Sheriff 's office. Voice mail let her know that it was past busi-ness hours and she should call 911 if she had an emergency. Jo left a message, explained what she'd heard, left her cell number. She hit the main road and hit the gas. Perhaps she'd conveniently get pulled over. At least then she'd have a better excuse for being late. Again.

WHAT'S VI HIDING?

Vi Mitchell reached out and rested her fingertips on the photo on her bedside table. The picture was usually hidden away, but since Randy's death she could not stand to have it so far out of reach. In the moonlight she studied her faded Henry. Tall, sturdy. Chestnut hair and hickory eyes. Her one great bad, the worst of the sins – and the worst of sins never felt bad going down. But done was done and couldn't be helped. Wanting was not having. She'd learned that years ago. That stupid saying about pearls and swine – they'd called it dead wrong. It wasn't that she'd missed the value of what had been laid before her. Just that she knew how ridiculous she'd look adorned in the finery, even if she'd been willing to pay the price. Or, more accurately, to let others pay it for her.

She hadn't believed what she said to Jo about Ilse Fuller. About the cancer eating up all the sin inside her. Embraced only by the thick blanket of the full quiet of the forest and the starlit dark of her room, the one she'd grown up in, to become a maiden and a crone and only a ghost of a mother, Vi knew her secrets hadn't been eaten. They'd just waited to come back around, sit fat on her chest. Tonight, Vi had the sick feeling that not just her luck, but Makah's, had run out. The past that had so long ago been laid to rest wasn't resting anymore.

On the other hand, she had led a good, long life here. Great, at times. Maybe it was time to say thank you and admit the good part of things was over. Maybe this was just payback come so late for her youthful indiscretions, and everything she'd turned a blind eye to over her lifetime. At a certain age you stopped believing silly things, like karma, had anything to do with anything reasonable. But late, late at night, everything seemed possible.

This year past she'd done plenty of weighty arithmetic on cold nights like this, eyes open and staring out the window watching the distant twinkle of lights on the old Fisher Point dock, away and below the stand of rare old-growth fir ringing the bay. It wasn't the trees Vi counted, but the years. And not those spent, but those to come. How many more vine-ripe blackberry summers? How many more strawberry-wine Christmases? She imagined them passing, one by one, and with each imagining her heart beat harder at the closing walls of panic. Only ten autumns of Makah left? After counting the years, it'd become counting the days. Her best guesstimate put her at about thirty-six hundred to go, if all that whiskey and pork fat left her alone a while longer. Each quick night was a tick on the chit. Sleepless long ones just like this, when the arthritis in her knees buzzed, didn't feel as though she were adding to her time on earth.

When the days grew thinner on the front end, examining those on the back end, no matter their flavor, became a comfort of denial. Hers was bittersweet. This past year the what-if bitter came in choking quantity, in the unexpected form of one Joanna Ford. Surprises like that made your pillow cool and nights short while the wonder of them lasted. When young Jo had appeared, Vi's wonder had hung around long enough to see what laid underneath the shine, to see the real test of the mettle. She'd become just what Vi imagined having a daughter might be like. As always, with that thought of family, her mouth soured.

Vi stared out at the moon rise coming up over the bay. The white spotlight right on her face. How do you force your will on someone else? You don't, that's how. She could no more force her wayward matronly love on Jo than she could on what she'd not intended and therefore didn't have as her own. She coveted what she couldn't have from afar, as she did the deer in her yard. She admired their grace as they grazed, their sweet-soft licorice eyes, and of course the gentle power coiled in tight muscle ready to spring. Over time she'd even earned the trust of two of the does, until they'd take seed right from her very hand. She'd been tempted to touch so often, reach the tips of her fingers to the soft brown pelt. But a little tame was still wild. The does belonged to the wild, and she could never really hold them. To even try would rankle base fight or flight instincts. She protected those girls too. Kept hunters off her land with warning signs and her own shotgun, when it came to it. Often during her long nights spent subtracting the remainder, she wondered what would become of her does when she departed.

Better to admire her distant little family and do what she could for it while she could. Embrace or not, the beauty before her still counted for every day she lived out.

But beauty didn't make the long nights peaceful, and it didn't make the sweet any less bitter. She hurumphed again and pulled her quilt up close, drifted into uneasy sleep that was disturbed only a few hours later in the dead of morning – when she woke with a start and only the ghost-memory of an unwelcome sound downstairs.

She sat up, listened hard. She knew something was off the second she put her feet on the battered oak floor. The wide planks were far too cool. She kept the house at a steady sixty-six in the winter. Quite a change from the way it had been a few years ago, when she'd finally given up on the wood stove and put central heating and new windows into the old farmhouse.

Add to the cold, Paula was not underfoot to demand breakfast.

"Paula honey. Hey monster. Meow meow."

Too cool floors and absent cat. This led Vi back to one incontrovertible fact – something was up. Vi had made a long living out of facts and reporting them. In small towns the truth might occasionally need a push or a plus. But the under-lying fact itself stayed just the way it started.

She groaned 'good morning' to herself and pulled on her pilled flower-print housecoat one arm at a time. She might feel like rushing to investigate, but it wouldn't do anything but aggravate her sciatica.

"Paula. Meow meow." She put on her most authentic Siamese cat accent and the meow came out sounding more like 'now.' Paula only had one word in her feline lexicon. "Now" served to tell her owner everything necessary.

Down the narrow stairs in the near-dark she went. Her bare feet hugged the worn wooden risers, fit just right into the rough crescent grooves at the centers. The flaps of her old housecoat shushed against the daisy yellow walls. Generations ago, when the homestead was erected, the Mitchell family ran a little smaller than her current generous sixty-five-year-old self.

As she descended, she grumbled and hoped to find a window open down-stairs. Even a door, and even if that meant a damn 'coon pilfering the garbage. She would accept just about any answer that didn't include the words "broken furnace."

The thin, gunmetal glow of the Pacific Northwest morning was still imminent, leaving her nothing to see of the first floor but lumpy outlines of furniture. Vi turned to the kitchen first. The back door stood open just enough for big Paula to wind her way into the yard and the forest beyond. That old door had its quirks of age, just like its owner. Certain parts were less than reliable.

Parts like the hit and miss latch she kept meaning to replace.

"Just how did you manage this trick, Paula girl?"

She gathered her housecoat and shivered against the creeping November damp. The cracked door was out of the ordinary. Unsettling surely, though no cause for alarm. Not on rural Makah Island, anyway. Not usually. Vi whirled around, glared at the empty living room, and finally laughed at herself. How many serial killers preferred fat old ladies? None that she'd heard of. Not even in the the Pacific Northwest, where wackos grew on trees. Vi checked her unease and put the worry where it belonged, with Paula. She turned back to the yard. Waited and hoped to see even a streak of golden tan in the gloom. But the gray and black forest kept to itself, crouched silent beyond the open door. Fog swirled around the waxy-green rhododendrons ringing the back yard, the way her beloved familiar was wont to swirl at her ankles around dinner time.

"Paula. Paula-girl, meow meow."

A sharp, lone bark from the Wojciechoski's Labradoodle a quarter mile away was the only reply.

"Humph." Vi grunted and stepped inside. "Well fine then." She didn't much look forward to breakfast by herself. She didn't like one bit the thought of Paula out all night. She could take care of herself, but coyotes had risked swimming the swift currents of the Colvos passage and found their way to Makah Island this year.

Well, Vi would start officially worrying, big worrying, anyway, if she weren't home for dinner. She flipped the silver switch at the base of Mr. Coffee. Pre-loaded the night before, it snorted and popped to life on the wood chop top. Her friend Connie Wilcox said putting the coffee in the night before made it taste pale and old by the morning. Vi said it was just fine as long as you didn't skimp and you added an extra scoop. Connie was fond of skimping and blaming the poor results on the dog.

She pulled two eggs from the breadbox, cracked them on the stainless-steel counter and beat them with a splash of goat's milk. She turned back to the cook top, reached up to the hanging rack for her mother's copper skillet.

"I'll be the prize in a box of Crackerjacks."

Every single one of her family's aged, beloved copper pots was gone. The bowl of eggs hit the counter with a thunk, sloshing everywhere.

She clutched her robe tighter and rushed to the dining room to check the cigar box she kept at the back of the china cabinet. Very few people would know what the contents meant about her. But the right people would know a lot more about the wrong things if they got hold of it.

"Shit." Vi stumbled backward and collided with the dining table. The yellow ceramic vase in the center wobbled, then toppled, then rolled to the floor and shattered. It had belonged to Grandmother Plancich. The loss hurt her less than imagining – no, knowing – who had that box now and what he could do with it.

Vi put eyes on the only other thing that could never be replaced, the faded photo of the two older brothers she'd lost to Lyndon Johnson's cowardice. Still breathing heavy, she checked that back door one more time. It was mullioned, just like the original farm windows. It split the world beyond into eighteen wavy, hazy portraits. None of them contained her wayward cat. She shuffled out for one last call to Paula, whose demanding meows would go a long way to comfort her.

"Come on Paula-girl. Breakfast. Meow meow." She waited at the door, a little longer this time, but it did no good.

She made her way over to the phone. Took it up, put a finger in the nine-hole. Stopped. The pots wouldn't be worth the insurance deductible. The secrets now gone would be repaid in pain and not money. Brian Stewart traded in a very different currency than the rest of the world. Randy was dead proof of that. Nothing to do now but be patient and watchful and wait for Jo Ford to settle her scores.

BRITTNEY ROEBUCK WILL SAVE US ALL

Jo fumbled her hand over her buzzing phone on the side table. She slid to answer, then shot a look to the other side of the bed. Laura wasn't there. Even if she were awake, she was supposed to stay in bed until Jo was up. But sometimes she forgot. Reason whatever they kept the house locked tight. She sat up, listened closely. She heard Frank's dry laughter downstairs, noticed that the air smelled like breakfast, relaxed, and answered the insistent caller.

"This is Joanna."

"Hi Ms. Ford – Jo. It's Tolliver. Larsen."

Tolliver. Right. Valerie's son and *The Quartermaster's* summer intern and toe-headed tree of a boy wonder. "Hi. Yeah. What's up?" She coughed, cleared her throat, and waited.

"Hi. Ummm, sorry to call early, but I thought you'd want to know – there's a body at Mill Creek."

Jo rolled out of bed and immediately pulled on the jeans slung over the bed-post. "What?"

Dead silence from the teenager. Jo heard car tires hiss over wet pavement in the background. Then, "Some hikers found a body at Mill Creek Ravine. It's on my trail to school – I ran past this morning, saw some cops. As soon as I knew what was up, I called you."

She crooked the phone at her shoulder as she grabbed her bra and awkwardly wrestled it on, the side with extra padding getting twisted the wrong way before she managed it.

"Do you know what time this was – they found it?"

"Not exactly. Maybe like seven something? Know it was just getting light." It was eight now. Jo had gotten her beauty sleep. "I'm heading out. Can you meet me there? Are you still there?" She threw on a thick sweater, tied up her hair, and remembered who she was talking to. "Or do you need to be in school?

You should be in school."

"I'm here already. It's fine. I asked Mom. She says if you're there, it's okay."

Valerie might be overestimating Jo's adult-in-the-room acumen. But Tolliver sounded like he might know more, and if he were serious about journalism, this would be a big deal for the kid. "All right. I'll meet you there. Give me about fifteen minutes."

She finished dressing, texted Vi, then pounded downstairs to find Laura working on a crossword with her dad at the kitchen counter. A common morning activity. He'd ask a question. She'd say a word that didn't have anything to do with the answer. It felt good to see it. Well, it felt good-bad.

Across Laura's chest, written in navy block letters, "It's 2am. Do you know where your TBI is?" Beneath that was a drawing of a human brain. They'd seen a poster with the joke on it at Laura's rehab hospital, and it had made both the women smile. So Jo went and had the shirt printed and presented it to her upon her return home from the facility.

"Morning." Jo declared as she wrapped Laura up from behind for a hug.

Frank tossed his pen on the counter. "You off already?"

"Yep. They found a body in Mill Creek Ravine." Jo filled her travel mug. "Thanks for making coffee. Can you stay to the end of the day?"

"What?" Frank's head swiveled. He looked to Laura, then back at Jo. "That's nuts. When?"

"Just this morning – now, I think. Got a call from Tolliver Larsen."

Frank stood, turned his back to Jo and headed toward the stove. "I can stay until the tide changes. Noon? Still real big swings right now."

"See you then," Jo conceded. She could take a midday break for research and writing at home.

"Jo?" Laura came around into the kitchen, hand running along the counter-top for balance.

"Yeah babe?"

"Good luck."

"Thanks." Jo hugged her again, then riffled through her messenger bag; two notebooks, two pens, and a digital recorder. She slung it over her shoulder, pulled on her pea coat, and raced through the door. She promptly raced back in and up the stairs. "Forgot my contacts," she called out.

Her vision was stellar, but her eyes weren't. One bright green, one bright blue, and both inviting unwelcome comments about how much she must love the Seahawks. Jo had gone on-theme and all-green for the temporary landing in the Northwest.

When she got to the north end of the Island there was just a handful of residents clustered at the barricade blocking the road winding down to Mill Creek Ravine. Twenty or so yards down, yellow caution tape was strung around fat old-growth trees, suggesting a perimeter. It started at the edge of the barely two-lane road near a trampled spot that might have been an old trailhead, freshly widened by several sets of boots pointing in all directions. Jo peered down into the thick expanse of fir dotted with ash and alder plunging into the ravine. It sloped away quickly. It was impossible to see much beyond the first hundred yards.

She stood on the other side of the orange and white sawhorse barricades, miles away from anything resembling meaningful access. She turned to Tolliver Larsen. His blue eyes were stuck wide open and he was even paler than usual, approaching translucence. His emerging Adam's apple nudged an inch up or down every few seconds.

"You okay?" She put a hand on his arm, and he blinked. This kind of thing buttered her bread – but most people remembered to be at least a little mortified by death.

"Yeah. I am. This is just kinda crazy. Hope I can help." He cleared his throat, then licked his lips. They were naturally ruby-red, as though the sweet vibrancy of his youth needed a highlighter run across his face just to make sure you no-ticed.

"You're as reliable a source as I've got around here. Heard anything?"

"Well," two ruddy patches rose on his pale cheeks. "One of the hikers was Sequoia Pfortner. She told me all about it, because she knows me, because she used to babysit me and my sister. Anyway, she told me she saw long, black hair. Said the body wasn't big. Maybe a girl, like maybe a teenager? And everyone's just sure it's Brittany Roebuck. She's missed all week at school."

"Okay. Can you get me Sequoia's number?"

"Yeah. No problem."

As he scrolled though his phone, Jo stared at the unremarkable trail head leading into the ravine. She thought back to Tucker trail, the stealthy return to her car yesterday afternoon. Two sketchy boys and their anxiety that the shit would hit the fan over someone named Brittany Roebuck. The odds this body wasn't that girl were as slim as Jo's chances of ever looking good in skinny jeans.

Last night Jo had researched Brittany, internet searches and the *Quartermaster* archives, social media. Senior in high school. She'd bragged recently on her Facebook about early acceptance to UW. She led the Spanish club, served for two years as an ASB officer, and qualified as an Academic All-American every semester at MHS, except last spring. She was also a cross-country stand-out. Jo remembered she'd done a piece on the team last season. Brittany had placed well at state for her personal time - last year.

What was missing from Jo's picture? The one Brittany had painted for the world, the one her parents were probably holding onto with a vise grip. How had she, presumably, died in a remote ravine?

"Tolliver, how well did you know Brittany?"

He sucked his lip and looked down. "Not super well. We were on cross country together for a few years. We used to meet up and run to school in the morning during cross country season. She was a good partner, at least for coaching. I'm like, a better runner for sure, because of her." He paused, hands on his slender hips. "She was a lot better runner last year, though. A lot faster." The poor kid's gaze had wandered while he talked. Now, he stood slack-jawed and vacant.

"Was Brittany who you were supposed to meet yesterday morning - your mom said your running partner never showed."

"Uh, yeah." Tolliver's bright-red mouth hung open just a little, looking like he was catching up with Jo on the math.

Jo kept pressing him. "I heard she was close with Ashley Sorensen. Do you know if she ever spent time with Tyler Sealth or Jered Brasier?"

"Brittany and Tyler used to be together, I think. And I think Ashley and Jered are going out."

"Really?"

"Yeah. I guess – when I think about it – " Towering over her, white and skinny as the aspen trees behind him, he wavered, then continued. "Brittany used to say what a tool Jered is. So I guess she knew him."

Brittany was apparently much smarter than her friend Ashley. "Okay. Good to know. So, did Brittany ever seem short of money to you – or maybe suddenly not short of money?"

"I don't think so? She always had enough to get whatever after away meets, when the team bus stopped at McDonalds, you know, if we had time before the boat. Sometimes she'd cover me."

McDonald's millionaire. Not exactly rolling deep, but teenager flush. There was no telling yet if that money came through her parents or by other means. Jo moved a pile of rust-brown needles back and forth in the dirt with the tip of her boot. "So, Tolliver. If this is Brittany, here, this morning – knowing what you do about her – what do you think happened?"

"Umm."

Watching his blue eyes turn bright, Jo's own throat started to tighten up. She realized her mistake. Tolliver was a just a sheltered Island kid. She'd gotten carried away, pressing him. Valerie would very likely be pissed off about Jo working her son over, and she had a right to be – because now the kid was actually crying.

She reached up and put a hand on his shoulder. "I'm sorry for your loss, Tolliver. Just keep your breathing slow and steady."

He tried to grin, bent his long neck. "Thanks."

"Why don't you go on back to school, or home for the day."

"Maybe in a minute." He paused and looked around at the gathered community. "It feels important to be here. I was gone when she went missing, you know? When she missed our state cross-country finals in Spokane. I hadn't talked to her in a while. I wish I had," he finished, quietly.

"Right. I'm sorry." She figured the least she could do was give him something else to think about. "Before you go, can you help me out with one more thing?"

He nodded, eager to please. She took his arm and led him away from onlookers. She pointed past the tape and into the woods. "Can you tell me a little about this place?"

"Yeah. It's land in the Makah Preservation Society. They own most of it. I think they have for a while."

Jo was familiar with the conservancy. They'd cornered more than two hundred acres on Makah over the past ten years. The woods on the Island ran deep and undisturbed.

He swept an arm along the edge of the ravine, where it curved up to meet the main road another sixty yards away. "It's acres and acres of watershed. The creek runs right into the Sound."

"And do a lot of people hike here? Is it used a lot?"

Tolliver's white eyebrows dipped. "I think they opened up a trail last year. It winds all over the Wash, up into Lost Valley, back down along the water through the Split and then into town. But it's a pretty serious slope here, and it's almost im-possible unless it's been dry. We used to come here when I was a kid. Always took the boat to get to the beach. Didn't go into the ravine a lot."

"There's a beach?" A beach where a man with a small boat might come ashore, for instance?

"Yeah. Pretty gravelly up on the shore. You can swing out off the madrona trees into the water when the tide's like all the way up and if the moon's totally full. But when the tide's way out it's sandy and nice."

"Thank you. You want a ride back to school?"

"No. I'm good. Is that what it's like to be interviewed by the legendary Jo Ford?"

"That's the friends and family version." Another tug of regret pulled at her. She'd gone too far with him.

He gamboled off to his car, a burgundy dinosaur, egg-shape straight out of the nineties and a bald spot covering the roof. One of the assembled folks waved, walked over and gave him a hug. Jo probably should have done that too.

She looked around again, thinking she might find another target for filler copy. She'd expected a crush of rubberneckers to show. Instead, the few people who had been there were already filtering away. Most visitors had left fresh-cut flowers at the base of one of the biggest trees. In contrast, this past summer, when a rare fin whale had beached out by the southern ferry dock at Queets Point, she'd had to park a mile back and hike along with a steady stream of on-lookers and volunteers. The response here, or lack of, stood out to her. In Baltimore she'd gotten used to shoving through crowds to cover a crime scene. Mourners, press, and the morbidly curious. She expected something like this happening in a small town, the potential death of one of their own, to create a minor crowd at least.

The road accessing the ravine dead-ended only a couple hundred yards away. Not a lot of car traffic, not a lot of foot traffic. They weren't far from the Reach, the hooked nosed jetty defining the north end of the Island. She'd reported a cap-sizing there last month. The Reach boasted wicked currents at every tide change. So not a lot of boat traffic headed to that beach Tolliver had mentioned, unless it was up from the south.

Not a bad place to hide a body. Maybe even a great place to dump a body. But if it had been a dump, the entire Puget Sound was a better bet and at anyone's disposal. If you had access to a boat.

Access. Everything she'd been investigating the last twenty-four hours seemed to boil down to access. Brittany had easy access to all the homes via the network of Island trails. No need for a car, and hence no out-of-place tire tracks. Small, careful girl, shallow or no footprints. The copper crimes were, for lack of a better word, respectful. No vandalism, no broken windows, nothing but the targeted items disturbed. Any thief with any experience would have plundered any valuables at hand. Any thief who felt a little bit guilty, a hint of compassion for her fellow neighbors, would have executed the burglaries with a little care.

She turned back to the scene and snapped a few photos. The green branches of the trees, the light trunks, and the dark in between, weaving its way through all of it. Bystanders, official police vehicles, and the lone Deputy Locke. Her head was turned, dark, wide-brim hat set back, thumbs tucked into her black leather service belt.

Another car arrived, a nondescript crossover making its way slowly toward the end of the road. Jo and Deputy Locke started toward it simultaneously. It parked, and after a minute or so, she recognized Kyle and Nancy Roebuck - Brittany's parents - as they got out.

IT'S THE KIND OF CLUB NO ONE WANTS TO JOIN

Deputy Locke approached Kyle and Nancy Roebuck, hands out and shepherding them back toward the vehicle. Kyle took a step back. His wife, gaunt, but still looking determined, didn't. He gently took her elbow. Brittany's parents stood, numb, waiting, as Brenda Locke spoke to the mic on her shoulder, presumably asking Hill what she should and shouldn't let them access.

Jo edged within earshot as Locke addressed them. "Mr. and Mrs. Roebuck, I won't ask you to leave, but I am going to ask if you can stay here, with your car."

"We heard – " Kyle got that much out. A fireplug of a man, his red flannel coat intensified the color rising in his face.

Jo held her phone low at her hip and snapped a quick photo as Nancy Roebuck's hand came up to cover her mouth. A one-dimensional silhouette set at the edge of the ravine where her daughter had presumably died, she wore a black hoodie, "MHS XC" in gold across the front. It looked at least a size too small for her. Through the gentle white fog hugging the dark bodies of the massive firs towering over her, the woman's despair leapt right through the camera.

Locke opened her arms, moved forward and herded the Roebucks backward. "Brenda please tell us something," Nancy insisted. "No one answers the phone. Not Hill, not our case worker. We just want to know what's going on."

"We're waiting on CID from Seattle to arrive. We've confirmed there's a body in the ravine. That's all I can tell you. It's all I know – for sure."

"And you don't want us here in case it's Brittany." Kyle's stout hand drifted upward, and Nancy pulled it back down to her side.
"We won't know who it is for a while yet," Deputy Locke answered. "And if we do need you, if we have reason to – we'll call you. I'm really sorry."

Locke inclined her head at both of them. "I am sorry. There's nothing more I can say. And you should be home. I'm sure your case worker will be calling you. She really should have already."

The Roebucks stood their ground. Brenda did too, her head down but her intention clear. The lost couple looked at each other, then toward the ravine. A few of the remaining locals started to wander over to them.

Jo outpaced them. She nodded a warm hello first to Nancy, then Kyle – who wouldn't look at her, wasn't looking at anything anymore except the middle distance and the bright yellow caution tape strung across it.

"This has to be awful, Mr. and Mrs. Roebuck. I'm sorry. I don't know if this is Brittany, but either way, I am so very, very sorry."

"Thank you," Nancy replied, thick, as though she'd said it so many times the words stuck like sawdust coming out.

Jo could describe that feeling in detail. The dull weight of it, the hate in it. But empathy wasn't her job. Getting the whole story was.

"I'm sorry," Jo repeated. "I know it's a bad time. I think for a while it will always be a bad time, though. Could I ask you a couple questions about Brittany?"

"Not right now," Kyle whispered. He looked to Nancy, and her bloodshot eyes.

Brenda Locke started walking toward them, shaking her finger at Jo.

"Could you tell me – was she still spending much time with Tyler Sealth?"

"No. She doesn't. We make sure of that. Let's go, Kyle." Nancy frowned at Jo as she replied.

"Even though Tyler's working with Luke Sorensen – her friend's father? She has to spend time there, on occasion?"

"Brittany told us she and Ashley didn't go into the shop. And we believe her."

"Of course." Jo played the last card in her hand. "What about Randy Fuller?"

"Ms. Ford, I think it's time to wrap this up," Locke stepped between Jo and the Roebucks. "Kyle, Nancy, please head on home. I promise you'll be getting a call with more information – soon."

Nancy spared another nasty look at Jo before she and her husband got back in their car and drove off.

"That was totally inappropriate," Locke said.

"That was me doing my job," Jo replied.

"If you want information, you should go through the proper channels."

"Fine." Jo held up her phone, walked off, and dialed Elijah Hill yet again.

Jo propped the phone in between her ear and shoulder and opened her notebook back up. She wondered where he was right now, down in the ravine or at the station.

"Captain Hill speaking."

"Hi. It's Joanna Ford. Thanks for taking my call." She cocked her bat and took a swing. "ID on the body you found – can you confirm that it's Brittany Roebuck?" Her reply was efficient and snappy. Even with the somber mood surrounding her, it was good to be stretching long dormant but well-cultivated muscles.

"No comment."

"Can you confirm a description – teenage girl with long dark hair?"

"No comment."

"Come on," she cajoled. "Don't leave the press out in the cold. You know we start chasing angles you don't like when you don't feed and water us properly." She scraped her blond hair out of her face with her forearm, ducked behind a hemlock tree for a break from the wind that was picking up.

"Look, Jo. I'm not stonewalling you. Just appreciate some time on this thing."

"Foot race with a suspect – so you're thinking murder?" She leapt deftly from conclusion to conclusion.

"We're not sure what it was yet. CID will take it from here. But we want a head start. It's all I can say, and it's not to be shared."

"Just background. I get it. But you know and I know and everyone else is saying it's Brittany. I can help you control the flow of information," Jo offered.

"So can our PIO," he came back at her flat. "You'll want to make sure she has your number handy."

"Will-do." Public Information Officers were notoriously stingy, guarded, and entirely unhelpful. Jo would do much better to keep things on the smooth with Elijah. One more try and she'd beg off. "Can you at least give me a cause of death?"

"We're still working on it. I'd appreciate if you lay off on any other speculation."

"I don't write speculation. Vi doesn't publish it. I know you're in the weeds today. Can we talk tomorrow? First thing? It's about Brittany Roebuck and Jered Brasier. I think I've got something Elijah. You'll want to hear it."

There was a pause and a rush of conversation in the background. She heard Hill shout something, but it was muffled. In a moment, he came back on. "Actually, just pass whatever you've got on to Deputy Locke. She'll relay it to me, and we'll follow up if it's anything."

Jo looked over at Brenda Locke. The woman's gaze managed to take in everything while appearing to see nothing at all. Competent. But low on the food chain. And not Jo's biggest fan at the moment. Join the club, Brenda.

"Nope. I'm serious about this," Jo said. "I'm not a hick junior detective. Call me as soon as you're available –"

"Don't take this personally," Hill cut in. "But I don't have the time. Let me give you this, though – I was wondering – I'm going to send you a photo. I want you to tell me if you recognize it. Strictly confidential. Disclose it, and you and I are done. We're looking hard for breaks here."

"Alright. I'll look out for it. Thanks." Placated, Jo clicked off. Maybe she wasn't as far out of the loop as she feared.

As soon as she hung up, her phone buzzed.

"Just what the hell are you doing out there?" Vi's shout carried through the cell and probably across the road.

"Nothing?" Jo looked around guiltily. The midday light had started to dim. She pulled up the hood of her raincoat. "At least nothing I shouldn't be doing."

"I hear you're harassing Brittany Roebuck's parents for a story?"

"That's not how I would put it."

"I don't care how you put it." Vi sounded seriously wound up. Her irascibility was usually self-conscious and good natured, but there was an edge in her voice this morning. "Stop and get out of there as soon as you cover the W's. It's disrespectful. As long as you work for me, you'll think about people before you think about anything else."

"Okay. Okay. Got it." She took a deep breath and leaned against her car. "Listen, Vi. Changing gears. Sort of. I've got a theory on the copper problem, how this all might go together..." She could tie Brittany to the means for the break-ins, and to Tyler, Jered, and the Sorensens. She could tie the Sorensens to the copper. But how did Randy and Brittany fit together? She'd only find out by chasing the leads she had. This was going to get sticky. But Jo never saw a sleeping dog without thinking about scratching it behind the ears. "I believe Brittany might be somehow connected to the copper break-ins, and I'm going to keep investigating that."

"You'll do no such thing, Jo Ford. Do you hear me?" Vi's pitch rose with every word she spat out. "And if it is Brittany who died out there, well, there's no way she could have been the thief. You can take my word on that. So, drop it."

"Sure." Drop the big lead. She thought about her lunch tomorrow with Beth Berge, Managing Editor at the *P.I.*. Beth's offer – well, two offers – sitting smack at the center of the table. "Wait – Vi what do you mean, if she's the one who's died? What does that have to do with whether or not she did the burglaries?"

"Nothing. Just – I just mean the Roebucks are good people. You don't have to make a damned federal case out of everything anyone says."

"Okay. Okay." She placated Vi with more assurances that she'd leave Britta-ny's family alone and clicked off. The first drops of water started to patter on the ground at Jo's feet. The surrounding trees let out a giant sigh as the wind rushed through them, and the rain started up in earnest. She climbed into the Volvo. As her windshield wipers pounded back and forth, she sat in the car at the side of the road on her phone and opened up her email. The promised message from Hill loaded.

Attached was a single photo. In it, an object sat on an off-white background. It was next to a ruler, measured about six inches long. Stainless steel, maybe just steel, maybe another metal Jo couldn't clock right off . But she did recognize the shape. Though the assembly was different, it was a very near facsimile to the tower in Luke Sorensen's workshop. Not all that dissimilar from the piece sitting in T yler Sealth's window.

Based on what she'd learned yesterday, Tyler and Brittany had a relation-ship, even if they were no longer dating. Island kids were inherently tight. They knew each other from the time they puked on each other's' shoes in pre-school to the time they puked on each other's shoes partying after senior prom. Tyler had access to melt down the copper and a sense of the value. Brittany might easily have been delivering the raw materials, the pots.

Cause of death would clear up a lot of questions. If Brittany was murdered, the likeliest suspect was already sitting smack in the middle of the table.

Jo emailed Hill back, hedging her bets – said the piece looked familiar, but she couldn't quite place it.

Because she couldn't quite place Tyler as a murderer, even with his shifty frenemy Jered Brasier making house calls. Whether Vi liked it or not, Randy was leading her suspect list.

She added in one more "call me" at the end of the email for good measure. She'd give more when Hill did. She checked her watch. Barely time to get home before noon and tag out Frank. It killed her to put a simmering investigation off until the next day. It killed her to think she might get to the bottom of it all and write an article that never saw the light of day, unless she screwed over Vi and went right to her good friend Beth Berge at the *P.I.*

Jo thought a little harder about screwing people. Where that road led, and where it ended. She sniffed, started the car, cranked the heat, and headed home for a cozy night in with Laura.

WHAT YOU MIGHT CALL A GUT FEELING

Long after going to bed and long after giving up on sleep, that night Jo woke several times to the high-pitched howls and yelps of coyotes in the distant woods. She listened closely. She thought she heard two distinct packs yipping back and forth. Whether they were simply being social or celebrating a kill, there was no way to know. After an hour of lying awake listening, she gave up, pulled on her robe and went to the window to wait out the light that always came so slowly here.

She stared from their second-floor bedroom window down at the bright yellow shrubbery ringing the yard. Vi had told her the name of the winter-blooming plant and she couldn't remember it. This morning she wasn't contemplating landscape so much as the state of her stomach. It vibrated this way, wired for sound, on three distinct occasions - when she thought about sex, love, or coffee. Jo hadn't even considered her first cup this morning. Which left sex and love. Sex had been off the table for the last couple years, until they'd moved here. And this wasn't about Beth Berge.

Jo was in love this morning. She'd fallen in love with her job again, overnight. Her gut, tighter by the second, was set on supernova; getting ready to pull her entire world together, then blow it all apart when she got a chance to write a real story, snag that byline in a paper than meant something.

Luke, Tyler, Jered. Tall men who knew more than they told. A dead body and Randy Fuller. The world's weirdest mystery. It all reminded her what it felt like to be on the hunt. She'd been a different person the decade she'd covered the daily police beat for the *Baltimore Sun*, before moving to the *Post*. She'd been a woman falling madly in love with journalism.

"Funny how God always gives us what we ask for."

Jo chuckled. Morning, Big Jack.

True enough. None of this was ever what she'd asked for, at all. Not Makah, not *The Quartermaster.* Jo didn't empathize with the willful ignorance of the small Island community. The persistence of their innocence annoyed her. Vi was her friend, but Jo didn't understand her.

The thefts she was investigating, in and of themselves, bothered her. They were so entirely juvenile. And in spite of – or perhaps because of – that fact, she knew there was more. Something she couldn't work out that lead her to worry about what might have become of Brittany Roebuck. Five thousand people surrounded by a mile-wide moat didn't lend credibility to any theories involving coincidence.

There was an easy way to cure her anxiety and her stomach, fortunately, and that was action. Jo stretched and popped, and the house did the same as it woke alongside her. The two-story farmhouse was more space than they needed. But she couldn't find better rent and it wasn't that hard to clean empty rooms. She'd left all their furniture in D.C. and leased out their town home turn-key when they'd moved West.

Jo tugged her thick, dishwater-blonde hair into a ponytail. She glanced over her shoulder at her wife, snoring with gusto. Her devastated septum had been jigsaw puzzled together as well as possible but deviated didn't even begin to cover it. She sat on the edge of the bed and ran a hand over Laura's brow, dotted her cute, crooked nose with a finger, and gave her shoulder a squeeze.

"I'll miss you today, babe. I could use your help on this, I think."

Jo was often out the door by the time Laura woke, but she chatted at her any-way because she missed mornings with her. She missed the ease of being middle-aged together with nothing left to fight about except whatever story NPR just aired and pattering back and forth about having Thai or Indian for dinner. She missed rock-paper-scissors for who had to leave their cozy brick town home and pick up the *Washington Post* and the *New York Times* from the driveway on snowy mornings. When it was particularly hot or cold out, Laura would come back from a ro-sham-bo loss with, "If you're so eager to read your own articles, you get the paper." Hard to argue with that.

But these days that never happened, even when Laura was awake. One or two words was the most she could hope for out of a sunrise heart to heart with her best friend. Sleep was come and go after the TBI, and not to be disturbed. When Laura did manage it, she slept like an otter, hand clamped firmly on Jo's. As though her wife might drift away in the long dark of the winter nights and the two would never find each other again. As though that had not already happened.

Jo reached over to the worn second-hand nightstand and popped open the case holding her moss-green contact lenses. Below her from the kitchen she picked up muffled sounds of dishes clanking and dog nails scrambling on hardwood. Her house was not her own, not really, and she'd tried to learn to be grateful for that. Frank was already here, ready for the day shift. Their dog Spot had probably already eaten enough scraps to spend the morning harking up pork belly all over the house. She'd have to apologize to Frank, yet again, for being late last night. Her excuses had begun to sound thin, even to her own ears.

She glanced again at her unconscious wife and wished for some reaction from her. Wondered what insight Laura would have into Makah that Jo was still lacking, some piece of shared Island past that might unlock the story. She blinked and rubbed her eyes and took a deep breath of morning that smelled like bacon and coffee.

Three years ago, Jo had started a day much like this one by blowing off a skeptical look from her father-in-law to snag yet another piece of bacon from the pan –

"I can't argue with you Frank, Rosie is one delicious pig. I could get used to this." Jo said, nudging Laura's dad with a grin.

Laura had wrinkled her nose. "Murderer."

"Don't talk to your Dad that way," Jo had replied.

"I wasn't. I was talking to you, Joanna Ford. You met Rosie. You *fed* her. How could you be complicit in her slaughter?"

"With boundless savory enjoyment." She snagged Laura by a perfectly an-gled hip and waved greasy fingers, which earned an anticipated increase in the horror stamped across her face. Fearless in covering genocide in Myanmar and too tender-hearted to eat the family pig. Jo's wife, A to Z.

"Stop." Laura wriggled free, smiling.

"Too bad Spot's not here to savor it with me." There was no way they were packing their over-sized puppy into a crate and stuffing him into a cargo hold for the five-hour flight from D.C. to Seattle. Though she was sure the dog would take to Makah like a pig to –

"One of you girls going to help with dishes?"

"Of course, Dad," Laura replied.

Both Tanakas busy at the sink in Frank's small kitchen, Jo refilled her coffee and wandered over to the dining table. The local paper, or the hilarious attempt at a newspaper, that Jo referred to as The Colloquial Master, lay open to a feature on sustainable alpaca farming.

"Hey babe," Jo called out. "Let's retire to Makah and spend our days reporting innovations in composting. This bad excuse for a newspaper probably makes great starter."

Her wife didn't respond. Jo flipped through more articles on local happenings, including a story that had a little meat on the bones. The large and once far-famed Kibo outerwear manufacturing plant on Makah had closed recently, after the death of the Stewart family patriarch. The son, Brian Stewart, had sold the business, putting hundreds out of work. The piece romanticized the deep Island roots the company had laid, profiled families that had worked there for generations, and the ramifications of the factory sitting empty while lean times plagued the vulnerable Makah middle class.

"Frank have you heard what they're going to do with the old Kibo plant?"

He turned from the sink. "Maybe a hydroponic farm."

Laura appeared behind Jo, rested hot soapy hands on her shoulders. "Hope they do something with it. It's a shame to think it would just sit there – and, umm, go to *pot*."

Jo craned her neck around and shook her head. "Couldn't resist, could you?"

Laura glanced over to the entry and her bright red Kibo jacket, manufactured right down the road. She'd been wearing it the day she and Jo had met ten years ago. Both had been covering the W. Bush inauguration for different outlets. Jo for the *Post* and Laura with the *Associated Press*.

"Well if Brian shut down Kibo," Laura said, "I'm hanging on to my old jacket, hell or high water. That thing is indestructible."

"Yes, but you're leaving it with me while you're running sorties and filing reports out of Baghram next month, right?"

"I still get to take your new Ray Bans?"

"Absolutely. I think I should just give them to you. You look like Christiane Amanpour and Gloria Steinem's love child when you're wearing them." Jo licked a finger, planted it on Laura's hand, and hissed. Then she stood and grabbed Laura by the waist again. Laura laughed and didn't fight her off this time, but pulled her tight and kissed her.

Laura slipped into the coat and flipped her sleek black hair out from under the collar. "Come on baconater. Let's go uptown and kill a couple hours on the porch at the Roastery. I have a list of people I want to run into."

Jo had smiled, happy to be led by the nose into whatever adventure her wife sought. "Your wish is my command, babe. At least while we're on vacation."

That January following, Laura had indeed gone to Afghanistan. A month after that, she was in a hospital in Ramstein, Germany. She'd stayed there for weeks, lingering in a coma. The roadside bomb that took out the transport she'd been on with the *AP* covering the Parwan Province had gone off miles from anything even passing as a field hospital. In the end, it hadn't been the politics, or the oil, or the religion or the war – but the two hours it took to get Laura any real help that caused the most damage. Lazy blood puddling like rain in the gray potholes of her brain had been what had turned Jo's sharp, funny, adventurous, wife into a volatile cross between a brilliant autistic toddler and a middle-aged woman with come-and-go dementia.

Twenty-four-hour care was a lot more affordable and a lot easier to come by in a small town, so they'd moved to Makah to find it. To Jo's horror and delight, Laura was doing better here. Her depression had already lifted, just enough, just a little. Just enough to hope about. The place Laura called home, the one-stop-light town, was exile for Jo but refuge for her wife.

Jo slid into her bunny slippers and pulled on an old Georgetown hoodie, made her way back to the window, still reluctant to face up to her day and the "I'm still sorry," she owed Frank for being so late last night. Again.

The sun was deciding to make a rare winter cameo this morning. The chickens growled and clucked as outside their run an old Jeep knocked a few times and died. Valerie Larson, the vet, here to check on their current bout of bronchitis. Jo wondered if she were the absolute last person out of bed on Makah.

At the far edge of the yard, Jo and Laura's proud mutt Spot hoovered the glistening salal ringing the grass. He barked once, then went completely batshit, spinning in circles, before plunging into the dense underbrush.

COME ON OVER, VALERIE

Jo hustled down the narrow staircase. She threw a wave to Frank on her dash through the kitchen, the back door, and out onto the porch.

"Spot. What the hell – what's up?"

His brown head emerged from the bushes, and he barked again. Then, Jo saw a flash of golden cream shimmy up a broad doug fir, followed by a black tail, crooked near the end - Vi's cat.

"Paula," she shouted. Spot came over, but the cat didn't. Jo trudged through the patchy, wet grass to the edge of the yard and waded into the thicket, arms crossed and peering into the treetops.

From behind her came a rich, merry voice. "She won't come back until she's ready. Vi'll be glad to know she's okay, though." The vet, Vi's friend Valerie Larsen, had joined her in the pursuit.

"Strong willed?"

"You bet. She puts Vi to shame."

Jo turned a three-sixty and announced to the forest, "Bacon for the first cat I see on the porch this morning."

"Good start," Valerie said as the two women returned to the yard.

Jo followed her over to the coop, tried to look like she was making a meaningful assessment of the situation. The lease on the sturdy farmhouse house had come with the chickens or no deal. Affordable places on Makah were one in a million. She was already stretching them thin paying for Laura's medications and therapies. So she'd signed on, then ironically jumped into the spirit by naming her favorite hen Foxy Loxy. Irony came around to bite her in the ass one morning when she'd found nothing but the bloody stump of Foxy's foot on the outside of the run. The next week she'd found the chickens quiet and lethargic, not an egg in sight, and promptly called Vi – who gave her a deserved hard time for condescending to a way of life some people fought for every day – and referred her on to the woman standing in her yard right now.

"So, Valerie. How's the herd?" At the sound of Jo's voice, Spot shot from around the back of the house and ran right past her. "Don't you dare mess with those chickens!" Jo's shout carried across the yard as her words rang through the crisp air.

The dog ignored her of course and darted right through the run. He skidded to a stop at Valerie's feet, who laughed at the commotion. He continued to nose along until Valerie snapped and he looked up, apparently puzzled by the nature of his transgression, before trotting over to her.

"Your brood's coming along fine," the vet reassured her. "Bronchitis is almost cleared up, the girls are looking much better. Another week, maybe, and they'll be laying again." She bent down to scoop up a rust-red hen that didn't seem to mind the woman poking and massaging her chest. "Heard you had a shoot-out with Happy at the store. Takes guts to mess with the McElroys."

Jo admired Valerie's ease with the chickens. When Jo stuck out a hand for an egg, she was likely to end up looking like she'd lost a street fight with a three-hole punch. "Can't really keep things to yourself around here, can you."

"Best not to try."

"You said Vi'd be glad Paula's okay. Has she been missing or something?"

Valerie became suddenly very absorbed in the hen she was holding.

"Valerie? Everything okay with Vi?"

"Yeah – sure. It's just that someone broke in and took her pots - you know the weird copper thefts? And when they did, Paula got out."

"Did she report the thefts? To anyone?" Least of all Jo herself, who was allegedly covering the story.

"No. You know how she is about law enforcement. I got the impression she didn't –" Valerie paused, seemed to simultaneously be sizing Jo up and collecting her thoughts. "Jo, I think she's hiding something. I think the break-in wasn't just about the pots. Maybe she was threatened, or something was taken she didn't want to talk about for some reason? She was defensive when I went over there - more than she usually is. I know I shouldn't have said anything to you if she hadn't, but you're – I trust you."

"Oh." Jo knew she should be pissed Vi hadn't trusted her, or curious about why, but for some reason Valerie's trust took her off-guard. "Well I'll ask her about it. Thank you for saying something." She dropped her gaze, kicked the toe of her slipper in the grass, wondering if this new trust would be long-lived. "So, has Tolliver said anything to you, about yesterday?"

"Not a lot. I've tried to get him to open up, but you know teenage boys. He thinks it's Brittany though. So do most folks. They were on cross country together. Used to run to school in the morning during the season. But she was always late. Drove him nuts." Valerie shook her head, dark mahogany waves bouncing into her face. She sighed, gently placed the hen she held onto the straw. "But he hasn't said much. Wish he'd just talk about it." She tugged off her work gloves and studied the mud before looking up. Laugh lines were just coming in at the edges of her soft brown eyes, a little deeper this morning than they'd been last week. "What do you think, Jo?"

"Well." The word hung between them as Jo debated how honest she wanted to be. Above them, a group of crows raised a shrieking ruckus, diving in and out of the trees before settling again.

"You think the same thing as I do, don't you," Valerie continued. Her voice thickened and darkened like the evening fog. "That I'm awfully glad I'm not Kyle or Nancy Roebuck. Just relieved to come downstairs this morning and find Tolliver and Alice going at it over breakfast."

"How are they, Valerie – aside from everything," Jo asked.

"Alice never met a soccer ball she didn't like." Valerie chuckled, or tried to.

"And Tol's full-time obsessed with his college apps. I think they don't really get it. Yet. What might have happened to Brittany - and what that means."

"No one gets something like that until you do."

"I suppose not."

"Where's he thinking about going to school?" Jo fumbled for small talk, a skill she'd never excelled at, that wouldn't make it seem like she was interviewing Valerie for a feature piece.

"Well, he'd take UW, and he's looking at Georgetown." Valerie nodded at Jo's hoodie, "But Pomona's at the top of the list. No offense, but twice the education and half the attitude." The vet's full lips twitched into a little grin, and Jo had a hard time taking the slight personally.

"Well, good luck. Hope he gets his top pick. I'm happy to write him a recommendation. My name doesn't go as far as it used to, but I'll help him any way I can."

"That's very generous. Thank you."

Jo was rewarded with a big smile, sunshine right through the rain coming from Valerie Larsen.

"No problem," Jo replied. "He's earned it. Anywa y, I've got to go, I'll be late for the boat. But can I get you a cup of coffee or something?"

"Yeah, sure. You bet. If it's on."

"I run almost exclusively on caffeine and the resentment of my fellow man. So yeah, it's on." Jo watched the dog sniff the squishy mud and straw-covered ground at their feet with the dedication of a coke addict cleaning up a mirror. "Come on Spotty. Time for breakfast." He looked up at her, then over at the other woman. He stood, but only to let out a giant sneeze before snugging his haunches back down again.

"Go on. I'll watch him," Valerie offered. "Just looking at you makes me feel guilty for being so warm."

Valerie's big barn coat looked a much better prospect and much warmer than the twenty-year-old remnants from her college days Jo wore. "Much obliged."

Occasionally Jo made an attempt to slip into the Makah patois, and failed most. It wasn't exactly the old-fashioned Andy Griffith aw-shucks and it wasn't the beating heart of Texas twang. It was a northern rural informality somewhere in between and it never came out of her just right.

Valerie pretended not to notice her cultural ignorance, turned to the coop, and then back again. "Oh – hey, Jo. Wait a sec. I've been thinking about those thefts. The copper pots. I might know how the houses are picked."

"What?" Jo spun on her bunny heel.

"It's not really airtight, but Vi and I are both in the Soroptimists? And we were both on the board a few years back. Actually, it's been a while, now, I guess. It was right after my divorce, and those couple years are a little murky. So it didn't come right to mind. But Vi had the idea one year to put together a home tour featuring the copper collections. We published a guide and everything. All the houses hit so far were in it, I think. I'm pretty sure, anyway."

Jo stared through the other woman. "Valerie, you two are close. Why do you think Vi hasn't told me what happened?"

"Well. I don't know. I think – she – she seems ashamed, for some reason, I guess." Jo must have looked stricken, because suddenly Valerie did too. "She can be secretive, Jo. That's all. She'd tell you if she could. You mean a lot to her. I don't know why she's being like this about it."

"Okay." It didn't make Jo feel any less like an outsider with Vi, but the exchange made her feel a lot closer to Valerie. "So, is there any way to know who was listed on that tour and who bought tickets?"

"I can get a list of the board members that year, definitely a copy of the program. It'll mean an hour or so in Connie Wilcox's dusty mess of basement. But I think I can help you."

"I'd really appreciate it. Thanks." Thanking sources was probably going to top the list of things Jo Ford did most often in her adult life, followed by cursing them.

She tossed off a wave and stomped into the mud room. She placed a hand on Laura's Kibo jacket, bright red and well-loved. As she so often did these days, she took just a second to hold and consider a sleeve and remember Laura – her wife, her real wife – wearing it. Before it had simply become another layer on the shell that hid her away from Jo and the rest of the world.

"What's going on out there? You wrangle Spot," Frank asked.

"I did. He was chasing Paula."

"Vi's cat? She'll be glad to hear the coyotes didn't get fed."

"Umm, yep." Jo pulled a couple mugs out of the dishwasher and paced over to the coffee maker. Next to it, Laura's collection of pill bottles lay scattered across the wood countertop. Anti-seizure, anti-anxiety, anti-depressants, painkillers, and of course a daily vitamin for good measure. Alongside Laura's collection sat Jo's. She broke into a new blister pack of Tamoxifen. Four years down, one to go. She popped the little white pill and chugged some luke-warm coffee.

"Can you take Valerie some coffee? I've got to get breakfast going if I don't want to miss the boat."

"Sure." Frank filled a tumbler, topped off his own, and put them both in the micro. "Order up." He grabbed the mugs and headed out the back.

"Hey Frank –" she stopped him halfway out the door.

"Yeah?"

"I'm sorry for being so late the other night. Late again, I mean."

A gust of wind and a clatter of dead leaves swirled across the porch, and the evergreens across the driveway roared to life. Frank raised his voice above them.

"Just don't make it even more of a habit, okay? Not so much my time, you know, as it is Laura's."

"Right. Okay," Jo mumbled. Forty-four and still brought low with the old, "I'm not mad, I'm just disappointed," coming from her father-in-law.

The glass storm door swung shut behind him.

Jo nuked her own cup of coffee, ran upstairs and hustled into her big-girl overtown clothes. Satisfied she looked good - but not too good - she ignored her guilt as she rummaged in the kitchen cupboard and pulled down a box of Bisquick. Distracted by the day to come, what she was and wasn't going to do, last night she'd mentioned oatmeal as a breakfast option to enthusiastic response from her usually quiet wife – only to shake the Quaker this morning and discover they'd basically run out. Change didn't always go over well, so she'd had to do some hard selling on pancakes with black-berry jam.

Frank came back in the house, they worked quietly on breakfast together as Spot wove in and out of her legs. Jo pulled out the emotional spackle and got to patching things up with her father-in-law.

"Big day, Frank. I better carbo-load."
"Okay. You make the pancakes. I'll scramble eggs. What's your big day? You look nice."

"Thanks." Jo's mind did some Cirque-du-Soliel contortions around her father-in-law's unwitting compliment and Jo dressing up to go see the woman she maybe, probably not, but maybe, or not, but maybe – no, definitely was not – going to sleep with. "I'm, umm, going overtown to run a few errands. But I'm shooting to get back on the four o'clock boat, if it's not overloaded."

Seattle would be a little bit of a shit sandwich, starting with the gynecologist and a mammogram. But she was wrapping with that lunch, just lunch, with Beth. Finally, if she had time, a stop at PNW Metalworks to play detective and follow up on that lead from Luke Sorensen.

Jo had even broken into the back of her closet to find a pair of slacks for the occasion. She'd taken her time picking out pants, a black sweater that actually matched her shoes that didn't have laces. When it wasn't mandatory, it was al-most nice to play dress up and sit at the big kids table. That's what the fashion TLC meant, nothing more.

Frank cleared his throat and studied the scrambled eggs intently. "Well call if you miss the boat, okay? Early kick off for Thursday Night Football. Hawks and Packers, shot at the playoffs. I'm hosting."

"You won't miss the national anthem, I promise." Jo held up three fingers, then turned to Laura, sitting at the table and staring at the radio listening to *Morning Edition* on NPR. "What are you and your Dad up to today, babe?"

Laura smiled over; crow's feet crinkled at the edges of her eyes. "Beach walk. Roastery and decaf."

When Jo did catch Laura in the mornings, she was downright chatty. Mornings were Laura's mini prison-breaks, the time her brain actually supplied the words to let the outside world know she was still with everyone in the here and now. It was Jo's favorite time of day. "I'll be sad to miss that. Grab me a moon rock."

Jo *would* be sad to miss it. Watching Frank and Laura's tentative, unsteady progress, hand in hand and heads bent as they strolled, was the foreground she loved best against the backdrop of tugboats, tankers, sailboats and ferries crossing the Sound. Laura loved the beach 'moon rocks' for their opaque inner glow. She had become an eagle eye at spotting the best. They'd amassed a sizeable collection in the giant glass vase dominating the corner of the living room.

"Would've been a good day to take out the boat," Frank said. "If it weren't in a county scrap yard."

"They found your boat – was it the one Randy ran into the Olympic?" Jo asked.

"Sure was. They pulled it up from the bottom of the Sound yesterday. Totaled. Filed a claim, but who knows."

"I'm sorry." Jo side-hugged Frank. He was half-way across the kitchen with a plate of eggs, and it was awkward. She gave up on making up and they sat down to breakfast. "Don't forget the sunscreen. Either of you. Clouds don't stop UV rays."

Jo kept one eye on the clock as they ate, then ended up sucked into a feature story about a U.S. raid on a terrorist base in Pakistan. Laura was still fascinated by anything to do with her old turf. Since the size of newsprint took daily papers off the table, and the computer gave her headaches, the radio was one of the only ways she could connect to the voraciously curious Laura Tanaka that had been. Jo almost couldn't stand to listen. Her wife could, and she liked to hold hands while she did. So Jo sat patiently listening and had mastered the art of not crying about six months ago.

The correspondent, the one who'd taken Laura's posting, signed off from Lahore. Jo shoved back her chair, swiped a sleeve at either eye. "Frank I'm leaving the dishes. You leave them too. I'll do them tonight after I get home."

He nodded, quiet.

Jo was almost out the door when she stopped again. The local affiliate had picked up the story she'd fed to the wire yesterday afternoon.

"An unidentified body was discovered on rural Makah Island yesterday morning. Hikers reported their find to the King County Sheriff's office, which has denied comment on the case. We'll bring you more details when they become available."

Love roiled around in Jo's stomach. This is what it feels like to be a real reporter, remember? She glanced over at Frank, head turned toward the radio. The story had caught his ear too. What would this death – presumably Brittany's death – mean to him, and to Makah? What did it mean to her? It meant she was covering a story that mattered. It also meant an as-yet unsolved, suspicious, probable homicide in the immediate wake of another suspicious death. That thought sent chilly fingertips of memory slithering down her spine. Of Washington D.C., a very bad man named Charlie Abish, and a Pulitzer Prize that came with a body count.

GATHERING WOOL: THE ITCHY KIND

She was tearing up the gravel driveway in the Volvo before she even checked her watch. Ten minutes left to make the ferry. She might be okay, if it wasn't overloaded with daily commuters. Miss the boat, late for the clinic, late for Beth. She cruised down the hill to the dock and was one of the last two cars to scoot on, just behind Vi Mitchell.

She zipped her jacket and pulled her hood up against the driving mist swirling at the back of the boat as it chugged out of the dock. She tapped her key on the rain-flecked driver's side window of Vi's Datsun pickup and raised her empty coffee tumbler.

Vi cranked down the window. "Running on empty?"

"Running late," Jo replied.

"What's new?" Vi flicked her wrist at Jo to back up and opened her creaking door. "Come on, let's go up. I could use the company."

Jo slowly followed Vi up the metal stairs and through the heavy steel door to the passenger deck. The older woman's outfit was a little quieter than usual, her standard loud, printed rayon top replaced by a faded black cotton sweater over brown polyester slacks.

They strolled toward the galley and queued up with the rest of the thirsty passengers. Jo had been shocked by her first cup on the boat. She'd expected something between day old 7/11 and Maxwell House and she'd been wrong. Even the Washington State Ferries took their coffee seriously.

Commuters and kids littered the blue and brown vinyl chairs and booths, reading books, frowning at laptops, and more often than not watching the ebony water slide by under the flinty sky. Mount Rainier wasn't out today. For the first two weeks Jo lived here, it had been hidden under clouds. She'd started to wonder if a giant mountain god had come and collected it unseen one night, plucking it from the rugged landscape as gently as Laura gathering moon rocks.

She gave an occasional wave and mouthed hello to people she recognized but didn't actually know. The checker she'd struck up a running conversation with at the market. The young guy with dreds who always seemed to be getting a cup at the same time she was at the coffee Roastery all the way over in Midtown, across from Frank's antique shop.

Jo had pegged four distinct demographics on the Island – lefty tech boom millionaire commuters, lefty blue-collar Washington every mans, lefty artist-hippies, and the multi-generational Makah rednecks who worked on barter and worked construction no matter how much rain fell. The truce among them was usually an easy unspoken one. The millionaires tolerated the perceived ignorance that came with the nativism of established Makah families, because they were willing to pay more than one kind of price for sumptuous bucolic seclusion. The folks with dirt under their nails ignored the millionaires' disdain because they were easy marks for over-priced construction projects and housekeeping. The working-class middle was the grease on the skids that kept either extreme from spending too much time together unsupervised. The hippies and artists snaked in and out of all of them like the familiar northwest fog, a peaceful cloud of weed-scented 'just be cool man' Xanax. But the real glue, what held it all together like Elmer's, was the choice all of them had made to live on the other side of the moat from the big city. The ferry, coming or going, brought them all together.

Vi steered them toward a quiet booth near the front. Along the wall were framed black and whites of Kibo workers from the nineteen forties. The plant had been given over for two years to the WWII effort, the machines and the Islanders manufacturing uniforms for American soldiers stationed anywhere cold, which was almost everywhere.

The two women hadn't said a word to each other since the car deck. Also unusual for Vi, who kept a running color commentary that, over time, had filled Jo in on a number of finer points of Makah life. The break-in she was keeping secret had visibly upset her. Jo wavered between going head-on and doing an end-run. Vi's bloodshot eyes and kindness, for all her irascibility, made up her mind, and she tossed a softball. "What are you up to in Seattle?"

"Well, I'll tell you what I'm up to." Vi came right back to life. "I'm getting smoked salmon for Randy's service. It was his favorite – just the one though, from Pike Place. He and the boys at that pricey tourist attraction in the center there are always friendly. Particularly the boy who sells the smoked goodies.

Randy went to school with one of the kids at the fish place a ways down, but he always said he just liked the smoke from the big shop most particularly, so that's what we're going to have."

"You're a good friend Vi. You really are. I'm sorry for your loss."

"Well, keep being sorry and then some." Vi shifted around on the vinyl seat as though she couldn't quite get traction. "And I hate to say it, you know I do, but maybe leave this all for Hill, Jo. Cold light of morning, time for me to think on it – it smells worse now than it did the other day. I don't believe Randy just hauled off and killed himself. But maybe what he did do was part of something you ought to steer clear of." Vi looked up at one of the Kibo photos above them, her gaze fixed and hollow on a group of workers clustered under a stand of winter-bare poplars. "You know Connie Wilcox called me first thing this morning? Said that when the cops went to Randy's place to search for whatever, they found a pound of heroin. Which doesn't make any sense at all."

"A pound of heroin?" Jo stifled a laugh. "Where would someone like Randy come up with a hundred-thousand dollars' worth of smack?"

"Someone like Randy?" Vi spat back. "You mean someone who's not quite right? Someone damaged?" The older woman leaned forward. "You ought to know better than to say something like that, Jo Ford. Your Laura's just as bad off as that boy. She got hurt on the job, and that's okay, that's just fine, and she gets all the compassion she deserves. But he got hurt because he's got a disease and now he's disposable. Not right that one of 'em means something to you and everyone else, and one of them doesn't mean shit. Randy's been clean for years now."

Jo sat back on the bench. Out the window she spotted a black and red cargo ship chugging right for them. The ferry picked up speed to outpace it. "I'm sorry, Vi. You're right. But that's a lot of drugs. A lot. Little more than personal use."

"Well I don't care what the charge is or isn't. Randy's one of us. And he's been clean for years now. He was a good man, though I know you don't think so. You or anyone else who - " Vi stopped short. She cleared her throat, ran a finger at her nose, and looked away.

"Hey – I'm sorry." Jo laid a hand on the older woman's knee. It was time Jo gave up what she'd heard about Randy, though she wasn't sure how it would go over. "The drugs – listen, Vi, I'm sorry to tell you this. When I went to interview Tyler Sealth about the copper pots, a friend of his came by. Jered Brasier?"

"Tyler Sealth is not friends with that little twerp. He's –"

"Beholden?" Jo filled in and continued. "I had an opportunity to overhear them talking about Randy – and learned that since he died, there's a 'distro prob-lem,' as Jered put it. So, if Randy was clean, he was somehow involved with Jered, and it sounds like they were selling."

"A-huh. Well." Vi tapped her foot on the green and white linoleum tile. The engines cut and the cabin quieted for a second. "You tell this to Hill?"

"I plan to. You implied the other day Jered was somehow connected to Brian Stewart – the Kibo heir? What's that all about?"

"You miss anything anyone ever says? Ever forget anything?"
The boat slowed. Their fellow travelers began to stand and shuffle their way down to the car deck. The boat shuddered as the engines reversed and it approached the dock.

Jo stayed put. "If I did, I wouldn't be any good at my job. What did you mean about Brian Stewart and Jered?"

"Nothing. Just spouting off. You know me." Vi patted Jo's hand, then stood. "I didn't know Randy was mixed up in anything, as far as Jered Brasier goes. Like I said. Perhaps it's best to let this all go." She glared then and pointed right at Jo. "And in case I wasn't clear, I don't care to hear theories about Brittany Roebuck and those copper pots. Now we know she –" Vi stopped, "You look elsewhere, or you stop looking."

What the hell was she supposed to go after, then? Jo had come to wonder if *The Quartermaster* ever did anything but echo the stories handed around the Island the week before it came out. That, and publish the high school sports scores. Or print legal notices. And disruptions to the ferry schedules. She wasn't surprised that small town news was different. But that meant her job was differ-ent. Vi focused Jo more on reflecting and reinforcing the culture of Makah than disrupting it or dismantling it. Scandal was fine, as long as it was about how the big broad world was encroaching. It was a journalism – if you could call it that – that Jo didn't understand, in a world she didn't understand.

But the more anyone, Jered or Vi, warned her off, the closer she wanted to get to this. So Jo lied. "You got it." She followed Vi to the stairs. They paused to let a pack of young boys shoving at each other clamor down. It was now or never. "Vi, why didn't you tell me you were robbed the other morning? I know that's why you're convinced it wasn't Brittany."

"Oh." Vi started down the stairs. "That. Guess I didn't think anything of it.

You've already been looking into it, I know that. So –" Her thick shoulders came up in a shrug.

Jo followed her. "So, when I'm investigating, one thing I love to do is talk to witnesses. Interview them?"

"I'll call you later. Sorry. Just a lot on my mind. How'd you find out?"

"Valerie told me, and she said they took your pots."

"Then there you go." Vi patted Jo's shoulder, opened the door to her truck and got in.

"They take anything else? Do any damage?"

"Nope. But they let my Paula girl out."

Pissed or not, Jo realized she'd buried the lede. "Vi. Shit - I can't believe I forgot to tell you. I saw Paula this morning. In my yard."

"You sure?"

Jo felt the little thrill at the payoff to her magnanimity, despite her own hurt feelings. "Yep. Notched tail, purple collar – a little robust? Definitely Paula. I would have picked her up, but Spot chased her off ."

"Probably better you didn't. She would've scratched the hell out of you."

"Even after I brought her all that bacon?"

"She knows that came from Frank." Vi seemed more like herself than she had this whole ride.

Paula's journey and reunion would no doubt make a fitting feature in the *Quartermaster.* Jo died a little inside. "Well she's out there. I'm sure she'll come home soon, alright?"

"Alright. Thanks Jo. And just to be like this – you have that article on the 50th Anniversary of the Island Quilters Collective ready yet?"

"Have it for you in the morning," Jo said, and died a little more. She headed for her own car.

She stumbled as they gave the dock a healthy nudge on the landing. Must be a new pilot. One of the passing crew members steadied her. Big and grizzled and sixty at least, his smile and his grip reminded her of her dad. The ferry always reminded her of Big Jack in one way or another. Twenty years at the Naval Academy and only a handful of days she could think of he didn't find time to get his Mastercraft out on the Chesapeake. As a little girl she'd get up in time to get out with him most mornings. Just Jo and Jack in the dark and the silence, the cicadas hours in bed and the frogs sleeping too. She'd work her small fingers at the knots of the ropes as the blowers on the inboards came to life and Dad set up the trolling rods. By the time it was light, and the rest of the world caught up, they'd be on their way back home. Jo smiling and Dad tying out the boat because her hands were covered in Croaker or Striped Bass guts, or cold from waving them in the air as they roared through the dawn, throttle wide open.

When she was older, she'd commandeered the ship and snuck out with girl-friends. A sunset cruise and Maryland blue crab right out of the pots off their dock made for an impressive date. Big Jack never mentioned it. By the time Jo was old enough to know what she wanted to do and who she wanted to do it with, don't ask don't tell was already the law of the land – and of the Ford household.

By then Dad didn't spend much time on the boat anyway. He didn't do much but sit on the dock after the cancer had taken Mom. Thank God he hadn't lived to see Jo through hers. That had been Laura's job, and she'd done pretty damn well with it. Every time Jo went in for her screenings, now, she wondered who would take care of her if she had to go another round. She panicked about it on sleepless nights, heart pounding in her ears in the silent dark; who would pay the bills, what would happen to them.

She startled as the same crew member tapped her window.

"You're up, ma'am."

The lane in front of her was empty. Behind her a line of cars sat patiently waiting for her to drive off, not a horn or a shout to be heard. Life on the water had a way of smoothing the rough edges. Sometimes just not enough. Well, she thought, Beth Berge would be smooth enough for all of it.

THE WEAKNESS IN JO

Driving over Pill Hill into downtown Seattle, the sun was too bright. Around Jo the traffic passed too quickly. The SUVs, mini-vans, delivery vehicles, hulking giants, all cruising by too close and in danger of clipping her mirrors or slamming into the back of her with the unexpected change of signals from green to red.

Jo almost kept driving past the iconic art-deco façade of the historic *Seattle P.I.* building. The giant globe in front shouting its gravitas, the gray concrete standing resolute under a deep blue sky, it was all too much of a contrast to her own weaknesses, the fatal flaws in her own internal architecture.

She slid the Volvo into one of the last remaining visitor spots in the garage, rested her head on the seat back, let out a hot breath. She could tell herself anything she wanted to. But deep down, where the truth hangs out waiting for you to stop by and have a heart-to-heart - she didn't intend for what already happened with Beth to happen just once.

Two months ago, that morning after, Jo had meant to stop. But in the many days between then and now, nothing about her situation on Makah had changed. Every week that had passed she found herself thinking more and more often about the Managing Editor for the *P.I.* – how Beth made Jo feel under fine white cotton hotel sheets.

She shook her head and started toward the stairs. Nothing was inevitable. Lunch could still be lunch. Just two colleagues catching up. She opened the door to the vaulted lobby. She crossed the black and white checked tile floor to the security desk. Beside her a massive wall displayed historic front-page headlines. Big national ones, of course, but local favorites too. The opening of the World's Fair. The ferry that rammed the West Seattle bridge. The Sonics winning the NBA championship. Mount St. Helen's eruption. Stories that made local news important, made locals feel important. Beside each front-page was a big photo of the journalist who'd bylined the article.

She stopped staring at what wasn't hers anymore and walked up to the massive front desk, anchored by a lone security guard.

"Hi. I'm Joanna Ford. Here to see Beth Berge."

The man was clearly unimpressed. "Wait here. I'll call her office."

"I'll wait here." She almost threw in, "and I won't touch stuff."

He called up, traded a few words, then set down the phone. "Secretary says Ms. Berge is headed down."

"Thanks."

Jo wondered how long she'd have to stand here soaking up other journalist's proudest moments, feeling her self-esteem and her resolve crumbling around her. The first time she'd given in to self-pity, it had only taken a handful of hours of staring into Beth's amber eyes. Catching up on the two decades since they'd graduated Georgetown. Since they'd called it off to take separate assignments; write other people's stories instead of their own. A few hours with Beth had been more than plenty of time for Jo to reignite an old flame and shake hands with the devil.

They'd started over the summer with get-reacquainted drinks on Lake Washington and Beth's hard-won concern. Jo's ex-girlfriend was soft enough to look at but cut like a diamond. When compliments were handed around, they were plenty effective. "I'd say you don't look a day older, Jo. But you do. You look older and better. Tired. But good."

Then, in Belltown, where they'd gone family-style on the best Thai dinner she'd ever had outside of Bangkok. Beth's first invitation had followed. "After I got back from Sinaloa, I wanted something different. I wanted to feel safe. I came home to Seattle and worked my way up. I've got a spot for you at the *P.I.*, Jo. Beat or stringer. Whatever you want."

And finally, waterside lunch at Salty's on Alki, early October light washing everything in gold. Watching the ferries cut back and forth across glittering Elliott Bay. Seattle shimmering in the background, and finally, the compassion she couldn't say no to. "I don't know what you're going through, Jo. I really have no idea. But I know you. And I know I can make it better, even if it's just for an afternoon."

Just a few hours were all it had taken to lay waste to the lifetime commitment Jo had made to Laura.

She didn't hide her smile when Beth appeared in her black pencil skirt to strut across the lobby. All curves and confidence, competence and ambition personified. Taller than Jo. Bigger than Jo. Better than Jo. They'd garnered sideways glances everywhere they went together in the nineties. She couldn't write it off to the old days to say with assurance it was the color contrast or the gay. Just plain old-fashioned envy. Jo had always excelled at dating up.

"Hey. Sorry I'm late." Jo said. "They were running with a boat down, messed up the whole schedule." She'd actually been late at the clinic. They'd had trouble with her mammogram, hadn't liked the fi rst set they'd taken. Jo wasn't ready to talk about that yet.

"No worries. Thanks for meeting at the offi ce. Can you come up for a min-ute? I'm waiting on an assignment to come back and I've gotta clear it for tomorrow."

"Sure."

Beth turned her cool gaze right on Jo as they rode up the elevator. She sensed the other woman's amusement at her discomfort, though it wasn't unkind. They hadn't stopped loving each other, after all. They'd just had other priorities.

They hit the top floor. Jo paused as the doors slid open. The newsroom hummed around her. She took a sweet and sour minute to soak up the familiar energy.

Beth took her elbow. "Come on."

They made it halfway in when some random white guy in a polo stopped them. "Hey Beth. I've got –" He looked harder at Jo. "You're Joanna Ford. The Charlie Abish-RICO-Pulitzer Joanna Ford?"

"Yep. I sure am."

He stuck out his hand. "Shawn Hansen. It's great to meet you."

"You too. What do you cover?" How quickly could she get him to switch topics?

"Asia-Pacific tech world. Waiting to make my big break. But who cares about me. I know you left the *Post*. What are you doing now? Freelancing?"

"Sort of." Dude was a dog with bone. How reporterly of him. "I'm over on Makah Island with my wife. I guess you could say I'm semi-retired."

"The way print's going? Good for you. But you're wasted over there. We could use you back on the battlefield. You ought to –"

Beth put a hand on Jo's arm. "Shawn we've got to get on. I promised this woman lunch and here I am making her wait. And I promise *you* I'm already giving her the hard-sell."

"Okay okay okay." He ducked his head. "Great to meet you. Hope I get to see you in here again." He waved around, saluted Beth, and rambled off.

"You feeling it yet, Jo? Even Shawn wants to see more of you." Beth walked on toward a corner offi ce looking out over lime-green Myrtle Edwards park and the storm-blue of Elliott Bay.

Jo followed a step behind and ran her eyes over all the men and women glaring at computers, talking on landlines and cells, sometimes both at the same time, and in general looking very invested in whatever task was at hand. She plunked down into an uncomfortable post-modern plastic chair opposite Beth's big glass-top desk. "Where do you want to eat? Please say we don't have to order in here."

"There's a sushi bar just up the hill," Beth responded. "Slow as molasses, but they'll speed up for me."

"Still know all the right people?"

"ABC, Joanna. Always be cultivating." Beth rapid-fi re clicked at her computer. "Here we are. Let me check one thing before we commit on this –" She grinned at Jo and then studied her screen for a minute.

Jo studied her. Making decisions. Running interference on articles that needed to be vetted, because there'd be actual blow back if they got something wrong.

"Golden." Beth clicked again, then grabbed her purse and came around her desk as Jo stood. She trailed a hand across Jo's stomach and breezed through the door. "You coming?"

"Yes. No – yes." Jo tried to laugh it all off and not to feel the pressure of the touch underneath her thick knit sweater. It didn't work.

The early afternoon sun winked off the towering glass high-rises downtown and the shifting surface of the Puget Sound just blocks away. It glinted off their water glasses and bounced through the restaurant. Around them diners clacked and clattered their way through business and casual lunches. Jo slipped easily back into her practiced professional role and at-attention posture. It was a conditioned response, surrounded by suits, crisp slacks and cashmere turtlenecks instead of ratty cargo pants and faded fl annel.

Desperate to get what she shouldn't be picturing out of her head, Jo homed in on the one thing that made her feel less like sex than guilt. The gynecologist appointment she'd just come from, and the diagnostic mammogram she wasn't worrying about. She'd had two other false positives in the years since the cancer had gone into remission. This would just be another bad read. No point in even mentioning it. To anyone.

"Thanks for meeting me, Beth. This is the perfect antidote to follow up the annual scrape and smash. The glory of being a woman."

"I hear that, all of it. We are the most glorious of the sexes." Beth's expression didn't hide her regard for Jo included in the statement. Her short black hair relaxed in thick bangs across her brow, and drew Jo's eye down over smooth taupe skin, past carefully shaped eyebrows –

Jo looked down abruptly, studied her half-eaten salmon poke bowl instead of the woman right across from her. She broke a sweat, and she couldn't even lie and blame it on the Tamoxifen.

Beth picked up the reigns. "So that body they found yesterday on Makah – between that and the boat collision, your little island is just lighting up the newsroom."

"I won't complain. First real stories I've had since I've been here. And I think the more I dig, the more I'm going to find. It all seems, right now at least, to come back to this sculptor, Luke Sorensen. The sheriff won't tell me anything about the collision or the body. But I think I've got another angle. Those copper break-ins I told you about last time I, um, saw, you." With the real world pressing in on her, Jo remembered how ridiculous it must sound to be taking all this so seriously. "Well – break-ins is a stretch. No one locks their doors, so I suppose you'd say trespass."

Beth blew a sharp, quick laugh through her nose. "I think I caught that plot once in a series about an old lady and her cats."

"I know. It's how they are." Jo snickered. "Keys in the car, houses open for anyone or her sister to waltz in and clean them out. But they love it that way, is what I'm picking up."

"You won't catch me writing invitations to be robbed, that's all I'm saying."

"The thief started small, one or two pots. Then this last heist," Jo paused at 'heist,' in reference to Vi's break in, and Beth's full, dark lips twitched.

"Fine. Laugh. But it's what I've got."

All of a sudden Beth's hand was covering Jo's, a striking, inviting contrast on the white linen tablecloth. She ran a finger over Jo's thumb. "Don't read me wrong. We all do what we've got to do, and you're working an honest day. So, tell me about your wild theories. Because when they're yours, they tend to pay off. Don't forget who you really are, Jo, under all that flannel."

"Thanks." Jo left her hand where it was and leaned her chin on the palm of the other. Then she sat back, sat straight up. She wanted to tell Beth Berge everything. She wanted her to be interested in everything she had to say, and she didn't want to stop there, and she wanted to be doing it all with a lot fewer people around.

"I'll listen to rural route stories any day anyway," Beth said. "The only thing I ever hear about are the bleeding hearts on the Seattle City Council snarling about growth management. That and how tragically underfunded our schools are, while Amazon and Microsoft are creating twenty-five-year-old millionaires weekly." She nodded. Her gold earrings swung back and forth, catching Jo's eye and reeling her in again.

Jo nodded back. Makah was a nice change of pace. But everything in moder-ation. Looking around her, out the window to the bustling Pike Place Market, she realized she was starting to overdose on rural. How long since she'd last been to Seattle? She couldn't remember immediately. Long enough to notice that the air here wasn't as clean and sweet. It was an odd thing to miss the smell of concrete.

"I've got a line on a girl, Brittany Roebuck. She's got means, opportunity." And the why? Jo hadn't gotten far on that but imagining was easy. "The age-old motive, cash, I suppose. Not like a few hundred bucks would go far against things kids want – cars, college tuition. And the old stand bys."

"Drugs and booze." Beth pointed her fork at Jo, and there they were. Collaborating. Jo stuck, spit balling with a partner and finding new angles. Could have just as easily been Jo and Laura, a few years ago.

"Yep." Drugs, sure but if Vi was right about what they'd found at Randy's, since when did white girls on the track team take up heroin? Randy Fuller, Brittany Roebuck. Tyler Sealth and Jered Brasier. You couldn't find a more disparate crowd. Society's one common denominator? Abuse. Drugs, alcohol, gambling... sex. Each and every one of them uniters, not dividers. Still, heroin didn't fit here. Jo was missing something.

"What's going on over there," Beth interrupted Jo's train of thought. "I don't mind watching the wheels turn, but I'd love to hear the story."

"Just drawing the picture that fits the puzzle pieces."

"You're holding out on me."

"Am I?"

"Yes ma'am. You always look so satisfied when you get it right. You look – completed. You've got the same expression for cracking a story and –"

Beth paused.

"Well maybe I'll get to see you make that face a little later this afternoon."

Jo chugged the rest of her water and rattled the ice. "So. Yeah. Anyway. Not the end of the story. I don't think Brittany was doing this all on her own. Copper pots aren't exactly easy to fence. It's gotta be whoever's stealing them is smelting them, then selling it overtown."

"Overtown?" Didn't Beth's eyebrow look smart as it arched upward? So well manicured. Jo pretended not to notice.

"Overtown. It's Makah shorthand for Seattle."

"You're going native."

Goddamn it, just let me breathe, is what Jo wanted to say. Instead, she played along. "Maybe. And don't think you're in on the joke at this point. You say overtown and you mean Tacoma, you'll get a quizzical look and a sad nod. Just a little in-group for you. I've got more, if you want it."

"I always want more," came the other woman's even-toned, unrelenting reply.

"Alright. I get it – I get you. Just –" Jo held up her hands, palms out. "I talk-ed to another kid, young guy, Tyler, who used to date Brittany. And Tyler just happens to work with a guy who just happens to have a smelting furnace. All of which produces money to buy, let's say, drugs."

Beth paused, stared at her, eyes traveling north and south. Resting so ca-sually on hair Jo had actually taken time to blow out this morning; then to her forehead, her eyes, her nose, her mouth. "Conspiracy solved. But apparently still not to Jo Ford's satisfaction."

Jo cocked her finger. "I'm not a big fan of coincidence, and on Makah? I can't see how they're not related. But if it is drugs?" The wet wind, the feel of the bulkhead digging into her back, and Jered's words came back to her. *"We've got a distro problem.... it's not long before shit hits the fan over pretty little Brittany Roebuck."* Did that imply motive, or just insider info about her death? "It begs the question of where murder comes in - at least how Brittany died – overdose, or something more vicious. Vi, my editor, doesn't want me on it. But there's something there, Beth. I know it."

"I'd run with that series for you, if you wanted to cover it like real news. Small town, big drugs? It's a hot angle. Get you back in circulation."

Going right to the *P.I.* would be the biggest fuck-you Jo could serve up to the woman who'd taken her in. "Well I don't know anything yet. Still all just conjecture." She poked her fork at her food but didn't take a bite.

"Seems like getting a look at the prelim autopsy might point you in the right direction."

"Sure, but that's hardly accessible to me."

Beth shrugged, tilted her head back and forth.

"Is it?" Jo asked.

"Might be accessible to me. What's a reporter without her sources?"

Real journalism. Real stakes. Pushing a story forward, not just regurgitating events. And making damn sure some young girl who got in over her head didn't end up a cold case. A little list of promises played in Beth's brown eyes, for Jo's benefi t. Problem was, she couldn't aff ord the mortgage on any of them. So, Jo dumped the clutch and slammed the conversation hard and awkward into another gear.

"Did you follow the Abish case?"

"Your Pulitzer series? Yeah," Beth said. "I did. How many bullpens do you think weren't chewing it over and cursing your name on the regular? When it comes to war-story swapping, yours is a trump card." Beth tossed her napkin on the table, signaled their waiter.

"Right." More fork-pushing ensued. The Abish break, the Pulitzer, were enviable. But her guilt over the still unsolved death of a District Court judge? Not so much. Laura - her wife - knew about that part of her past. Understood about it, what it meant to Jo.

Beth didn't of course and kept pushing. "It's not the only work you've done that's world-class. Why do you think I want your byline – and you – so badly?"

Jo shook her head and subsequently had to swipe her bangs out of her face. Beth's eyes followed the movement.

"Fine. Don't answer."

The waiter appeared with their check. Jo started to rummage in her bag for her wallet, stalling for time. She still hadn't found her resolve about this afternoon, one way or the other.

Beth pulled the little black folio across the table. "I've got it. Anything I do during the day is on the *P.I.* This is business. I'm going to win you over. You're going to write for me. It'll do us as much good as it will you."

"I don't know about that."

"Listen." Beth snapped the check closed, and once again put a hand over Jo's on the table. "I know what all this back and forth's about. You're good at hiding yourself, woman. But you're not that good. Having your body's nice. Having your mind would be divine. But you can leave your heart right where it's at."

Jo stood, abruptly. The scrape of the chair legs across the floor screamed in her ears. No one else seemed to notice.

They started toward the door. Beth's hand rested comfortably at the small of Jo's back. They paused on the sunny corner, Elliott Bay shining below them and skyscrapers towering above. Beth stood too close and Jo didn't step out of reach of the smell of her perfume.

"Look. Beth. I have to go. I have to get to PNW Metalworks and chase a lead. If I can tie Brittany to the break-ins –" the rest seemed like a lot to explain while Beth stared at her. About Vi, and Randy, and Jo wanting to help.

"You went with green," Beth responded.

Jo looked down at her not-green sweater, puzzled.

"Your eyes. You went with all green. Used to be blue in D.C.. Perfect, cerulean, blue."

"It seemed right for Seattle."

"Well, I miss naked Jo Ford. Blue and green. It's like getting two of you for the price of one."

Funny way to put it. These days she felt like she was living a life for two, running a life for two people. But not the way the other woman meant it.

Then, before she could think any more about it, Beth kissed her. She took her time about it, and Jo let her. She wrapped a firm hand low on her waist, slid it slowly down to her hip, and Jo let her. She didn't feel like she was cheating on Laura. She didn't feel anything but Beth's soft mouth and her warm touch, because she didn't feel like this was her life. Not really. How could it be? Just as Jo really started to forget about how none of this was okay, started to think about how she wouldn't have to spend the afternoon lonely and wanting and scared, Beth stepped back. She looked down at her slim, gold watch. "I have an hour. The Four Season's across the street."

More accustomed to the Island fishbowl than she gave herself credit, Jo glanced around the busy city sidewalks. But as crowded as they were, there wasn't anyone to take note of her indiscretions.

THE GUILTY PARTY

"I can't stay, Beth. I have to make the four-o'clock boat." Jo sat idling in the parking lot of PNW Metalworks replaying that fleeting moment of denial earlier this afternoon. She still hadn't decided if the disappointment on the other woman's face had been because she'd turned her down, or the half-assed nature of the excuse.

"You've gotta do what you've gotta do, then." Beth's hand flew from Jo's waist. Jo had reached out to take the other woman's arm, to apologize, to say – something – but she was already steaming away.

"Beth –" Jo didn't know what more to say. Didn't know the right way to apologize for not cheating on her wife. Jo could still feel Beth's hand on her hip, the pressure of it. She was glad she'd walked away – but she could still feel the warmth of that hand, pulling her toward what she wanted.

Bright sun winked off the windshield, blinding her as she reviewed what she had so far on the thefts and trying, unsuccessfully, to focus on that – instead of what felt an awful lot like a lover's spat with a woman who wasn't Laura.

A dump truck came to a stop beside her, accompanied by the loud pop of the pneumatic releasing. She jumped in her seat. She'd gotten lost twice on the way to Harbor Island, home to the Port of Seattle and most of the heavy industry on the south side of city. She'd navigated over and under rusting metal viaducts, turning several times after dead-ending at fenced yards with shipping containers piled four-stories high. Twice, semis had blared their horns as she sat at stop signs turning her phone around and around in her hand trying to figure out which unmarked road was which.

It was already half-past three. Jo was out of time to make the four o'clock. She texted Frank, then flipped through her notebook. There wasn't much to review. She had pictures of Brittany, Tyler, Luke, Randy, and Jered on her phone, and a prayer someone inside was in a sharing mood.

The warehouse before her was dotted along the front and side with metal designs. The most prominent, centered on the half-block long building, was a copper Seahawks logo that had aged to green.

Inside, the place buzzed with white LED light, and smelled like sheet metal, sweat, and Lava soap. She stood in a small ante-chamber office listening to AM sports talk for a minute, then rang the bell on the counter. A clerk came through a door behind her and ducked behind the burnished stainless-steel counter.

"Help you?"

"Hi. My name is Joanna Ford. I'm a journalist, and I'm looking into some copper that's gone missing over on Makah Island."

"Heard about that. Easier ways to get your hands on the stuff, if you ask me."

"Well, I would like to ask you for some help, if you have a minute."
The guy shrugged, and the PA cut-in on them. "Front office line two, front office line two." He held up a finger at Jo and picked up the phone.

"Yeah man, we got that."

Through a panorama window behind him, she could see an expansive store-house of sheet metals, rows of tubing, and wheels of wires in a Crayola box of shades of gold, silver, and bronze.

She considered the candy dispenser in the corner. While the clerk talked she played twenty-one questions with herself trying to deduce what might be in the two red-topped glass buckets. Both selections were far faded from whatever their original shade had been. One was definitely chocolate-based. The other might be – her eyes wandered up to the three-year-old Sea-Gals calendar on the wood-panel wall. She recognized some of the offensive starters, kneeling with their helmets, and decorated with cheerleaders. Yep – had to be Skittles in there.

"Baker's dozen, sheets of PVQ stock. Give us about an hour to pull it." He hung up and started punching at a keyboard. "Yeah, so, what you need?"

"A friend of mine on Makah says he buys copper ingot from you guys for his work."

"Woulda been Luke or Terry?"

"Luke – has he been in lately?" She finished the sentence on a friendly up-note. What she really wanted to know was whether he was buying or selling more or less than usual. But if they were on a first-name basis with a customer, well, better to do an end-around.

"Seen him just a week or so ago." The clerk pulled off his Kibo beanie and ran a hand through his long hair, which looked in better shape shine-wise than Jo's.

"Buying copper? Selling it?"

"Neither. Bunch of bronze and some sheets of aluminum."

"Okay. Anyone else?"

"You like, looking to solve that who-dunnit or something? Luke told me it was stumping the local five-oh, last time he was in."

Funny. Luke had told her he didn't know anything about the copper thefts. "Umm. You could say that. A friend of mine, her house was broken into. And the pots were in her family for a couple generations. And – they let her cat out. The sheriff 's office has better things to do, but you know, I guess it's kind of personal?"

"Sucks, man. Sorry. We get folks who try to fence, but not very often. Usually just junkies still strung out, red eyed and a trunk full of obvious cut-off from meters, ground rods. The other day some asshole dragged a downspout in here. We don't take scrap like that. Almost always bad news, and we don't want to lose our license."

"How about anyone new coming in recently to sell legitimately?" She opened her phone and fl ipped through her Hogan's Alley of suspects. He shook his head at all of them.

"I mean, you'd have to have like, a real set-up to smelt that stuff," he followed up. "We don't really pay much attention if you come in with legit goods."

"But do you keep a record. Could I look?"

"Yeah. Got a book here, we record everything. Gotta."

He pulled out a fat, over-filled three ring binder. Jo looked up at the yel-lowed-plastic Mariners clock on the wall. It was four now. She wouldn't even make the five-fifteen boat at this rate. But Vi seemed really desperate this morn-ing. If Brittany were involved, maybe this really could help Randy somehow. Jo owed it to Vi to be thorough.

He slid the binder over to her, and she moved off down the counter. She at least had a date to start looking, sometime around when the first theft had occurred in October. To be safe, she flipped to the page about a month before it. It left her about thirty pages to check. She scrawled down the names through the week following the first break-in. She flipped to the date of the second theft and did the same. Finally, to Vi's recent burglary.

She scanned the columns of names she'd jotted. Six people who overlapped all three date ranges. Only three others that hit two of them. She pulled the sheets and looked up at the clerk.

"Any of these names new, or folks you don't know as well?"

He paged through. "This kid. Says he just started working with copper."

"Kind of unusual to be wearing a hat in a driver's license photo?" Jo looked more closely at the scanned picture. It showed a young – girl – she thought. Black eyes, dark hair under the cap. Nowhere near the twenty-one years claimed on the card. More like a dead ringer for the yearbook photos of sixteen-year-old Brittany Roebuck.

"Aw man. You're right. I totally missed that."

"Can I take a picture?" She already had her phone out.

"Sure. And I'll be on the lookout for this guy."

"You do that. And if he does come back, would you give me a call?" Who they reported what to was their business. This was hers. And Jo didn't think the girl in the photo was going to be back to PNW Metalworks. Ever.

Back in the day, this would have been the moment for the big reveal. When she'd hand over her card from *The Post*, and the recipient paused and scrambled to say more to the Important Journalist. Instead, she handed over a thin-stock card from *The Quartermaster.* He tossed it on top of a mess of pink receipts on the counter.

"Sure. I'll call if I see him."

"Thanks for your time." Jo smiled like she meant it, nodded and headed out the door. Sources used to approach her. She used to have to decide who to call back. Those days were over.

Pride zero, investigation one. Brittany was in on the copper – but given the timing of Vi's break-in, she had to have been working with someone. Somehow the more she got on Brittany, the more she wondered about how she died. The more her ambition to solve the puzzle turned to nausea. She thew herself into the car, shot off an apology to Frank about the time, and headed to the ferry, praying the commuter lines wouldn't be too long.

Her prayers weren't answered. Not a lot of them were, lately. If she were meting them out, she'd trade being home late for a clean second read on that screening this morning. She got into line about a mile from the dock, pulled a schedule from the visor. Six-o-five boat was the best she was going to do.

With a gut-rumbling, bloated cry, the late six-thirty boat shuddered out and away from the dock. Second by second, the smell of creosote was replaced by the smell of brackish water. Out her window, the porthole was split by two gray bars of painted steel. Rust had established itself around the perimeter. Outside the horizon was split as well. Blue-black water, dim jagged green tree line, dark sky and black clouds.

Teens in black and gold MHS uniforms screamed and laughed and clanged their way up the steel stairs to the passenger deck. A man in a dented matte-red Toyota pickup looked up from the fat novel he read to smile at them. His manner and his long, narrow, yellow teeth reminded her of the man who'd come knocking at their door at 319 C street on Capitol Hill in Washington D.C. one cold December night. The man she'd later come to know as Charlie Abish's go-to enforcer, who Laura had turned away from their doorstep like a hustler selling magazine subscriptions.

BACK IN THE DAY

The dead, dry cold of D.C. in January might as well have been Maui sunshine to Jo. The silhouettes of bare trees against streetlights outside their townhome seemed starkly romantic. Buicks across the street idling clouds of exhaust at the late night "car wash" run by their neighbors made her laugh and feel like she was on the right side of a Capitol Hill insider joke. For Jo, right here and right now, life was coming up Miracle-Gro blue ribbon roses.

She was at the heart of a story that was going to break and break big. Laura was home from Afghanistan, finally, and here to stay for months. Though, at the moment, Laura was pissing Jo off. In the kind of way you get pissed off with someone when really all you're thinking about is whether or not it's still too early to hit the sheets.

"We don't have enough time to get out to Ravi Kabob," Jo scolded her girlfriend. "My guy said he can keep the Jennings and Bryan server open ten minutes, tops. If I miss the window, he'll spook." She clicked her Blackberry yet again, waiting for the little gray screen to tell her that her source had actually delivered.

"Yes," Laura admitted, before continuing to tempt Jo. "But also, I need palak gosht. And they only have it on Fridays. And I neeeeed it. And samosas. I absolutely need samosa, too. Ravi's the only thing decent outside Pakistan. It's been a week of stateside bland and I can't even."

"We'll go after I get the lists. I'll drive."

"And park when we get home?"

"Yep. While you were gone, I discovered a hidden spot, only two blocks away. It looks like it blocks a driveway, but it actually doesn't."

Laura wrapped Jo up, crushing her in a bearhug, added a playful nip on her ear. "Thanks. And I hope you know I'd never make you miss a break. I can't wait to see what you fi nd. How'd you get Michael to give you access?"

Jo smiled. Partly because Laura was still gently fretting at her ear, and partly at her own brilliance. "I told him what I thought Abish was up to – and what Jennings's firm was doing to grease the skids. Did a little digging on Michael's family, how he ended up connected to Abish in the first place. Turns out his dad was a very happy union boss for UFCW local 152 in Jersey. Until Abish decided he wasn't his guy anymore."

"Then what happened?" Laura released her hold, picked up a banker's box from the loveseat and the ten file folders of purloined tax documents on top of it, set it all on the floor, and sat down.

"Michael's dad ended up taking an early retirement. After he mysteriously broke his leg getting out of his car - about a mile from the store in a dark Walmart parking lot. Two years out from full benefits. Had to sell the family homestead, entire sad story of the American dream gone south - and voila. Michael, the eldest son with a grudge, gives me access to Jenning's client list."

"It's not who you know – it's what you know about them that gets Jo Ford her story."

"Every time, babe." Jo shoved aside a pile of unfolded laundry and sat down next to her girlfriend. Two months into shared domestic bliss and chaos reigned. They had one bed between them, two of everything else, and zero dressers all stuffed into a small apartment. The only thing they'd bothered to make permanent was the living room office, with dueling laptops, a printer, a radio, and a television atop what was meant to be a dining table. Laura's return from assignment with the AP had been welcome, if not a little cramped.

She started to take advantage of the close quarters and answered Laura's flirting with some of her own, when her phone buzzed from the dining table. Jo reluctantly pulled herself away from a deeply tanned neck and looked up.

"Go get 'em, champ." Laura winked at her and smacked her hip.

The burner Blackberry, as Jo referred to it, was alight with good news from a number she instantly recognized.

"OK," Jo texted back.

She dropped into her office chair and refreshed the open browser on the laptop that Michael, her source and IT admin at Abish's go-to law firm, had left for her at the *Post*. Before her eyes appeared a Jennings and Bryan internal web page with a complete and search-able client index. She expanded the alpha link and let out a whoop.

"Yes."

Laura darted over, grabbed the digital camera off the table.

Jo scrolled through the frames as Laura took photos. Michael had explicitly forbidden her from downloading anything.

Half-way through, a sickly chime sounded, filling the small front room in a distorted minor key. The women looked at each other. The chime was followed by aggressive knocking.

"So that's what the doorbell sounds like," Laura said. She crossed the room, peered through the peephole. "I have no idea who this guy is."

Jo waved her aside, took a look. She rocked back on her heel as the *boom boom boom* of the large man's knock resumed, startling her. He stood surrounded by the weak yellow of their porch light, an empty sidewalk beyond. "I don't know him either."

"I'm here to speak with you Ms. Ford. I know you and Ms. Tanaka are home." The words were muffled by the solid wood door, but the deep voice on the other side easily carried through. Jo was caught between fear and reassurance, and fear again – that Laura was here, and she wasn't doing this alone. And that Laura might somehow end up getting hurt.

"He's definitely not a cop," Laura said.

Jo eased back the curtain and checked the window. The man waved at her. It wasn't friendly, and no cheery smile appeared on the face of the tall, thick-necked stranger asking to have a heart to heart at eleven pm on a Friday night.

She waved back and continued looking him over. It was dead winter and the walk was slick with ice. Below his overcoat Jo noticed he wasn't wearing dress shoes, but thick rubber soled boots, jeans. And a sweater – no tie, and that was it – she was used to seeing this man in a suit. "I know who it is. Dave something. The investigator for Jennings and Bryan."

"Whoa." Laura grabbed Jo's phone, put it up to the window, and pointed at it.

The man shook his head. Laura nodded at him, pointed to the phone again.

Presently, it started to buzz. Laura handed it to Jo. "Talk to him, I'll get the rest of the lists." She picked up the camera, then set it back down. A 404-error had replaced the data on the laptop screen.

"Yeah. Okay." Where her girlfriend had acquired her giant brass ovaries, Jo had no idea. But she looked forward to growing a set of her own, once she figured it out. For now, she put some muster in her voice, answered on speaker.

"Good evening, Joanna."

"Hi, Dave. What – umm – what are you doing at my house?"

"I'm sorry if I scared you. But you know how it is, when something just won't wait."

"Okay. What won't wait?" Jo tipped back the curtain again. Dave was staring right at her, the bulk of him maybe four feet away through a single pane of glass with spiderwebs of frost at the corners. She almost stepped back, almost let the curtain fall, but realized it would be way worse *not* to know what the guy was doing.

"I'm here on behalf of Jennings and Bryan. They're concerned that you're doing something that might land you in jail."

"Like what?" Jo asked.

"Illegally acquiring private data."

"Oh," she replied, wondering exactly how far the *Post* would go, or rather how much they'd spend, to protect her. Putting together a RICO-worthy case on a guy who'd been on the cover of Time more than once would move a lot of papers – but even sky-high circulation wouldn't get her out of criminal charges.

Laura walked over, pulled the curtain open all the way and faced off with Dave through the window. She took a picture of him with the camera she still held, as she spoke toward Jo's phone. "Neither one of us has any idea what you're talking about. But it was really sweet of you to come out here in the cold. Hope you're getting overtime."

With that, she took the phone from Jo and hung up. Dave lingered on the porch. He held a fist to the door but didn't knock. Then, he turned and disappeared into the night.

"We should work fast." Jo grabbed the camera and plugged it directly into the printer. A few clicks later and sheets of paper began sliding out of the machine.

"I'll settle for frozen pizza tonight and brunch nehari from Ravi in the morning. You've got these jokers. Sending some giant white dude over late at night? Classic intimidation move." Laura grabbed a couple sheets off the printer and a highlighter. "You think Michael set you up?"

"Maybe. Clearly, they knew someone was doing – something. Why not just pull the server offline or change admins, if they were suspicious?" Jo took the rest of the stack, settled onto the couch next to Laura. She shuffled the papers, unfocused, worried that she'd gotten a little further up shit creek than she'd thought. She didn't dare text her source Michael – and didn't know if she should be pissed at him or scared for him.

Laura put a hand over her knee, kissed her cheek. "Come on – let's start on these lists. If they had anything actionable, Dave and his cold toes would have been here serving you a subpoena, or the cops would have been here with a warrant. The best insurance policy we can get is to find something solid."

"We?"

"Well. You. But Dave knew my name too, didn't he?"

"I hope he slips on a patch of black ice and breaks his ass," Jo muttered.

"There's my girl," Laura said, nudging Jo with a sharp elbow.

"Owww."

A frozen pizza and half a bag of tortilla chips later, Jo started to snap her fingers. "This name – this company."

Laura looked over, rubbing at the base of her neck with one hand. "Solomon Holdings Corp?"

"Yes. I recognize that. From a filing in – " Jo shot off the sofa. She rearranged file boxes until she hit one she'd labeled "Ohio." She dug for a minute, then, "Cuyahoga County. A Solomon Corp was named in a suit brought by a voting rights group. Something about the ballot counting machines – "

Laura interrupted her. "Ohio? Jo, check out the country code for the number listed here for Solomon. That's Saudi Arabia. And –" She stood, started tapping her fingers on her thighs.

Jo's eyes followed Laura as she paced the tiny breadth of the floor. She loved on Laura's face as it swam in and out of focus on whatever it was that she was putting together. Her eyebrows knit and relaxed, the smooth plane of her nose gliding to a tip that twitched every time her lips pulled down. Long legs striding back and forth in soft blue broken-in Levi's that still had pink dust from the Pakistani hills in the seams.

They were this close from cinching the story tight, and she was this close from swatting the papers out of Laura's hands and calling the entire thing off for the night, to welcome her live-in girlfriend home for the seventh – or was it technically eighth – actually, more like tenth – time that week.

Laura smirked at her. "I know. But just hold your horses. I think we can tie this back to Abish directly. Where do you keep the files on his incorporated subsidiaries?"

Jo pointed to a box standing in for an end table with two small lamps resting on it.

Momentarily, Laura thrust a folder at her. "Tabuk, LLC. Solomon Corp's biggest holding. Check them out. I remember meeting this German guy at a bar in Riyadh who worked for them for a year. Said he got paid $10,000 a month in American, cash, to play Call of Duty in an empty apartment. He thought he was about to get lucky that night. I told him I already had a blue-eyed hottie waiting at home."

"Lucky me?" Jo tilted her head, then turned her attention to the file.

"Lucky you indeed, Jo Ford." Laura sat down next to her, ran her finger down the dossier on Tabuk that Jo had pieced together, connections that had taken on brand-new 4K UHD definition. All of them linking Charlie Abish and the legal firm who did his bidding to a whole new world of international sins.

The ferry hit the dock on the other side of the passage, engines reversing, pulling it back from full impact. A car alarm came to life. A blaring signal to the everyday commuters that an outsider was in their midst.

Lucky Jo had stuck on the case and paper-trailed her way to a Pulitzer. Her source, Michael Pulaski, had gotten killed, and so had Sonya Petrosyan, the federal judge presiding over the Charlie Abish case. Michael's murder was solved. Patroysan's never was. Every attendee at every White House Press Corps dinner could be jealous of her all they wanted. They could have her fame, and the guilt that came with it.

Thanks partially to her work, and mostly to intrepid federal prosecutors, Abish was charged with enough class A and B federal felonies that the individual states of Pennsylvania, Ohio, Michigan, New Jersey, Illinois, and Virginia had all declined to file charges. Twelve allegations alone were drug and firearms-related RICO violations. Nine were computer fraud. Five related to identity theft. The IRS even threw in with three tax evasion charges.

By the end there were teams of reporters from every major daily covering all angles of the story. A young hotshot from the Chicago Tribune thought some in-discretions might have been missed. She'd taken pains to locate and interrogate the guy who groomed Abish's four Irish setters. Was it such a stretch to believe that the man most believed ordered the murder of a federal judge also abused animals? Apparently not.

Jo stared out the porthole again. A molting gray gull came even with the boat, gliding, flapping, and finally pulling away on a draft of air to scream off into the distance and join her sisters swooping away into the night.

Her phone buzzed. Frank. *"Got Laura with me at my house. Missed kickoff."*

Shit. She floored it up the hill from the dock and hoped she could quietly sneak in and pick up her wife. She wasn't up for another discussion with Frank about her general tardiness. It was already dark, it was cold, a perfect night for a fire. Curl up and recall those early, ecstatic, glory days with Laura. It was a familiar Ford-Tanaka repast, both of them reveling in it. Any time she talked about her Pulitzer, Jo gave Laura half the credit, because Laura deserved it.

They'd spent plenty of nights together sharing bottles of wine and laughing about it, crying about it, caught up in how much they admired each other. What a fantastic team they had made. Tonight, though, it'd be scotch for Jo, hot cocoa for her wife, and only Jo's side of the story being recounted. Still, it sounded intimate. It sounded nice.

Jo flipped on the radio and clicked over to KIRO. The Seahawks were up by a touchdown at half-time. Maybe Frank would be in a forgiving mood.

LATE FOR DINNER

The Packers had started the second half against the Hawks with a pick six. That, and Jo being two hours late – Frank wasn't in a forgiving mood. At all. For the second time that day, she started a conversation off her back foot. "Frank, I'm really sorry. I –"

"You're always apologizing," he said. "Don't know you're actually sorry."

Laura stood silently between them in the small entryway of his house, staring at the floor. From the living room just around the corner, Jo heard shouts, cheers, and then vigorous boos directed at the football game.

The cloudy atmosphere on the face of the man across from her began to darken.

"I'm disappointed in you, Jo." Frank looked her in the eye, then over at a mute Laura. He rubbed his forehead with a weathered hand, and that missing index finger. "The way you treat my daughter."

Jo reached for Laura's hand, and she didn't take it. Damn, Jo was tired.

Frank went from rubbing his forehead to rubbing the back of his neck. "Laura's a blessing to me. But I think she's a burden for you. I wanted something different for her, too, you know. But that doesn't matter to me. But I think it does to you. I think what you wanted from your marriage was different than what you got, and you can't square it."

Jo stared up at the spartan cut-glass light fixture overhead. One thing journalists didn't do was stop someone when they were telling the truth.

"I love Laura, and you love her too," Frank continued. "But that's just a part of what she needs. You're not up to all of it, maybe you oughta just say that. I'll move Laura in here with me, and you go and make your life right by you. I won't stop you from visiting, won't stop you spending as much time as you want with her. But I will take responsibility for her if you can't."

He'd gone one step too far. She jammed her fists into her coat pockets to stop herself from pointing her intact index finger in his smug face. "That's not exactly a fair way to put things, Frank. You're pissed because I made you late for *football?*" Somehow her hand had escaped her pocket, and she was pointing at him. Jo tried to keep from yelling and couldn't quite manage it. "I understand you're not used to trying to juggle a family and a career. I messed up today. Again. But I won't be put down for wanting to feel like I have my own purpose in the world. Or that I'm less for asking for a little help." Jo wanted to go on. She could go on, and on and on, but ended with the ever-impotent whine, "I'm doing the best I can. And I think – I hope – Laura understands that."

Laura nodded. Then, she started to cry. She reached out a hand, took Jo's, the one that was waving in Frank's face, and squeezed it as tightly as she could manage. Which wasn't a lot of pressure, but it was enough.

Some gray-bearded guy Jo didn't know stuck his head out from the living room. "Everything alright out here?"

No one in the entry responded. Slowly, he ducked back into the other room.

Jo snatched Laura's red Kibo parka from the coat rack and helped her into it as she spoke softly to Frank. "I'm sorry I was late. Again. If you'd prefer, I can call around and see if I can take Laura to Vi's tomorrow for a half-day. Maybe she can do rounds with Valerie."

"Someone else'll work good, until you start calling in late on them too." Frank held up his hand again as Jo prepared to lose her damn mind on him. "But I don't want that. Like I said, I want to be with my daughter. So I'll see you in the morning."

"Yep. See you in the morning. Go Seahawks." Jo raised a fist in the air, opened the door for her wife, and followed her out.

That went well.

Thick wool socks on oak hardwood, Jo padded across the kitchen to set a pot on for pasta. She'd done her best to hit reset on the ride home, chirping about the weather. The fight with Frank had maxed Laura's struggling frontal lobe. She and Jo were both barely hanging on right now. No reveling in the glory days tonight.

Monday. Spaghetti night. She hadn't known the first time she'd made spaghetti on a Monday that it would become a weekly deal. If she had maybe she would have made risotto instead, or mac and cheese. She hunted in the cabinets and came up short. Routine was Laura's jam now, and messing with spaghetti night was asking for trouble. But it was late. Maybe she could slip by with a noodle-format change. Maybe her wife would catch on to her melancholy and decide to go with the flow. That's how it would have gone in the past. Laura showing up to make it right when Jo wasn't. She reached into the cupboard above, grabbed a box of bowties and dumped it into the boiling water.

"How do you want to top your pasta, babe?"

Just a wan smile in answer from Laura as she traced the paisley pattern on the red and gold place mats with the tip of her finger.

"Parm from a can? You know it's my fave. Never could sell you on it though." She kept acting like this was all good, situation normal, and brushed a hand over Laura's shoulder as she crossed the warm yellow kitchen to grab a bag of salad from the fridge. Laura smiled up at her again but offered no response. Jo clung to her gratitude that she was here with her at all.

"How about we try pine nuts. I'm always too lazy to toast them, but they're still seriously high class. Gourmet all the way, and that's more your style." She'd had this exact conversation a hundred times. She did quick math in her head – Laura had been home from rehab for almost two years now – so maybe nine-ty-eight times.

"I am going to pull a fast one on you with the salad. Don't care what you say – or don't say – we're having arugula with lemon and olive oil. None of the Boston lettuce holds up out here in the winter, so we're going to power through, power ranger."

She brushed her fingers through Laura's salt-and-pepper bangs, which Jo had started cutting. She had to say she'd gotten smart at it. Maybe not enough to do her own – but then again, no one on Makah looked twice at self-cut bangs. Her wife certainly wouldn't. Jo missed her wife looking at her – or more accu-rately – seeing her. Having an opinion and saying it. She missed opinions, good ones and bad ones, and she missed clever affection, intimacy, and even nuanced anger. After the day she'd had, she missed compassion too. Even if she didn't deserve it. Then again, isn't that what love is?

As she so often did now, she imagined the scene between them differently. Imagined things as they were before it all went south in her wife's mind. She imagined shining scissors at the ready at her forehead, and Laura's scandalized voice and the horror on her face glancing over Jo's shoulder in the bathroom mirror. "Let me save you the time and I'll just get a bowl for the next pass."

Maybe that's what Laura would say. More likely something a lot funnier. It was why Jo had fallen in love with her in the first place, after all. Her now long-gone wicked-dry, wicked-smart sense of humor.

"Let's make this dinner a party." She grabbed her phone off the table. They'd be just in time to catch a little bit of *All Things Considered* on NPR. Laura and Audie Cornish had actually been great friends when they were all in D.C. It would feel a little as though they were accompanied by familiars.

Before she managed to find the right app on her sea of home screens, the phone buzzed.

"What's up, Vi?" Jo stirred oil into the pot with the noodles and then fished in the cupboard for the Parm.

Vi blustered on the other end. "I told you that dumbass County Mountie didn't know a suspect from a lampshade. Now I hear they're laying Brittany's death on Randy. And that's not just wrong, it's stupid. And offensive."

"What?"

"Yes ma'am. Connie heard from Peggy down at the liquor store that they matched his prints to some made up piece of evidence. Dollars to donuts that overtown wannabe sheriff's never even read *To Kill a Mockingbird*. Even my cat knows Boo Radley never did it." Vi's words poured out fast and ran together, started to slur, actually, as her volume increased.

Jo chose to ignore all the literary irony rolled up in that statement. Honestly, she wasn't all that surprised about Vi's big news. She glanced back at Laura, paying rapt attention to this side of the conversation, an emotional-intensity Geiger-counter getting set to peg red. She clicked down the volume on the call and lowered her own voice. "Matched his prints to what?"

"Who knows what. Nothing is my guess. Just a lazy place to lay convenient blame."

Jo sighed. Not many people cared this deeply about a man who used a chain-saw as an accessory like a new spring scarf. "I stopped in at PNW Metalworks this afternoon. Brittany Roebuck was definitely fencing the stolen copper. I'll give Hill what I've found. I'm not sure if that clears Randy for anything, but I think it might help?"

"How's that supposed to do anything? It's all just going to shit anyway." Vi sounded ever blurrier on the other end of the line. Sounded drunk, actually.

"You're welcome." Jo glanced over at Laura and it sucked all the sarcasm out of her. *Thank you, Vi, for giving me an excuse to walk away from cheating on my wife again today,* would be the better sentiment. "Look. I don't mean to doubt you. But how do you know Randy isn't involved? You said yourself it looks more complicated now. If they've connected him to Brittany somehow –"

Jo covered the speaker on the phone and whispered over to Laura. "You want to earn your keep and set the table, hon?" It was a joke they'd made for years. Jo had stopped making it for a while when Laura returned from the rehab facility, but it was back in rotation. She'd moved on from thinking any topics were too sensitive. She put silverware, plates, and napkins in front of Laura.

She heard the stove hiss and turned her attention back to the pot that was about to boil over. Shit. The pasta water was past opaque. She crooked the phone in her shoulder and dumped it out into the colander in the white porcelain farm sink. She missed the angle and winced as hot steam seared her wrist. She dropped the pot with a clang, flipped the faucet to the other basin and ran the water as cold as she could, exhaling as it bathed her stinging forearm.

"It's just ridiculous is all," Vi insisted. "Break-ins or murders. The only per-son with less brains than that Sheriff is Randy. And he was stupid but not mean. Ilse raised him better. I guess it doesn't matter though. Don't know what does anymore. Randy dies for nothing and looks bad doing it. Whole damn island is falling apart –"

Jo tuned out the rambling, raging woman on the other end. She grabbed for the Parm on the counter and missed, catching the edge and dumping most of the can. Little white sprinkles covered the cooktop and the floor. *Damnit.*

She tried to give Vi credit for her faith in Randy, her loyalty. It seemed a pleasant way to see the world. After her time in D.C., Jo would believe it if you told her Santa Claus was real and intentionally spreading cancer across the globe. When it came to people, anything was possible.

"Vi, I'm sorry. I don't know what more I can do. Hill's already turned Brittany's death over to Criminal Investigation. I'll tell him what I came up with about her selling the copper. I can try and see who's on the other side of the investigation, but honestly, I don't know what I can do. I was already planning to take another run at the Sorensens, and Tyler Sealth. The sheriff can shake his trees and I'll shake mine."

"Well Elijah Hill better hope a brain falls out of one of them. It's stupid what they're making of Ilse's boy."

Jo switched the phone to the other shoulder and dumped a jar of Ragu over the pasta. She stirred and whacked the side of the pot with the wooden spoon and picked it up to go to the table. "Hey, Vi. I'm really, really tired and I still need to get Laura dinner. I'm sorry but I need to go."

She heard a clatter of silverware and plates behind her. She turned to investigate, just as Spot shot through her legs to do the same. She tumbled over him and landed on her elbows and her knees with a nerve and bone-quaking smack. Her phone skittered across the polished oak fl oor. The stainless-steel pot holding dinner sailed through the air and ricocheted against the dining table, splattering a chunky bright-red streak of sauce across everything in its fl ight path, including the ceiling, the walls, the table, the dog, and Laura.

"Shit." Every joint in Jo's body checked in to let her know how unsatisfi ed they were with this turn of events. She gasped and struggled to catch her breath, fl at on her stomach as she checked back in with her body to see if anything had gone irreversibly wrong. All the while, her wrist throbbed where it was already burned. Spot circled her, whining, then licked her face, before stopping to shake and send chunks of tomato fl ying onto any surface in the house that wasn't already red.

"Shit."

She looked up to see horrified confusion cross Laura's face, big fat tears sitting in her eyes, and heard a quiet keening beginning at the back of her throat.

"Jo? Everything all right over there?" Vi's confusion only added to Jo's frustration.

She sagged against the table leg, picked up her mobile. "It's fine. I have to go." She didn't wait for an answer and clicked off.

It wasn't fine, of course. Nothing was fine.

Laura's keening picked up in intensity. Now the dog began to circle her, bowing and pawing and whining. Laura began to cry in earnest and Spot let out a series of sharp barks.

"Damnit, Spot. Just shut the fuck up already!" Jo struggled to her feet.

She pointed at Laura, the most illogical recipient of her anger. "You shut up too, alright? It's just spaghetti sauce. That's all it is, and it's a goddamn mess that will take forever to clean up, and I'm the one who's going to do it. All of it. So stop crying right now, Laura. Because if anyone gets to cry over this it's me, alright? It's my goddamn turn to cry, you hear me?"

Laura shook her head and kept at it, hands now covering her face, probably because who in the hell would want to see all the ugliness that was Jo Ford, standing in their kitchen yelling at her innocent, addled wife? Jo wasn't the one who'd really lost everything, after all. Laura was. Laura had lost a career too. Laura had lost intrigue and acclaim and prestige and passion, and a lot more than that. Remembering that right now didn't make Jo any less angry. It made her more angry.

"Go." Laura slapped a hand on the table. She stood, slowly, and walked out. Probably just as pissed as Jo that she couldn't storm out.

Jo stomped her foot, because if she didn't do something else with it, she was going to kick the damn dog. She stomped once more for good measure, turned, and stalked out, through the kitchen, the mudroom, and finally tore through the back door and into the cold, clear night.

Hands piled on top of her head and face to the sky, Jo took her turn crying, and then some. Good thing she was in the middle of nowhere, because she could just stand here and do it in peace. She could cry all she wanted, because right now she really, really wished she'd said yes to Beth Berge today. She could have had Beth this afternoon and felt guilty about it, instead of not having her and feeling guilty anyway. What the hell was she saving herself for?

She could cry about turning her down professionally as well, out of all kind of loyalties, real and imagined. She could cry because she was scared to spend the rest of her life on this rock in the middle of nowhere writing about quilting shows – because if that mammogram came back bad, she was probably about to leave behind a career that ended on a low note and a marriage that ended on an even lower note.

She could cry because she was sick and fucking tired of feeling so goddamn selfish every single day. And tonight, most of all, Jo could cry because she was so thoroughly and desperately alone, even though she laid her head down next to a beautiful, loving wife every single night.

Eventually, Jo stopped crying, and started to laugh. She laughed until her stomach hurt, and until she started crying again. Then, she wiped the snot from her face that had become crusty with the cold. She walked back inside to her figural, and now literal, mess of a life, to start cleaning up the house, the dog, and of course, Laura.

TUESDAY MORNING COMING DOWN

Jo and Laura sat at the kitchen table the following morning, silent, an assortment of beverages before them. Jo had no way at all to hold her head that didn't hurt. It had taken her a couple hours to scrub the physical evidence from last night's great unraveling. During that time she'd also finished a bottle of wine, then that promised glass of scotch. Still, her hangover was as much emotional as it was anything else. She was still angry. She was still everything. But it all had a hollow feel to it. She'd run through her passion as fast as she'd run through the wine, and she was as empty as the bottle laying dead in the recycle bin.

At least she'd managed to put Frank off with a promise to bring Laura by the store later. She opened the *Seattle P.I.* to pull out the crossword puzzle.

All her nice, wrung-out hollow filled right back up with rage, and frustration. "Son of bitch. "

A sidebar below the fold opened with the headline, "Body found on Makah Island identified." A picture of Brittany Roebuck accompanied the story. The King County Sheriff's department must have released the name late last night. Likely right before the print deadlines, by the spartan nature of the story. Little more than Brittany's name was included. No cause of death, no mention of persons of interest or the investigation. Not even a jump to back story on Brittany.

"Son of a *bitch.*"

Laura squinted at the paper. "The body?"

"Yep. And that prick Hill didn't even give me a heads up they'd be dropping the ID." Jo steamed over to the radio, hoping to catch the headlines and any more info on Brittany. She considered calling Vi, Hill – anyone she could lay into, and sat back down again as her dehydration and headache rearranged her priorities. The truth was, she wasn't on anyone's notification rosters. Her impotent rage wouldn't change that.

"Kyle and Nancy," Laura whispered, rearranging Jo's priorities yet again.

Brittany's parents. Right. This wasn't about her. "Yeah." Jo caught the little sag in Laura's shoulders and stood. She tossed the paper on the table, and wrapped Laura in a hug. "You know them?"

"Kyle. Growing up."

"I'm sorry, hon."

"Vi's right." Laura's insight was more concise than ever.

"About what?"

"Why."

"Why what?" Jo's attention had wandered out the front window to Spot, nosing around at the edge of the woods.

Laura slammed her fist on the wooden table.

"Babe." Jo put her own hand over it, softly. "Sorry I got distracted. But hey."

Laura frowned. Jo waited. Her wife's mood swings were fast to come and go.

"The copper. Brittany. Why, Jo?"

"I think Hill's working on that." Mysterious photos or not, clearly Hill had chucked her out of the loop. Jo pouted a little more.

Laura shook her head. "He's who. You're why."

Jo sank back down into her chair. She stared at Spot, happily patrolling the yard. Constantly on the hunt. It was his nature, after all. She'd been denying hers for a long time now. And that wasn't Laura's fault. It wasn't Vi's either, or Elijah Hill's, or Beth's. It was hers, and she didn't even need a pithy shot of wisdom from Big Jack to revile herself and her pity party. So what next? That part was easy.

She grabbed Laura's chair and dragged her across the floor right next to her, and leaned her head on her shoulder. "You always were the brains of this operation. I'm sorry about last night, babe. I really am. I love you."

Laura leaned right back. "Love you, Jo."

Vi came barreling like a nasty spring storm into the *Quartermaster* office later that afternoon. Jo had just arrived herself after dropping Laura with Frank. Their brief exchange could either be described as terse or gruff, depending on how finely you wanted to slice it.

Jo walked the whole twelve feet it took to cross the office to the coffee maker resting on the slender, faux-wood grain countertop. She waved the empty pot at

Vi, who squinted at it, eyes a little bloodshot. She looked in worse shape than her employee. She scowled, and then nodded. "Thanks. Ran out a day ago. Haven't even been to the store. What happened to you last night, anyway?"

Tough question to answer. Best to stick with the truth, and keep that simple. "I tripped over the dog."

The fine, dark wrinkles lining Vi's thinning upper lip grew dense as they drew together. "This isn't kindergarten. I won't make you share." Vi ripped herself out of her rain coat and threw it onto the back of her massive leather chair. It creaked under her weight as she sat. "Next order of business. Time to start thinking about what we're going to do for Brittany. We'll take letters, of course. I can help Kyle and Nancy with the obit, if they want. Can't imagine. Just can't."

Looking at Vi now, pushing papers around her desk, pulling at her rayon slacks and eyes circling the place like a dog missing its bed, Jo wondered if the woman was telling the truth about that lack of imagination when it came to grief.

Jo's inbox pinged. A new message from Beth. *"Know you've got to be pissed about that ID article on the body that ran this morning. Sorry I didn't tip you off. Hope this helps."*

Was this supposed to be some sort of apology – and for what? Jo clicked open the attachment. An interdepartmental memo from the King County Coroner's Office to Criminal Investigation. Topline results from the autopsy. She could go to jail just for opening it. She read on.

"Based on current information, cause of death is respiratory arrest. Initial toxicology panels are pending. Presence on the body of what preliminary testing and observation has evidenced as a non-medical grade trans-dermal delivery system for fentanyl analogue has been noted and is likely a contributing factor to cause of death. No additional illnesses or abnormalities are reported or present upon initial examination. Notable trauma includes fracture of the fourth rib and damage to costal cartilage on the right side, likely result of poorly administered life-saving measures. Time of death is estimated between six and eight days prior to administration of this exam. Further testing –"

Her phone buzzed. *"You get my email? Call me, then go talk to Brian Stewart."*

Jo didn't have any intention of calling Beth Berge. She glanced out the window. The boat was in. A stream of cars hissed by, sending up little rooster tails from the asphalt.

"What's got your attention over there?" Vi hauled herself out of her chair. She poured two cups of coffee and walked over to hand one to Jo - who immediately clicked out of her email.

"Probably best if I don't share details. But are you sure it was heroin they found at Randy's?"

"It's what Connie said she heard."

Translation on that game of telephone? Unreliable. Jo picked up another loose thread. "What can you tell me about Brian Stewart? Must have pissed off a lot of people when he closed down Kibo."

Vi turned her back, sat, and began paying rapt attention to her own computer. "Nothing to tell, except bunch of folks lost their jobs. But not even pissed off folks around here will tangle with the Stewarts."

"What's that mean?"

"Means money insulates you from a lot of things. That's all," Vi mumbled.

"Maybe. But not everything." Jo had taught that lesson herself. "It's been a couple years now – why hasn't Brian sold the building?"

"Who wants a couple hundred thousand square feet of nothing but liability on an island?"

"Why not convert it? Re-zone it. Turn it into housing. Makah could use it." Jo had written four articles in the past year about the skyrocketing cost of living on the Island and the ever-disappearing middle class.

"Who's going to pay for that? Not Brian. He's not the landlord type."

"Didn't Makah just come up with a million in pledges for that sculpture park by the library?"

"Sure did," Vi answered. "But the line for putting your name on public art's a lot longer than putting it on a wall in Section Eight. Lot of rich people don't want the family crest next to poor people, addicts. Seniors. Must think their conditions are catching."

"Sure. Okay. Or– maybe Brian's already figured out another use for the place," Jo pondered.

"Maybe. By the way, Valerie said she dropped off that Soroptomist brochure. You make any hay there?"

"Haven't had time. Subtle change of subject, Captain Obvious."

"How's that?"

"I've got a more than a few good reasons to be interested in Brian Stewart. I start asking about him, you zag. First on the boat, and now." Jo sipped her coffee and stared over the rim. Vi still wouldn't look at her.

"Alright." Jo held up her palms. "I'm sorry Not to pry, but are you okay?" Vi looked as hungover as Jo; puffy eyes and a shiny pall to her face.

"I'll be fine. I will. Just tired, I guess." Vi slumped, then smiled a little.

"Okay." Jo smiled back. "I'm sorry." She swiveled back and forth, back and forth in her chair. She wasn't even close to dismissing a link between the burglaries and Brittany's death. She'd get to Brian Stewart later. She dug the crinkled Soroptimist brochure out of a drawer. Ten xeroxed pages, just starting to yellow at the edges. She thumbed through awkward but enthusiastic descriptions.

"Kathy Matsuda will display a very nice collection that includes a rare original 19th century copper cauldron, used to cook apple butter as a method of preserving apples since there was no refrigeration...."

Within ten minutes Jo had learned enough about copper and 19th century cooking techniques to feel like she could take on the best and brightest on Antiques Road Show. But she found the really valuable info on the back page. Of course.

A list and short bios of the Soroptomist Board. Vi Mitchell and Valerie Larsen. A few other Makah well-knowns, and the name that jumped right out at her. Melissa Sorensen. "Melissa is the Former Environmental Safety and Health Assistant Manager at Kibo Outerwear. She currently studies nursing at Seattle Central. Her husband Luke taught art at MHS, and now sells his work in galleries throughout the Northwest. Illustrations by their daughter, Ashley, are seen throughout this brochure."

The entire damn Sorensen family was up to their pale Scandinavian noses in this thing. It was time to head back to Lost Valley.

Before heading out, Jo circled back to the autopsy. She hit the Google and refreshed herself on fentanyl. It fit the bill way better than heroin. Brittany Roebuck had died of a potential OD. Randy Fuller had enough of the drug in his house to kill a herd of elephants. Jered and Brian suddenly had a distro problem. Another coincidence on an Island far too small for even one to carry water.

Jo dove down the rabbit hole of research on opioids. What had started as housewives getting handsy with Percocet had evolved into a crisis for white America. Fentanyl was the lethal little brother of the more popular oxy derivatives. Impossible to manufacture without a more than passing knowledge of chemistry and equipment that wasn't exactly available on Amazon. And it seemed to raised a lot of questions from the DEA if you could get your hands on the machinery and raw goods - fentanyl was mostly imported from China along with shit televisions. The powerful synthetic was popular now as a standalone, a way to cut heroin, and even as an addition to pot. Trick was it made meth look like a cute little cousin when it came to lethality. Incidental contact with even a few grains of it, uncut, could cause a fatal overdose.

Small towns and opioids went together like flame and smoke. Middle America was already decimated. And ready or not, Makah Island, it looked like the epidemic had jumped the moat.

The alarm chimed on her phone. Three o'clock. Should be enough time to catch Ashley after school and still pick up Laura – early.

"I'm off. Going to interview Ashley Sorensen." The Roebucks had gone to Bellingham to stay with Nancy's sister. So, Ashley was the closest she was going to get to the girl at the heart of the matter.

It should have set the woman off – at least earned Jo a warning. But Vi didn't look up from her computer when she waved her off. She'd been typing at the rate of maybe ten words an hour. "Okay. Good luck."

"Thanks."

When Jo jolted her way to the end of the rutted Sorensen driveway in Lost Valley, there was no sign of Luke's spattered Abstract Expressionist work truck. Just that boxy Subaru. No lights on in the workshop, but the kitchen and a bed-room upstairs in the house were lit. Thin white smoke came up through the stove pipe on the moss-covered roof of the beige two-story Northwest 1980s contemporary. The air was acrid and deep, sweet and sharp. Frank had told her that was Washington hardwood burning. The sign of a good, hot fire.

Jo could see her breath in the freezing drizzle. In the perpetually muffled silence of the valley, she could hear it as well. She knocked on the battleship-gray steel front door. The sound echoed into the house, hollow and loud. It was met by the predictable barking of two large dogs.

"Hang on."

The door opened on a girl who looked in worse shape than Jo had seen her last week. The dark circles under her red-rimmed eyes were now deep purple. One look in those anime-style oversized pupils and even Nancy Reagan would have pegged her as an enthusiastic drug user, high on her taste of choice. Jo wondered how long ago it had started, and when she'd lost control of the habit.

Ashley sniffled and wiped her sleeve across her nose. "Can I help you." She didn't really even ask. The words just fell out of her mouth like rotten teeth and piled on the ground between them. The abject dispassion in her manner left Jo without a response or a question. First time for everything.

"I'm Joanna Ford, from *The Quartermaster.* I stopped – " She sighed and her breath hung between them. Ashley Sorensen likely held answers to a million questions swirling like mountain clouds in Jo's head. But she had just lost her best friend. The kid looked strung out.

Ashley brought the sleeves of her black MHS hoodie up over her thumbs and crossed her arms. Her straight barn-mouse brown hair hung lank and un-brushed past her shoulders, her brown eyes flat, dirty mud puddles.

Jo started over. "I'm sorry for your loss, Ashley, and I'm sorry to bother you, but –"

She heard feet pounding down carpeted stairs, and down the hallway came none other than Jered Brasier. He wore only white tube socks, shamrock green sweatpants, and a thick gold chain hanging onto his pale, hairless chest.

"Hey Ash, is it my pizza – " He caught sight of Jo and sneered. "Snatch-lady. Shoulda known by the stupid car."

"Jered Braiser. Shoulda known by the bad smell."

NOT ALL MEN, BUT DEFINITELY THIS FUCKING GUY

Jo thrust her hands into her pea coat. What the hell was this guy doing half-dressed alone with Ashley Sorensen? She knew the answer, but she didn't want to.

Ashley stood between them, watchful through giant saucer-eyes with dilated pupils. Jered's nasty behavior couldn't be reserved only for Jo. She wondered when Ashley had crossed paths with him. What the first conversations had been like. When they'd first turned to what he could do for her, promises he made to her about how sweet life could be. She wondered when they'd subsequently turned to what she could do for him, as was always the case with dealers and users.

Jo raised her voice to the boy. "Ashley and I are talking. You can go back where you came from. Better yet, you can leave."

"I go when I wanna, and I stay when I wanna, bitch." His head and his torso swayed back and forth like a drunk cobra's.

"So do I. And I think what I see here comes awfully close to a charge of statutory rape. If you 'wanna' stay, I can call Captain Hill and ask him about it."

"You listen to me, snatch-lady." Jered took Ashley by a bony shoulder and pulled her further into the house. "I know you're slow, but you should not be saying things like that to me."

"My name is Jo. I know you're slow, but I'll expect you to remember that in the future. Maybe it will stick better when your lawyer reads it to you from the harassment complaint I might chose to file, on top of the statutory charge."

Jered stepped outside, right up in Jo's face, torso still snaking back and forth. He shouted directly at her. "Did you not hear me when I told you to leave?"

"Did you not hear me when I asked you to leave?" Jo leaned close enough to look up into the yellow whites of his dark eyes. She drilled her index finger into his scrawny chest. She could take him any day – and as Vi liked to say, twice on

Saturdays. And today, taking him, taking anyone, down a peg, seemed particularly appealing. That little ball of razor-wire rage she'd drowned in a bottle last night shook itself off and started spinning, fast.

Ashley squirmed on stick-figure legs. "Jered, come on. Leave the nice old lady alone."

Ouch.

He bent down and laughed right into Jo's face, and for three seconds she had a contact high. "I don't know about nice, but yeah. I ain't got time for beatin' on old ladies." He looked down at his feet. "But goddamn it bitch, now my socks are wet. You better fuckin' watch yourself." With that he shoved Jo, hard.

She almost tripped on the cracked concrete of the walkway but caught her footing. Then she pulled her phone out of her pocket and thumbed it on. She held it up and took a picture before either kid knew what was happening. "No, Jered. You better watch yourself."

"Bitch, you give me that phone, and then you leave." He stepped toward her. Ashley continued to cower in the doorway.

"Come get it. And when I finish kicking your ass, then you can leave." She stepped right up in Jered's face. Big Jack had taught her two approaches to this kind of situation. *"Joey, you can turn the volume way up, or you can turn it way down. But either way – you act – and you act like you mean it."* Jo's guts weren't sending her even one vote for turning down the volume right now. She was dialed up to ten, and that felt right. That might have a little more to do with some anger issues she had to work out than it did with good strategy, but she wasn't about to second guess herself now.

Jered stared at her, little flickers of impotent anger dancing in the wide pupils of his eyes. Jo stared right back and filled her mind with thoughts of Laura and everything they'd lost and everything they'd never have. She thought about cheating on her wife, and then yelling a her. She thought about that mammogram. She thought about Brittany's parents and their only child, strung-out and dead at sixteen. Nancy's hand over her mouth at Mill Creek, surrounded by trees and gray gloom. She thought about nothing but despair, and she let it suck her totally dry, nothing left on her face except the dead-eyed void of a woman with very little to lose.

Jered blinked.

Jo inched even closer, until her jacket was touching his pale ribcage. "I'm here to talk to Ashley. Not you. Move along."

"It's alright Jered. Just let her stay. Meet me at the cabin in a minute."

He spun on Ashley almost before she finished speaking. His open hand came down across her face, and she bounced off the doorway.

"You don't tell me what to do either, you hear?"

She raised her hands to ward off another blow, but Jo was one step ahead. She grabbed Jered's outstretched arm and went with his forward momentum, which carried him face-fi rst into the heavy steel door. She let go of his arm and grabbed a handful of his greasy hair. She cracked his head into the door once more for good measure before pushing him outside and letting go. He reeled backward and tripped over that crack in the sidewalk Jo had missed. He fell on his ass, and stayed there.

Jo stood directly over him. "Ashley, go get whatever clothes Jered came with. He's leaving now."

The girl hesitated, then disappeared up the stairs. Jered stood, slowly, still a little tipsy on his feet. Jo heard Ashley's footsteps coming back down the stairs by the time he'd recovered himself.

"You're dead next time I see you first, bitch."

Ashley handed Jo a pair of Jordans and a puffy Seahawks stadium jacket. She tossed them on the ground in front of Jered.

Jo considered his threat and hedged. "I'm writing up everything I saw here today. Anything at all happens to me, to my car, my house, or even near me or my car or my house - I get a hangnail – the write up and the picture in my phone goes right to Hill." She didn't have any illusions about Jered staying away from Ashley, or Hill's ability to make a statutory or an assault charge stick based simply on her say-so. But Jered was an idiot, and that made the threat good enough. "Get the hell out of here."

He'd already shrugged into the coat and was hopping around trying to get his shoes on. He sneered at Jo, then started walking toward the tree line. He got about fifty feet, then turned back. "Suck it you fat dyke."

"Only in your dreams." For the life of her, she couldn't figure out why Tyler or Ashley were in any way intimidated by this boy. There was another player on the game board. Jered and his distro problem. He was dealing, but no way was he at the top. Jo swung for the fences.

"Hey Jered. Does Brian Stewart know what you've been up to with Ashley?"

Jered froze in his tracks.

Nailed it.

He flipped her the bird over his shoulder, and stalked into the black mouth of a nearby trail head.

The whole exchange left Jo with way too much current in the line. She turned to Ashley, whose saucer eyes were now platters. The red imprint left by Jered's palm was already fading, but it had to hurt. It hurt Jo, certainly, to look at it. She rested a hand on the girl's shoulder. "Come on. Let's put some ice on that."

Jo sat on the coffee table in the Sorensen living room facing Ashley, who had thrown herself into the corner of the sofa. She held a frozen bag of peas on her cheek, absently twirling the lank hair that fell to her shoulders. Behind her the window framed a panorama of Lost Valley, green pasture fading into fir trees in the dying light.

The world's loudest dogs turned out to be two German Shepherds, now curled in front of the wood stove. Jo had gone to add a log, but Ashley had waved her off .

"Ashley – where's your mother?"

"Sleeping. She works graveyard in the ED at Harborview hospital."

Jo glanced toward the stairs. The house wasn't that big. "She's – sleeping?"

"She has some help. I think this month it's Benzos."

"Ah." Jo grimaced. Ashley had conveniently picked up her bad habits at home. "Then you don't see her much when you're in school."

"Yeah. Not anymore. Not since she had to start working overtown."

Jo kept fishing for a responsible role model in the teen's life. "What about your dad? Where's he?"

"Who knows. At the cabin. Fishing. Doesn't matter, even when he is here, he's out in the shop."

"Okay." Jo shifted around on the edge of the table. Ashley didn't offer her a more comfortable seat. "I want to say again how sorry I am about Brittany. We're putting together a special edition for *The Quartermaster,* if you'd like to contribute something."

"I don't know. Maybe. You know anything else about what happened to her? Or like, why her, you know?"

"You don't think she died accidentally?"

Ashley fished around in the pocket of her hoodie with the hand that wasn't icing her reddening face. She pulled out a small vape pen and glanced quickly at Jo. "You mind?"

"Ah – no. It's your house."

The girl took a hit. A massive cloud of strawberry-scented white mist drifted out of her mouth and through her nose. "I mean, everyone says it was Randy Fuller. That he killed her." A smile tried to creep onto her lips, and she almost giggled. "Sorry."

The change in the girl was too instant to be organic. Pot had come a long way since Jo's college days.

"Has anyone said anything to you about why they think he killed her. Or how?" Randy's potential motive still eluded Jo. So had anyone else's. Tyler didn't seem like the jealous-ex type. Randy was too simple, and Jered too – something.

"I just heard she probably OD'd," Ashley replied. "But when the cop came to talk to me about Brittany, he was asking all kinda questions about Randy too, if we knew him and stuff ."

"Do you think he did it?"

"Probably." Ashley shrugged. "He's crazy, right? Isn't that enough of a reason? And who cares about him. Brittany's dead too."

"You're right." Jo sighed. "I'm sorry Ashley. Did you have a chance to see her recently? Before she died?"

"Like, say goodbye or some shit?"

"Umm. Yes." The kid's mood swings and lack of empathy weren't exactly a surprise, given the makeup of her world and obvious drug abuse. But was it genuine lack of control, or an act?

"Last time I saw Brittany, her and dad and Tyler were out in the workshop. The smelting furnace was full blast and I got hot. So I came in to do homework."

Wow. Came in to do homework? And had Ashley meant to throw Brittany directly under the bus? Jo watched her, looking for tells, but it was like watching clouds. The changes in her expression came slowly, and Jo couldn't be sure she wasn't putting meaning over the shapes. "When was that?"

"Like a couple weeks ago."

Jo no longer believed a word coming out of this girl's mouth. But perhaps she could push her into more useful lies.

"Do you know why Brittany was breaking into those houses, stealing and selling the copper?"

"What?" Ashley paused for a very long drag. "No."

"But you knew about the break-ins?"

"Umm." The girl stared out the window at the jagged horizon. "I don't have to talk to you about, like, any of this. Why are you asking, anyway?"

"Because it's my job. And, to be honest, I could really use your help." Jo decided to lean hard on that, stretch it to see if she could get a few more questions in. "You're a source. Anonymous, deep background if you want. I don't have to tell anyone what we're talking about."

"I don't –"

Jo interrupted, quickly, keeping Ashley off pace. "As far as you knew, did Brittany use drugs?"

"No way. Ne-ver." The girl's response was quick, and firm.

"You and Brittany, Tyler – Jered, never partied? Not even weed? You don't think she just overdosed?"

"Nah." Ashley shrugged, and once again the vape pen appeared along with the smell of artificial strawberry. Her ragged, chipped nails were fake red too, over-bright. They matched what Jo took for an emerging hickey on her neck. Jo looked a little closer at the mark. And thought a little harder.

"She never, say, used fentanyl patches?" Slow-release patches were hugely popular with recreational users. Like Ashley, apparently.

"Umm. No way."

"How about you, Ashley?"

"Me?"

"Yes, you. It's understandable. Senior year in high school is stressful." Jo was now stretching the very limits of her sympathy.

"No. I don't. Just – this." The girl held up the vape and nodded, and Jo still wasn't buying it.

"Jered never pressures you into anything else?"

"Jered? No. He just kind of hangs out sometimes. We're not that close."

"Could have fooled me. I'm sure he's your dealer. But he's not your boyfriend?"

"He's not a dealer. We're, like, off and on. He's not the smartest guy."

"Did he have a relationship with Brittany?" Maybe he'd dated her, and Brittany had broken it off with him? Maybe he'd just lost his temper. That damage to the girl's ribs could have been CPR, or it could have been something else. Maybe they had been on the way home from a burglary that morning, or maybe he'd just followed her on her cross-country run. Jered kills her right at Mill Creek, flees the scene. Randy stealing the boat, sheer, convenient coincidence – correlation without causation.

"Brittany and Jer together? Fuck no. No way she would have messed with him. She was still hung up on Tyler. Or someone. Anyway. No."

Jo leaned forward on her elbows. "Why are you dating Jered? Ashley, you used to be a very good student. A good kid. How long do you think you can keep this up, with him, the pot, the fentanyl – whatever else you're using?" Old year-books put her on the Honor Roll and in Key Club last year. Salt of the earth on her way to the University of Washington along with her bestie Brittany, if that's what she wanted.

Ashley took the frozen bag of peas from her red face, set it on the couch next to her and pulled her hoodie tighter. She didn't respond and didn't look like she intended to. That question had been meant as a little more food for thought anyway.

Over by the fire, both of the dogs stirred. The larger one, mostly black with only a smear of gold on her underside, padded over and sat by Ashley. She stood.

Upstairs, Jo heard footsteps. Then she heard socks on carpet coming down the stairs.

The petite, bedraggled woman who appeared had to be Ashley's mother, Melissa. Same barn-mouse brown hair, but this styled into a blunt pixie framing narrow brown eyes, the same color as her daughter's.

She stopped at the landing, hand over her forehead. She swayed just a little. "Who are you?"

"I'm Joanna Ford. I came by to see if Ashley wanted to submit anything to *The Quartermaster* for Brittany Roebuck's tribute." Jo held out her hand.

The other woman didn't take it. "I need to get ready for work. Ash needs to start dinner. Could you wrap it up?"

Ashley stood. "I'm not making dinner. I've got somewhere to be."

"You'll be where I tell you, when I tell you. Your father might stand for that attitude, but I won't." Melissa finally seemed to actually notice her daughter. "What happened to your face?"

"Nothing," the girl responded, eyes averted.

All four ears were up on the two dogs now at at Ashley's heel.

Jo's thumbnail sketch of the Sorensen family was starting to shade in quite nicely. "I know you're busy at the moment, Mrs. Sorensen. But if you had a minute in the next couple days, would you or Luke have anything to contribute for Brittany?"

"No."

Jo waited for Melissa to elaborate. She didn't. "Okay. I'll head out then. Ashley, if you want to give me anything – at all –" Jo held out a card to the girl.

Melissa scowled at Jo and took the card from her. "I'll let you know."

Jo nodded. The dogs escorted her out the door.

Jo tore down the Sorensen driveway and headed home. As she barreled around evergreen-lined corners and curves, she reviewed what she knew. The copper pot thefts were a shiny distraction, the collateral sin. The fentanyl listed on the autopsy memo - the patches – they had to be the steady bass drum pounding out the through line on this story. She needed to know where it was coming from. Jered was the obvious first step, but not the last. Beth had mentioned Brian Stewart. Vi had avoided talking about him. And Jered had practically jumped out of his skin at the mention of his name.

As she thought about Beth, she subsequently thought about the two yellow and green sponges she'd gone through wiping down spaghetti sauce plastered tothe walls of her dining room last night. Her little lust-frustrated temper-tantrum. Ultimately, she thought better of making that particular phone call. There were other ways she could get information on Makah.

BRIAN STEWART MAKES HIS ENTRANCE

Arms crossed and stance wide, Brian Stewart surveyed the sun coming up over the world before him. Though the steep southern shores of Makah Island cut sharply away below the deck of his home, he had no fear of falling. The view he commanded here, solidly engineered by the fine Stewart men before him, took in place and time alike.

The Kibo fortune had been built by men who were determined, ruthless, and most of all, commanded an almost magical relationship with the laws of supply and demand. Sole heir to that empire, Brian Stewart spent much of his time evaluating the changing laws of economics and his forefathers' approach – profiteering but socially conscious Keynesians each and every one of them.

Brian represented a new iteration of the Stewart man. This late in the game, this late in the history of the human species, he embraced an unabashedly objectivist free market view of capitalism. There was no stopping the fall of Rome. Accepting this reality freed him to live and to run his own realm efficiently and profitably.

A magnificent illustration of the poverty of humanity created by the ravages of late capitalism and primacy of the supply and demand relationship stood before him now, whining about his latest failure. To sum up Brian's thoughts on the subject as Jered Brasier brayed on, good help is hard to find.

The boy was sunk into Brian's very expensive Italian leather couch, legs spread wide and arms slung over the back. His body language did not convey nearly enough remorse or appreciation for the hard work and finery surrounding him.

"I'm sorry," Jered whined. "I left the bricks at Randy's like always. It was like, not predictable, or foreseeable, or whatever, that he'd fucking go batshit and kill himself. I didn't think it would be a issue, man. Like I was actively solving a problem, because Harmony's got a new dick to ride, so she's on a fucking tear right now and there was no way she wasn't going to get her nose all up in the stash at my place."

"Two flaws in your excuses," Brian said. "The biggest one is that you made a move without telling me. If your mom's going to be a problem, you come to me and I tell you what to do. Second flaw is you didn't put two and two together when Randy killed himself, and move to clear his house before the cops got there," Brian explained. "Do you see how those problems are synergistic?"

Jered stared at him.

He waited patiently for the kid's dim synapses to fire, which they did, eventually –

"If I told you that I left the product at Randy's, you would have told me to move the shit in time."

Brian nodded. "Well done."

Did Jered even count as good help? No. Barely adequate. There were several advantages to operating on Makah. One of the disadvantages was the supply   of adequate labor. Jered, sadly, was the best Brian could do at the moment. Demand, hampered by the heavy hand of the law, was fettered. Therefore, the supply of competent middle managers with experience distributing illegal drugs was similarly anemic. On the job training was Brian's constant burden.

Jered studied him, warily, as he circled him on the couch. He did at least have good instincts. Brian took Jered by his greasy hair and pulled his head back, exposing his fish-belly, acne-spotted neck and sharp Adam's apple. He paused to give him a beat to imagine what might happen next. Fear thrived in the imagination when you gave it time and fuel – and kept things unpredictable.

He let go of the kid's mange and grabbed firmly but not aggressively on to his shoulders, gave them a warm little squeeze and a pat. "But hey, mazel tov, Jerr Bear. You tripped and fell into winning the fucking lottery. Hill's got Randy on the fentanyl, connected it to Brittany Roebuck, and he'll stick with that. Why rock the boat when he can walk out of it all clean?"

"Shit. Yeah. Right."

"We've still got to sweat it out." Brian continued his lesson. "If it keeps breaking right though, all this blows over. That dead girl? People will cry about it, but in their dark little hearts, they'll blame her. And her parents. And move on. People always move on."

He sat down opposite Jered, perched on the coff ee table opposite the couch where the boy was sprawled. Brian had cut down the big Hemlock for the piece himself, milled and dried the wood. Start to finish the table was his creation. He knew that you can't hide the flaws in imperfect materials. You can still work with them though, turn them into useful tools with guidance, creativity, and patience.

He waited again for Jered to connect the dots and realize the additional complications in the situation.

"I think we – I – have another problem," Jered confessed. "That new snatch at *The Quartermaster*. I think she's getting like, too close."

Brian picked up the Seattle daily from the neat pile on the table. He took a seat near Jered and opened it up. He crossed his legs, sat back with it held out in front of him like a friendly grandpa. "You're right. I'm not surprised. I've been waiting for Joanna Ford to get bored with our little Island."

Jered leaned forward, tapped his finger on the table. "Well, I'm telling you, she keeps turning up. At Tyler's, and Ashley's. Like she knows something. Or at least knows where to look. I'm telling you man, she's a problem. We should take care of her."

"You're in charge of making decisions about how I do things now?" Brian started folding the paper. "You know, you or I can only fold a piece of paper seven times. No matter how big or small it is. It can only take so much shape-changing before it says, 'enough.' After that, well, you can fold it again, but it requires a lot of force."

He smacked Jered across the face with the paper. Unpredictability inspired sharper critical thinking and strategic planning skills. "I know how many times I can change your shape, Jered. I know exactly what I can get out of you or anyone else. And most importantly, I know when to use force. What you don't know, but I do, is when I need to apply a lot of force." Smack across his face again. "Do you want to find that out? When I need to use a lot of force?"

"Jesus fuck man – no. I'm sorry, okay?" Jered sat at attention, blood-shot eyes wide.

Supply fear; demand respect. A balanced equation. "I like that you're starting to try and use your brain, but please don't get ahead of yourself. Let me tell you our next steps. You're going to pump the brakes. You're going to tell our Makah buyers that they need to chill out. They get just enough fentanyl to keep them unhappy and needy, and the rest goes off -Island. They'll do an autopsy on that Roebuck girl, so I need to switch up the fentanyl analogue. That's going to take me a minute."

"OK, man. Got it. Watch the supply."

"You talk to Tyler?"

"Yeah. He knows what's up. He's filling in."

"Good. Now get out of my house." Brian folded the paper neatly and picked up a copy of the Economist. He was behind on his reading since all this shit with Randy had gone down. If the man had just done as he'd been instructed, Brian wouldn't have had to pick a fight with Vi Mitchell. Then again, investigating the leads they'd acquired was already yielding dividends. Speaking of –

Jered was half-way across the living room and into the kitchen when Brian called out again.

"About the other thing – stay away from the reporter. She's three times smarter than you are, even before you started baking what little brains you had to begin with. If she's decided to try her hand back in the big leagues," Brian shrugged. "If she even looks at you, you call me."

"Yeah, okay man." Jered paused. He looked at Brian's feet, sniffed, ran a finger under his nose. "Uh – Brian? I probably ought to tell you something else, then."

"Yes. You probably should." Brian rubbed at his eyes He'd been up all-night re-jiggering the fentanyl recipe. Why couldn't things ever be easy?

"The newspaper lady snapped a couple pics of me and Ash. Nothing spicy, but if she shows them to Hill and gets feminazi about the statutory shit, it might be, like, a problem."

"Like a problem." Brian crossed his arms and stared hard at Jered. "*Like* a problem."

"Yeah."

"I think that's more of an actual problem than it is like a problem. And you know exactly why, don't you? Take a minute. Think it out."

"Nah I don't need a minute. It's because it fucking sucks to have that fat dyke have something on me."

"Dikes are engineering tools. Don't be an asshole. What else?"

"And it means –" Jered paused. "It's bad for business?"

"Let me help you." Brian's necessary patience was wearing thin. If he weren't a man down already... "It's not just bad for business. It's bad for you. If Hill arrests you for what she's got, you go to jail. You'll decide you don't like it all that well. You'll be offered a deal, and you'll take it. Which is bad. Mostly bad for you.

Because unlike that useful shit for brains Randy, people will believe you if you point at me. So I'll have you killed before you can talk. That's what it means. That's a little clearer?"

"Umm. Yeah. Real clear, man." Jered swallowed hard.

"You know," Brian walked up to his current employee, close enough to smell the ghost of cheap aftershave and incompetence. He was almost a foot shorter than the clown, and yet he towered over him. "Now that I think about it, this isn't the first time Ashley's caused me problems, is it? Get her in line or cut her loose. If you don't, I will. I've got plenty of leverage on the Sorensens."

Jered bobbed his chin up and down. "I will. I will. But, like, what do you want me to do about Ford? Because I don't want to, to go to jail."

Brian walked right up to the edge of the plate glass panorama window fronting the living room. When the fog wasn't so thick, it commanded a breathtaking view of Mount Rainier and the entire south Sound. The Stewarts had built the compound at Dixie Heights decades ago to ensure security – but also to remind generations to come of the importance of perspective and place in the world. Far above it all, the boats, homes, even the planes, all looked like little toys. Brian knew exactly where he belonged and what to do.

"Just do your job, Jered. I'll take care of Joanna Ford."

I LOOK ACROSS THE WATER, AND I THINK OF ALL THE THINGS

Frank and Laura were up and out by the time Jo was coherent and dressed Friday morning. She was tired lately, sleeping harder and later than she ought to be. Frank had left a note on the kitchen counter. Since the weather was supposed to turn sunny, they were down at Plancich Bay if she wanted to join them. She tapped the little scrap of paper, smiled at how much more personal it was than a cold, sans-serif text.

Jo scanned the sky as she stood on the porch. The air was wet. The trees were bent and spoke back to the steady breeze. Popcorn puffs of clouds raced by as she surveyed the serene oval of blue above the clearing defining the property.

She plunked down on the top step, deciding if she wanted to head out to Plancich Bay, get back to chasing a story that was heating up fast, write up her notes, follow up with Tolliver's hiker friend, chase down Brian Stewart, or just sit here and think about what her life had become. The step creaked beneath her. Spot came up and nudged his brown snout under her elbow. She wrapped an arm around him and leaned in, fingers wrapped in his wiry mutt fur.

The dog's ears came up. She followed the swivel of his head. At the edge of the Technicolor green clearing, past the chicken coop, she saw a flash of gold and a flick of black disappear into the forest. Had to be Paula. She stood to go after the cat, but before she could, she and Spot both looked over at the sound of tires on gravel, their next guest temporarily hidden by the tall evergreens edging the driveway. He stood at attention and his whole ass wiggled. A few seconds later Valerie Larsen's old wood-paneled Jeep emerged.

The creak and slam of the door rang off the house and the trees as Valerie got out, shining chestnut hair bouncing along with her. She stuffed her hands in the pockets of her jeans. Despite Jo's bundled layers, her visitor wore only a purple v-neck tee and a lightweight jacket.

Jo met her halfway across the drive. "Chickens are doing great."

"I know." Valerie grinned and shrugged. She inclined her head to the sky high above them. "It's been three days straight of dark and rain, and I'm getting a little stir-crazy. Steve's got the kids this afternoon. Nice morning to be on the water – and Tolliver mentioned you might have a particular interest in, say, visiting Mill Creek Ravine?"

Jo took a second look at Valerie and decided the woman was insinuating what she hoped she was – a once-over of a crime scene from a hard to get angle. Tolliver must have held out about Jo grilling him, because Valerie still didn't seem at all pissed.

Jo glared up at the sky, wondering what secrets it divulged to Islanders that it hid from her. Her eyes and her weather app told her it was supposed to rain all day. She checked her skepticism and put her own hands in her pockets. "Sounds good."

Valerie's freckled nose twitched. "You want to change shoes. It'll be squishy in the low spots. I'll ride you up to my place if you want. We can walk down to our dock from there. Save you the gas. I've got to be back this way later to get Alice and Tolliver."

"Alright." In for a penny. Jo let the dog back into the house and stopped in the mud room to swap into boots and lock up before she joined Valerie in the Jeep. Resting on the back seat was a massive, black raven head. It was crumpled and bedraggled and missing a patch of feathers on the top. Momentarily she realized it was papier-mache.

"Tolliver's the MHS mascot," Valerie explained. "He was practicing his cartwheels in costume in the yard and landed wrong. I'm taking Riptide here over to Connie Wilcox for some TLC." She reached forward and nudged a cassette back into the player on the dash. "I don't know if Green Day's your thing. Tolliver's been into 'classic rock,' as he refers to them."

"Ooof." Jo covered her stomach and winced.

"No kidding. I'll spare you what Alice said about Madonna last week."

"Thanks," Jo laughed. "And thanks for taking me out to Mill Creek for a fresh perspective. I'm having trouble tying all this together. The thefts, and Brittany."

"Vi said you think she was the one behind the break-ins. I just can't believe it."

"She needed drug money." Case closed, for Jo, on motive. "But let me ask you something. A friend of mine insinuated Brian Stewart, the Kibo guy, might have something to do with all of this. Does that sound right to you?"

Valerie drummed her fingers on the thin steering wheel, out of time with the music. "I'm not sure. What did Vi say?"

"What do you think she said?" Why would Valerie immediately make a connection to Vi?

"Don't manipulate me, Jo." Valerie smiled, waved at a truck headed the opposite direction on the highway. "I've got a few years on Tolliver, and I don't like it." The vet glanced over as they came to a stop sign. "But I do like you. So just ask what you want to ask."

"I thought I had." So Tolliver had spilled the beans. Or Valerie had carefully extracted the information from him. Given this last exchange, Jo thought maybe the latter scenario might have been the one that smoothly played out over a cheerful dinner table. Maybe there was a little more behind this woman's ever-ready smile. "What would Brian Stewart have to do with all this?"

"I really don't know. But he makes Vi nervous. And a lot of other folks too. I've never had a reason to cross paths. Think I'm glad about it."

"Alright. Thanks for being honest. Not everyone is when they talk to me," Jo added.

"Yeah. You bet." Valerie turned off the highway, started sloping up a long drive that widened as they rolled along.

Jo smiled at a ray of sun streaming down on the open, emerald green hillside stretching up behind Valerie's house. She lived up in the Wash, a swath of the Island still bare from the clear-cutting that had decimated Makah a hundred years ago, before forest stewardship became all the rage. Without the omnipresent tree cover and south-facing, when the sun came out it washed the entire four-mile square patch in light.

She covered her eyes against the bright glare. Eight hooves and two black horses pounded toward them as they got out of the Jeep. Valerie walked over to the wooden split-rail fence to say hello.

"The one with the white blaze is Aggie. The big boy next to her is Saturn." She took Saturn gently at the ears and pulled his head down to her chest, gave his neck a scratch. He pushed toward her and chuffed.

Jo smiled but stayed a step back. Annapolis wasn't known for its horse to people population density. Her one childhood visit to a petting zoo ended in tears when a pissy llama had nipped at her ponytail.

Valerie dished out equal time, ran a hand over Aggie's nose, and started toward the woods. "Trail head down to our boat dock's just past the barn."

They made their way through more pasture, goats, sheep, chickens, geese, and passed what Jo thought was a rabbit cage. How the Larsens even had time for anything other than animal care baffled her.

"Welcome aboard the good ship Artemis. You want to pilot?" Valerie nodded at Jo. "I remember Laura said something once a while back about your Dad being in the Navy. You grew up on the water?"

"Actually, I did. In Annapolis – and that would be great." Jo hadn't driven a boat since they'd left D.C. She'd sold Dad's place in Maryland after he died, everything that came along with it, and never looked back. The current vessel didn't have much on Big Jack's Mastercraft. But the old two-seater bass hauler was well-maintained and cut the chop of the midday water smoothly.

Valerie eased back the throttle. They idled and Jo took over. She pushed them back up to speed and gave a little test torque on the wheel. It was tighter than she expected for its age.

"Do you think I'd drag you out into the middle of Colson Passage in a hunk of junk?" Valerie laughed and nudged Jo's arm.

"No. Sorry," Jo replied. "Just checking out the equipment." She pushed them a little faster. To her right, the jagged green landscape of Makah slid by. Here and there stood a house or a little cluster of cabins perched on aging retaining walls along the rocky shore. Other than that there was nothing but bright sun, blue sky, fresh air, and the thrum of the motor. She sat back and let the water have its give and take, disappointed when Valerie pointed to their destination, a small inlet well-hidden by a wall of evergreen.

The stern of the boat caught some yaw with the current flowing off the natural jetty, and Jo cut their speed. The surface of the water shifted with the current and tide, but as soon as their wake died the place was silent. From the nearby trees a raven let out a harsh gurgling caw. It was answered from the far Western shore of the mainland.

The little bay south of the Reach was protected by a thin hook of land crook-ing out on the north side. The peeling trunks of the madrona lining the white-shell beach were a sticky crimson in the brittle winter sun. They were dominant along the craggy shoreline, leaning toward the passage as though they'd been listening to a secret for a very long time. From the neck of one hung a long, frayed rope, likely the remnants of the tire swing Tolliver had mentioned. Up past that a deep gash in the hillside took shape, the ravine lined with old-growth fir and hemlock. It was a native, wild piece of land.

Jo beached them and peered down into the frigid, winter-clear water and the rocks below. Valerie shucked her shoes, rolled up her jeans, and vaulted into the shallows. She tugged them a little further up while Jo hauled a small anchor over the gunwale, then made her way across the bow and on to dry land.

A straggling length of yellow caution tape waved in a thicket of glistening salal. Either people or place had decided its warning and authority were irrelevant.

Jo started up the hill where an overgrown path lead into the forest.

Valerie came up behind her. "Not many people come here in the winter."

"More in the summer?"

"A few. Used to be more popular. High school kids loved it. Then the county put out the wind-pattern map from the ASARCO plant down south. Turns out the Hook here caught a lot of it. Soil's contaminated all up and down the shore. People stopped coming as much."

"Laura mentioned that. Arsenic, right?"

"Yeah. Remediation would cost a fortune. So —" Valerie shrugged. "We get cancer, and we deal with it."

Jo stopped, huffing mist into the sweet air. There it was again. That weird indifference to death she'd clocked when Brittany's body had been found. "You deal with it? Seems like you don't deal with it."

"What are we supposed to do to fix it? You have a few million bucks to spare?" Valerie pushed roughly past Jo and continued upward.

"No. But wouldn't this qualify for something from the EPA, the state?"

"Makah stopped turning to the government to fix our problems as soon as we figured out that all they do is make more of them."

"Did you grow up here, Valerie?" She certainly sounded libertarian enough.

"No. Over on Mercer Island."

"Just been hanging out with Vi too long," Jo needled.

"What's that supposed to mean?" Valerie scowled at her over her shoulder, and picked up her pace.

The pitch got steeper. Jo grabbed a tree branch for purchase on the slippery needle-lined path as she followed.

"Nothing. I've just never heard that particular style of Makah Libertarian coming from you before."

"I guess on an island we learn to solve our own problems." Valerie's shoulders began to creep upward.

"Fair enough." Jo slammed the brakes on investigative reporter, reversed back into friend zone. If Valerie could be honest with her, she might try the same thing on for size. "Can I ask you about something - it's not city mouse country mouse. I'm just curious about how everyone's reacted to Brittany. And that whole ASARCO cancer business."

"Yeah. Sure. What about it?"

"It seems like everyone's reaction is - stunted. A girl dying in Baltimore, or D.C., maybe it doesn't get noticed. But in a small town? It's all I've heard people talk about, but still, it's not what I expected."

"I hadn't really thought about it." Valerie paused. "I know what you're saying though. About how it is overtown. Someone's daughter can die, and it's just someone's daughter. It's not Brittany from down the road, a girl we all knew from sports and birthday parties and pancake breakfasts. But that's how it is with everyone, here. We notice when everyone dies. They aren't just someone, they're someone you know's aunt, or sister, or your kid's elementary school teacher. When you read the obits in the *Quartermaster*, if nothing else the name rings a bell. We're closer to everything, really, on Makah, I guess. Even losing people. I mean murder is different. It is. But when death comes around, well –"

"It's just another part of the ecosystem," Jo concluded.

"Yeah." Valerie started hiking up the trail again. "What a great question, Jo. Thanks for asking. I'd never really thought about that before."

"Ummmm, no problem," Jo replied. People rarely thanked her for asking questions. It stunned her into silence for a while as they trekked on together.

Jo put her hands on her hips and inclined her head at yet another string of yellow plastic circling a tight clump of ferns. "This must be where Brittany was found."

"I suppose," Valerie replied. A stillness matching the tenor of the place came over her. Jo saw her sneak a hand to the back of her nose, then her eyes, and heard her sniff quietly.

They'd come to a clearing in the trees. The forest floor was covered in prehistoric sized ferns, deep emerald, bright moss at their feet. The plants formed their own canopy over the soft ground and left no way of visible passage, a close veil stretching to the crest of the hill. The soaring maples offered an ethereal quality to the light, dappling the forest floor in dancing patterns from the bare branches. In the summer it would be a cathedral of green stained-glass as the golden day filtered through the leaves. It would be lovely.

It would be the kind of place someone just a little sensitive, someone who felt nature called them to create in its image, might love. Might find poetic, and peaceful. She could picture Tyler Sealth here. Gazing at the trees with longing and loneliness, and quite possibly regret. Randy Fuller, not as much.

Valerie was first to break the reverie. "Not that I want to pile on Randy, insinuate he killed her or anything. But Brittany being found up here and just died of an overdose?" She shook her head. "I don't know. It's an awfully strange place to come to use. Tricky to navigate the terrain, that high."

Jo stuffed her fists in her pockets. "I agree. I think she was killed." She parsed her words, careful not to talk in too familiar terms about the circumstances of Brittany's death. "Or at least someone was there when she died. You'd have to be pretty strong to get a body all the way up this bank. And I think you'd have to care about Brittany to go to this much trouble – and I'm still trying to find a way she and Randy might have ever crossed paths."

"Well I don't know if whoever did this really cared about her. But you'd have to know Makah pretty well. You probably wouldn't be from overtown." Valerie took a knee. She ran her fingers over the blade of a fern, stroked it, and sighed, pinched the bridge of her nose.

"A local." Jo tried to make out the path at the top of the rise. "Can you get to the road from here?"

"Not really. It'd be even tougher going than it is from the beach."

"Where does the trail lead?"

Valerie gestured off to the south. "This forks about another twenty yards up. Left hits the top of the ravine. One of my favorite spots on Makah. You go right, it takes you kind of anywhere if you know your way. Heck, we could get back to my house if we wanted. Tolliver's all over the north end during training season."

"A little muscle, a little creativity." Jo turned in a circle. She'd huffed her way up here. "You'd have to have time to do this, with no one asking where you were." She listened to the maple branches rattle as a breeze came through.

"I think I want to go now." Valerie ran a hand through the carpet of dead pine needles.

"Yep," Jo replied. She'd seen what she needed to.

"If you're up for it, I'd like to clear my head a little," Valerie said. "Up just a ways more, it's really something. I don't know if you've been up at the top here when it's sunny – there's a panorama of the Olympic mountains that just takes my breath away every time."

"Sounds good."

Valerie started off again, glided on while Jo chugged after, leaving behind the clearing where Brittany had been abandoned, and their heavy sobriety.

As they curved around a sprawling hawthorn bush, Valerie glanced back. "Just to make offensively light of everything, I've been a little depressed myself all week. I thought the chickens had completely stopped laying. There was no good reason I could figure for it. They just up and totally stopped –" she swept her hands across her body dramatically, "which isn't usual at all, even in the winter. I hadn't planned to butcher for another season. I just couldn't figure it." Her tone took on a tenor Jo knew well herself, running through a stream of possible answers to a problem and disliking all of them.

"So, now what?"

"Now what is a grounded-for-a-month sixteen-year-old boy underfoot. It turns out Tol's been collecting the eggs every morning to sell to the neighbors – and save up the money to buy video games. Alice was helping, but she finally sold him down the river during their daily dinner fight last night."

Jo looked sharply over at the other woman. She figured Brittany had an accomplice, because the burglaries hadn't stopped after her death. Her initial formula for Mill Creek had nearly taken Tyler right out of the equation. But what if there'd been someone else in on it? Jered kills Brittany and tasks Tyler or Randy with clean-up duty? Or, Tyler kills her, asks Jered for help – and that's what Jered holds over him? Thinking about a young girl being considered disposable to even one person hurt in a fuzzy way, in a place she couldn't locate. Thinking about two people teaming up to erase Brittany Roebuck's future brought the ache right to the center of her chest.

They took yet another turn and the trail opened wide in front of them. The cliff where they stood jutted up over the swift waters of the Colson passage. Jo's breath was instantly stolen by a vista of the snow-capped Olympics. It held its own with her visit to the Swiss Alps on her honeymoon with Laura a decade ago. The world seemed to carry on forever, over the vast stretch of evergreen of the Kitsap Peninsula. Though they were at least fifty miles away from the mountains, Jo wanted to reach out and scoop a snow cone from the top of the peaks, crystal clear in the piercing winter air, blinding-white and razor-sharp in definition against the cornflower sky.

"Wow."

Valerie turned, hands on her hips, smile glittering like the Olympics beyond. "I know. Can you believe it? Never gets old. It just does it for me every single time."

Jo nodded. From far below, the sharp smell of wood smoke drifted up.

PRETTY LOW, EVEN FOR SOMEONE LIKE YOU

"You excited to catch your mom's show tonight at First Friday?" Jo sat on the edge of the tub drying Laura off . Manipulating a towel required a surprising amount of strength and dexterity. Usually Laura did this, another part of her occupational therapy, though she wasn't allowed in and out of the shower by herself. Tonight, Jo wanted that intimacy, to feel as though they were sharing a moment before they headed out for their big family date night.

First Friday art gallery walks were not to be missed on Makah. The primary commercial hub on the Island, known as "Uptown," consisted of five restaurants, four bars, three hardware stores, two grocery stores, a mélange of service stores, and six art galleries. The native priorities and tourist proclivities were clear, and art remained a huge commercial driver of the tenuous economy.

At the very least the monthly events were a great excuse to get out of the house on a dark winter night. After their family feud this week, Frank had laid out a path to peace and suggested they all meet uptown. Jo had happily signed on to the treaty.

"I know your dad can't wait," Jo followed up Laura's non-answer. Frank had been talking for weeks about the Hana Tanaka retrospective opening tonight at one of the bigger Makah galleries. Many of the works were from the extensive collection that rotated in his antique store, but quite a few would be on loan from Makah residents who owned a piece of Hana's thirty-year career. Many of the paintings were of landmarks on their own properties. Regal, shady stands of old-growth timber, sleepy ponds ringed by willows, proud barns captured at sunrise. Others were ubiquitous Makah views of Rainier, the Olympics, or the green and white ferries, depicted so many times in so many mediums that Jo, looking at them, felt as if she were gazing at self-portraits crafted by the Island itself rather than its residents.

Hana's pieces had become definitive in the Makah canon. Her subjects were the Island's most shared geographies, but more than that, shared cultural experiences, and often tackled by aspiring local artists. Proud shepherd of that heritage, Frank made himself a regular drop-in at the gallery during installation. He'd fussed at Jo for a month about how they were curating the paintings, which were displayed by chronology versus subject. His non-stop grousing revealed exactly how attached he was to Hana, still, through her work. How much Frank missed his wife. How the show was bringing a piece of her, who she was to him, and to their community, back to life. It would be a good night to try and start things over with him.

She finished drying Laura, both of them now smelling like Ivory soap and citrus. Jo started to brush out Laura's damp hair. She was careful about it, gentle on the ropey, jagged scar running from her hairline at her ear to the crown of her head, as she worked to lay the part right. She pulled a thermal down over Lau-ra's head, ran her hands down her trim sides. Finally, enough padding now, on the Makah bacon and eggs diet. Laura had lost so much weight in the hospital, in rehab. The first couple of weeks home, Jo had cried every time she dressed her. The stark, hard bones of her ribcage were still a detailed architecture of everything lost. Her broken wife had healed, but only on the surface.

Jo pulled Laura close. She ran the tip of a finger down the slalom course of her shattered nose. They'd done well with the reconstruction. But you could still feel the damage. She held her tight, tighter, and leaned in and kissed her. She blew right past the one-second love tap. Laura didn't pull back. She rested her hands low on Jo's stomach, moved them around to her waist. Jo slipped her hands under the thermal. Let herself feel Laura's body, lost but familiar. Her own body, with its own scars and shames, that she trusted Laura to love. As they kissed, she started to pull up on her wife's shirt, to lift it back off again.

Then, she felt tears sliding down her nose. It was past sundown, the early northwest winter night dark around them. Laura's most vulnerable time. Intimacy, sex, big emotions, were always hard on her wife and completely overwhelming even on the best of days. Laura had said, once or twice, when she'd started to cry because it was too much, that it was fine, that they should keep going Jo had never had the heart to push through.

"It's okay babe. You okay?".

"Sorry."

"No, don't be sorry. No way. It's fine. I'm glad we had a minute. It was nice."

"You still love me, Jo?"

Jesus Christ. It was quiet in the house, outside too. Not even a rush of wind to keep the world spinning, yet Jo still had to hold on tight if she didn't want to be pitched off the ride. Both of them really were just hanging on by their fingertips. Jo took her wife by the shoulders. "Laura, yes. I love you. Like I love coffee and bacon and Spot and oxygen." It was a start, but way back in those inky eyes, Jo saw she hadn't gotten the job done. And she could. She could, because she did love Laura. She'd asked herself that question before, and never questioned the answer. "This is hard. It's really hard. I'm really sorry about what happened the other night. Sometimes I have no idea how to cope with – this. I don't think you do either. But it's what we have. And I'll take it because I'm with you. Okay?"

Laura nodded, a slow up and down of her chin, watchful. "Okay."

"Okay. I love you." Jo grabbed a tube of lipstick from the vanity, hopefully signaling a close and a transition. She didn't want to dwell, here.

"Love you," Laura murmured, and smiled.

Jo smiled back, only inches from Laura's face. She leaned close to paint Laura's lips, threw on some mascara for her as well. It was Friday night, after all. Everything looked good. Situation normal, not fucked up. She kissed her on the cheek once more for good measure. "Come on. Let's go get some culture."

The cloud cover had rolled in that afternoon and kept the cold in from the day. Jo pulled her scarf tighter against freezing pellets of rain as their trio jostled through pale white faces on narrow sidewalks on their way to the Chautauqua Gallery. In addition to the Tanaka retrospective, Luke Sorensen had a show up and was scheduled to make an appearance. Jo hoped she'd have a chance to talk with him about his daughter, and Tyler.

First Friday was a boisterous outing for housebound Islanders in the winter. Shouting kids and reunions of friends, they filtered through the restaurants and the galleries, and finally into the bars. Tonight, she listened a little more carefully to the conversations around her, filtered them through Valerie's perspective on the whole thing. Hushed speculation tumbled from drawn lips in every passing conversation she overheard, which she expected. But the tone wasn't gossip-excited or the pearl-clutching 'that poor soul' variety. Instead, many were scowling and grieving, sharing their own honest stories of mourning and loss.

At the front of the gallery was a large glass vase with a hand-painted sign asking for donations for Brittany's family. It was already more than half-full. Outside, a sheet of rain pelted the plate-glass front window. A gust of crisp air blew in with the next patrons through the door, Valerie Larsen and her ex-husband. For a reason Jo hadn't yet clocked, divorce was as common as Scandinavian surnames here. Many couples stayed friends, then married other divorced friends in a bizarre overlapping matrix that Jo only saw as incredibly awkward. Still others, despite the tiny geography, managed to never see each other again. The many-faceted ripples of this small pond still rocked her boat every now and then.

From across the room Valerie mouthed a 'hello,' shot her a smile and an enthusiastic wave, before three gray-haired women wearing pastel alpaca scarves matching their raincoats swallowed her up in merry hugs and surprised, happy greetings.

Jo waved back, made humble apologies to Frank and Laura about not listening to them about going before you go, and headed to the bathroom. Island plumbing was as likely to be on septic as sewer, and even larger establishments had limited facilities. At the front of the long line she saw Luke Sorensen. If he saw her, he didn't acknowledge it.

"You still around?" Happy McElroy queued up right next to Jo and looked ecstatic about it.

"Still here," Jo replied. "I'm just as happy about that as you are."

"Too bad. Heard you were hassling the Roebucks about Brittany. Pretty low, even for someone like you."

Why were so many people so determined to convince Jo to lose her shit all the time? She stepped into the woman, who shrank back. "You know what? You don't know —" Out of the corner of her eye, Jo caught sight of Frank and Laura, holding hands and entranced by one of Hana's paintings.

"I don't know what?" Happy squared her shoulders, regained her ground.

"Nothing," Jo said. Right here, right now was for Frank, and for Laura. And her reasons for finding out the truth about Brittany were her own.

"Yeah, that's what I thought," Happy sneered up at her. "Tough enough when you're hiding behind Vi and her paper. Chickenshit when it comes down to it."

"Yep." Jo leaned against the wall, felt the dim hallway closing in on her. Finding a better work-life balance might be a reason a lot of these people moved to Makah. But it sure as hell wasn't working out for Jo Ford.

She stood up straight again as Luke's muffled voice rose and came through the thin bathroom door a few feet away. "Your mom's not right about much, Ashley, but if she won't bail you out of whatever trouble you're in, that's fi ne with me. We're not made of money. You know this isn't the time for this, and you're not in a place to be making demands right now. We're going to talk when I get home."

The toilet flushed. Luke threw open the bathroom door and jostled past the waiting women.

Wasn't the time for this? When was the right time in any family for a teenager to be hustling cash out of her parents? Jo cast another glance at Luke. What could possibly be so sticky in his world right now?

Jo took care of her business, then edged her way back through the crowd, over to the table with box wine, water crackers, and a small wheel of bedraggled brie. Luke's serene gulls soared overhead. The place was otherwise quiet, but at the back, Jo strained to hear. An assortment of ornamental quilts on the walls and the cluster of coat-clad bodies muffled the sound. Within moments he concluded. A round of polite golf-clap applause ensued and Luke began holding court in a cluster of female admirers.

"Prick." Laura stage-whispered at Jo, unsuccessful with the volume control. Two or three people looked over. When they figured out the comment was coming from Laura, the corners of their eyes softened, they glanced at Jo, and moved on.

Frank joined them, raised his glass of room-temp Chard at the popular artist. "Hana never liked him either."

"She ever say why?" Jo asked the obvious question, hoping she'd unlocked a wealth of Makah insider goods.

"Not really," Frank responded. "They worked together for a while at MHS, but she never said anything specific."

No help there. Jo turned to Laura, who started to scowl furiously.

"Because –" Laura clenched her fists.

"It's okay babe. Take your time." Jo caught Laura's eye, but her wife wasn't in the mood to be placated. Occasionally, when she had too many words to get out, none of them could get out.

"He. Ugh –" Laura stuttered again. Finally, she took in a big breath, looked around. She pointed at a cluster of gulls fl oating in a near corner. Luke had given them a blue-ish cast.

Jo tilted her head, walked over to read the plaque, "Paloma," then walked back to her family. "Weird title for a bunch of seagulls."

"No." Laura slapped Jo's arm. "The artist," she hissed, loudly.

Frank cleared his throat as a few more bystanders tossed off interested glances. Neither he nor Jo actually cared what people thought, but Laura hated it when people stared. Understandable.

"Okay. It's not a big deal," Jo said. "Let's table it and circle back in the morning."

"Fine." Laura nodded. "Thanks." She looked at Luke again, and rolled her eyes, then grinned at Jo.

Frank hooked an arm through his daughter's elbow. "Your mom's stuff looks good up in here, doesn't it?"

Jo stood next to them, and here they were, a little family unit again, all of a sudden, all of them gazing at one of Hana's larger oil paintings. Willapa Harbor, overlooking Makah's little downtown at sunrise. She'd been thick with the paint on the water, giving it a little more indulgence and a little less realism. Gone more on the warmer side, shades of rose and indigo glowing on the horizon and portending a sunny day to come.

"I'm sorry, Frank. For being late the other night."

"I know. Me too. I know you have it tough. But that's hard for me to see sometimes." Frank sipped his wine and studied a piece foregrounding the old general store at the main four-way in town. Laura's mom had chosen to capture the red of the blinking traffic lights as they flashed against a clouded sky.

"I don't want to stop living my life," Jo said. "But I don't want that to be at Laura's expense." They moved on a little, to a small portrait of a ferry coming into the dock at sunset.

"I know. Just hard to make it work sometimes." Frank cocked a thumb. "I saw you start to get into it over there, with Happy?"

"Yep. I'm sorry about that." Jo chugged half her wine. "I know it's not the place – but can I try to explain something to you? I'm not trying to start something. But I –" What? What was Jo trying to do here?

"Just say what you need to."

Not quite as warm an invitation as she hoped. "Everyone on Makah thinks a lot more of my ego than I do. I know I'm still learning how it's done, here. But problems like you've got shouldn't just be written off with a shrug and an aw-shucks. Those copper thefts weren't cow-tipping, Frank. They weren't climbing the radio tower on a rural Saturday night. Add to that, there's a dead girl. Drugs, and the assholes who deal them. For me, the most important thing is finding out why she died. Even if she did overdose, and I think there's more to it than that - I want to know why."

He looked away from her, back at another one of his wife's pieces, this one a glittering Sound on a sunny day and sea birds wheeling across the sky. "Maybe so. And you know what? I've heard Laura give that same little talk about the world, every time we told her we didn't like her out on assignment. So maybe that's how you feel and it can't be changed. But maybe you ought to leave all that up to someone else." He laid a hefty hand on her shoulder. "I love you Jo. So does Laura. And you know what? You two could be happy. You'd fit right in on Makah, if you wanted to. But I don't think you do. I think you want to write big important stories that shake things up, and not take responsibility for what happens after you do. And that's okay. Just hard to make that work on an island."

"Vi Mitchell told me it's our responsibility to take care of the community." Jo crossed her arms and didn't quite sound like a whining five-year old as she responded.

"It's the 'our' in there that's important," Frank said. "If you're telling me that you want to know what happened to Brittany because you want to make it right, not because you want another shot at the brass ring? You're telling me that, we're having a different conversation."

"That's what I'm telling you." Fake it until you make it, right?

He stood quietly, and he didn't take his eyes off Jo. "Alright. I'm tired. Know our girl is too. Think they're getting ready to close up here. Let's head home. Are we calling tonight a win?"

"Yep. We are. Definitely." Jo polished her crappy Merlot and hurled the cup toward the compost. She took one more glance at Luke Sorensen, made a mental note to follow up, and followed her family out the door.

AT LEAST IT GETS BAD BEFORE IT GETS WORSE

Jo, Frank, and Laura huddled together in the parking lot and stared at the flat rear tire on the Volvo. The gravel lots on Makah held all manner of hazard. Like the bent nail winking at her under the orange glare of the streetlight above.

"You guys go back to the gallery. I'll change it out." Jo headed toward the trunk and opened the hatch.

"Think they're closed up. Rather not take this one into the bar." Frank nudged Laura, whose eyes were wide, but sagging and puffy at the same time. She leaned against her dad, on full sensory overload and staring absently at the flat tire. When she blinked it was a slow, dazed little motion. Across the alley, the Alibi was jumping, live band cranked up and people packed onto the back patio. A loud bar now could send her into an hours or days-long spiral of uncontrolled emotion.

Jo looked around for an alternative. Except for the bars, Makah rolled up the sidewalks promptly at nine pm. She ducked below the hatch and wrestled out the spare and the jack.

Valerie Larsen's Jeep rolled by, then stopped. She, her ex Steve, and Tolliver piled out. Valerie looked pained as she scoped the situation. "Of all the bad luck. Do you need some help?"

Jo dropped the spare, which rolled a foot and plopped over. "I know it doesn't look like it, but, uh, no. Thank you." Then, she looked over at Frank, huffing little clouds into the cold night air, Laura huddled next to him. "Maybe you could give these two a ride home?"

Frank walked over to Steve, shook his hand, and they exchanged comfortable man-pleasantries. Valerie came over and put her arm around Laura. "We'd love to." She scowled around the lot, the dark alley, then at Jo. "It's late. We could squeeze you in too."

"It'll take me less than twenty minutes."

"Okay. If you're sure." Valerie nodded over at Steve and Tolliver. Frank started toward the Jeep, and the boys crowded into the back seat.

Jo walked Laura to the car and buckled her in. "See you at home in half an hour. Get right to bed, okay?"

Valerie took Jo's arm as they walked around to the driver's side. "I'm glad we ran into you guys. Text me when you get home, will you?"

"Yep." Jo waved one more time to Laura and headed back to her own car as they drove off.

It ended up taking her twenty-five minutes to change out the tire, with the cold and dark, but it was relatively pleasantly spent. The band was good, plenty loud enough to hear, and about every five minutes someone would wander over from the Alibi patio and ask her how she was getting along. A couple patrons even offered to buy her a beer. She finally took one of them up on it.

She plunked down into the driver's seat and turned the key. She was met with an extremely disappointing *click click click click.*

Dead battery and flat tire? Someone was messing with her. Jo thought back to her interaction with belligerent Happy McElroy.

She sighed and grabbed a flashlight from the glove box. She popped the hood. Everything looked in place – wires to the battery seemingly unmolested. She popped the casing to the engine, checked over all the pieces that moved. All tight, all present and accounted for. Maybe the battery *was* just dead.

She leaned against the car and dialed Frank.

"Hey I've got a dead battery too, I think. I'm going to head into the Alibi and see if I can get a jump, or a ride home."

"Well Valerie's still here. I can stay with Laura and she can probably ride you home or give you a jump."

Jo heard something muffled follow up Frank's response, and he came back on the line. "She says she's up for it. Already dropped off Steve and Tolliver."

She looked across the alley again. The band had just started the second set, and things were getting late-night rowdy. Her odds of finding a ride home or a sober helper were slimming. "Sounds good. I'm going to head into the Alibi to wait. It's cold. And I could definitely use a drink."

More muffled conversation ensued, and Frank came back on. "Valerie says she'll be there in maybe twenty, she's gotta stop for gas."

"She knows where to find me." Jo tapped off. She turned to give the new spare tire a kick for good luck and headed into the rowdy bar.

Jo had gotten used to decent music on Makah. The live bands lured out of old barns and garages weren't just bad cover hacks rehashing others' creativity. She wasn't surprised to be enjoying the rolling Petty-inspired song she'd started paying attention to as soon as she had a whiskey in her hand. She was surprised to see Tyler Sealth on bass, and vocal back-ups.

"Her love was the kind that left you in shreds. Ah, the things you learn too late on the road to regret."

Jo finished most of her drink during the harmonica solo. She left her glass on the shining live-edge cedar bar as the band finished up. She bumped and nodded her way over to Tyler, deciding to make productive use of her free time. Successful investigations had just as much to do with keeping on sources, cultivating trust, as they did bad guys messing up and leaving a paper trail. She came next to him and didn't wait for him to acknowledge her.

"How long have you been playing?"

He finished half his bottle of Rainier in a go. The shine of his eyes told her it wasn't his first of the night. "Since I was a kid." Tyler turned to her and shrugged. Same un-brushed long black hair and black jeans she'd come to expect on him. The hoodie had been swapped for a loose, buttoned-up flannel.

"You're good." Jo stood next to him, again off to the side. Always trying to work the kid from an angle.

"Yeah. Maybe." He finished his beer, set it on the bar, and held up a finger for one more. "How would you know?"

Good question. Jo had been a pretty hardcore Cougar-Springsteen junkie, but what East-coast late eighties girl hadn't been? "Where did you learn how to play?" She heard the door to the Alibi open and close behind her, and the jukebox blare to life.

Tyler cast a quick look over her shoulder. "My mom. We done here? I already told you. I don't have anything to say."

"Maybe you do. Maybe I'm actually interested in you, and I want in on the ground floor. I'm guessing you'll have your own work up across the street, someday. Or maybe I just like you."

"Why would you like me? You want something, that's all."

"It's a free country, for now. I can do both. It's my job to get to know people, and fast. From what I know so far, I like you." That was partially true. He was clearly committed to his art. To writing his own story, his own ticket out of the despair he'd grown up with. Dump though it was, he chose to live in one of the most beautiful spots she'd come across on the Island. And that was saying something.

"If you want to like me, go for it. Hope it gets you somewhere."

"Maybe it will." Jo looked up. This time Tyler smiled down. Just a flicker in his black eyes. "I hear they've got Randy Fuller for the break ins, and for Brittany's death. That doesn't seem likely at all to me."

Tyler shrugged again. "Me either."

"Why not?"

"'Cause Randy's not a bad guy. He didn't do those break-ins, and he didn't kill Brittany," he replied.

"You seem awfully sure about that. You know something?"

"Nope. I'm just a decisive kind of dude."

"It's just that I don't want to see him wrongly accused."

"Why not?"

This kid was filled with good questions. Despite what she's said to Frank, she didn't really care all that much about bat-crap crazy Randy. On the other hand, the Islander done-wrong angle seemed a good one here. The wild man had two fan camps. People who smiled at him but were afraid to talk to him, and people who smiled at him and picked him up when he put his thumb out on the highway. He was woven into Makah. He was one of them. She did care about Randy though, in her own way. And she cared about Brittany, too. Because Laura did. And Frank, and Vi, and anyone who meant anything to her around here.

Jo spared another glance at Tyler out of the corner of her eye. She remembered his wistful look across the Sound and out to Rainier the other day. She thought back all of five minutes to his syncopated solo and backing vocals on a song about making bad choices. Maybe a little honesty might work.

"Because I hate unanswered questions. I hate people getting one over on the rest of us. It's my job to answer the questions. It's my job to make things right. And I could use your help."

"It's your job to sell papers."

"It's not, Tyler. It's not why I chose to write. It's why I care about making sure nobody takes the fall for something he probably didn't do."

He nodded and finished his second beer. "Alright. You're a decent person. But that still doesn't mean I know anything. Or that you know anything."

She was just about all the way where she needed to be with him now. Finally. "Yeah? Here's what I think I know. These copper thefts, someone's not just hauling boxes and boxes of pots overtown to dump and trade. Luke's set up to convert them. You work in Luke's shop. Brittany Roebuck was your ex-girl-friend, and I know she was the one selling the copper at PNW Metalworks. What I don't know is how Randy fits in, or where Ashley and Jered fit in. Can you help me with any of that? Because right now everything I know points to the fact that Captain Hill ought to be looking awfully hard at you, and not pawning this off on Randy."

He was silent for a moment as he looked down at her. Behind her, the door to the Alibi opened and closed again with a rush of cold air. Jo decided to play the last card up her sleeve. Ask him if he had any clue at all why a figurine matching the one on his window was found on Brittany Roebuck. Before she could, Tyler tossed his empty bottle in the bin. It shattered, loud and hard. "You need to back off. I gotta go."

She looked right up at him as he tried to step around her. He threw ten bucks on the bar and hustled out the back door a lot faster than someone just looking to avoid pointed questions.

Jo threw a little more cash down and followed Tyler out. Valerie would be here any minute anyway.

She plowed through the back door. Tyler was already gone. The patio was empty. That was odd. The band hadn't laid off that long ago, there should at least be a few folks lingering. Jo looked around the parking lot. No sign of Valerie. She looked down at her phone.

A cold hand that smelled like a hungover ashtray closed over her mouth. "Said you better see me coming, bitch."

THAT'S GONNA LEAVE A MARK

Bright moonlight penetrated the swaying tops of the evergreens in the clearing where Jo stood. She was flanked by Jered Brasier and just the man she'd been looking for, Brian Stewart. Under his custom Kibo parka, very visible in the waistband of his jeans, was a sensibly sized, reliable-looking semi-automatic.

When Jo had found herself sandwiched between Jered and Tyler and Mount Rainier last week, it hadn't occurred to her to be scared. Now the feeling announced itself like storm-driven breakers. Wave after wave of *I think I might be in real trouble here.*

She hadn't been given much choice about their walk into the woods. After Jered grabbed her, Brian pistol whipped the back of her head, which now pulsed hot and tight. She knew they hadn't gone far. A hundred yards give or take. She took that as an encouraging sign that this was going to involve more shaking-down than murdering. On the other hand, there had already been one dead body found on Makah recently. Jo had observed during her time in Baltimore with the *Sun* that death was often a contagious condition.

Brian paced for a few seconds, did a bad job of looking like he was struggling to gather his thoughts, and started talking. "Hi Joanna. I'm Brian Stewart. Big fan of your article on the senior center last year, with all the profiles." He didn't seem at all sincere about the compliment. "You know Jered."

Jered gleefully gripped her arm, fingers and long grimy nails digging into her bicep.

Brian continued pacing, medium-long strides on his medium-long legs. In another situation entirely, this middle-aged man would have been fairly unremarkable. "You two seem to keep tripping over each other. I can't really get by with the way things are, you winding people up." He finally stopped moving. "So I'm asking if you might consider changing your priorities.

If you just go back to writing about quilt shows, I can guarantee you'll never run into me or Jered again. Alright?"

Jo leaned into denial. She was scared but decided she just didn't have time for it. Not now. "Is it winding people up about the break-ins, Brittany Roebuck's death, Randy's, or the fentanyl that you're concerned about?"

Jered tightened his grip. "Shut up, snatch."

Enough. She could find out quickly just how serious this whole thing was going to get. "Get your hands off me, you little shit weasel." She stomped her heel into the inside of Jered's ankle and shoved off at the same time, sending him stumbling into the wide trunk of a nearby tree. He grabbed a low branch and kept his feet. His teeth gleamed in the moonlight, and he came back at her.

Brian laughed and waved him off. "She had a right to do that. No one's being held against her will here. We're just talking. But she does need to understand some things before she goes." He turned to Jo and swung a tight, powerful left hook that drove her right to the ground.

There was absolutely no point in trying not to cry. This was not a pass yourself off as a tough guy moment. Tears poured out of her eyes. Blood poured out of her nose. She crouched on all fours and let it, because she didn't want anything near the bright pain engulfing the entire right side of her head. Her ear rang, and her heart kept time to the little drips of red making a puddle on the ground between her hands. She groaned, started to feel dim and nauseous. Though Jo wasn't a godly woman anymore, she prayed she wouldn't throw up. She couldn't imagine the world of hurt that would open up.

Nearby, she heard Jered laughing like a goddamn hyena.

Brian stood over her. "You know, some people won't hit a woman. I think that's sexist. I'm an equality-minded guy. Hell, I voted for Bernie Sanders. Viva la rev-o-lution, ladies."

The broad toe of his work boot connected with her soft stomach. Jo caught an inch of air. She came down hard. The bad cheese and shitty wine she'd had earlier came up. Her vomit drowned her puddle of blood, turning it chunky, and a darker shade of red.

She moaned and rolled onto her side. Jo tried to feel like the cool night air was doing anything to salve her burning face. She coughed and choked and spit up a little more. Her nose felt overstuffed with hot, soggy cotton. Jo closed her eyes, pain taking precedence over everything. Brian and Jered were talking, though she couldn't hear them. She did hear the flick of a lighter. Great. They were going to have a smoke and celebrate the size of their dicks.

Cool air came in through her mouth. Her breathing slowed. It was maybe a minute before she opened her eyes.

Brian rolled his cigarette between his fingers and nodded down. He nudged her screaming stomach with his boot. "Harder than it looks in the movies, isn't it?"

Jo had only been punched twice before. Once in fifth grade arguing over a football game, and once by one of the lobbyists she'd sent to jail in the course of winning that Pulitzer. Apparently, some people were a lot better at hitting girls than others.

She planted a hand on the rough bark of a tree behind her and struggled to her shaking knees, then to her feet. She leaned against the tree and kept breathing. Hands on knees that were still sore from her trip and fall the other night, Jo remained quiet and studied the ground. Then she heard a slide of metal and a click. She looked up.

Jo hadn't spent a lot of time at the barrel end of a gun. None at all, actually. It was mesmerizing. She grasped the abrupt possibility of instant mortality in a way she never had before – not even during the cancer – as she stared into the skinny cylinder of black infinity. It seemed to return her hypnotized gaze. A disembodied voice floated like a lazy ghost into her ears. Her eyes stayed locked on the gun as Brian spoke.

"Let's just be really clear. Jered tells me you have some photos and some stories about him that make him uncomfortable. He also says that you keep showing up in places that make him uncomfortable."

"Yeah." Jered popped his chest.

Jo flinched.

"Shut up." Brian continued, "I don't like it because it means he might get in a spot and say some things he shouldn't. Here's the deal. You talk to Hill about Jered and Ashley, you keep digging on Brittany or Randy, and one Ms. Laura Tanaka gets put out of her misery."

"What?" Jo murmured.

"He's saying we'll end your retard wife, bitch." Jered's skinny chest snaked back and forth under his puffy coat.

Jo sprung toward him, head-first. He easily side-stepped her drunken stumble. She tripped, crashed back down to the ground that came up fast to meet her shoulder.

Getting to the bottom of a story always involved some hard work. Now, here she was, at the bottom. Down in the shallows with the nasty creatures that lived under the rocks, face smeared in blood and dirt and dead pine needles. It was where the good stories lived. But Laura? No. Jo needed time to regroup. Breathe, and think. She looked up at Brian, could see the cigarette smoke flooding from his nostrils. She held up a finger, stalling more for oxygen than time. "I understand what you're saying."

"That's really great to hear. Thank you. Now, unlock your phone and hand it over," Brian replied.

"I don't –"

Brian nudged her again with his boot, this time tipped her over onto her back and aching shoulder. *Damnit.* Slowly, Jo did as she was told. Slowly. She was having a hard time getting back to her feet. There was a way out of this, but it wasn't here and now. From the cold ground, she watched Brian's fingertip plunder her digital world.

He looked down at her. "Here's something interesting. From a Beth Berge at the *P.I.*? I'll go ahead and CC myself on this."

Jo closed her eyes and heard a little swoosh.

Brian pocketed the phone. "Sorry about all your photos. And all your emails. And your voice mails. And all your texts. And your contacts. Not sure what you've got backed up. Guessing some of it. If you do have photos of Jered living in a cloud somewhere, and you decide to restore them, I can now remind you that I have an email that looks an awful lot like you and this person Beth committed a prosecutable offense."

Jo looked up into the starry night sky. She kept breathing. She finally managed to stagger up the near tree and keep her feet.

Brian came right up next to her, right in her face. Jo hated herself for it, but she turned her head away, cringed just a little bit as he stood almost touching her chest.

"Let's recap. I have your wife and whatever you've been up to with this Beth gal hanging over your head. You have nothing on me but speculation, and some creepy pictures of a young guy with his shirt off. You're not law enforcement. You're not even a real journalist anymore. You've got nothing to work with. You steer clear of Jered from here on out. I hear there's a missing cat you can chase."

"Okay." She'd back off until she could she could see straight again, find a way to protect Laura.

Then all bets were off when it came to this ego-centric fucker.

Brian stepped back. He turned to Jered.

"Get over here. Give Joanna something to take the edge off. I feel like we've fucked her up a little bit."

"Hell yeah." Jered stepped up to Jo again.

She backed away.

Brian's gun reappeared. "I don't have to kill you. I could just shoot you in the foot. You might think 'yeah, but then they'd nail him on ballistics.' But the other part of that story is you never walk right again."

Jo let Brian take her by the chin. He smelled like patchouli and privilege.

"Open up."

She didn't. Brian pushed a finger against her tender cheek. She cried out, then did as she was told.

Jered reached into a pocket. He pulled out a plastic dime bag. In it were a few small, opaque red tablets. She looked up into his slippery eyes. She caught a whiff of weed on his breath. She was beginning to really hate that smell. He grinned at her, chuckled, and put one of the tabs in her mouth. "Bet you don't swallow. In this case, that's gonna pay off ."

It tasted faintly like fake strawberries. Brian held her by the face for – thirty seconds? A minute? Longer? Jo kept her eyes on his the whole time. They were brown, the color of weak coffee, a shade lighter than his wavy chestnut hair. There wasn't much else to them. As long as she stared at him, she didn't see anything behind those eyes. Not even hate.

She had plenty of hate for both of them right now. *I'm going to burn your rural shit-show house of cards to the ground, Brian Stewart.* Jo made that promise to herself and to Laura. And then, the world slipped away from her.

Jered and Brian both stepped away. Neither one of them intervened when she slid all the way down the tree she'd been leaning against. When the world stopped spinning, she spit out what they'd given her.

For a minute, Jo didn't feel much of anything. All of a sudden, she realized – well, she didn't feel much of *anything*. The pain in her head and her gut were there, but that was okay. She knew Jered and Brian were still there too, talking. Jered pointing and laughing. It wasn't good, sure, but was it bad? It was a pretty night, after all. The wind shushing around. A little cold, but it smelled like cedar trees. The sweet dirt and the shiny leaves were soft against her face. She closed her eyes. The dark was nice. Really nice.

She heard hollow thunks on the forest floor. From very, very far away came a voice, shouting. "What the fuck, you guys." The voice swooped toward her. "Jo – hey, Jo." A big pair of hands rolled her onto her back. One hand brushed all the hair out of her eyes. She saw a part of a moon, and some stars, and some clouds. And then, holy shit, big as life right in her face, was Tyler Sealth. He looked so serious. He disappeared; the voice swooped away again.

"You're not going to kill her, are you?"

"Nah. Don't be dumb as you look, Ty." Jered Brasier's voice slithered into Jo's ears. "We're just gonna let her have a little fun. Plan was to dump her at the Alibi for the closers to deal with, but it looks like you've got that job now, man."

A cigarette dropped next to Jo's face. The smoke made her eyes water. Then, a boot appeared. The same one that had kicked her. She heard the crunch of the pine needles as it twisted out the butt. Brian, the boot's owner, was suddenly whispering in her ear. "Nice to meet you, Joanna. Let's not do this again."

"Okay," she murmured. Doing this again sounded like an absolutely terrible idea. At least the part where she was being punched and kicked sounded awful. Right now, though? Right now was not bad. If she could stay here, right in the here and now, not worry about tomorrow, or being blackmailed, or Laura, or Beth, or her dying career? Well, she'd do that. She'd just float around in this pleasant cloud and everything would be fine. Jo hadn't felt this good in a very long time.

She heard some shuffling and some cracking twigs and leaves. Then, Tyler and his funny, fuzzy black eyebrows filled her view screen again.

A second later, he lifted her by the armpits. He stood her up against the tree. He took her under the shoulder and made her walk.

"Come on. Let's get you home."

Jo figured she would never, ever hike in the woods of Makah, ever again. She also figured she'd never again be so glad to see the scuzzy back patio of the Alibi and the old wood-paneled Jeep parked in front of it. Or the woman leaning against it.

"Oh my God. Jo. *Jo*. What happened to you?" Valerie Larsen rushed forward, leaned under her shoulder, and took her from Tyler. Which was good, because they were both seriously flagging. Whatever Jered had given her was wearing off very quickly. The aftermath was fucking atrocious and she was completely exhausted.

They got to the Jeep and Jo rested against it.

"What the hell happened," Valerie asked.

Jo wasn't sure who Valerie was talking to, but she'd let Tyler go ahead and field that one.

"It was Jered Brasier and Brian Stewart," he answered.

"Oh."

That was Valerie's response? "Oh?" Not, "Who the hell are those guys, and why did they take a woman into the woods and beat the shit out of her?" Jo brought her head up gently, slowly, tried to stop the world from fading in and out, getting ready to ask those follow-up questions.

Then, she actually *looked* at Valerie. Abruptly, she changed tactics. "Why are you crying?"

"Why aren't *you* crying? My God – Jo. Look at you."

Jo looked down. There was blood all down her pea coat, her jeans, even splattered on her boots. Stuck to all of it were dirt and pine needles. Her upper lip was warm, her neck was sticky, and her mouth tasted like she'd licked an old key.

"Yeah, so, I'm going to leave now." Tyler spared a glance at Jo. "You're okay?"

"Not really," she responded. Her tongue filled up her entire mouth. She sounded, and still felt, a little slurry. "Thanks for the help. Could have used it a few minutes sooner."

"You're fucking welcome."

"I'm not –" Jo tried to take a bigger breath in. Bad idea. Pain wrapped her abdomen in a giant, fiery hug. "I'm sorry. Really. Thank you, Tyler."

Valerie pulled a Kleenex from her pocket, licked it, and swiped Jo's nose, dabbed her eyes. She tilted her head at Tyler. "Where did you come from – how did you end up out there?"

"I ran into Jo at the bar. After I left, I was sitting in the car, umm –"

"Smoking?" Jo offered.

"Yeah. I saw Jered and Brian grab you. I thought for a second, and then decided I'd follow. Listened for a minute. I knew you were going to get what was coming to you. Here or somewhere else. But I didn't want – I didn't want anything really bad to happen."

"Anything really bad – " Valerie yelled –

Jo interrupted her. "Bad, as in what happened to Brittany Roebuck?" The connection had become striking as Jo's head cleared.

Tyler shook his head. "I'm going."

Valerie stepped in front of him as he started to walk away. "At least help me get her into my rig."

He nodded. Valerie opened the passenger door of the Jeep.

"I can do it." Jo brought her foot up about six inches. Stopped as everything between her bra and her knees seized up. She almost fell over.

Tyler caught her under the arms and lifted her onto the seat.

Valerie shoved in between them and brought Jo's knees around. She took her wrist, laid two fingers over it. "Jo, do you have any injuries other than what I can see on your face?"

"Brian tried to punt me like a football, so my stomach's a little sore."

"Anything else?"

"He hit me in the back of the head. With a gun."

"Okay." Little beads of moisture reappeared at the outer corners of Valerie's eyes. Her fingertips moved gently upward from the base of Jo's neck until they both winced. "Yep. Got you good. Did you pass out?"

"No."

Apparently satisfied for the moment, Valerie turned back to Tyler, standing with his hands in the pockets of his jeans. "I'm going to give her the once-over, get her home. If you want to go, go."

He glanced over her shoulder at Jo. "Sorry this happened to you."

"Me too. Thanks, Tyler."

He made his way to his sad Nissan sedan, lonely in the empty parking lot.

Valerie studied Jo, big brown watery eyes scanning her face as she gently prodded it. She ducked away, grabbed a red box with a bright white cross on it from somewhere in the back of the Jeep. "Lucky for you, you've got Makah's one and only vet and EMT all rolled into one. Chickens to car accidents, I do it all. Let's get you checked out, see if we need to have Bonnie open up the clinic tonight." She opened the kit, fished through, and put on a pair of exam gloves. Then, she pulled out a small flashlight, which she promptly shone right in Jo's eyes, one after the other – and, of all things – grinned.

"Are your eyes usually two different colors?"

Shit. Of course her contacts were history. Jo nodded. "Yes."

"Okay. Pupils are good. Same size. A little constricted, which I wouldn't expect."

"Jered – Brian had him give me something. I spit it out. I'm guessing fentan-yl. I can see what all the fuss is about now."

The other woman stilled, didn't acknowledge what Jo had said, really. Then, she held up an index finger, orbited it side to side. "Can you follow this?"

Jo could. "How long have you been a volunteer first responder?"

"Ten years now." Valerie disappeared into the back of the Jeep again, reap-peared with a gallon of water and a roll of paper towels. "I don't think Laura ought to see you like this." She wet a towel, took Jo's chin, leaned in close, gently ran it over Jo's face. The towels were bright pink when she was done. "A little better?" The vet smiled again, more like she was trying to force the reflex from Jo than she actually meant it herself. It was still beautiful.

Valerie's smile, her kindness, it made Jo forget about how much every part of her body hurt. Most of all, it made her want Laura. "Yeah." Jo sniffed and that was the wrong move. A wad of bloody snot slid down her throat. She gagged and spit it up onto the shining black asphalt.

"Sorry."

"Don't be. I calved a breech this morning. You've got nothing on that." Val-erie offered her the water. "Have a drink, unless it makes you sick. Shouldn't."

Jo took the water, but she couldn't hold it very still, despite Valerie's help. What did make it to her mouth was the best thing she'd ever put in it.

"Alright. Almost done." Valerie had started to tear up again.

Jo must look like a damn wreck. "Is it that bad?"

"No. No – I don't even think this is broken." Valerie took off her gloves, delicately ran her soft fingertips at either side Jo's aching nose. "I'm sorry. I must just be tired."

An invisible hand rustled the treetops. Across the alley in the woods, un-derbrush cracked. Then, a tense silence. Four glowing green eyes looked back, reflecting in the moonlight. The eyes disappeared, a flick of two white tails, and the crackling and rustling resumed.

"I'm going to lay you down now, Jo, if that's okay. It's probably going to hurt." Valerie's jaw tightened as she eased Jo back along with the seat.

It did hurt. It hurt like a bitch.

She brushed aside Jo's crusty coat. "Is it okay if I check your abdomen?"

Just what Jo had wanted ever since she'd moved to Makah. The lady who took care of her chickens assessing how tight her abs were. Or, more accurately, weren't. But it would either be Valerie laying hands on her right now or Jo wondering all night if she were going to wake up pissing blood. "Okay."

Valerie slid her hands under Jo's sweater. They were dry and cool when they hit Jo's red-hot stomach. She sucked in air through her teeth and the hair on her arms stood on end.

"Sorry. How badly does this hurt?" She pushed on one side of Jo's abdomen, in the middle, and then on the other.

"Bad – but not too bad."

Valerie slid her hands up further, to Jo's ribcage, and pressed around. "Anything hurt?"

"No."

"You feel cold?"

"No."

"Okay." Valerie leaned over Jo, close. She brushed a hand across her forehead, smoothed away her sticky hair, then gently brought her blood-caked coat around her and buttoned it up. "I think you're fine to go home tonight. Check in with the clinic in the morning. Especially if you get weak or disoriented."

"Will-do. I'm up on the protocol."

"Of course." Valerie squeezed her hand, closed the door softly.

"Thanks," Jo squeaked when Valerie climbed into the driver's seat.

"Anytime," she answered quietly. "You want to call Frank? He's been expecting us at your place a while ago."

"Right. Yes." Fuck. "Can I borrow your phone? Brian took mine."

"Oh - sure." Valerie didn't look at Jo, just pulled up Frank's contact and handed her phone over.

Jo closed her eyes as they drove off. "Hey Frank. Yeah. It's me. Sorry I'm late."

A HIT DOG WILL HOLLER

Elijah Hill looked up from his desk as Jo came into the tiny Sheriff's station, pointed at her with his pen. "Heard about what happened last night. Just about to give you a call. You here to press charges?"

"No. I'm here to get information," Jo replied. She'd dozed most of the morning with a cold pack on her face and one on the back of her head, like a damn ice cream sandwich and her brain partially frozen.

When she thawed out, she headed right for Hill. Brian Stewart had decided to kick a dog. She wasn't going to whine and slink away. Jo was the kind of mutt that whipped right around and bit you in the ass.

"I can tell you that raw meat doesn't work." Hill reclined in his chair. "That looks like it hurts. All seriousness – you okay?"

"It does. And I am." Jo invited herself to take a seat. Her knees crunched right up against the desk, but there wasn't really anywhere else to put a chair. "But Brian Stewart and Jered Brasier beat the shit out of me last night. Then, Brian blackmailed me. Then, they dosed me. Judging by its popularity around here, and how I felt, I'm going with fentanyl."

Brenda Locke looked over at her from her desk a couple feet away. Jo recognized the that-must-hurt tenor of her sideways glance. She'd had to park a block over from Hill's office and walk, because the farmer's market was on this morning and town was jammed. Two small children had pointed at her along the way. The bruises were already coming in under her eyes nicely, and her right eye was totally bloodshot. Half her world had a sickly, pink tinge to it.

Hill sat forward, leaned very close to Jo's face, shaking his head. She flinched and leaned back. Even in the safety of a police station she was jumpy.

"I'll arrest Jered and Brian for assault and battery on your word. Criminal coercion too. That's no issue."

"Actually, it is an issue." Ten years ago, she'd written the biggest story of her life about a small man who got very big by pulling exactly the same shit Brian Stewart was up to on Makah. This was how they did it. This was why anyone blinked even one eyelash when Jered came around. Leverage. Breaking the chain depended on them leaning on the wrong person – the strongest link. Jo hadn't broken with Abish, and she didn't intend to now. "Brian's got something on me. I don't think you're surprised about that. I think he's got something on half the people on this island. The question is, to protect himself from what?"

"I can't comment on that, specifically. Just background, and you won't have to ask anyone around here twice to get the same answer. We believe Brian's moving opioids on and off the Island. Specifically, fentanyl. Which I think you've already pieced together." Hill ducked his head and tapped his pen on his notepad, twirled it through his fingers.

"Well, piecing things together is what I'm paid to do," Jo said. She thought about the averted eyes she'd encountered when she mentioned the Kibo heir's name. Vi, Tyler, Valerie, hell, even Jered. "I've started wondering, if he might even have something on you, Elijah."

Brenda Locke looked over again. Hill rearranged his giant gun belt. "Let's take a step back."

No thanks. "How does Randy Fuller fit into all of this, by the way? You seized a nice amount of fentanyl at his house. But why do you think he killed Brittany? A random fingerprint? Cause of death is a pretty weak connection."

"Cause of death? How'd you put Brittany together with the fentanyl?"

Jo had walked herself into a spot. Maybe she wasn't as put back together as she thought. "Makes the most sense. Thanks for the confirmation." Hill didn't respond, and that was what she'd come here to see, the way his face looked slack and caught out. She pressed on. "Okay sure. Randy Fuller as the universal bad guy on all of it. Makes sense. But, because you know, of how my *face* looks this morning, I'm having a harder and harder time putting him at the top of the food chain. What I think, and what I think you know, is that Randy was a mule for Brian Stewart."

"Yes." Hill acknowledged. "But what you sent me about Brittany selling the copper – it doesn't mean Randy wasn't in on the burglaries too. But that does strengthen the link between them. So, thanks. Helps with motive. What if he and Brittany were in it together, got in a fight over profits? Despite what Vi Mitchell thinks, Randy wasn't a saint. He was a criminal. Just like the boys who assaulted you last night."

"Elijah do you seriously see Randy Fuller and his chainsaw, and Brittany Roebuck in her MHS track hoodie, getting together to cook up this little enterprise? You can tell me yes, but it'll just prove you're full of shit."

Over at the filing cabinet, Brenda Locke covered her mouth in a half-cough.

Hill just sighed. "Wish you'd reconsider filing charges on Brian and Jered."

"Not yet. But I do intend to when the time's right. I just need to know, Elijah - if I go out on a limb, are you going to be the one to snap it, or catch me if I fall off?"

"If you bring us anyone who will talk, if we get anything that sticks, I guarantee you I've been looking for a way to rid Makah of Brian Stewart for a while. But Jo, there's a reason it's taken so long. We had someone come forward, we arrested Brian once. Then the guy actually moved to Canada so he didn't have to testify. I don't want to discourage you. I want you to be careful. Think this through."

"Right. Speaking of careful." She started to elaborate, ask for what she really needed, then had to stop and pull herself together. Still, her voice was thick. "Now I'm going off the record. I need you to keep an eye, two if you can, on Laura. Please."

Hill nodded. He tapped his pen against the half-full coffee cup on his desk, stained and well-used. He ran a hand over his head. "That's what Brian threatened you with?"

"Yep."

Hill flipped up the edge of his keyboard. It clattered down.

Brenda Locke stopped blending into the background, came and stood next to her boss. She was only about a head taller than he was sitting down. "I'm there every day, Jo. I'll park at your driveway between dispatch."

"Thank you."

"I'll cruise the Porter whenever I can," said Hill "We can't promise you anything, Jo. We could, if you'd file charges."

"You know I can't. Yet. You know why. But at least you know I lock my doors."

"If Brian decides to come after you, a locked door won't do you much good."

Jo's split lip and blood-stuff ed nose drove that point home hard.

The more you have Joey, the more you have to insure it.

Man did Jo miss Big Jack right now. The thought of her dad still being here, stepping in, larger than life, kicking those skinny boys' asses like a couple screw-up cadets and making everything better, cinched up her throat. Dad had taught her long ago about fighting her own battles. But when she was younger, he'd always been there, backing her up.

Tyler had been there, last night, backing her up. Valerie too. Hell, Vi was the one who'd started the Makah giving tree, when it came to Jo. All of them were scared as hell. All this had started as a way for Jo to exorcise some demons. It was going to end by getting rid of Makah's.

Hill conceded to Jo's silence. "Alright. You need to do what you think will keep your family safe. I get that. One more question. You know anything at all about that picture – that sculpture I emailed you? That, and a fingerprint we can't match on evidence at the scene – they're the only outliers we've got."

"You mean besides Randy's lack of motive and capacity?"

"Can you help me out? That's all I'm asking."

There was Tyler again, floating in and out of her blurry vision last night. An unmatched fingerprint – that ruled out Tyler, he'd been arrested. As well as Luke, Jered, and Brian. "Not yet. But I was just headed out to follow up on a hunch."

"Mmmm hmmm." Hill tapped his pen, acted like a guy who was good at getting information out of people, and waited quietly.

Jo acted like someone who was also good at that game and responded with a question. "Just curious. You happen to talk to Luke Sorensen at all, about the break-ins?"

"Of course." Hill put his thumbs in his belt. "He and Terry are the only guys who could convert the copper."

"Where did you talk to him? At his workshop, or –"

"At home. Driveway, actually. Caught him a little early in the morning back from fishing. He'd just come up empty out off Willapa Harbor."

"Okay. Have you asked him – or Ashley – about Brittany Roebuck?"

"No. Why would I? We're pretty damn sure where she got her hands on her drugs. And we're pretty sure we've got the guy responsible for her death."

Jo hot-footed around in her head, couldn't come up with a way to follow-up without hinting even more clearly that she knew too much about the details surrounding Brittany's death. "Okay. Just wondering."

"Right." Hill stood, grabbed his raincoat and his hat. He stopped right next to Jo on his way out, put a hand on her arm. She was sure it was meant to be comforting, but after last night, she couldn't help but jump.

"I'm sorry for what happened to you, Jo. Stay in touch."

"Yep." His sympathy was a little too much. She hustled out and into the Volvo for her next nerve-wracking stop of the afternoon.

NOTHING TOUCHED THE TRIGGER BUT THE DEVIL'S RIGHT HAND

At the end of Tucker Trail this afternoon there was no million-dollar view of Mount Rainier. Instead, sheets of rain showered down from the clouds into the Puget Sound, which churned black, erupting in white caps. It pounded against the bulkhead under Tyler's cabin, splashing up the wide timbers and over onto the patchy grass. At a crumbling dock twenty yards down the rocky shore, a metal dingy thunked against a rotting wooden pylon. Jo wouldn't have taken it out on a calm day. It hadn't been here on her last visit. Was it Tyler's?

The wind tore under Jo's upturned hood and ripped it down. She was wearing one of Frank's spare coats. It smelled like outside and fish guts. This morning at the hardware store that ran the new cleaning service, she'd dropped her pea coat off to be sent overtown. The pale teen behind the counter had stared at her, then slowly placed it in the rolling canvas bin with the rest of the clothes. Jo had bagged it, but there was blood smeared all over the plastic. In all her bruised glory, she'd leaned forward to whisper, "This is my first murder. You won't tell anyone, will you?" The girl did not laugh at her joke.

The wind ripped at her again. Her head still ached, and the cold was making it worse. She tugged at her hood, placed a hand on her head as she walked across the gravel and up onto the porch.

Tyler opened the door before she knocked. "You look like shit."

"Thanks. I came to thank you for helping me out of a tough spot last night."

"If you have to." He glanced toward the sheets of rain, and then up at the trail she'd just come down. "But I know you're not here to thank me, you're here to ask questions." He turned his back and Jo followed him in. The window in the wood stove in the corner glowed red-white. A wall of heat surrounded it, pushing back the cold gust of sea air with contempt for its intrusion. This time the cabin was hazy with smoke, warm and close, and

Jo knew she was going to be at least half-way high before she got out of this hotbox. Her phone - Laura's borrowed phone - buzzed in her pocket. *Short, short, short.* Frank. She'd check it in a minute.

Tyler stood in the cluttered kitchen, fingers tapping at the sides of his dark skinny-leg jeans. Jo invited herself to the threadbare couch butted up against the window. She winced as she sat. Her stomach felt like she'd done two-hundred crunches with a hot anvil resting on it.

She leaned her elbows on her knees and looked up. "So first things first – really – thank you. Since that's out of the way, did Brian or Jered have anything to do with Brittany's death?"

"How about no?" Tyler just laughed, turned abruptly away from her.

Jo half-laughed back at him. Blood started leaking out of her nose. She pulled a spotted kleenex out of her pocket. She had exactly no time left for any of this. The only way she was going to get clear of Brian Stewart, get Beth and Laura clear too, was nailing him to the wall. That started with cracking Tyler. "Then why were you and Jered so worried about her, that day I came by last week?"

"Don't know what you're talking about."

"You two were right out on the bulkhead – Jered said, I think exactly, 'we both know shit's going to hit the fan over pretty little Brittany Roebuck.'"

"Jered's an ass. He was just talking to talk, pretending like he knew some-thing."

"I agree he's an ass. But is he a killer? Seems like a guy who might lose his temper, go too far."

"I don't know. But you're fucking nosy, and you know what –" Tyler kicked at the foot of the dining table, side-eyed Jo. "I don't have to tell you anything more about minding your own shit. If Brian can't teach you that lesson?" He held his hands in the air.

"Fine. Enough about Brian. How about the Sorensens?"

"I don't know what they'd have to do with all this."

"Are you covering for your friend, or your boss? Where's your car?

"Danno's garage." He threw his chin in the air. "Luke's not my boss."

"What is he? Your friend?"

"No." His eyes flicked to her for just a second.

"So, Luke's not your friend. But you know what, Tyler? I think I am."

Desperation radiated from him like the heat coming off the stove.

Jo felt it just as clearly, because as she worked to get into Tyler's head, the hollow need clanged off the tuning fork in the center of her own chest.

"Thanks, but I'm good with who I got," he answered.

"Seriously? Jered Brasier? Really?"

"You know what? He used to be a great friend. We were in baseball together when we were kids. I used to sleep over at his house." He shook his head and turned, walked two steps over to the run-down yellow Frigidaire and pulled out a can of Rainier. He popped it, fidgeted off the tab and threw it onto the peeling linoleum. He polished half the can, and pointed it at her. "Jered and I were in the same class, until he got held back a couple times."

"What happened?"

"His mom, that's what. Harmony spent about a decade on weed and booze, then got into meth. Now she's big on fentanyl. She used to show at our baseball games loaded. Toward summer she'd take her shirt off and just sit in the bleachers in her bra. Not a sports bra – like the Vicky's kind you don't wear in public. I mean, guess it was nice or whatever that she even came at all. But Jered didn't last long in stuff, once he got to middle school."

"I'm sorry to hear that. Jered's an asshole, but I'm sorry to hear that."

"His dad's already been in for like, ten or something, for killing a guy drunk driving." Tyler made his way to the stereo and put on an actual record. The guy on the cover looked like he'd stepped out of an ad for Budweiser, confederate flags, and chainsaws. He flipped a kitchen chair backward and sat down, and to Jo's great satisfaction, looked like he was settling in. "So how about you, Joanna Ford. How many people you know in jail?"

"A lot." She'd put a few there herself.

"Yeah you're real funny. If you want to be friends with someone, then don't be a bitch. I've got four – mom, dad, and two cousins. I bet you already know that." He throttled his beer consumption but kept drinking like he meant it.

Jo pushed on her stomach, eased herself back on the sofa. She put her hands in her lap and clicked her thumbnails. "None."

"How about gone to rehab? And not summer camp rehab. Like, court mandated."

There was that one guy at college, probably named Chet, one of the editors on staff with her at the Hoya. He'd been kicked out senior year for coke. A couple folks she'd known in the newsroom at the *Sun*, and the *Post*. None of them had lost their jobs.

Jo figured they didn't count in this situation. She'd covered a lot of crime in Baltimore. Then, she'd gone home. She caught a little echo of Frank's lecture. About sticking around where you stirred things up.

Tyler kicked the rest of his beer. "Your dad ever smack you one across the face for crying after you dropped a fly ball?" He went back to the fridge. This time, he offered a can to Jo.

She took it and immediately put it to the side of her face. "Thanks. And, no. Dad never hit me."

"I figured. So, then, what's the worst thing you and your best friend in high school ever got up to? Cigarette behind the gym?"

Nailed it. But Jo didn't answer, because that question also poked a sore spot. The worst thing her best friend in high school had done was join the Navy. She'd had to watch Big Jack tear up over how proud he was of him. Dad hadn't teared up when Jo had announced her plans to go to Georgetown.

He took her quiet as a confession, put his head back and laughed his ass off. "I thought so."

Outside, the rain kept on. Tyler eyed her as she drank her beer. Stereo-guy clanged and moaned on about the devil's right hand. She stood up and stood over Tyler. She had no illusions about intimidating him, but the beer had hit her stomach hard and fast, and her eyes had started to burn in this tiny hotbox. She felt half like a god and half like a hungry wildfire.

"Fine, Tyler. Point taken. I'm not from Makah. I'm not of Makah. I didn't grow up in an after-school special. I've had all the damn lectures I'm going to take about that. But guess what. I don't care who's in-group here, who belongs and who doesn't. I'm going to find out what happened to Randy. To Brittany, what she did and didn't do, and I'm going to talk about it, because I *get* it. When people get side-ways on Makah, they have a hard time getting out. I don't want that for you. Or anyone else, because there will be a someone else. And I have a strong suspicion that if you help me out, we both get out from under Brian Stewart."

"How stupid are you, lady? Take a look in the mirror this morning?" He stood, grabbed an ashtray and a half-smoked joint. He lit it, took a drag and held it for a while before exhaling and downing most of his beer. "I'm sorry about everything that's happened. You know that. I know you do. But you still shouldn't come here asking me for help."

Jo took a big breath in. Her stomach and ribs screamed.

The shock from last night was catching up. She was decompensating, totally blowing her boundaries, and she needed to stop. Or not. "I'm just looking for some information. I'm screwed here, and so are you." Laura's borrowed phone buzzed, again. This time it was a call, not a text; she'd had her number forwarded. Could be important. She ignored it again as Tyler spoke.

"You know what, Joanna Ford? You're right. We're both screwed. So you ought to leave, and you ought to let the police do their job. If they can." He snorted, but did not laugh.

"Is that an or-else?"

"You know it is, but not from me."

Jo wandered into the kitchen. On the blistering paint of a windowsill she noticed again the little metal mini-Tetris. She picked it up, turned it over in her hands. It was cool to the touch and at war with its own order. A conflicted geometry barreling straight for a singularity. She was a little at odds with herself, wondering how its twin had ended up in Brittany Roebuck's pocket. Was it love, a token of affection from Tyler? Was there still something going on between them? Or was it something else? Inside her coat pocket, her phone buzzed. *Short, short, short.* Frank, again. That probably wasn't good.

She tossed the little statue up and down in the palm of her hand. "Could you answer for where you were during the break-ins? The morning Brittany died? Not that I'm asking. But Hill might – if I take your advice and hand what I know over to the police."

"Ask Luke. He'll say I was with him. So tell the cops whatever you want." He chuckled and rolled a joint back and forth between smudgy fingers.

"Tell them you mysteriously found money to get your car fixed?"

"That's money from Luke. He pays me. Not much. But enough. And he lets me keep the work that's good, that I've done. He's going to help me get it around, galleries and stuff . Help me get into UW or somewhere. You know, Jered thinks if you get enough stuff, get enough people afraid of you, you're made. I don't. If I'm going to get off Makah, not just move, but get away from it, if I'm not going to end up like Jered, that's how it's going to happen. Meeting people who don't spend their Saturday nights scoring whatever they need to bring them back from how they spent their Friday night."

She set the little figurine on the table in front of Tyler. "You know they found something that looked just like this in the pocket of Brittany's hoodie."

"What?" His head swiveled fast from the gray haze outside. He cast his dark eyes right on hers. She'd finally pulled the right lever. He seemed almost genuinely surprised, though.

"Yep. Since we're friends, I'm giving you a heads up."

"You haven't said – they don't know where it came from?"

"Not yet. You want to tell me?"

"I gave one to Brittany, I made it for her, when we were together. She must've still had it. Seriously. That's the whole story."

She took off her coat and threw it over a metal folding chair, one of three not completing a set. She turned to the sink and pulled on the faucet. It shuddered and water spat and hissed from a broken aerator. In Tyler's world, friendships seemed highly transactional. Jo tried showing a little value, stepping into the shoes of a mother who was long absent. She waited for the tap to run hot. Tyler didn't pay any attention to her until she started in on the Jenga-tower of dirty dishes spilling onto the countertop.

"Lay off that. You don't have to do it. You don't live here."

"I'm not going to fiddle with the levels on your stereo. I'm addressing the super-fund site in your sink. You live in a shithole. Do that long enough, and it gets to you." She glanced around. "I think you know what a metaphor is."

"How'd you know about –" he nodded at the little statue she'd placed at the center of the table and started peeling the label off his Rainer bottle. "That piece being on Brittany?"

"I'm friends with Elijah Hill." That was a little bit of a stretch. But Jo was warming up to her theme. "He asked me if I'd seen anything like it. I told him I hadn't. So right now I'm the only link between this –" she pointed a sudsy finger at the statuette. "And you – when it comes to the the law. What do you think about that?"

Tyler sniffed and swiped at his nose. He finished his beer in a gulp and took a big pull on what was left of the joint, drummed his fingers on the rickety table. "I think someone like Jered, when they know something like that, they use it to get more out of you." A wash of rain clattered against the windows of the cabin. Tyler and Jo both watched as it filtered down the single-pane windows. He turned back to her. "I think you're more of a pain in the ass. I think you'll try and use it to get someone to do whatever you think the right thing is. But you're still just trying to get something out of me."

"And?"

"What if I don't do whatever you want me to do? Will you rat me out?"

"Remember how I told you that I didn't like people paying for things they hadn't done?" Jo didn't turn away from the sink, or her work there. "I don't want Randy to catch the blame while the real asshole walks and talks his way into whatever crime he's going to commit next. I don't want that for you either, Tyler. But you're not helping me help you. Why not?"

"You're okay. I'm sorry I hassled you. So just leave it."

In her coat on the chair next to Tyler, her phone buzzed yet again.

He glanced over at it. The beer and the weed had already outpaced her. She hadn't seen him this far gone at any point. The kid's pupils were a mile wide. Despite him tuning into her finally, and getting anxious about the figurine she'd asked about, a smile tugged at the corners of his pale, thin lips as they both listened to the phone buzz.

"Sounds like you got some business of your own. Maybe you ought to handle that before you get into mine."

"You're covering for people. Come on. I'm not stupid." Jo could still paint a picture that looked a lot like Jered accidentally killing Brittany and strong-arming Tyler or Randy into helping with clean-up duty. "I don't think any of them are the kind who'd cover for you, whether or not you were in Little League together. So who's looking out for you?"

"I am."

"You're not doing a very good job."

"Neither are you." He tilted his chin, obviously at her colorful, aching face. He laughed, just a little, and wobbled as he stood up. He burned down the rest of the joint, smashed it out in the overflowing blue plastic ashtray. He went to the fridge and grabbed another beer. He stood right next to her as he spoke. "I'll handle what I need to handle. You're right, about how I need to look out for myself a little better. And I appreciate you not giving me up to Hill. But you need to stop coming here. Please." He didn't glance back at her as he strolled off through the dark, wood-paneled living room and down an unlit hall. She heard a door close.

The sponge in her hand looked like it might do better for a visit inside the reactor at Chernobyl, but she reloaded it with soap and worked on the dishes. She focused on scrubbing from a plate what might be green spaghetti sauce or might be mold. Either way she was glad for the scalding water turning her hands red. She hunted through drawers for a clean kitchen towel. They were empty save mouse droppings and the occasional scratched and dented pot or pan. On a last try, she found one, stained and threadbare. She laid it out on the curling orange-fleck Formica and stacked the dishes to dry.

Jo shrugged back into her coat. She was getting somewhere with Tyler, finally. He'd cave and give up what he knew, and soon. She fished a business card from her back pocket and wrote her cell number on the back. She set it on the table next to the fragrant ashtray and walked out.

She checked her phone. Two texts from Frank – Laura was going nuts over the fact that they were out of yogurt – could she stop and pick some up? A call from the gyno, and a call from a Seattle area code, a number she didn't recognize. Maybe Beth, calling her back from the office?

"Yes, hello, Ms. Ford. This is Jeannie from Dr. Phyllis Nokes' office. You've been referred to us for a consult. If you could please give a call back to schedule an appointment..."

Jo hung up. She stood on Tyler Sealth's crumbling porch and stared absently at the water. Rain poured down, obscuring everything more than a few feet off shore. She stared at Laura's blank phone a while. She thumbed it open. The screen saver – the two of them decked out for the White House Correspondents' dinner, both of them in the nicest dresses they'd ever owned. Jo had been invited to sit in the nosebleeds the year the Abish story had broken, and the year following. She flipped to the browser, searched the name of the doctor. The top hit was clearly the one most relevant to her. "Dr. Phyllis Nokes, Clinical Oncology, University of Washington Medical Center..."

That crappy little boat was still thumping against the dock. Bouncing around, tossed by the angry waves, tied up and just pounding and pounding against what wouldn't move. Jo thought it'd be a nice idea to free it from its misery. Fire it up, take it out into the middle of the Sound, and never come back.

THOSE DAMN PAPER VESTS

All the waiting. It defined Jo's every experience with medicine. Squirming on a hard, plastic chair waiting for her first booster shot and ignoring her mother's scolding. Drumming her fingers on the kitchen counter, waiting for her oncologist's office to call with results from the first biopsy she'd ever had. Or, head in her hands, doubled over in a pleather chair dying to hear when, or if, Laura would come out of a coma. And now, squirming on sterile, thin paper, perched atop an exam table, pulling and tugging at an offensive blue paper jacket in a futile attempt to cover any part of her cold stomach and chest.

All the waiting. It never suited her. Now, she waited for a doctor she hadn't even met to feel her up and confirm her worst fears had come true all over again. She'd been lucky the on-Island clinic even had an opening for her in the visiting rotation.

Jo waited, knowing what was coming with the cancer. The constant ache in her body, physical and emotional. The dead-tired, physical and emotional. The love and the pity. The medical bills it would take them years to pay off – again. And most of all, all of those goddamn *pills*.

"You bring the Connect Four?" Laura asked, rummaging through Jo's bag that was way too small to hold the favorite game. A therapy staple, Laura still enjoyed playing, even though she was kicking Jo's ass on the regular at this point.

"No – sorry. I forgot it. How about you do some jumping? Your OT says you've been slacking." She smirked. A few seconds later, Laura smirked back.

Jo hopped off the table and helped her search, finally came up with a slinky. The perfect low-dexterity fidget toy. She had one in her bag, one in the car, and God knows how many under the couch at home. She handed it over, climbed back up, and resumed waiting.

Hands clutching and un-clutching the beige sides of the padded table in the corner of the small, white exam room, she shifted back and forth. She realized she was slumping and fixed her posture. Surely doctors appreciated patients with good posture. If nothing else, sitting up helped minimize her anxiety over the little fl ab of stomach overfl owing the top of her jeans. The fluorescent lights above her buzzed and flickered. She tugged at the crumpled paper under her legs and tried to straighten it out.

"Want it?" Laura held the slinky out to Jo.

"No. Thanks."

She studied a poster on the wall that illustrated the various stages of cancer, from, "Hey no problem, stage one means a few months of misery and off you go with the rest of your life," to "kiss your kids goodbye, it's end-stage, it's everywhere, and it's curtains for you." The decorative border of the poster featured a series of ever-larger, then ever-smaller dots that mesmerized her. They reminded her of the tattered fishing charts she'd seen tacked up in every store on Makah. The dots indicated the fisher's chance of catching something growing larger or smaller along with the moon and changing tides. Jo got up, bare feet on the cold tile floor, padded over to her bag and her notebook. Something about the notes she made at the Sorensens – she reached in for her notebook and her borrowed phone started to buzz. Damn. It was Beth –

"You can have a seat, please, Ms. Ford." Jo's back had been turned to the door, and she jumped a little - she hadn't heard the doctor come in. "I'm Doctor Nokes. Phyllis if you prefer. The clinic kicked your case over to me. I'll be taking care of your exam and overseeing your tests today, and the results, through any treatment options we may need to explore."

The woman held out a hand. Jo held her paper jacket closed with one of her own, which ripped it, and shook with the other. *Explore treatment options.* She pictured herself as she'd seen her mother go out, head bare and patchy, hanging over their bathroom toilet. Jo's Kodachrome featured grasping white porcelain and simultaneously trying to wave off a fretting, helpless Laura. At least last time around, her wife had been able to hold the hair she'd been able to keep.

"We're seeing you because we've found a couple things in your current mammogram we don't like to see. And because of your history." Nokes bent her head and flipped through papers clipped into a sky-blue folder. "I'm going to do a more thorough exam than you might have received previously, which will include an ultrasound. After that Sally will take over, get your blood samples, and you're all done." The doctor set down Jo's chart.

"But before we start – can I ask about the injuries to your face?"

"Legitimately earned. And I have talked to law enforcement."

"Do you feel safe at home, Joanna?" Nokes looked over to Laura, fidgeting in the corner.

Wow. She'd heard countless doctors ask Laura that question and then glance at Jo. It was routine at the rehab facility. TBI patients came in for check-ups with all manner of bumps and bruises. Jo was shocked at how it made her ashamed just to be asked the question. And now she wondered what happened to women if they answered, "no."

Jo didn't feel safe on Makah, but that wasn't what she was being asked about. "I do. Absolutely."

"All right." Nokes stared at her, met her eyes directly, and held them for a while. "If you could lay down for me?"

Jo shoved her hands to her burning stomach and managed it. She sniffed away tears building at the edges of her eyes, though a few got loose. She pulled yet again at the damn jacket that had absolutely no staying power against her breasts or gravity. She examined the flecks on the bone-white drop ceiling tiles and looked for a pattern. There wasn't one.

The oncologist paused again when she saw the fading green bruise checkering Jo's abdomen. "Whatever you've been up to, it looks like it hurt."

"Long story. But it won't happen again."

Nokes's gaze lingered on her stomach a while longer, and Jo's face. "You're going to want to take care of yourself a little better, Ms. Ford." She reminded Jo of her fourth-grade teacher. Both women had the air of a gray-haired British woman you addressed using a title.

"Yep." Jo closed her eyes. She gasped as the cold ultrasound goo hit her breast. The woman standing over her didn't apologize, just shoved the wand around her chest and stared at the black and white screen next to her. Jo glanced over a few times, but the grainy image just reminded her of thick fog and dark forests. Mill Creek Ravine, and a dead girl.

In the quiet, she heard the phone in her bag buzz out a quick voice mail notification. She looked over at Laura. Jo started to cry. She closed her eyes and pretended the message wasn't from the other woman she'd been seeing.

While her brusque nature might have started a little disheartening, after a while Nokes's sure and steady execution calmed Jo down. She realized she was used to being forced by courtesy into answering a slew of irrelevant, and maybe inappropriate, personal questions during exams and tests while half-dressed. She remembered being off her guard and led into a conversational corner once when she was younger, and ended up coming out to a random old white guy with a pelt of black hair on his arms filling in for her usual gyno. He'd been right in the middle of the scrape when she'd squeaked out why she was absolutely sure she wasn't pregnant. Jo had actually felt him pause.

So maybe the down-to-business bedside manner wasn't so bad.

"All set." The doctor sat her up.

"Thanks."

"Alright. Get on out of that vest of shame we've got you in, and we'll talk."

"Okay."

Nokes clicked the door shut behind her.

Jo shrugged into her clothes. The phone buzzed yet again. Before she could stop her, Laura started to paw through Jo's bag.

"Need it?" Laura helpfully handed the cell to Jo, who was relieved to see the screen was black.

"Nope. Thanks." She took it, tucked it into the pocket of her jeans, smiled when the nurse came through the door.

"Here to bleed you dry." Sally, according to the name tag, smiled and clinked three large, clear vials.

"Right." Jo eyed the vials. The phone lit up through the pocket of her jeans, buzzed again.

"Get it," Laura urged her.

"No, it can wait."

Sally waved a hand to the bed. "You can be on your phone while I stick you. It'll distract you."

"Umm – alright." Jo stuck out her arm. With her free hand she clicked through to voice mail. "Ow." She winced at the jab.

"I'm in. Easy breezy from here."

Sure. Easy breezy. Jo clicked the volume all the way down. Beth was already talking.

"... your message. Look. I've been thinking. I spent a day really pissed at you. I got out of Mexico because I was sick of being so damn anxious all the time. But you know what? I also get a little sick at myself for bailing out on my friends down there." The line went quiet for a few seconds. "If you need to keep on the story, Jo, keep on it. Just promise you'll give the *P.I.* first crack when you hit pay dirt. So, good luck, and if you need me for anything, I guess I'm here. I've got you covered. Alright. Bye."

Jo glanced at another chart on the wall. This one a flayed human body, exposing the lymph system and all the places it could go off the rails. She'd expected Beth's wrath. Her sympathy was nice, but in a way a much more complicated proposition.

"All set." Sally unsnapped the band around Jo's arm. "Mickey mouse or plain?"

"Is that even a choice? Mickey Mouse." Jo smiled at the woman and her wild, full, frizzy red hair. She liked Sally, she decided.

"Obviously." Sally tossed the bloody cotton ball in the trash and patched Jo up. "Doctor will be right back."

"I want to schedule you for a surgical biopsy next week, Ms. Ford." Nokes sat on the spinning stool, Jo in a chair opposite, holding hands with Laura. "I located a couple areas of concern. With your history – the imaging was conclusive – and I'm sure we're going to see some things we don't like in your blood work." She finally put the papers aside. She crossed her legs, clasped her hands, and stared right into Jo. "I'd like to be aggressive."

Jo nodded.

"We'll get you scheduled as soon as possible and begin treatment as soon as possible. Certainly, before the holidays."

Jo kept nodding. Right. Christmas. There was still going to be Christmas. The oblivious world would go on about its business.

"We'll schedule you in Seattle for the biopsy. It'll be a quick outpatient procedure. But you'll need someone to drive you that day."

"Okay." She did a casting call in her head, and landed like a bird on a hot wire when Beth's was the name that stuck, and Beth's offer. *"If you need me for anything..."*

"I need to tell you that at this point I don't expect this to be a false alarm. Sally's got some information for you to take home, resources you'll want to access. This is a lot of information, even if this is your second time around. I'll see you in a week or so. I'm optimistic about this." Still no smile from Dr. Nokes.

"Yeah. Me too. Totally."

"Stop at the desk on your way out and set up the biopsy. One thing at a time, Joanna." The doctor nodded again, shook her hand again, dropped the chart in a pocket on the door and walked out.

Definitely the way to describe Jo's life right now, one thing at a time.

"All set." She took Laura's arm, helped her stand.

"It's okay, Jo." With her thumb, Laura clumsily wiped at the tear tracks on Jo's cheek. "It's okay."

"Right babe. It's okay. Let's get home."

WE ALL SAW IT COMING

Jo dropped Laura with Frank and promptly fled. She sped past the turnoff to the Wash, marked by a sagging barn covered in faded spray-painted psyche-delic murals. She passed the driveway leading to Brittany Roebuck's house. The mailbox was barely visible above a tower of wreaths, stuffed animals, candles, and laminated photos that circled it and spilled out into the weeds leading down the drive. Jo's tender nose started stinging. She pinched it, sniff ed, and shook her head.

Back to the story. Back to the only thing less dangerous than her own per-sonal life. Jo's first stop was going to be Lost Valley. It was late afternoon. Tyler and Luke's on-duty art time, and Ashley probably home from school. Maybe she could get them all in the same room, work them against each other, Ms. Marple-style. The copper, the furnace, the connection to Brittany, Jered's jack-in-the-box cameos and his blunt wrath – Tyler was an axis and there was no way Luke or Ashley had clean hands.

For all the crying she'd done today, her eyes were painfully dry. Her contacts rubbed like the salty, rough skin on a beach pebble every time she blinked. She flipped down the visor. She looked in even rougher shape than she felt. The mass of a bruise covering the side of her face was green, yellow at the edges. She fumbled in the center console with one hand, searching for a little bottle of contact solution she wasn't sure would be there. Getting the red out would be a good start. Run a brush through her hair after that, and she'd at least look somewhere between bag-lady and presentable.

She slowed and threw on her blinker. Cars streamed by on the right shoulder, rushing to catch the boat. The longer she sat there, the stupider she felt. Who the hell stumbled around looking as strung out as the kids she was pumping for in-formation? No interview plan, no gotcha-research. Definitely the wrong attitude.

Finally, the traffic dwindled. She was clear to turn, but she didn't. She paused in the middle of the highway. She flipped off her blinker and took her foot off the brake, rolled slowly forward on the main road. She ought to go home. She had no business here, and she had obligations.

A truck horn blared, and she slammed her foot back onto the brake. She'd drifted into the wrong lane. The other driver swerved around her, horn still ringing in her ears, the sharpness of it shredding her mess of confused thoughts.

Over the towering evergreens, filling up everything, came the deep, blaring horn of the ferry. It startled her almost as badly as the truck had. The boats, the water, always brought her back to Dad. *"It's never the sin, Joey. It's always the cover up."* Big Jack again, clear and loud in her head.

Jo had a metric ton of reasons she ought to go back home. She also had a hunch. And she had no idea how many more stories, large or small, she'd be around for. She stomped her foot on the gas and swung the car into a hard left, directly toward the silence of Lost Valley.

A delicate mist wound through the forest. She parked behind the lone, squared-off white Subaru she presumed to be Ashley's, and Luke's truck. The flat *whump* of her car door died away into nothing. The close sound of her breathing and the crunching gravel beneath her boots were now familiar. She surveyed the Sorensen property as the light of the afternoon waned. Without the sun, there were no shadows to crawl from the lurking shapes. But Jo still saw them.

Though it would be twilight within the hour, there wasn't a single light on in the house. The two-story workshop crouched like a predator against the tree line and the darkness of the dense woods beyond. It stood a pale, windowless metal husk, set off against the brilliant emerald pasture beside it, dotted with rocks, and tufts of scotch-broom that would be brilliant yellow in the spring – but now were spiny green finger-skeletons spreading across the field.

Jo fidgeted with the hem of Franks' borrowed jacket. Flashed back to her morning spent under the sterile, diagnostic gaze of Western medicine. There was nothing to be done about what-ifs and cancer. There was something to be done about the right now. Something she could do for someone else. Her determination outweighed her burgeoning flight instinct that wanted nothing more to do with situations that might end with bloody noses.

She started with the house. She knocked on the heavy steel door. The sound was booming, hollow and empty. The two large dogs barked and barked. No one was home, and she knew it. She crunched her way over the gravel walk to the workshop, knocked. No answer. She bet the door was unlocked. Yep. It opened to a gloomy interior. Light snuck in from narrow win-dows along the roof line. Shadows lurked everywhere. Above her soared dark iron birds. In front of her stood the ruins of the off -center, off -balance behemoth tower of Luke and Tyler's combined divine inspiration, that apparently had come crashing down. She groped along the wall at her side and found a bank of switches, threw up every one. A blaze of buzzing light doused the shop.

"Luke? Tyler?" Jo expected no response and received none.

The air was rubbed the wrong way, like wired fur on the ridge of Spot's spine. She shivered and peered around. Infrared heaters looked down on her through crimson steel mesh. They'd been on, but not for a while. The door swung closed behind her and the clang reverberated off the walls and through her, down to her toes that lifted off the ground just for a second. Once more, she faced-off with panic and told it to take a back seat. She heard the dogs in the house resume their objection to her intrusion on the silence.

"Luke? Tyler?"

The sculpture that had dominated the space was now a wreck. Half-disas-sembled, it looked even more chaotic than it had whole. Large pieces of it lay at scattered angles near the base. Why would Luke, or Tyler, or both of them tear it down now? She looked forward to asking. Though the place was empty, and she shouldn't be here, Jo had the notion there was too much to learn before she could even think about leaving. She crept deeper into the shop. On a work bench in the back, next to a huge metal box she recognized from Google searches as the smelting furnace, sat a set of gleaming copper pots. Bingo. She started toward them with swift, bold strides, and then stopped.

"Oh God. Damn it. *Fuck.*"

As she cleared the edge of the self-battling sculpture, she saw the body sprawled at the base. White skin, blue lips, wrapped in his standard alt-lost-boy uniform. Black skinny jeans and black hoodie, pulled up over the disheveled black hair of Tyler Sealth.

Jo knelt down before she knew what she was doing it. She put three fingers at the clammy skin of his neck. Recoiled not just from the texture, pliant and damp, but from the naivete of the action. He was clearly dead. Touching him wasn't a wise thing to do. She noticed though, right next to where she'd lay her fingers, right under Tyler's ear, was a small, clear patch. Some of his hair was stuck under it.

She worked to slow her breathing, belay her horror. She fumbled for Laura's phone in the back pocket of her jeans. She pulled it out and promptly dropped it. The screen cracked, splinters of glass creeping out across a bright image of the two of them, both atop camels in front of the red stone Treasury in Petra. She stared at it as her hands grew colder. Jo closed her eyes and took in all the thin, insufficient air she could stand. She dialed.

"911, what's your emergency?"

Jo stared at the silver corrugated ceiling as she relayed her grim find to the operator, who promised to dispatch someone immediately.

In all her long years reporting she'd never discovered a body. But she had stumbled into plenty of stories. Curiosity began to retake her. Jo had very little time.

She snapped photos from all angles. Captured shots of the table with the copper pots, the massive sculpture dominating the space, and panoramas of the entire workshop. She didn't touch anything, tried not to move around much, but digitally scoured every cluttered work bench and sharp scrap pile. She wiped her cheeks with her sleeve, only now realizing that she'd been crying. Angry at the boy, at herself. *Dammit, Tyler.*

The door of the shop flew open. Jo leapt an inch off the floor, spun around, crouched and ready to fight.

It was Luke Sorensen. "What the hell are you doing in my shop?" Outside, Jo heard cars tear up the driveway, throwing gravel against other cars as they came to a sudden stop. Before she could answer, Elijah Hill barreled in, hand resting on the gun in his belt.

"Don't know why Tyler would try to take that thing down himself." Luke Sorensen sat looking shell-shocked on the gate of his pickup. He pulled a beat-up pouch of tobacco and papers from the back pocket of his work pants. He fumbled opening it. His rolling technique looked practiced, but his hands lacked a steady confidence. Little auburn bits of tobacco floated onto the gravel at their feet. "You want one?"

"No thanks." Jo smiled reflexively. She said no the way you say no to cake when you're on a diet. Fast, before you have a chance to regret it. Then, she did regret it. "Actually, sure." Her heart couldn't get the beat right and her hands were already shaking. A little nicotine couldn't possibly make things worse.

"Spliff or straight?"

Tempting. Jo was thin and dry inside, untethered by Tyler's death. She glanced over to Luke's workshop, open door exed by yellow caution tape. Just inside the open door she saw Hill and Locke, each on cell phones and pacing. As much of a relief as it would be to take the edge off, getting loaded right now would be one step too far in her attempt to deal with the traumas of the day.

"Just tobacco would be great." She pulled up a seat next to her host. Both were waiting to give statements to Hill about Tyler Sealth.

He finished crafting the cigarette and offered it up, re-lit the zippo. She leaned toward him. He could have just as easily lit a match on his rust-gold beard stubble. Those sky-blue eyes really were something. His pupils were pinned, and he was clearly high already, on what she wasn't sure. Otherwise, mixed with the smell of the fresh cigarette and fresh sweat, the guy was pure, uncut Washington catnip for women who made that kind of lifestyle choice. Luke bent to his work. He licked and sealed the second smoke, and now it looked a lot more like old habit. Routine was routine. When your extremities felt like someone else was pulling the switches, it went a long way.

Jo pulled on the cigarette and was instantly reminded of the soothing power of habit. The first drag practically took her head off. The second was just like coming home. She pulled a fleck of tobacco from her tongue, wiped it on her jeans. "Why was Tyler taking the sculpture apart?" She threw her pitch up a little at the end, as though she had no idea why the kid was trying to get rid of a smoking gun.

"No fucking clue. I mean, I'm pissed about it. Because he's gone, and now it's gone. I couldn't get it right again, without him. We worked that piece together for a long time. You liked it?"

"I did. A lot." And its little brother, perched in Tyler's window to the world. Jo put her sleeve to her nose that had started to run, took another drag.

"Everyone liked it," Luke said. "Guess I'll try – it just seems like – " he considered his cigarette, pinched with his thumb and index finger. Both had grime embedded, both had knuckles that were chapped, well-worked. "Seems like I ought to rebuild it. If I can."

"How long had Tyler been here, this afternoon?"

"No idea. I was out hiking near the Wash."

"Alone?"

"Yeah. Alone."

"His car's not here, so, do you know how he got here?"

Luke glanced around. He took a drag, closed an eye as smoke drifted into it. "Probably got a ride. Maybe from Ash."

"Is she here?"

"She isn't now. You want to wait for Hill to come back for this interview?"

"Sorry. Habit." Jo waved her cigarette in front of him. Half-way through it, and she was flying high and feeling a lot better about life.

Both of them looked toward the workshop. The flood lights outside had come on as night began to fall.

Jo checked her watch. Hallelujah. She wasn't late. Yet. "I'm sorry about Tyler. I didn't know him that well. But I know he had a lot riding on you, and his work."

"Yeah. He had it, you know. It. If he'd kept at it. Stayed off the bad shit."

"He was using again?"

"I think so. He'd started to act like it. Moody." Luke chuckled. "Moodier, anyway."

"That wasn't my impression." Jo took one more pull at the cigarette. She ragged the butt out on the sole of her boot. She didn't trust her balance right now if she'd had to pick it up off the ground. She also didn't trust anyone who was already trying to write off Tyler Sealth as just another OD. That made two swings Luke had taken at Tyler's cause of death. The question was though, was Luke doing the set-up and selling her on it, or being set-up and trying to get out from under it?

"But then, you didn't really know Ty, right?" I did. I knew what he could do. Fucking kid. Fuck." Luke smashed what was left of his own on the tailgate. He stood. He picked up his kit and started on another roll. Jo saw this one was just shy of one hundred percent weed.

"I guess I didn't know him that well. I just thought – " Jo shrugged. What was the point of finishing that thought? Whatever Tyler was or wasn't doing, it was over now. Forever.

Luke flicked the zippo open and shut, open and shut. "Let me guess. You thought he was an alright kid? That he would make it, if someone just gave him a chance? Overcome all the obstacles, get clear of his family and live to tell? Yeah, you really picked up on something. W e all had that impression."

"I'm sorry, Luke, for your loss. I'm not trying to piss you off ."

"Well I am pissed. Tell Hill I'm in the house when he wants to talk to me."

Pissed at whom, wondered Jo. Luke walked off, into the dark house. The dogs shouted his arrival.

She checked her watch again. She did not want to call Frank and have to tell him she'd be late. Her run-in with Brian had sealed the family peace pact. Guess it took taking a beating to convince Frank she was actually serious about her work.

She walked over to the workshop, head still in the clouds from the nicotine. The high was nice – or at least at this exact moment, she didn't feel like crying or breaking something. She knocked on the metal door frame. The silence had been replaced by squawking radios and cop talk. Hill and Locke were waiting for investigative reinforcement from Seattle. They seemed to be making good use of the down time. Little black and white numbered tents dotted the space. Jo kept her eyes on the floor, or up at the soaring gulls. Tyler's body was still there. Still asking her why she hadn't done more.

"You guys mind if I head out? I want to get home to Laura."

Hill came over to her. "You'll come in tomorrow for a full statement, and won't leave the Island in the meantime?" He flipped through his notebook. She'd given him the top line just after he'd arrived.

"Sure. I'll just murder someone else before I stop by Brittany Roebuck's service tomorrow, then swing by the station. Are you going, by the way?"

"Yes ma'am."

"It's a little weird, right? Tyler – " Jo inclined her head to where the body lay.

"How do you mean?"

Jo recognized an invitation to hang herself and declined. "Just odd. Just, it feels familiar, but out of place, doesn't it?"

"We don't know what happened here. What do you mean by familiar?"

"Nothing," Jo said. "What would I know."

"Right." Hill followed her out to her car, opened and closed the door for her. He didn't step away when she started it up.

She rolled down the window.

"Jo maybe it's time you stepped back from this."

Her bump from the nicotine was gone. So was her patience, and frankly, her stamina. "Elijah, maybe it's time you stepped up to this. See you tomorrow." Jo rolled up her window and drove off.

BRITTNEY'S STILL WITH US IN SPIRIT

Thunder rumbled, metal squealed, panels clacked and slammed as staff rolled out the ancient wooden bleachers inside the Makah High School gymnasium. Jo stood quiet and melancholy under warm yellow lights against a white cinder-block wall, her figure camouflaged by years of blending into backgrounds to better observe uncensored honesty. Above her a sharp-eyed, razor-billed raven perched as secondary witness, shining midnight black and purple, painted in relief against a cream background. Over it, in block letters shadowed in gold, were the letters MHS. On the opposite wall a faded red, white, and blue triangle Kibo logo presided over a faded thank-you to the Stewart family for their generous support.

Two-hundred metal chairs were already set up on the freshly polished golden hardwood of the gym floor, empty and facing a stage covered in native flora. Forced winter blooms of vibrant white rhododendron, champagne dahlias, white tulips, even sprays of yarrow anchored the sides. Evergreen boughs swagged the front. The podium jutting up in the middle of it all was wrapped in black and white velvet; beside it stood a tripod frame bearing the weight of a larger-than-life photo of Brittany Roebuck. She wasn't tall, but lean and muscular. She stood in a purple and gold UW sweatshirt on the ratty track circling the high school football field. One hand an empty fist in the air, the other raised too, clutching a large gold medal that hung on red, white, and blue ribbon. Her long straight hair pleated and laid over her shoulder, her smile was wide and her clear blue eyes shone in triumph at whomever was behind the camera capturing her elated moment of victory.

The Quartermaster had run a special insert in this week's edition with memorial tributes to Brittany from friends and family, all filled with "I remember the time we..." -prefaced snapshots of Brittany's loves, hates, conquests, and misadventures.

She would be remembered as her parents, friends, and community wanted to remember her. Jo had seen more recent photos of the girl on her social media. Brittany's athletic glow had lost its luster in the past year. More often than not, dark eyeliner was poorly applied to cover dark circles over hollow, high-boned cheeks.

Intermittent over the loudspeakers came snippets of classical music. Then the heavily synthesized opening bars of a K-pop ballad, "Rain and Cry," by one of Brittany's favorite artists. How appropriate.

Muted clumps of mourners began making their way inside. Jo stayed where she was, hands shoved into the pockets of Frank's smelly, borrowed coat.

"You need to stop coming here. Please." Tyler's voice played on repeat in her head as a steady stream of people filled the gym. She thought about Islanders and the pained, intimate tolerance the small community had for death. She wondered if she'd be able to pack a gym full of locals when the cancer got to her. Probably not, once she shoved their faces in the cozy drug-den they lived in. And she was going to show them the truth, because it was probably going to be the last thing she did. Beat cancer twice – there wasn't a snappy colloquialism for that, because it just didn't happen often enough.

Across the gym, she spotted Elijah Hill. He spotted her, started to move off in another direction. She threw discrete observer out the window and put some hustle into her step, apologizing to people as she brushed by them. One or two gave her a less than pleased look. She finally caught up with Hill near the back-side of the bleachers.

"Good morning, Elijah."

"Good morning Jo." He inclined his head.

"Anything more, anything at all you can tell me about Tyler?"

"This is a funeral. Give it a rest." Hill tucked his fingers into his heavy, leather duty belt, shifted his weight. It creaked and complained.

"I won't give it a rest. You know I won't. Because, breaking news, I can't."

He pulled her to the side, almost under the bleachers. She could hear the stomping of feet and the shifting of the wood overhead.

"You're not going to do this here." Hill swept his arm at the filling gym.

The crowd recalled the diversity at the ravine where Brittany was found. Surely only a handful of these people actually knew the girl or her family. They were here to mourn the hurt to the community, the stab at their insular safety, as much as they were the offensive, out of place loss of youthful promise.

"I will do this here. This isn't just a couple kids and a run of bad luck," Jo said. "Tyler didn't OD. It wasn't an accident. You know he had ties to Jered Braiser and Brian Stewart. Same as Brittany. Same as Randy."

"All I'm saying is that you'd do well to at least pretend to buy-in to the community here, the way they do things. You think I don't want to establish a new world order? Only thanks I get for that – or you get – is thanks for closing the door on your way out. Ask the last officer that was posted here. It's a good place. I like these people, a lot. If you want to help, play the long game here. Get a little smarter about it."

"Sounds like a reasonable way to say I should half-ass this." Jo caught her own voice rising and hit reset. Sort of.

"I know you liked Tyler. But whether you want to hear it or not, accidental overdose. Clear cut. Off the record for now, but you can expect a release, maybe tomorrow. We found a wrapper in his pocket, Jo. For a fentanyl oral dose. He was doubled up."

"Hey what does that remind you of? Oral doses and leaving people completely fucked up?"

"Jo, if you can tell me why Brian would want Tyler dead, I'll consider it. Until then, shortest distance is the best theory of the crime. The kid used before, started up, thought he had longer before the patch kicked in."

"He just decided to get totally pegged in the middle of Luke Sorensen's workshop. Not at home, not out with friends? Just right there in what even I think would be the worst place ever to get your party on?"

"Like I said," Hill repeated, slowly, "Maybe it's time you learned a little about people here before you start making assumptions. This isn't D.C.. Hell, it's not even Seattle. These artist folks, that's exactly what they do. Take a little of their drug of choice and let the inspiration flow. It doesn't mean the ODs aren't a problem. It just doesn't mean it's murder, or anything else."

As he talked, Hill had edged them further and further under the bleachers. Jo knew why he was doing it, and she couldn't say he was wrong. The place was almost filled, and it was quieter now than it was during set-up.

"Flowing on fentanyl? I don't think that's what Thompson was mainlining in Vegas."

"Yes, on fentanyl," Hill responded. "Lot of kids, even on Makah, have problems they'd rather forget. And if his dealer went off and killed him, or Brittany, don't you think they'd go to some pains to cover it up a little better instead of leaving them to be found?"

"Maybe they took just enough pains to try and pin it on Randy – or Luke." Escaping problems, she understood. Maybe he was right. But Jo didn't think so. Jo thought the Tyler she'd caught sneaking longing looks at Rainier, caught looking scared when Jered showed up, was the real version of the guy. If he'd been trapped, if he wasn't apprenticing with Luke maybe – but whatever else was going on, Tyler had a light at the end of the tunnel. That, well, that she envied.

Hill shook his head. "Now you're telling me Brian had something against Luke, too? You're just shotgunning theories. That's not how I work. Not how investigations work. You should know that."

"Investigations work by asking questions until you know all the answers," Jo asserted. "What about the hair under the patch on Tyler's neck? Seems like an addict would be a little more skilled at their craft."

"Kid was high. Probably wasn't worried about a couple of pulled hairs."

On the other side of the gym, Brenda Locke came in out of the cold. Hill nodded to her, took the chance to make an exit. "Stop by later with that statement. Have a nice day, Jo."

How likely was that? Jo pouted behind his back, tossed off a "yeah, you too," as he walked away.

The Roebucks had arrived and were exchanging hugs and hand clasps. She started over, intending to offer – something. She wasn't best friends with grief, but they'd sat next to each other in church for a long time now.

"Kyle, Nancy – I'm so sorry. Brittany had a lot of potential."

Nancy Roebuck didn't look like she had a second for Jo's well-wishes. Her husband, Kyle, rubbed his hands together, managed an answer. "She did. She was going to be an exceptional woman. She was going to be anything she wanted to be."

"I know she was close with Tyler as well. I didn't spend a lot of time with him, but I gathered he cared about Brittany quite a bit. I gather most people who met her did. I'm sorry."

Kyle tilted his head to the side, confusion beginning to spread on his face. Before he could ask the question Jo had queued up in his mind, Brittany's mother interrupted. Her voice was low, her jaw tight. "Look. We're sorry to hear about Tyler Sealth. We are." Nancy paused. Jo recognized a woman working hard to keep her shit together, avoiding a complete shame-faced breakdown in public. It was like holding up a mirror. Nancy continued, hand clutched in her husband's and white knuckled. "But dating that boy – it was the start of things for Brittany. Things we didn't want for her. I don't know if you have kids. If you can understand that. How it feels to have your little girl's name smeared by someone because she likes to see her own name in big print."

"I'm sorry if Brittany wasn't the girl you thought she was. And I understand what it means to lose the person you loved," Jo admitted, easily. "The promise of who they were."

Kyle's flush peaked, then he paled. "Frank and my dad worked together at the Kibo factory in the 80's. Laura was maybe five or six years ahead of me at MHS. I'm sorry for her. But you have to understand – you have to see – what happened to Brittany isn't supposed to happen –"

Jo cut in on that familiar song and dance. "On Makah? Or anywhere. It's not, Mr. Roebuck. But it is happening. All I want to do is stop it – and be a part of telling Brittany's story, and Tyler's. Because he didn't ask to die either. His family wants him back just as much – "

"That's where you're wrong." Nancy interrupted her, voice shaking now. "The Sealths, they're what's keeping the drugs here in the first place. They've got nothing better to do with their lives than work and get drunk, or high, or whatever else when they're off shift. As far as I'm concerned, one way or the other, Tyler killed –" she stopped, and couldn't seem to get the rest of the sentence out.

Vi Mitchell shoved in between all of them and took up the slack. "It's Sealths that built your house, Nancy. And the house next to yours. Tough day but that's the truth."

Nancy, tissue clutched in a tight claw of a hand, bared her teeth. "A house that isn't worth shit anymore, Vi. A house that's silent. No teenage girl giggling over cartoons like she's still ten, or sobbing over a loser boyfriend who deals drugs, like she's sixteen and already washed-up. Tell your friend here –" she looked Jo up and down, then sneered. "Tell her she's got some nerve –" she looked like she wanted to continue. Her mouth opened, closed.

Around them, people were beginning to stare. Mostly at Jo. At her heated exchange with the Roebucks or at her mangled mug, she wasn't sure. She wished she'd worn a sign around her neck, *Talk to me if Brian Stewart is also black-mailing you.*"

"That's enough." It was Valerie Larsen's turn to cut in. She nodded at the

Roebucks; placed a hand on Jo and Vi's shoulders. Her two children stood silent and pale a few paces away. She turned to them. "Alice, Tolliver, go sit with your father." They nodded and shuffled off. "Nancy, Kyle. I'm sorry. More than sorry, and I don't even know how to say it. You should be with your family now."

Valerie spoke quietly to the stricken parents, and they wandered on toward the waiting row of chairs.

"You two – outside." Valerie actually pointed. Jo actually understood why Spot always did exactly what she said.

The trio made their way through the nearby double doors and into the misty drizzle.

Vi didn't lose a second. "Right here and now, Joanna Ford? At a funeral?" Vi was right in her face, breath day-old sweet and nose tinged purple.

Jo came back twice as hot. "With Tyler that's two kids dead. You may want to just cover that up. But I don't. Asking people to be aware of the dangers around them isn't creating the dangers. Pretending Tyler isn't a part of this, that his death didn't count – maybe, Vi, you ought to think more about what *The Quartermaster* isn't writing about, instead of what it is." Tyler was being ignored in more ways than one. Today was a packed gymnasium for Brittany. Next week was a small grave-side service for a man that Jo was certain would include no more than Vi and a handful of blue-collar locals.

"You little shit," Vi croaked out. "How dare you talk to me about Tyler Sealth. How dare you turn a favor into an agenda. You selfish –"

"Both of you stop. Right now."

Jo cast her eyes right to the ground as Valerie interrupted.

"*What* is wrong with you?" Valerie addressed Vi. The women were so focused on each other Jo might as well not even be on the planet. Both stood with hands on hips, leaning toward the other.

"What's wrong with me? What's wrong with her?" Vi glared at Jo.

"Let me tell you exactly what's wrong, because I guess it's hard." Jo held up her fingers as she ticked off her talking points. "Two dead kids. Randy's suicide. Burglary. Drugs. Murder. And this –" Jo pointed at her face. "That's what's wrong with me."

"Sorry to put you out," Vi sneered. "But this place is my home. These are my people getting hurt. They're not stories, they're not a way to feed your damn insatiable ego. You just don't learn, do you?"

"If you think that's all there is to me, you've got no business running a newspaper –"

"Time out." Valerie made the appropriate gesture, then glanced apologetically at Jo. "She didn't mean that." She turned back to Vi. "We're not going any further with this. We have a *funeral* to be at. There's a time and place. And this isn't it."

"See that's the problem —" Vi gestured at Jo, "that this one never will un-derstand. You'll never understand Makah. Because you don't want to." Vi took a few steps, planted her finger in Jo's shoulder, leaned in close. Her eyes were bloodshot. "Why don't you take a while to yourself. Think about what kind of reporter you really want to be. I'll cover your assignments this week. I've been covering them most of the month. Ever since you started getting your fix by stirring the shit."

The drizzle was starting to accumulate on Vi. A drop fell from her hooked nose. Behind her, the football field stood out technicolor green against a rust-colored, muddy track.

"There's something we don't disagree about," Jo spat back, gleefully. "Maybe I'll take more than a few days off . I can think about *who* I want to write for, as well as *what* I want to write, while I'm at it. I started all of this for you, Vi."

"You want out? Fine by me." Vi spat at the ground. It landed next to Jo's boots and mingled with the mud and rain.

Valerie's thick lips were pulled into a thin line. "Damnit." She glanced at Vi who had started walking away, then suddenly swooped toward Jo. She hugged her, fierce and silent, before she trotted after the older woman.

Jo just lingered in the rain, arms dead at her sides. She was torn up about Tyler's death, she was torn up about maybe dying herself, leaving Laura behind. Struggling with the fact that she'd really abandoned her wife already, and most of all, about all of it happening on this goddamn depressing rock in the middle of career nowhere. Maybe it was time to give Beth Berge at the P.I. exactly what she wanted.

Jo watched the two women standing in the open doorway of the gym, exchanging words she couldn't make out. For just a second, she saw the warm yellow glow and the full bleachers inside, and caught a high-volume snippet of Brittany's beloved, cheesy, synthy, K-Pop ballad. Then, the door closed with a whoosh and a snick. Jo stood, quiet, and listened to the rain patter around her.

THAT FEELING WHEN IT'S LIKE YOU'VE BEEN SOMEWHERE BEFORE

Jo sat alone in the Volvo staring out over Wilapa Harbor and Makah's twinkling uptown across the bay. The little cluster of buildings grew fuzzier with the waning light and the incoming fog. Sailboats bobbed in the marina, lights on the docks already coming up in the gloom and bouncing off the shifting waters. She'd pulled over at the quiet overlook across from town, too riled after the debacle at Brittany's service to call it a day. She'd sat there maybe an hour, just thinking things out. She was getting close. The momentum, the unraveling, everything was escalating.

There had been a moment just like this, when she'd been dogging Charlie Abish and all his cronies, when she'd felt just like she did right now. It had come the day after her source, Michael Polaski, died. The day after she'd visited him in prison and just about a week before Federal Judge Sonya Petroysan went missing. The bad guys had gotten antsy and started taking desperate steps to ease their anxiety. That included the disappearance and still unsolved murder of the judge that had been presiding over Abish's case.

Jo's solution for the woman's death was simple: apparently just like Brian Stewart, no one treated Charlie Abish the same as everyone else and lived to tell the tale. Except perhaps Joanna Ford. Some of that was luck. A lot of that probably had to do with traveling in nowhere Pakistan and Afghanistan with her wife for more than eight months when the indictments had started coming down.

Whether her survival was wits or luck, the minute Jo got on the right track, a lot of interlocking pieces of Abish's operation had started falling apart. Before he'd been murdered, she'd wrestled a lot of secrets out of Michael. Then she started following up on them. The FBI got smart and started following her – and well, the rest was literally history in the Newseum in D.C..

The sun had set while she strolled down memory lane, sketching out the parallels between Abish and Brian Stewart.

The gray of the clouds pressing down on her was darker. The late afternoon mist hiding the trees and the shores beyond began to thicken as the temperature dropped. The car began to fog. She turned up the heat, stared down at her phone, her appointment confirmation on Friday for the biopsy. She needed a ride.

Jo should know better than to be thinking about Beth Berge right now. Than to let lust, and maybe a little bit of love, drive her decisions. *Should* know better. But Jo had heard lonely whisper her name in the middle of the night. She'd heard Beth whisper her name in the middle of the night, too. Staring at that biopsy appointment confirmation, it was easy to make up her mind about who she wanted to listen to a little more right now.

Jo owed Beth a call back to apologize for jamming her up in this whole blackmail problem. But did she also need to apologize for not sleeping with her last time she saw her? If Jo were being honest to anyone, including herself, what she really wanted was to tell Beth that cancer was back. To ask her for help.

There were a handful of folks who could take her into Seattle for the upcoming procedure. Frank, Vi, even Valerie. But she didn't want just anyone there with her when she woke up. She wanted someone familiar. She was supposed to be asking for help, right? And she wanted Beth to help. She wanted to talk about how kids here kept dying and how she wasn't getting anywhere with the story. Tell her she was sad, and lonely, and washed up – and ready to say yes.

Jo ran a finger over the cracked screen of Laura's phone. She'd changed the background to a picture she'd found on Instagram. Brittany and Tyler at homecoming a few years ago. She dismissed a voice mail from Frank, one from Vi, and dialed Beth.

"Well if it isn't Joanna Ford. Lose my number?"

"Beth –"

"You left me hanging. I get to give you a little trouble for it."

"What exactly did you expect out of this? Out of me. I don't think we covered that."

"What exactly did I expect out of sleeping with a married woman? Too smart for her own good, who can't even think about how to make a move on her wife, because they haven't had a decent conversation in two years? Because both of your brains are on the fritz and neither one of you can handle sex? I don't know, Jo. I think I thought you were having an awfully bad time of it, needed something to take the edge off. I took the opportunity when I saw it."

"Okay." Jo put a hand over her face. It was a fair answer. There was no fair response. What the hell was fair, anyway? What did Beth owe her, or vice versa? The real question was, in the currency and context of what constituted her marriage these days, what did Jo owe Laura? What did Laura owe her, if anything, anymore? And exactly how was she supposed to collect on that debt?

She hadn't been trying to wait her out, but Beth broke the silence first. "I'm not trying to hassle you. I'm not here to break up your marriage, or fall in love, or – I don't expect anything. I care about you, though. I don't need you Jo – I just want you."

"I don't know what to say. I'm sorry."

"You don't have to apologize to me."

There was certainly more than one way to take that. Jo didn't want to pick any one of those choose your own adventures. "Listen. I don't know what to say about any of that. So – I guess I'll apologize about this whole thing with the email and Brian Stewart instead."

"Before you start apologizing, Jo – what the hell happened?"

Jo gave her the Reader's Digest. She had to click up the volume when the other woman responded.

"I didn't know it was like that. I'd heard Brian Stewart had himself a little kingdom out there." Beth paused. Jo heard the bustle of a legitimate newsroom in the background. "He's got enough old-school money to have a reputation. The family, anyway. And from what I hear, it was never good. Kibo's been a front for plenty of bullshit over the years."

"He sure has the sheep penned on Makah."

"I know you're thinking about rocking that boat, hon. But maybe this time think twice. Drugs – they might have put money in Abish's bank account. But dealing with Abish is a lot diff erent than dealing with distribution chains, the bastards on the ground. Jo – I've seen what happens – " Beth started to sound younger. Raw, even. Everything more on the surface. The way she had when they met. "Mexico taught me a lot. That's all I'm saying."

"I'm sorry I got you involved." Past Jo's fogged windshield, the lights of the smaller boats on their buoys bounced up and down as a larger trawler crawled in for the evening.

"Don't worry about that email. I can cover my own ass. Who's taking care of you?"

"I am." Jo started laughing, Tyler's words coming out of her own mouth. She laughed for a long time, and then she started crying. She kept telling Beth to hold on. Then, she decided, what the fuck? You only live once.

"Beth, can I stay with you, this Friday night?"

From the other end of the line came distant voices on other telephones, and a knock. "Hold on."

Sure, Jo thought. I'll just keep holding on.

"Sorry. Just wanted to close my door."

Great. Hopefully everyone at the *P.I.* had been privy to the entire opening of this conversation.

"Why the change of heart? I kind of got the impression you were calling us off. Not that I wouldn't miss me, too. But you're all over the place. *All* over the place. What's up with you? Really."

"God. I need – want – to stay with you, because, I actually –" Jo stopped. Her throat clicked when she swallowed. "I have a surgical biopsy. That last mammogram, it didn't turn out so well for me. The breast cancer –"

"Jesus, Jo. Of course – what else can I do? How can I help you?"

"Take me back to that bar on Lake Washington, on the cut."

"Before or after the biopsy?"

Jo laughed, and that felt okay. "Both, maybe. Can you order up some sunshine?"

"I'll look into it. Do you want me to take you – to the appointment?"

She almost started laughing again, because her first thought was, no, that'd be crossing a line. Apparently, she'd set up rules for herself and whatever it was she was – or wasn't – doing with Beth.

"I don't know. Yes. No. Maybe."

"You don't have to decide now, magic eight-ball."

"Okay. Thanks."

"Of course. And we can talk about Brian Stewart, and what in the world you're thinking."

"Thanks."

"You know it. Mi casa is your casa, Joanna."

"Thanks. For everything. I'll – I'll call you. Thanks."

"Anytime hon."

Jo hung up. She set Laura's borrowed phone in the console. All the threads of her life - what she had, what she didn't have, were flying apart faster than she could decide which was which – while everything with Brittany and Tyler seemed so intertwined she couldn't find a way in.

It was full dark out there. The clouds were high, blocking the stars. Too early for the moon rise. The only light came from town. The orange and white from buildings and street lights strained and muted through the fog and reflected off the rippling water in the bay. The bright blurs slipped on and off the shifting black surface, appearing and disappearing, illuminating nothing.

VALERIE TAKES A TURN AT THE MIC

Valerie Larsen read Jo Ford right off, all the trouble she was going to bring her. She was bringing a lot more for Vi Mitchell though, and Valerie couldn't figure out why. It frustrated and hurt her that Vi, a woman who she'd become so close with over the years, was simply refusing to be honest, or to ask her for help. She was clearly struggling; with Randy, with Jo, with Paula missing, and as Valerie was also coming to suspect, with her drinking.

But her struggles didn't give her a right to how she'd behaved that afternoon. Valerie had driven Vi home after the service and stayed, and she intended to get to the heart of all of this one way or the other.

"You owe Jo an apology," Valerie said. "She's right. About everything. You were just as out of line as she was."

"Phhhhht." Vi slammed two coffee mugs on the wood top and filled them. "Sixty-odd years on Makah and most of them running this damn paper. I know this place. I know what I'm about. We've all been humming along just fine without Jo Ford."

"Maybe. But maybe things change."

"Damn right they do. A week ago I had my cat. I had my pots and my pans and – that's plenty of change. No need for more." Vi coughed and glanced out the kitchen window. She'd done that three times since they'd come in the door. Not hard to guess she was hoping to see Paula out there. "And respect for your elders ought not to change, ever."

Valerie stood, hands wrapped around her coffee mug. A prized Otis original, one of the few still around from the famed Makah potter. She coveted Vi's set. She walked around the kitchen island and laid a hand on her friend's arm.

Vi laid one of her own over it; finally softened up. "Don't rub it in."

Valerie leaned down and kissed her cheek. "Just take some time with it. Then call her up. Be honest with her. You both deserve that."

"I've been honest. Enough. This has nothing to do with lies."

"It's not lies I'm talking about," replied Valerie, though she suspected Vi had told her some. Why she wasn't sure, but if Vi Mitchell couldn't handle saying something it had to be awfully painful. "It's your ridiculous secretive nature. It's you being scared for her and turning that into anger. It's perfectly clear to me how much you like Jo, what kind of expectations you have. You want her to take over the paper. You want her to run it the way you have. But she's a little too distracted to catch on. And oh, right – she's stubborn." Valerie winked at her, then wandered into the dining room. "Why were you so set against Jo investigating here in the first place? Why wouldn't you at least let the Sheriff come by?"

"You know why. The man's not helpful. Those pots. I don't know. I thought maybe it was a joke, you know, a prank gone too far."

"You're really going to try and sell me that?"

"Speak clearly, woman."

"I think you had a hunch this was all going to lead exactly where it did. And Jo's the one willing to take the risks, and you're just chicken. I don't blame you. She looked awful when Tyler Sealth hauled her out of those woods." Valerie blew across her steaming coffee, then took a sip. "You know, there are a couple ways to end up on an island. You can land on purpose or you can shipwreck. Jo's shipwrecked. And she's looking for any way she can find to get off Makah. You can either build the raft for her, Vi, or you can give her a reason to stay."

"I said speak clearly." Vi slapped the counter and glared.

"I don't want any of this to be true any more than you do. But I have Alice and Tolliver to worry about. I want to know how to stop these drugs. I want to know how two good kids ended up dead." Valerie started to pace. "I came here for a reason, too. I came for safety. And to find a little peace. Maybe Jo's disturb-ing the peace right now. But I think we need it."

"Your kids are going to be just fine," Vi grumbled.

"Oh – like I was just fine?"

"The way you grew up – it's not the same at all. And look where you are now. Look what you managed to do with your life. You better be as proud of yourself as I am of you, Valerie Larsen. What happened later, with you and Steve – happens. Kids get over it."

"Maybe." Valerie finished her cup and set it in the sink. "But what about when they don't? What about Randy? You ought to be thanking Jo for trying to help clear him of what she can – not berating her."

Vi leaned against the counter. Stared into her coffee. "Makah broke that boy, and – I suppose you're right. I suppose it's time all this, with Makah, and the Stewarts – I guess maybe I'm a little stuck in the past. Henry keeping everything in check. I keep seeing Brian as his son, and not his own man."

"Not a very good, man." Valerie said. "I think it's time we were honest about Brittany, too, and the thefts. I believe Jo. She's very good at what she does, and she's committed, and passionate. I think you've been waiting for someone, Vi, for a long time. I don't know why, but I just have that sense. Maybe it is Jo. Because she's definitely got the guts to do what needs to be done."

"What I've been waiting for's always been right in front of me. That's how that always works, isn't it?" Vi managed a big smile. "In your case, you fought for what you wanted, and you're doing fine with it. Like I said, it's not my business, but I'm proud of you. I thank you for talking me around all this. Hard to give up what you know."

"It is." Valerie rinsed her coffee cup, hugged Vi. "Speaking of pride. Time to go grab mine. Steve took them to the Dairy Queen. I bet he let them eat hot dogs. I'm sure they're both loaded with sugar by now ."

"Stick 'em on Saturn and Aggie and tell them not to come back until it's dark. Best way to fix kids is wear them out."

"It's a plan." Valerie put on her barn coat and opened the back door. She fingered the bright red string tied around the knob. "I think we need more than superstition and tradition to protect us these days."

"I know. I'll call Jo. I will. And Val, will you call her, too? Something in that girl's still not right. Besides what you might call the obvious – you know, with Laura."

"I'll check in on her, Vi, but you need to do your own part. Before you wreck a good thing. Before it's too late. Okay?"

"I'll get to it. You're good girl, Valerie."

"Thanks. For everything you've done for me, to get me where I am today. I love you Vi. I do. I hope that helps with all this."

"Yes ma'am. Both ways, on that. Thank you."

SOMETHING JUST OUT OF REACH

"I'll be back on an early boat Saturday morning." Jo was already late for the ferry, but unable to make her feet walk out the door. She didn't need to stay over with Beth tonight, before the biopsy. But she wanted to. And she was going to.

She wrapped her arms all the way around Laura, as tightly as she could get them, and hung on. Laura squirmed and frowned.

"It's okay, babe. It's just a simple test, and then we'll know what we're dealing with. It'll be fine. It's just that I'll miss you." In some ways it was easier to lie to her wife now. In some ways it was harder.

"Love you, Jo." Laura hugged her a little harder, then let her go.

"I love you, Laura. So much."

Her last words to her wife before she'd headed to the boat, crying the whole way. She stayed in her car and kept at it as the ferry slid swiftly through the silent, smooth waters of Puget Sound.

Jo cried a little more, after she and Beth had sex that night. While they had sex that night. She lay in another woman's bed, shoulders shaking as Beth held her, dark, still, and immersive as the water Jo crossed to get to her.

The afternoon following the biopsy was an almost pleasant fugue. The left side of her chest didn't hurt yet, but there was a ghost of an uncomfortable intrusion, like a purse that was rummaged through for something that was never found.

She tried to pay attention but couldn't really, as Beth managed her discharge from the clinic, asked about aftercare, gathered the paperwork, helped her from her obligatory wheelchair into the car. She slept most of the ride back to Beth's condo downtown and most of the afternoon. The sky was blue, but the day was windy, something blowing down from the north and serious about letting

December know who was boss. Jo fell all the way into sleep as the building popped and swayed and the clouds rushed by around her, head in the clouds twenty floors up.

When she finally woke in the dark of Beth's apartment later that evening, Charlie Abish, the man whose sins had won her so much acclaim, was on her mind again. Why, in her post-opp drug-addled state, she thought of Abish and his crimes she couldn't say. Certainly it had nothing to do with her own sins.

Outside the door to the guest room, she heard murmurs from a television and saw flashes of light in the hallway. She shifted, winced, and marveled at how well she'd slept. She looked around. Her eyes adjusted to the dark but not to her environment. She pivoted out of bed, slowly, and made her way, still slowly, to the bathroom. When she reemerged, the television was off. There was also a throw blanket at the foot of the bed. Jo carefully draped it over her shoulders. She fumbled around in her bag for her phone.

"Hey Frank. Yeah. It's me. I'm still good. Can I talk to Laura?" She'd texted Frank before the biopsy. Beth had texted on her behalf afterward.

She heard shuffling on the other end, then, "Hi Jo." Laura sounded thin and scared.

"Hey babe. It's me. I'm totally good. I'll be home first thing."

"Sure?"

"Yep. I promise."

"Okay. Love you."

"I love you too, Laura. Hug Spot for me."

"Okay. Bye."

"Bye babe. Love you."

Jo sat in the dim with the blanket over her shoulders and swiped at her wet cheek. She was semi-dozing again when her stomach rumbled. She rubbed her eyes as she walked down the hall. Stared at the view she hadn't taken in when she'd arrived. The lights of Seattle tapered away below them to the dark of Elliott Bay and the twinkle of the smaller towns across the water. It was striking and almost dizzying as she peered out over the edge to the world falling away below.

"I have won ton soup to drown a family of four. Will that be enough?" Beth skirted the island in the kitchen and met her halfway across the apartment.

Jo was already out of breath. Perhaps venturing out for sustenance had been ambitious. "I'll let you know after I finish it all." Won ton soup was exactly what she wanted. She and Beth had ordered in Chinese a million times to their little D.C. sublet in Foggy Bottom, after Jo's mom had died. The other woman had remembered.

"Sit down, hun. You look terrible." Beth took her shoulders. Jo sagged against her, and she absorbed her weight as though it were nothing.

"Thanks." She sank down into the couch and closed her eyes.

"Wine's a no-go, but how about some Gatorade?"

"Orange?"

"You know it." Beth left her with a pat on the knee and returned with a full glass.

Jo took half of it in a go, then leaned her head back and closed her eyes again. She could smell pot stickers and the soup, and she wanted both. The heat was turned up – she was warm enough, all over. Beth had always liked it a little on the hot side. The floors on Makah were always cold, and so were her feet.

There were newspapers scattered across the shining, live-edge wood coffee table in front of her. The *P.I., The Times* – both New York and L.A. For a while she heard nothing but Beth bustling in the kitchen. Then she heard Elsa and Ari introduce *All Things Considered*.

They ate on the couch, tucked under a blanket together. Jo couldn't eat on the couch with Laura. Her coordination just wasn't good enough. As they ate, Jo decided not to worry about cancer and Makah, but instead what it meant to be having an affair. This wasn't sex, what was happening tonight. This was an affair. Jo was someone she'd never thought she'd be, doing something she'd never thought she'd do. She already pined for those few pre-anesthetized anxiety-free seconds she'd spent this morning.

She fell asleep trying to figure out how to tell Laura about what she'd done. She woke who knows how much later when a violent gust of wind set the building to swaying and popping again. Beth was still next to her, quietly reading a magazine. The dinner dishes were cleared from the coffee table and her Gatorade had been refilled.

Jo fished in her pajama pocket for her phone. She dismissed a voice mail notification from Vi. She was much more with it, felt like taking advantage of having Beth near. "I think my food-coma's wearing off. You up for talking something out with me?" Jo knew she had all the pieces to complete the puzzle, she just didn't know how they went together. It was that time in an investigation when all the possibilities were getting in the way of getting to the truth.

"Of course. But are you sure you are?"

"I won't be up for anything else until this thing on Makah is finished."

"Okay. But after that, it's bedtime." Behind Beth, the lights of Seattle's Great Wheel spun, glowing green, blue, red, white. "Where you want to start?"

"It's all tied together," Jo insisted. "I have to start somewhere, and I'm starting there. But first I've got to unravel it."

"Alright. Talk it out."

"Let's say the thefts are where it starts," Jo began. "Brittany did the break-ins, and the fencing through PNW Metalworks. She had help, at minimum from Ashley. Tyler had to know about it, maybe Luke. Though I can't imagine he was actively involved. He's stable, doesn't need the money badly, as far as I can tell. And if he did have access to the stolen copper, why keep buying it from his wholesaler?" She smiled. It was nice to have this again, someone to ramble to who could make sense of it. "Theory one. Three kids get in over their heads, they fight amongst themselves, age old tale. But why would you murder someone to avoid a B and E charge? Ashley's not what anyone would call a good kid. But she's not simple. Now, Jered, her boyfriend." Jo paused as the threads started to wind themselves back together. "Jered might know about it all through Ashley, but he'd hardly get involved. Running the fentanyl was way more lucrative. I think Jered wouldn't want anything to do with crime that quaint."

"Your boy Brian Stewart seems like he likes to take care of loose ends," Beth said. "If Brittany's using the cash she gets from the thefts to buy drugs, ends up getting arrested, he's worried it'll come back to him?"

"Definitely a possibility. But that's a winding road. And if that were true, why try to give her CPR after she OD's? Why not just let her die? By the way – thanks for sticking your neck out for me. Reading that autopsy spared me a lot of false starts."

"Of course, hun. This story is a good one for you – you deserve a shot to get it right."

"Thanks." Jo snugged in a little closer. "But let's get back to theory one. Let's say Brittany, Tyler, Ashley, Jered, and Luke all knew some or all of what was going on with the copper thefts."

"Let's say," Beth nodded along. "They're going along fine, and something changes. Brittany dies as a result. Then Randy. Then Tyler. What changed, in each circumstance, to motivate someone to kill them?"

She couldn't answer the first question. But what changed after Randy and Brittany's deaths? Jo. She'd come around and started pushing Jered, and Tyler – *"I'll handle what I need to handle. You're right, about how I need to look out for myself a little better."* Had he called Brian's bluff, or Jered's, and paid for it?

She thought back to her hike with Valerie up Mill Creek Ravine. Someone who cared about Brittany had left that body someplace beautiful and peaceful, where eventually she'd be found. Someone who cared about Brittany had tried to save her life after she overdosed. That whittled the list to Tyler, maybe Ashley.

"Maybe," Jo started over again. "Maybe it really was an accident. And the cover-up got out of hand. That could hold water. Brittany and Tyler are still secretly seeing each other. She OD's at his place. Tyler tries to give her CPR, then gets scared and puts her in his boat? Or, Brittany OD's with Ashley, and she enlists Tyler to try and cover it up? No – she would have recruited Jered, and he would have gone the path of least resistance."

Beth tilted her head back and forth. "But if it were Tyler, why would someone then kill him? Revenge for Brittany's death?"

"Kyle and Nancy, her parents, they're the only ones I've come across with that kind of motive. And they've been up in Bellingham with Nancy's sister, except for Brittany's service."

"So motive and means gets you nowhere in particular, yet."

"No." Jo regrouped, glanced back at her borrowed phone. "I've been flipping through these pictures from Luke's workshop. I've got to be missing something. Help me out?" She looked up, caught Beth's eye.

She was studying Jo. She reached out and ran a finger under her bangs. "Love to." She nudged with an elbow and moved in closer. They huddled next to each other over the phone.

There really wasn't anything you could call evidence. Just machinery, art, art in progress. That hulking asymmetrical sculpture half-destroyed. Assorted pictures, maps and charts on the walls. She'd taken pictures of Tyler as well as the workshop, and they were hard to look at. She kept fixing on his blue lips, his pale neck, the square fentanyl patch sticking up over his t-shirt collar. But the more she did look, the easier it got. She didn't like that.

"Is this okay?" She turned to Beth, immediately regretted it. Her chest pinched with the movement and she yelped. Jo put a hand to her side. "I think the local's wearing off ." She took a shallow breath. "I mean, are you okay look-ing at these photos? I know you saw a lot in Sinaloa, and you left for a reason. So, is this okay?"

Beth smiled. "It is. I did see a lot that I didn't want to. But it made me a better journalist. And maybe I just don't know enough about it – but Jo I don't see anything here that points to anything but a simple overdose. I really think you should let this go. Let the system, the police, take care of it. If Hill's got the wrong guy, it could very well fall apart eventually."

"I can't believe a black woman just said that to me."

"Touché. Fine." Beth pinched Jo's shoulder. "But you can still walk away. Cover the story, but don't drive it. I'll print your byline, either way."

"Solid plan. But giving up isn't the way I want to go out. You know, I think I get it, more, now. How I fit in on Makah. How a real journalist fits in there. Brian's been running his game, fearless. Hill's a good guy, but toothless. That leaves me. We're not just here to regurgitate events, Beth. It's our responsibility to shine a light if no one else will. You can't tell me that's not more important now that it's ever been."

Jo shifted around. Beth did the same, until they faced each other. Their couch in D.C. had hosted plenty of discussions that had looked and sounded just like this one.

"Sure. We are." Beth traced the yellow shadow of a bruise on Jo's face with her fingertip. "But you're not really in fighting form right now, are you?" She put a tender hand on the fresher wound on her chest. "Sometimes we need to take care of ourselves, first. Or let someone else take care of us." Beth moved closer, grazed Jo's jawline with her lips. "There's something breakable about you Jo. Just under all that tough-girl skin that keeps it in. It keeps it in, but it doesn't stop it breaking." She moved her lips from Jo's neck where she'd been whispering what Jo wanted to hear, up to her mouth, to finish the sentiment.

The thought of someone else taking care of her stuffed-up Jo's nose and closed up her throat. She reached out and ran her fingers over the other woman's smooth calf, over her ankle, down to her foot and pretty manicured toes. It was the first time she'd touched Beth that way in a long, long time. The way you touched someone you loved, not someone you lusted after.

It's everything you want, she thought to herself. You can have everything you want and never be lonely. A wife. A career. It can be like it was.

You can be like you were. It would hurt, sure, it would feel wrong for a while, but that would pass. How are you going to do it all alone, when you get that call later this week? When the biopsy turns up what you know it will turn up? And how long are you even going to be around? Why end your days the hard way? Stop lying. Stop keeping secrets. Stop wanting what you can't have, and just have it. Just take it, Jo.

She slid her hand back, pulled away from a kiss that was moving toward much more. She could lust after another woman. That was bad enough. But she could not love Beth Berge. Any, every action that followed from that decision, to feel love for this woman who wasn't Laura, would be means and ends without any possible justifications.

She had to stop. Jo had known as soon as it began that this couldn't last. Sex, she could confess. Her marriage could have a chance to recover, once she came clean. But this wasn't sex. It was more, and it was going to decimate her world if she didn't stop and start telling the truth.

"It's never the lie, Joey."

The cover-up was where the shit went down. With Abish, Makah, and now with Jo, if she went that route. What would she have to do, to cover this up, if she didn't tell Laura what she'd done?

Through her drug-induced fog of contentment, through her guilt, through her desire, through her pain and her fear, it came to her. She knew who'd killed Brittany Roebuck and Tyler Sealth, and why. It wasn't drugs. It wasn't money, and it wasn't power. It was good old-fashioned love, Jo's style of love. With all its temptations and all its nasty, unintended consequences.

Someone who cared enough about Brittany, loved her, in his own way, enough to leave a body behind, and try to save her life – but with enough at stake to try and cover it up. She'd missed it because she'd been too close. She'd been looking for the big twist, the elaborate agenda, and glanced right past the disgusting reality of the everyday. Jo simply hadn't wanted to admit what people like her were capable of. The predictability of it all turned her stomach.

"Beth, I can't do this." Jo sat up, pulled her legs to her chest.

"Do what, hun?"

"Be here with you. Like this."

"What exactly is 'like this?'" Beth matched Jo's crossed arms.

"Like we're a couple again. I'm so sorry. I can't."

"Mmm hmm. I can see how you could misinterpret this." Beth stood.

She took Jo's glass with her to the kitchen and refilled it. "I think you've got the wrong impression about what I've been looking for. I don't want to steal you away from Laura. I don't want you waiting for me when I come home from work, dinner on the stove. I want this. You come, you go, and so do I."

"But – this morning. Tonight –"

"No strings doesn't mean I'm a bitch. I'm still your friend. Gotta be I love you still, too, because you can't be the way we were, when we were together, and pretend that just disappears with time. But whatever you thought was happening here, it's not. Consider me a vacation from your troubles, Jo. Not a cure for them."

"I'm not using you, you're using me?" Jo Ford, the incredible shrinking woman.

"Something like that. I think it's time we got you to bed." Beth stood, helped Jo up, then walked away.

CLOSE DOESN'T COUNT

Jo woke alone in the early morning gloom, dressed herself, and snuck out of the apartment. A walk of shame for the ages.

It would have been worse if she didn't have something else to feel shitty about, and something else to focus on. She hadn't seen past her own guilt and self-pity in time to save Tyler, who'd been covering for the guy who could get him that big chance he needed – Luke Sorensen. She didn't feel like time was on her side, either, when it came to Ashley Sorensen and what she was now sure the girl knew.

The engines on the ferry cut, painfully slow as it coasted the rest of the way into the dock. It was just past nine in the morning. Still mid-winter dusky. She raced the Volvo up the hill coming off the boat. As she cruised through a tunnel of evergreen trees, head resting in her hand propped against the window, she thought about all the times that she'd been desperate to see Laura.

When they'd first gotten together. After Laura came home from long assignments overseas. Young, frustrated love that couldn't cope with separation.

Then, after Jo's dad had died – waiting at Dulles for Laura to step off the plane and hear "it's going to be okay" coming from the one person who could make her believe it.

And running down the hall in the hospital in Germany, rushing to hold Laura's hand, even if she couldn't hold Jo's.

This morning, Jo's loneliness for her wife was excruciating. Now, when she deserved the comfort the least, and wanted it the most.

She sped down the drive, ignoring the clever Burma-shave haiku signs painted by her neighbors about keeping it at a steady fifteen. The pressure cooker in her chest collapsed when she saw Frank's truck in its usual place, and a light on in the kitchen

Jo slammed into the back door on her way through and paid for it. Her left side caught on fire, still tender from tweaking the stitches last night. Despite the truck outside, the place seemed empty. She caught her breath back, yelled up the stairs.

"Laura? Frank? Spot?"

No answer from any quarter. She turned back to the kitchen, stalked to the customary note-spot next to the fridge. "Walk." Next to the notepad was a chewed ball-point pen. Jo let out a deep breath and took another one in. She resisted the urge to tear the pad into a handful of ticker-tape parade of 'what did you think karma would send you' confetti.

She set it back on the counter and willed herself to calm the hell down. It wouldn't hurt her to wait a while for them to come back. That was a good idea, actually. Have some breakfast, get her head right, get some perspective.

But inside Jo, a clock was still ticking. She thought of her informant on the Abish case, Michael Pulaski; crusty-funny Sonya Petroysan, the murder that was never solved. When Abish had started cleaning his mess, he'd been thorough.

She suspected Luke Sorensen was also a thorough kind of man, because shame was a powerful motivator. Brittany had been the starting point. But he'd more than likely killed Tyler Sealth along the way too, to cover up what he'd been doing with Brittany. He'd wanted what he shouldn't and decided to have it anyway. If Ashley knew, though, how thorough would he be in covering it all up?

Luke was responsible. Luke and his fishing charts. Luke, former MHS art teacher, in a district where all the employees were CPR certified. Jo had done a piece for *The Quartermaster* on the annual spring training course. Luke and his cabin in the woods. His brand-new affinity for conflicted art. Denying he knew about the break-ins, most of all casting suspicion on Tyler. He'd planted those sculptures on the bodies. Luke put Brittany in that ravine, taken a risk when he should have just put her in a shot-out Yeti 500 and given her a watery burial. Leaving Brittany where she could be found – it was the kind of thing a father, someone who knew Kyle and Nancy, would do. He couldn't stand the thought of Brittany never being found. Even if he was a rapist, he couldn't bring himself to disappear her forever. Randy was just coincidence.

It all fit. It was the cleanest explanation she'd come across yet.

As soon as she ate, as soon as Laura came back, Jo would drive to the Sheriff's office and stage a sit-in. Hill would hear her out.

She rummaged through the breakfast cupboard and grabbed a packet of oatmeal, splashed some water in a bowl and nuked it. She'd eat in bed, didn't trust herself not to fall asleep at the table.

Jo scowled when she got upstairs. The bed wasn't made. If she didn't do it, Frank always helped Laura do it. Jo was adamant about Laura living in order. If her world were well-ordered, maybe her mind might catch on.

Didn't matter today. She scarfed the oatmeal, downed a glass of water and a handful of Motrin, and laid down, ecstatic to put her head on the pillow.

It was gloomier, almost dark in the room when she woke. In the perpetual twilight of winter days here, judging time by the light was a non-starter. She looked for her phone on the hand-me-down bedside table, then realized it was still in the pocket of her jeans.

Christ. It was past two pm. No word from Frank. She listened to the house - still nothing from downstairs. If Laura had come home for a nap, Frank would have sent her upstairs to be with Jo.

She got up and didn't bother to change out of her rumpled clothes, already dialing Vi on Laura's borrowed phone that her wife maybe really needed. Jo careened down the stairs as it rang, now thinking about Jered Brasier and Brian Stewart. *"He's saying we'll whack your –"*

"Hey it's Jo."

"Thought I'd hear from you sooner than later."

Jo rubbed her forehead. "I don't – look – I don't have time to talk. Have you heard from Frank or Laura?"

"No ma'am. Everything okay?"

"Yes. No. I don't know."

"What the hell's wrong, honey?"

"It's just that when I got back from Seattle this morning, they weren't here. But Frank's truck is." Jo cast a glance at the Toyota. Twenty years old and in as good condition as the day he bought it.

"Probably just caught a ride, went for a walk. Nothing to worry about. You call up Rick Bunker?"

"No. But you're probably right. Good idea."

"Usually am."

"Anyway, Vi, I'm going to keep calling around."

"Nothing to worry about. Sure they're just watching the Huskies game in some man-cave somewhere."

"Yeah. Thanks."

Jo hung up. She opened Glympse on Laura's phone to send Frank a location request. She left a message for Hill, then commenced calling Frank's various good buddies. After she ran through those, she started calling guys he knew casually, playing telephone tree and grabbing the next number from the guy who'd just finished the conversation with some version of "let me know when you get ahold of them."

When she hung up on the last call and the last in the chain of friends she'd ever heard Frank mention, she sank down onto the sofa, and finally let the thought she'd been holding back with all her might materialize. She needed to find Jered Brasier, make sure he had nothing to do with her absent wife. But she also needed to find Luke. And Ashley.

She couldn't wait here any longer. She scrabbled around for her keys. Almost panicked, she racked her brain for where they possibly could have gone between the car and the kitchen – when she realized she'd left them in the car.

Outside, the rain was picking up. Unable to deal with the fishy smell of Frank's coat any longer, she grabbed Laura's red parka. Why wasn't it with her? Stop, Jo. Stop. No one takes a dog and an old man with them on a kidnapping. Laura's fine. It's fine.

That's what she told herself as she fired up the Volvo and tore-ass for town. True to Northwest form, when she got there, the rain wasn't stopping anything. The Saturday farmer's market was jumping and so was the traffic, most of it headed out of town. It was past three and the sky was already darkening. She snagged a parking spot farther than she wanted to take time to walk and cruised through the happy, oblivious North Face clad wanderers, searching for Laura's shining black hair. Nothing.

She stopped in the middle of the bustle, closed her eyes, took a breath –

"Ma'am - are you okay?" A teenager with blonde dreadlocks staffing the goat-milk tent leaned over an assortment of cheeses and soaps, looking very genuine in her concern.

"Ummm. I don't know. Sorry." Jo threw up her hood and hustled on. She had no idea where Jered lived. But she knew where to start looking for him. She didn't imagine he made a habit of hanging out with the midday crowd at the Alibi, mostly seniors taking advantage of breakfast specials, but it was worth a try.

The place was dreary day-lit. Rarely a good look for a bar. As expected, the tables were dotted with gray-hairs chugging the crappy, cheap coffee. The bar itself had a couple die-hards anchoring the same stools they'd certainly abandoned only a few hours earlier. She paused on her way to the back patio.

"Anyone seen Jered Brasier today?"

A guy with a red face, redder eyes, wearing a stained puffy jacket shook his head. For a second Jo was concerned the movement might tip him off the stool. No one else responded. She continued on, through the back door, to the empty back patio. She couldn't help casting her eyes to the gap in the trees she'd come stumbling out of, agonized and bloody, less than a week earlier.

She dialed Hill's cell again. Straight to voice mail, again. She could call 911, but they wouldn't take a missing person report seriously for at least another twelve hours. Not while Laura was supposed to be with Frank. More likely they'd start asking how things were in the house. She'd have to tell them all about her being late all the time, fighting with her father-in-law, who'd wanted to take custody. But Frank wouldn't take Laura. He just wouldn't. She dialed the old pre-911 number Vi had slipped to her, that went straight to Deputy Locke. She got through, and hastily explained the situation.

"Hey yeah Jo," Brenda responded. "I don't like hearing that, no. I'll keep my eyes on for Frank and Laura. I'll go sniff around right now."

"Thanks Brenda. And will you ask Elijah to call me?"

"Sure will."

She jogged back to the car, hand pressed to her incision. Well, she jogged a few steps and then started sucking wind, had to walk the rest of the way. Her nap was already wearing off. Tired or not, Jo was headed straight to the only other place she could think to lay her hands on Ashley, Jered, Luke, or anyone else who she could shake to end this clusterfuck.

She laid hard on the gas on her way north to Lost Valley.

...AND DEFINITELY THIS FUCKING GUY

When she got to the Sorensen's, the entire property was quiet. Trees, pasture, house and workshop dim and deserted. Luke's truck was there. So was Ashley's Subaru. She frowned at the sinister landscape, where she'd already been in a fist fight and discovered a dead body. She closed her eyes and put her head back against the seat, already drowsy. Even if it wasn't a great idea to snooze in the driveway of a man she suspected of murder, it still sounded nice.

Instead, she got out to the car. Did a three-sixty. House, woods, workshop.

The phone buzzed in her back pocket.

"Frank. Where the hell have you guys been?" Jo felt relieved and shitty, like she'd just crashed through the floor of a bad high.

"We were just out walking. Wally flagged us down, asked if we were up for a little spin in the boat. We stopped at Hunter's for wings and the Huskies game after. Then Brenda Locke comes busting in, said to call you right away. I left a note."

"'Walk' was all it said, Frank. Not 'walk, boat ride, and Hunter's.'"

"Sorry." The warm sound of the crowded bar filled the silence between them, grated against the isolation of standing alone in a stranger's driveway. Of course they'd been right across the street from where she'd been looking. Her classic M.O. these days – miss the shot that matters by a hair.

"Alright. Can I talk to Laura?"

"Oh yeah sure. She's been asking about you all day." She heard Frank hand the phone over, a muffled, *"Jo."*

"Hi. Where are you?"

"I'm up in Lost Valley. I'll see you at home soon. I miss you, so much. Love you."

"How's Beth?"

Not, "How was the biopsy, what did they say?" No. Laura Tanaka asked

Jo Ford the question she meant to ask, and for a reason. Jo fell back against the car. Shame finally caught up with her. The real kind, the nauseous kind. She was out of time, out of rope. She was going to have to pay for what she'd done, and you know what? She should. Just maybe not over the phone while she was half-searching for a murder suspect. "She's fine. Still interested in me writing for the *P.I.*, but that's off the table, as far as I'm concerned."

"Okay." Laura sounded perfectly placated. Jo waited for her to continue, but she didn't.

Instead, Frank came back on the line. "So, we'll –"

Jo heard shouting from deep in the woods. "Hold on, Frank."

"Get back here – let me – "

"No –"

From inside the house came frenzied barking from the dogs. She turned around to see if she could - and promptly tripped over -

"Nooowww."

"Jesus H – fucking – Paula – what the *hell*."

Arm pressed at her side that had begun to ache from all her non-prescribed activities, she bent down to scoop up the cat. At least something good could come of this day. She caught her around the middle, but she yowled and swatted her hand.

"Dammit, Paula" Jo held on as the cat squirmed and generally did every-thing to aggravate Jo's sore body.

She threw open the back door of the Volvo, tossed her in, and closed it before Paula could make an escape. She leaned back on the car, panting.

"You alright out there?" Frank sounded more amused than concerned. "Fi-nally solve the mystery of the missing cat?"

"You know what, Frank –" By the skin of her teeth she pulled back on the throttle. "I'll see you guys at home, okay? I just want to check something out. I'll be there in like twenty."

"Alright."

Jo clicked off . She studied the forest, tried to figure out where the shouting had come from. She was sure it had been two voices. A man, and a girl. She thought back on all the interactions she'd had with the Sorensens, running con-versations through her mind. Running. Trails. Plenty of people had trail heads on their property. She remembered Jered walking toward the tree line after she kicked his skinny ass, what she'd learned about Ashley after he'd left –

"Where's your dad, Ashley?"

"Who the fuck knows. The cabin. – "

The cabin?

She scanned the thick stand of trees again. Sure enough. Just a vacuous hole leading – somewhere. Somewhere near where she'd heard that shouting. She crossed the drive and stepped into the early night of the forest.

Jo smelled cedar and heard gentle rain pattering the leaves above on the trek along the path. The dense, brown pine needles on the forest fl oor deadened the sound of her footsteps. A hundred winding yards or so in, she found part of what she was looking for. In front of her stood what Ashley had called a cabin, and Jo would have referred to generously as a shack. From it, she heard two voices. She snuck closer, toward a window in the back.

The light through the dirty glass was thin, blue-white and dimmed by the dark wood paneling on all four walls inside. It was enough to make out cha-os. The tiny cabin looked like a pack of raccoons had fought to a bloodless death. Old fi shing charts and a map of Makah were ripped and strewn across the washed pine fl oors. Overhead a broken light bulb clung to its socket. A puke-green and yellow upholstered chair was giving her four wooden middle fi ngers. And a stained, blue-striped mattress hung limp, halfway off a tilted metal box spring. Looking at that mattress was like looking at an oily coil of black, head-less snakes. She knew that there was every chance that this had been where Brittany Roebuck had taken her last breath.

Jo was close enough now to see and hear Ashley and Luke tearing into each other.

"Just stop fucking lying, Dad. You don't have to lie about it anymore, be-cause it's done. Slutty Brittany is dead now, but you had to fuck it all up."

"Ash – " Luke collapsed into one of the chairs that was still upright. "Did you mess with Brittany's dose?"

"I didn't think it would kill her. But too bad. And she's out of your life now. It's fi xed."

Shit. Jo rummaged through her pockets until she found her phone. She missed the code when she tried to click in, remembered it was Laura's, and fi nal-ly got into the camera app to start video.

Luke ran his hands over his face, scrubbed through his fresh beard. "Ash I'm so sorry. I really am. You were never supposed to know."

"Yeah no one was supposed to know, right? You fucking perv."

"That's not fair. It's not how it was."

"How was it, Dad? That's what I'm asking. How was it? What, did you like, love her?"

"Yes."

"*Whatever*," Ashley howled. "I mean, but seriously, whatever – it doesn't matter." The girl seemed to collect herself, then started to wail again. "She was my best friend. And Mom –" Ashley lunged toward the little table against the wall and grabbed a slab shaver. The fishing knife was only large enough to be useful. But depending how old it was, it was more than sharp enough to do real damage. Big Jack hadn't let Jo start handling them on her own until she'd had a month of practice under tight supervision.

She pointed it toward Luke, but her stance wasn't aggressive.

"I'm sorry, Ash. I am. Really. I came out here today to try and make it all right." Luke held his palms up, then reached into his pocket. He pulled out a small handful of what looked like, had to be, fentanyl lozenges still in their wrappers. Either that, or he was about to do something really dramatic with sugar free candies. "When Tyler told me that he knew about me and Brittany, as soon as he did, I just started thinking about who else might know. And I knew you did. I *knew* it. I couldn't see how I could still keep in the clear, with you knowing. And I couldn't ever hurt you – how I could ask you to keep this secret? I couldn't."

"You're seriously going to kill yourself?" Ashley sounded disgusted. "You're a real stand-up guy, Dad."

"That was the plan."

"You can't –"

"Ash, I don't see another way –"

"No, I mean you can't. You fucking sick coward. You can't just bail. I'm so sick of dudes just *bailing*."

Jo kept the video rolling. Half of her wanted to see Ashley finish the bastard off. She began to wonder at what point she should stop and call 911. Despite her wish for frontier justice, now was probably right.

"I'm not bailing. I'm taking responsibility. But I just want people to understand how we felt about each other. For Kyle and Nancy to know she was loved. I'll cover for you too, Ash, if you'll let me.

I'll say I gave her the wrong dose, accidentally."

"I don't want that." Ashley stepped closer to her father, knife tip angled straight at his throat.

Jo stopped the video. Holding her breath, she crept away from the cabin, dialed 911. Nothing. She moved further toward the house, hoping Luke had any kind of capacity to deal with what was going on in there. Still not connecting. She turned back to the cabin as Ashley burst through the door, followed by Luke. Now, she held the knife to her own neck.

Father and daughter intently focused on each other, it still didn't take Ashley long to spot Jo and her bright red parka – a beacon against the green, brown, and black of the forest.

Ashley looked from Jo to her dad, back again at Jo. "Why are you here –" Ashley frenetically scanned the woods. "You alone? You call the cops?"

"Why would I do that," Jo asked. Ashley approached her with the knife. Luke didn't stop her. "You did. You're lying."

Jo took a step back, tried a lie. "Okay. I did. So just let them sort this out, Ashley."

"She fucking called the cops," Ashley yelled at her father. "And I'm not done. I'm not done with this."

"She's okay," Luke called to Jo. "She's just a little too high on the wrong stuff . You should probably go."

"Okay." Jo began to back away. She hadn't meant to escalate the girl. Tick another bad choice on Jo's tally for the month.

Ashley flicked the knife toward her father. He ducked his head at her; started in the opposite direction, and Ashely followed him down the trail.

Jo checked her phone again. Nothing. She darted into the cabin, snatched a pile of papers Luke had been waving at his daughter while he whined about atonement. She tucked them in her coat and stared down the slope toward the beach, then started heels-first down the muddy trail after the Sorensens, grabbing on to tree trunks and branches for purchase, paying for it as her tender side roared at her to stop.

The rain and wind picked up intensity the closer she got toward the shore-line. She could hear the two still arguing. She skidded to a stop behind a tree a dozen yards from a crumbling dock, checked her phone again, dialed 911 again, which rang but never connected.

"I don't have a fucking plan, Dad," Ashley screamed, the wind blowing hard off the Sound carrying her words and her urgency. "I just want to talk."

"What else have you got to talk about, that can't wait?" Luke said. "Come on, Ash. As much as you want it to, and believe me on this, time's not going to change the truth."

"Fuck you." The girl kept the knife at her throat. A little dribble of crimson appeared at the tip.

"Fine." Luke climbed into a small boat bouncing on the choppy water.

"Start it," Ashley insisted.

He ripped the cord and fired up the outboard.

Once he sat down, Ashley climbed in. "Go."

The girl was going to kill them both. Accidentally or intentionally. Ashley was right about one thing – Luke didn't deserve to bail – he deserved to look Kyle and Nancy Roebuck in the eye. Then again, Jo didn't owe Luke or Ashley anything. Why should she risk her life for two shitty people who were basically strangers? But she did owe Tyler. And she owed Laura, and Vi, Valerie, Frank – that meant she had a debt to Makah. To the community. Ashley needed help more than she needed to die. She, and Makah, needed someone to care.

There were two other boats tied out. She climbed down into the larger using her right hand to try and steady herself. She sat on the aft bench and stared at the Evinrude, glad for the recent refresh with Valerie. Dad only ever had inboards. She ran her hand over the throttle, twisted it right, then came to the shifter, clicked it to neutral. She took the starter rope and gave a gentle tug, feeling for tension. She shifted to get a better angle for the pull. Her toe squished on some-thing. She looked down – grabbed the fuel line and pumped.

She could still hear Luke's boat, but the sound was fading with the horizon. She stood and hauled on the rope. Nothing. She held her hand to her sore side and tried again. Nothing. A gust of wind came through, amplifying the harsh shriek of a passing gull and the increasing static in Jo's head.

She closed her eyes and stepped back in time. A Ford vacation in sunny Florida and a bass fish fry at the end of the day. They'd only had outboards at the small marina, and Big Jack took it as a teaching moment. *"Engines need two things, Joey. Air and fuel."*

Right there next to the damn shift lever. She pulled out the choke and ripped one more time. Her knees gave way as the incision at her ribcage split open. She collapsed on the bench and waited for the dizziness to pass. Jo goosed the throttle, waited for it to even out. She tucked her phone into the interior pocket of the jacket with Luke's papers, zipped it tight, and turned the boat out into the darkening afternoon.

The entire surface of the Sound was obscured by motion. The shifting waters and the steady, bone-chilling wind worked against her progress. The boat pounded over every whitecap. Every thump resonated through her body to end in her miserable chest. Jo hadn't given the motor any time to warm up. She pushed back a little on the choke and froze when it began sputtering. She caught some fumes, but it smoothed back out. She didn't want to mess with it again, though she wondered exactly how much gas she had.

The sound of her motor and the whine of Luke's were all she could hear. There were no other boats in the slim, swift-watered passage between Makah and the mainland. Even the birds had retreated from the mist and the blustering storm charging in. She, Luke, and Ashley were each in their own world. Each bound to a one-way trajectory by choices made, running from the consequences of actions they couldn't take back. She ought to go home, but she couldn't. She ought to give what she knew over to Elijah Hill and hope for the best, but she wouldn't. Jo wasn't going to do that. The ache that had been building in her chest propelled her forward through the profound anxiety that what she was doing right now was very, very reckless.

Through rain that was fast turning to sleet, she could barely see the ratty skiff making its way north, toward the dangerous currents coming off the Reach. Two hunched figures rose and fell along with the swelling waves. Luke's boat was half the size of what she'd commandeered and no match for the Sound in this kind of weather.

It had to be past four o'clock already. There wasn't much light left in the day, an hour at most. Jo figured it'd be too dark to make out anything, any kind of reference point on the land a lot sooner than later. Now she looked around for a side light on the bow. Nope. Backlight? No. She hunted at her feet for a flashlight anywhere. None. *Shit.*

A massive swell tossed her boat up, down, and she caught air. Then she pitched side to side as the wind picked up. She ducked her head from the driving rain and held on until it passed. When she looked around to see how Luke's boat had fared, it was gone.

Jo twisted the throttle and slowed. She scanned the horizon where she'd last seen them. The fog on the water blended everything together like a wet, gray, watercolor. The misting, freezing rain worsened the effect. The lack of contrast made her vision stupid. Jo cut her motor almost all the way and listened. Nothing but silence and screaming wind.

She couldn't see the other boat, couldn't hear it either. Just the plop of the waves against her own hull. Then –

"Dad! Dad!"

She looked toward the sound of the voice. Luke's boat hadn't gone any-where. It had capsized, caught by the surge. He could have easily banked into it sideways, looking to roll it. Or just as easily been out-piloted by mother nature. She could make it out, now, the silver metal see-sawing in the restless water. She saw Ashley's dark head bobbing next to it. Where was Luke?

Jo trolled toward the prone vessel. She searched at her feet. A short coil of moldering rope, a fishing rod missing the reel, and a single weather-beaten oar with a split running half its length. No life jackets to be found.

"Ashley." Jo called to the girl. She edged in even closer, throttled the motor to an idle and shifted into neutral, praying it wouldn't die. She'd never get it started again if it cut out.

Ashley looked at her, then away, head swiveling left, right, and back again. "Dad!"

"You need to get out of the water." Jo picked up the oar and maneuvered it over the side of the boat. She gasped as the torn biopsy incision flared under her arm.

Ashley grabbed hold but continued calling for her father.

"Ashley, get in. We'll keep looking for him."

The girl nodded – or was she just shaking from the cold? Or was it Jo shaking from the cold? Ashley grabbed the other end of the oar, but before getting any closer to the boat, she was swallowed by a whitecap.

"Dammit." Jo could still feel her holding on. Through the ripping, hot agony in her chest, she heaved the oar forward. Ashley surfaced, sputtering. Jo reached for her with her right hand, her left arm plastered to her side in a hopeless attempt to control pain and fatigue dimming the edges of her sight. The girl latched on to her with both hands. Jo heaved again, tumbling her up into the boat.

Jo sat panting, crying, moaning, teeth chattering, trying to catch her breath despite the staggering cold, and the warm, wet squishing under her jacket. Ashley lay prone and shivering.

"Luke!" Jo tried to peer below the murky, agitated water, tried to catch a glimpse of anything that might indicate he hadn't been taken by the Sound.

The girl pulled herself onto the forward bench. "Dad!"

The distant eastern and western shores were barely visible. The threat of passing out, giving in to exposure, losing their way in the mid-channel fog, was very real. Jo would not risk whatever time she had left for Luke Sorensen. She shifted the motor out of neutral, wincing at a fresh stab of pain.

A white hand shot out of the water. Long fingers clutched the side of the hull and they pitched toward the pull. A moment later, Luke's head surfaced. He grabbed on with his other hand and hauled himself up. Jo barely had time to shift her weight against his as he flopped over the side and collapsed into the boat.

She'd yelped and tweaked the throttle at Luke's sudden appearance. They were careening toward the capsized vessel. She grabbed the tiller and hauled the rudder to the side. They skimmed the edge of the other boat. Jo righted the course and brought them back around toward what she was mostly sure was Makah.

The three soaked occupants huffed and shivered as the rain and the dark deepened around them. Jo sat at the aft, Ashley and Luke huddled together on the forward bench. Heads almost touching, neither was paying her any attention.

She wasn't sure what it would mean for her when that changed. Jo had yet to hear, "holy cow, thanks for pulling us out of the drink," or more particularly, "this isn't your boat, and why the hell were you following us, anyway?" She didn't like that.

They droned on toward a shoreline with indistinct features that blended together in Jo's blurring vision. She glanced at Luke, glowering at her.

Ashley glanced at her dad and didn't say anything.

Luke put his arm around the girl.

Jo was flagging. She needed to be off this boat. Every whack from every little wave was killing her. In the gloom, she barely caught sight of a trail of white smoke, not too far north of where she thought the dock was. She kept it lined up with the bow. In her near sight, she noticed Luke and Ashley whispering to each other.

"You need to go further south." He gestured toward her two o'clock.

Jo sped up, but not in the direction he indicated. The faster they went, the less footing anyone had to be making trouble. All of which begged the question, what would happen when they got to shore? If they got to shore. How long could she really keep them moving – and how much gas was in this thing in the first place? There were way too many ways Jo was set up to die out here.

"You need to go south." Luke shifted on the bench and pointed again.

"I know." Jo couldn't feel her ears or her nose anymore, or her lips.

Luke looked down at the splintered oar. Ashley looked at it, then at him.

Jo was the first to get a hand on it, but it was the broadside and her grip was frozen and weak. Jo's boots slid on the bottom of the boat grasping for purchase as she struggled to get another hand on the weapon. Luke had grabbed the slender handle and with better leverage he wrestled the weapon out of her grasp. Pale blue eyes wide and wild, he held up his prize, ready to hit a grand slam. The oar came swinging toward her. Before it could connect, Jo hugged her arm to her screaming left side and plunged headfirst into the bottomless black of Puget Sound.

TIGHT BUT NOT RIGHT

"Come on, Jo. Wake up. You're fine. Up and at 'em."

Jo was not fine. She felt like a chicken breast that had been tenderized while the bird was still alive. Her chest simultaneously ached and blazed white-hot. It was the only thing about her that was warm.

"Time to wake up Jo. Eyes open. Come on. Didn't know you were this lazy."

She felt a hand at her shoulder, the side of her body that didn't feel like it had been through a paper shredder and taped back together. She opened her eyes to see Elijah Hill. Behind him, nothing but solid charcoal sky through a rain-smattered window. They were pitching up and down. Jo was rolling back and forth, but she was secured somehow, laying on a hard bench. She heard the crackle of a radio, a blip, voices, and an answer. They were on a damn boat.

"I'm not lazy. I'm fucking exhausted." She shifted, realized she was wrapped tight in scratchy blankets. She closed her eyes again. Immediately they shot open wide. The blankets were very scratchy. Everywhere. She blinked, rapidly. Her eyes were raspy. Then, she realized, no contacts.

"Your secret's safe with me." Hill kept his hand on her shoulder. "I'm sorry. It was a little uncomfortable getting you out of your clothes. But you're fine. You're safe. But you weren't going to be. We staunched the bleeding and got you warm and dry as we could. We're headed to Seattle to get you fixed up."

Jo tried to calculate how many different people had seen her naked in the last few days. Too many. Through closed eyes, she asked. "Luke and Ashley?"

"Down below with another officer."

"How'd you find me? When did you find me?" Jo ought to be dead right now. That splintered oar should have been the last thing she'd ever seen.

"Laura's phone. Brenda stayed at Hunters to grab some dinner. The Huskies game went into overtime. Frank checked friend-finder to see if you were still at Sorensen's – saw your little dot go from land to water. That's when Brenda called me. Seems like you owe your life to UW losing that game."

"She call you on that phone you never answer?"

"It's called boundaries, Jo. Anyway, what the hell were you all doing out there? Damn stupid time to be on the water. I saw Luke take a swing at you with that oar. That's assault, and I can hold him on it."

Behind her closed eyes, Jo saw again the cabin where she knew Brittany Roebuck had died. The broken light bulb, the ratty wood-paneled walls – and that stained mattress hanging off the rusting bed frame. Case closed right there, more than likely.

"I went to talk to Luke, Ashley was there, and things escalated. We have to talk to them now, Elijah. You – do." She wished she sounded more forceful. Her throat was raw, and her sinuses – well, whatever crap had been left over from the black eye and bloody nose was long gone. "Ask him about Brittany. And Tyler. Now." Jo saw the window on this closing. Once they were back on land – there would be regret, reality, there would be lawyers. She struggled to sit up. She couldn't. Whether that was engineered for her protection, or just her fundamental lack of core strength – she laid back down.

"I can't, Jo. Not the time or place. They're both a little roughed up too."

"Then stop the boat, and I will. I know he killed Brittany. Tyler knew what was happening between them. I pushed him into confronting him. Luke killed Tyler to cover it all up. I found a letter – " *Shit.* Double shit. The letter had been in her jacket. Which had taken a bath along with her in the Sound. "Did you get Laura's parka?"

"We did. It's in a locker with the rest of your clothes."

"There were papers in it. Inside pocket."

Hill thrust his chin at the tall guy at the helm. "Slow it down, Barrett."

Jo rocked a little as the engine cut. Apparently, her Elliott Bay-Watch stunt had earned her some street cred.

Hill stood and moved to a row of gray metal lockers a few feet away. He opened one and pawed through the red jacket. Jo started to cry, seeing it. She'd never been this far away from Laura in her life.

He unzipped the inner pocket. From it he produced a cell phone and crinkled, folded papers, all damp but intact. It was like a damn advertisement for Kibo. Jo held out her hand. Hill considered, then handed them over. She began to read.

"Brittany and Ashley became friends a couple years ago, when they were freshman. They were both on cross-country, had algebra together. Brittany didn't live far, so they got rides home together all the time, and you know, they just got close. Kinda the same happened with me and Brittany. I didn't look for it, but you can't stop love, you know?

Britt started coming out to the shop more when my work started to sell last year, I really got in the flow. Really liked that Tyler was so into what I was seeing. The collaboration was great. We'd smoke and work, and before I knew it, it was dark and past dinner time. So the girls got unsupervised girl time, and I think Brittany liked the freedom. Kyle and Nancy are good parents, I want to say that. I don't think it was about escape. I think it was about teenagers wanting space.

I know it was Ash that got Brittany into the drugs. I'd seen her change, seen her get moody, moodier than I knew she ought to be, even, and I just didn't do anything except use more myself. It's bad knowing my own daughter developed a habit and I didn't do anything. It's worse knowing she dragged Brittany into it too. By the end I loved her. I really did. I still miss her. I hope that all this will at least end up with Ash getting help.

When Britt started using, that was when she started coming out to see me in the shop. At first she'd bring Ashley along – I think she probably coaxed her along. Brittany would start talking to Tyler, but then she'd kind of end up near me. She and I would end up talking while Tyler and Ashley hung out. She'd run a hand along one of the birds, one of the sculptures, and just stare at me with those blue eyes of hers. She had these big lips. She used shiny pink gloss. Sometimes she'd put some on while we were talking. She knew she was off-limits, and I did too. But there's something about that wanting that's almost more satisfying than having.

The girls had been hanging around some afternoon in the summer, and after they left, Tyler and I smoked a little, parked our asses on the work bench and shot the shit. I knew Tyler and Brittany had dated. God, I can't think about her that young. It's not how I saw her. Brittany moved a way Ashley and other girls her age didn't, yet, like a woman, like her hips had come in, you know. I couldn't really think about Tyler being with her. Or any other guy.

I asked him about her. I just wanted to hear about her, that was all. I could *see from how he looked at her sometimes that he was still into it, but not into it in a pathetic kind of way. More that it had been good while it lasted, but he knew it was gone. I could dance to that tune.*

He says to me, "It was good. Brittany's a good girl. Dating her, she felt like she had her shit locked down. Tight, you know?"

It was that word. Tight. He said it, and it burrowed into me like a goddamn tick. I don't think I even said anything back, just nodded as that goddamn word got deeper and deeper in my mind. "Tight, you know?"

I tried to work some more after Tyler left. I couldn't. Ashley had already eaten dinner and holed up in her room by the time I called it quits. I threw on some Page and Plant and picked up the guitar and tried to jam, but there was nothing. Just kept hearing about how tight Brittany was. Kept seeing those fat, shining, pink lips, and kept getting tighter myself.

The next few days I knocked around in the shop, but I still couldn't work. I'd look at the birds and I'd see Brittany's hand gliding over their smooth, hard, heads, her nails painted the same shiny pink as her lips.

Then, couple days later, there Britt was in the shop again, but this time no Ashley, no Tyler. She was high, you could tell that. There she was, high, giggling, just staring at me – like she knew what was in my mind. I knew it was over. I knew I was going to have her. I had to. I couldn't think about anything else, and I couldn't work. And as soon as we got together, when I was with Brittany, the way forward just came to me. It was like I was back in it, you know?

She always talked a lot. Ran on in this stream of consciousness way. I didn't mind it. I liked it. Melissa never talks to me anymore. Melissa doesn't give a shit about me, anymore, I don't think. Our shit marriage is my fault as much as it is hers, and I'm sorry for that too.

But Brittany was into me. Brittany was smart, and sweet, and into me. And I got to be real into her, too. And I got to love her. Jesus Christ, Tyler was right about her. It wasn't much, it wasn't right, I know, but I loved her. I did, and I'm sorry. I just want everyone to know she was loved."

What a pathetic train wreck.

The motion of the boat, the water, was getting to Jo. She took a few deep breaths and her nausea passed. She handed the letter over to Hill. He read the first page, stood abruptly, pounded down the stairs to the lower deck.

Jo started to nod off again. She had her answers. She wanted done with all of it.

After a while, Hill returned. He stalked to the wheelhouse, motioned for the pilot to bring them back up to speed.

He put his thumbs in his belt and stared down at her.

"Hell of a thing you've done, Jo."

"I guess. I've got one more thing, and maybe I'll regret it. But I want to press charges. Against Jered, and Brian."

"You sure?"

"No. But I need to do it."

Hill crouched down next to her, face to face. He was a handsome guy, really, in a way that she didn't think Luke Sorensen ever was. Close up, Hill was too kind-looking for the work he did. Aging slowly into midlife. He touched her arm, on his hand a thick, soft, yellow-gold wedding band with nicks dulling the shine but not the glow. Jo wondered if he had kids.

He sighed, then nodded. "Alright. I'll take a statement when you're back on your feet. Brenda says Frank's on his way to Harborview to meet you when we get there. They'll catch and release you, most likely."

"Did Brenda say if Laura's with him?" Ungodly Jo offered up another prayer.

"I think so." Hill glanced out the window. The lights of Seattle were close. Jo could make out the taller buildings, glittering glass during the day and lit sentinels at night. "We're about five minutes out from Elliott Bay. Try to sleep it off a little more. And – thank you."

"Sure." She closed her eyes. Wisps of thoughts swirled in her head. Luke, Ashley, Jered, Brian. Randy and Tyler. She couldn't untangle it. Probably because it couldn't be. Because one thing had led to another and another until they all burned each other down. Brian had just been the one to light the match.

It'd make a great story. Jo could have at least a weekly byline in the *P. I.* for months, filling in with color, the why, whenever things got slow with the cases or the trials. But Luke wasn't the story she wanted to tell. *Makah* was the story she wanted to tell. Tyler's story, in particular. There had to be more than a handful of kids like him to talk to. Lost in the middle, fighting money and drugs and inertia, just trying to find a way out. Those were her stories now, and probably the ones Vi had been wanting her to tell all along. She had a feeling Randy's was far from complete. His would be the first one she'd start with, figuring out exactly why he was dead. It was all still too much coincidence for her to accept suicide.

It was night now, completely black on the sea. The buttery lights in the small wooden cabin were up. Under different circumstances, it might have been charming. The boat slowed as they approached the dock. Jo couldn't wait to get off the water. She couldn't wait to wrap her arms around Laura, either, no matter how much it hurt. That was the only thing left in her entire world that was absolutely clear.

THERE'S NO LAW AND ORDER TWIST, AND THAT JUST MAKES IT ALL WORSE

For what she hoped was the last time, Jo piled out of her Volvo parked in the gloom of Lost Valley. Luke's workshop sat dark. Menace had been replaced by a hollow sense of decay; despite the sunny day the yellow sheet-metal walls were flat and dull.

Jo wanted more answers from Ashley. More why. More about Randy Fuller, in particular. When did you give up on a story before it was finished? Never.

She knocked at the house, already expecting the booming of the barking dogs to preface her arrival. Instead, from inside she heard only whimpering, panting, and pacing.

The heavy door swung open.

"You're Joanna Ford." The small, dark-haired woman was far more alert than Jo's last encounter. Melissa Sorensen vibrated alert this morning.

Jo shoved her hands into the pockets of her pea coat and nodded, once, slowly. "Yes."

"Come in. I owe you a little more than a cup of coffee. But it's a start."

Gratitude had not been what Jo was expecting. "Ah – sure. And, um – call me Jo." She followed Melissa into the kitchen. The woman's movements were controlled and efficient as she pulled a mug out of the cupboard, filled it, and handed it over.

"Melissa, I just wanted –"

"Before you even start – I knew he was sleeping with someone –" Luke's wife tapered off , then took a sharp breath in through her nose. "But I had no clue it was Brittany." She picked a sponge out of the sink and began rubbing small circles over the cook top and a stain that looked like it wasn't about to go anywhere soon. "You cleaned up my mess for me. What I ought to be saying here, is thank you." She finally looked up at Jo, brown eyes even darker than they'd been only minutes ago.

Despite the outwardly friendly gestures, Jo was sure she hadn't misjudged the anger. It was there, but it lay carefully controlled, far below the surface. She kept her silence, still unsure where this little show of gratitude was headed.

Melissa continued. "Luke ought to be dead for what he did to Brittany. To Tyler. And - to me. And to Ashley. *Bastard*." She scrubbed harder, before throwing the sponge with a wet *thwack* into the sink.

Maybe the anger wasn't so far under the surface.

"Melissa —" Jo waited to see if the first-name basis was going to fly. The woman kept her gaze fixed out the kitchen window to the sun-lit valley beyond. "I'm sorry. I really, really am."

"What have you got to be sorry about? Nothing. It's Luke that's sorry. It's me that's sorry. It's me that's giving up a job and a life and a world to move back home with my parents, because how the hell do you think I can ever show up anywhere on this Island again? Forty-five years. This is my home. I went to school with Kyle and Nancy Roebuck. And now I can't look either one of them in the eye. How could I? If I were them, I would have already come around to kick my sorry butt. Twice. It's not *you* that's sorry."

"You're right."

"You're not here to listen to me whine. What can I do for you."

Before Jo could answer, the two German Shepherds padded in, nails clicking on the hardwood. They took turns at the stainless-steel water dish. Then they looked up at Melissa, black ears perked. "No." She pointed toward the living room. They trotted directly to side-by-side beds. She stared at their retreat. "Those dogs never used to beg. Never used to bark. Not when I was home. Not when I was at Kibo. When I had work on the Island, it was good. Even between me and Luke. It was all okay before I had to start commuting. Then I turned my back, and I let my house go to hell. I left my daughter alone with that absolute waste of a man. And now she's just as bad-off as anyone. Ash isn't going to spend another second here digging herself deeper. Neither am I."

Jo jumped at the opening in the angry monologue. "It's Ashley I came here to see, actually." The house was quiet. But in between Melissa's low-voiced invectives, she heard occasional footsteps upstairs.

"That's not going to happen."

"I just have a couple loose ends. Randy Fuller —"

"This business is done."

Jo touched a hand to her tender side. The new stitches burned. "I don't think it is done."

"I'm grateful to you, Ms. Ford. But not that grateful. As far as I'm concerned, as far as Ash is concerned, this is all over."

"I certainly feel for you, Ms. Sorensen. But Ashley lied to me. About the copper, about Jered Brasier, about Brittany. And I think there's more than that. I want to know why. Don't you?"

"She lied because she doesn't owe you anything." The volume finally started to edge up on Melissa's voice. "She was high on everything you can get high on when they took her off that boat. You can't hold anything she said against her. You know Hill came through here and pulled all kinds of drugs out of her room. She's been expelled from MHS. Have to get her GED now, if she still wants to go anywhere. And you can know for damn sure she won't be leaving our house for anything except church. It's past time I brought God back into our lives." The woman's voice bounced off the walls by the end of the proclamation.

Jo thought God was maybe as far from any of this as you could get. She stood, intending to head upstairs to find the girl, when Ashley appeared on the landing and strutted into the kitchen.

"I'm not going anywhere with you, Mom. I'm staying here. With Jered." She glowered at Jo. "As soon as he's out."

"Your father might have stood for that attitude. But I won't. Not anymore. You'll go where and when I tell you, because otherwise it's the court that will. Don't think I won't turn you over. After everything you've done."

"Dad deserved everything he got. And so did Brittany." Ashley chucked the cap of her water bottle across the counter, went to the fridge, filled it with milk, and slammed the door. "I'm done covering for him. Jered's the man in my life now."

"You shut your mouth right now, young lady."

Ashley continued. "I'm sick of people telling me what to do. I'm sick of you. I'm sick of this house. I can live with Harmony, with Jered's mom, and you can't stop me. I'm staying on Makah. You're as useless now as you've ever been."

The teen was anything but the zombie of a girl Jo had encountered on the rainy afternoon a couple weeks ago. She was wearing a tank top, tight, and Jo scanned the skin that showed. Not a mark, no redness or irritation anywhere that she could see. Of course, Ashley would be on her best behavior. But there was a fresh edge about her. A hum that reminded her of – Randy Fuller, the few times she'd talked to him. Ashley was desperately trying to get clean.

"I know I've let you down, Ash," Melissa said. "But that's no excuse for this. I know your father –"

"Dad's an idiot. Brittany didn't care about him. She and Tyler were still all crazy about each other. But her parents wouldn't let her date him. She was just mad at me for making her sell that copper overtown. That's all. They both got what was coming to them." Brazen, Ashley looked right at Jo as she said this. Then, in a fi ne imitation of Jered, she thrust up her chin and stared down her mother.

Jo realized the girl was just begging her to push the issue, to uncover more ugly to punish Melissa. Happy to oblige. "Ashley what else do you know about Brittany's death?"

"Shut up, Ashley, and you stay that way." Melissa thundered at her daughter. She came around the counter and took Jo by the arm. In the living room, the dogs stood, shook themselves out, and fixed their brown eyes on Jo.

Ashley sneered at both of them and shrugged. "Brittany should have been more careful about how she used. Bad business to trust junkies to remember what they bought." The more she talked, the more she sounded like Jered.

Jo did the math and took her shot. "Is Jered the kind of father you want for your child?"

Ashley grinned. "Yeah you are clever. Meaning I ain't telling you shit. Jered's a good guy, deep down. He acts like he's a baddass, but he's not."

"Did he have anything to do with Brittany's death?"

"Shit no. Like I said, he's all show. I wear the pants in my family."

"Was Randy involved?"

Ashley began to laugh. "You're so smart and you never learn. You not figure out yet that Brian Stewart's the boss here? He wants you to do something, you do it. Dad needed help. He was a fucking wreck over Brittany. Dumbass couldn't even wrangle a body dump. Jered and I show to the cabin that morning – ignorant you know, of what had happened –" Ashley looked anything but ignorant. "We saw Dad sneak out of the house that morning. So Jer and I followed to see what we could learn –"

"Shut up, Ashley." Melissa's wiry fingers sunk into Jo's bicep. "No more. You're leaving. Now." The smaller woman was strong, and Jo sure as hell wasn't up for any kind of combat. Mentally or physically. More importantly, she heard two low growls building as the dogs started toward her from the living room.

Jo tried to get off one more shot. "So Brian had Randy —"

But Melissa clamped down harder, nudged Jo in the rib, and Jo wasn't in any kind of fighting form. She shook her arm free and walked toward the entryway. Ashley didn't follow, but Melissa did.

Jo turned to her. "Who do you think your daughter was really bad mouthing in there? Do you think she was angry at her friend? Or at her father?" The answer was neither. "She was punishing herself, Melissa. Ashley's smart. She's smarter than Jered. How he's manipulated her into staying with him, I don't know. But I'd guess it might be tied up in making Luke – and you – pay. And feeling like she's got someone, something, she can control. But she can't control Jered. Or Brian Stewart. You need —"

"My family's none of your business." Melissa replied coolly. "I said thank you for exorcising that snake from our lives. But you've worn out your welcome. Don't try to contact me or my daughter again." Melissa shut the door in her face.

Stay away from the Sorensens? Not a problem. Jo nodded once, slowly. She studied the clear blue sky as she headed for the car. Ashley would be doing her penance, that was for damn sure. But it wouldn't be anywhere near enough to make up for Brittany, or Tyler. She got in the car and dialed Hill. He picked up in three rings.

"Hey Elijah. That extra set of prints you found with Brittany Roebuck, on the fentanyl patches?"

"What about it?"

"Did they match Luke?"

"Nope. Nothing yet, but we're still working on it."

"You're planning on running them against Ashley Sorensen?"

"It wasn't a priority, but we will. DA's still working out charges on her." Hill's voice was a little bit quieter now. "Hate to pile on a family that's already at the bottom of the heap. But if we can actually tie her to Brittany's death – the Roebucks deserve anything they can get."

"They sure do. Thanks, Elijah."

"Anytime. One more thing, Jo. We got the full autopsy back on Tyler. Overdose. Nothing that says otherwise. Luke denies any involvement, and his story on it hasn't changed at all. You could say Luke had a hand in it, and you'd be right. But legally, there's nothing I can do. I'm sorry. I think the kid just couldn't take it. Relapse isn't a long road."

"Oh," was all she could manage. "Okay. Thanks. Has Luke said anything more about Randy Fuller?"

"Nope. All he'll say is it was all his fault. Sounds like he's covering for Ashley to me."

"Ashley's insinuated that her dad contacted Brian after Brittany died – that Brian – and Randy – helped dispose of the body."

"If that's true then Luke won't say a word about it. We all know Brian's making sure of that."

Jo's panicked search for Laura confirmed that assumption. "Right. Okay. Thanks."

"Take care, Jo."

She hung up. Never in a million years had she expected any of this. Two people dead, more in jail, and major daily headlines out of a few measly petty thefts. But it had never been about the thefts, not really. It had been about the drugs, and the lives being burned like dry kindling to fuel the addictions. The thefts, even the murders, Randy's suicide, Tyler's overdose, were just collateral damage. Just the ever-telling secondary misdeeds. When she'd put on that first fentanyl patch, Brittany Roebuck probably hadn't seen any of this coming either.

Jo pulled out of the Sorensen driveway and headed home.

HEY, HEY, HEY PAULA

"Put that cat on a diet, would you? She's a chunk." Jo bent down to pet Paula, stretched out at Vi's feet on the porch. The cat swiped at her. Jo shook her head and handed Vi a cup of coffee. Not to be rude, she waved at the deer graz-ing near the ring of rhododendron skirting the edge of the older woman's yard. One of them ignored her completely. The other flicked a tail, and she'd swear it wasn't random. It almost felt – insolent. Jo smiled. This place was getting to her.

"Nonsense. Svelte as your mama, aren't you Paula-girl." Vi looked up from her roomy Adirondack chair – it looked custom built to her dimension – and pointed Jo to the other.

It had to be at least fifty degrees, despite Christmas knocking on the door. The sun and clouds had played leapfrog all morning. Plenty warm for a North-west al fresco chat.

Jo didn't mind it. After the month she'd had, the shadow on her horizon she'd yet to face, being outside felt preferable to being locked inside, staring at the walls.

"You get a call back yet on that biopsy?" Vi cut right to it.

"Yep. "Re-run, only worse the second time around. Late stage two invasive cribriform carcinoma. Early stage three, if you're less optimistic about things. Hasn't metastasized though, so, hey, good news. I'm going in on Monday to talk about next steps."

"Gonna be tough, however it shakes out. Where you thinking about getting your TLC?"

Her boss really was a better interviewer than Jo had given her credit, all these months. "I'm taking Laura with me now. She likes Dr. Nokes."

"Glad to hear you're learning new tricks. You'll be glad for her."

"I already am." First Abish, then Sorensen. Men who'd let their inability to deny themselves anything, ruining the lives of everyone around them. That wouldn't be Jo. Laura wouldn't be collateral damage. "You're right. I might need a little help with things. With the –" Jo paused and cleared her throat. "The cancer. Laura. Figuring out how to not make a mess of living here. Stop pretending I'm just a tourist."

"Good girl."

"Vi, I don't know what you know, or don't, or - it seems like you put together what's happening with Beth. What happened, with Beth, I mean. And I don't know what you think of me. I know what I think of myself –"

"Not my job to think anything of you. That's for you and Laura and your God, if you've got one, to sort out."

"Okay." Vi hadn't exactly absolved her. But what she'd said about not being judgey seemed true to form. "Speaking of secrets. You mentioned you'd learned your own lessons about that?" Jo watched the other woman's eyes. They stayed plastered on those deer.

Vi chuckled. "Touché. Brian Stewart isn't the only person on this rock who understands the concept of leverage. I know Frank's been filling your head with his ecosystem crap. He loves that metaphor. It's a little on the nose, but he's right. About balance. Long as what I got balances even with what Brian's got, well, I think the applicable term would be *ho-me-o-stasis*." Vi drew the word out and winked at Jo.

Jo's hand dropped to her pocket, to the rough outline of the object inside. The small sculpture that had been on Tyler's windowsill in his hovel to the view. She'd actually gone to Tyler's place yesterday, just to see the mountain, and the small sculpture, one more time. The cabin was open, of course. She'd helped herself to the sculpture. There was no one else who'd miss it, after all.

Jo swirled the last of her coffee in the mug. The deer's ears winked this way and that. She thought about the Sorensen's dogs. Sweet, until they weren't. Ashley curled into the couch, telling Jo everything she wanted to hear.

"I'm sorry about Randy, Vi. I don't know how you wanted the story to go, but I know you wanted some kind of meaning to it. Brian having him clean up after Luke's mess with Brittany – I don't think there's any meaning in that. Or justice for him. Or you."

"Or Ilse." Vi stood and gathered her flowered house coat. She strolled to the railing of the deck, Paula at her ankles. The morning mist was long gone. The sun was out, but it didn't give much light. "Luke ruined more than one family.

And you're the one who's done the most here to make that right. I was stupid, how I behaved. I was scared to do what I had to, and I made it worse for you, Jo. I'm sorry for that."

"Yeah, well. I'm still here. Randy, Brittany, Tyler, the Roebucks." Jo saw their hollow eyes, their heartless shuffle across that crowded gym floor. Those people were done with life, even if it wasn't done with them yet. "What a goddamn way to lose a kid. Luke was the Roebuck's *neighbor*. A man they trusted. I can barely stand to leave *Laura* with someone new. But to leave your daughter with someone, to know how that had ended up? I'll be honest, Vi. I don't really know what to do with myself. About being sick. But it's Tyler and Brittany – they're really getting to me. Brittany, I know I couldn't have done anything. But Tyler – it's like I've been standing out in right field for a year waiting for a fly ball, and I get one, and it just falls right out of my glove."

"Bases loaded, to boot."

"Yep." Jo folded her hands in her lap and tapped her thumbs. "I'd convinced myself that nothing I did on Makah would ever matter. I was wrong. I finally did something that mattered, and it pushed Tyler Sealth to overdose. Jesus."

"I haven't started singing yet, Jo. You're making a start. Anyone's struggled with drugs will tell you, and they're right, that Tyler's choices were his own."

Jo nodded. "Maybe. Jered's at least going to jail, and he'll have a conviction on his record. But I don't know about Brian Stewart."

"Listen. Here's what everyone knows, and what you're not going to get anywhere but here. Stewarts been doing what the Stewarts do even longer than I've been around. Brian's old man, Henry, he kept a handle on things. At the factory and in the drug trade. Kept a balance between what he sold to the Island and what he gave us. Kept Makah floating when it looked just about ready to sink. Hell – he bankrolled the grocery store for an entire year after the GM took off to Mexico with the goods in '76. But Brian doesn't seem to have that same inclination. I thought he'd be more like his old man. I thought maybe Randy'd be the worst that ever came of it all. But I was wrong. And I'm sorry for that. And now Hill has Luke *and* Randy to use for blame, and he'll just let them wear it. All the folk on the Island whose kids never get sent to school in second-hand jackets will get to keep feeling superior about the pitiful Island rednecks. They'll get to say, 'at least we're not those poor people,' and carry on, clueless as the day they drove their German cars onto this rock."

Jo couldn't do anything but stare. "You should have told me this. All of it," she finally said.

"When? When you came over for a little coffee talk like this? When you said, 'yes Vi I'd love to come over for a piece of pie?' Because I don't remember any of that. I told you any of this before you learned how things work here, you would've gone charging off at Brian Stewart like a drunk bull. Could've all gone a lot worse, on that front."

"Still – "

Vi waved her off. "Yes. Yes I could've told you all of this. But I don't know – would you have understood about Makah and community? Or would you have just seen another shitty little rural town taking one on the chin, destined to suck air until we died like the rest of Rockwell's America? I let you do the work you needed to do. You think I could ever tell you anything?"

"I'm sorry. Things have really slipped out of control, I think."

"Are we talking about you, or are we talking about Makah?"

"Both."

"Yes ma'am. Because apparently we're all bad at asking for help."

"I think I've got it covered, now." Jo ran a finger around her coffee, took the second step on the long road to confession. She'd admitted to herself what she'd done. Now, to another person, and as soon as she could get up the guts, to the one who mattered. "I don't intend to keep secrets. If Luke Sorensen didn't teach me about what happens when you cheat and lie –" Jo paused and cleared her throat. "I know I'll need help. I know how to ask, now."

"Good girl. I was dead wrong, how I went after you about how you went after things. I see that now. But no one ever wants to pull tall weeds. Brian's got a fistful of nasty, slithering, poisonous skeletons hidden away. Don't know about you, but I'd rather mine stayed hidden. And that makes me weak, I suppose."

"I don't think it makes you weak, Vi." Jo would never consider this woman weak when it came to anything. "But I think it makes you vulnerable. What good did keeping anyone's secrets do Tyler? Its already all over the place. What Luke's done, why he killed Brittany. How did anyone think it wouldn't come out?"

Vi finally swiveled her gaze over to Jo and clucked. "Sorry to poke the bear, honey. But what you got up to with that woman overtown – did all the what-if consequences stop you? Knowing you'd be keeping something from Laura -

from yourself?"

"No. Apparently it didn't stop you either, Vi. Whatever it is Brian's holding over you."

"I did what I did. I've spent my fair time atoning for it. I never expected to get out from under it, but I did try." Vi misted up. "You see now, what I'm saying? Listen to me here. Really listen. When the devil's everywhere, locking your doors doesn't make a spit of difference. Good gets where it's going to go, and so does bad. The Roebucks lock up, they don't, it wouldn't have kept Brittany in. It sure won't bring her back." Vi's gaze wandered to the dense woods, then off to the clouds soaring by, fast, above them. "Brian Stewart's hell on wheels. And he'll get his, in the end. But we've all got a little sin operating in us, don't we? What about when the bad's inside the house, Jo? You went and locked it all in with you, good and tight, until all you heard was the king of lies whispering about that sweet little number Beth Berge. What'd that get you?"

"Nothing good."

"That's right. On the other hand, I'll bet you my beloved Paula girl that there isn't a deadbolt to be found inside the pearly gates."

"So which applies to Makah, Vi? Which is the reality? An evil trap or a perfect oasis?"

"I don't have a clue, Jo. But I'll tell you we've got it heads and tails over you mainlanders. For a couple reasons. One of them being, we've got you. And I'll fess up to this – what you might consider reality, truth versus how you see the truth – it's never been much use to me out here."

IT'S COMPLICATED

When the winter sun did appear over Makah, it was perpetually setting. The thin, campfire quality of the light made Jo feel as though it would disappear any second. It was glorious while it lasted, a cinematographer's dream. Green was greener, red, redder, yellows in shades she hadn't even seen back east in the fall.

Mossy sticks, rust-colored fir needles, lay scattered over every inch of the yard. The ubiquitous pattering rain last night had been followed by a hardy windstorm. After Vi had left, Jo had sat next to Laura in bed, trying to read a book. Eventually she just gave up and listened to the howling trees.

The wind had also kept Laura up much of the night. Jo had checked all the locks on the doors before bed, worried Laura would wander if Jo dozed off. She'd paused at every door to ponder what it might be like to spend an entire day, or more particularly night, with them unlocked. She thought about the way the dark in the Pacific Northwest was so, so quiet. No crickets or cicadas to say *'everything well tonight, just as always,'* or on the flip, signal danger, or change, when they cut out.

A carpet of brown maple leaves covered the chicken run this morning. Jo was clearing it out and throwing down straw where it had bogged up. She waved to Laura, sitting on the back porch with Spot. The sun and relative warm had him wound up. He'd tear-ass around the outside of the entire house, then tumble in front of Laura belly-up to receive appreciation for his physical prowess. At one point he brought her his ball. She took it, and her throw was surprisingly good. Vastly improved, in fact.

One or two of the hens were near Jo, hunting for any good grub the new-ly-soaked ground might offer. The braver ones were used to her now. She smiled at them clucking and pecking. She stripped her work gloves, shoved them into the back pocket of her jeans, and walked over to Laura.

"Just you and me today, babe. You want to hit up Salish Point? There's something I need to talk to you about."

The storm was bound to have churned up plenty of sea-treasure for Laura to discover. Their beach walks made Jo believe in hope. The crisp cool air, the rocky terrain, the slow pace, stopping to bend down, stand-up. All of it helped Laura's strength and balance. They were good for Jo in about the same way. When they were quietly walking side by side, it was like nothing had ever changed. Those moments, when the water teemed with bright, white-gold light, alive over the blanket of blue, strolling with Laura's hand in hers, those moments were right. She could take in a few more and appreciate them and not wish to be somewhere else. For the first time since they'd arrived on Makah, Jo didn't want to be anywhere else. She hoped too, after she told her about Beth, that Laura would want her to stay.

"Yeak okay. We should talk," Laura replied.

"Yep." Jo latched the chicken run, came to sit next to her on the porch. She didn't look at her wife, who didn't look at her. "You gave Spot a run for it Have you been working with your dad on your arm?"

"No. With Wendy."

"Oh." Laura's OT Wendy was more on the case than Jo thought. "Okay. Well, come on. Daylight's wasting." Jo grabbed coats and keys from the mud-room and ten minutes later the Ford-Tanaka trio was waterside.

They weren't the only ones with the idea. A couple dozen Islanders were smattered here and there along the rocky beach looking over Mount Rainier. Spot barreled out of the car to sprint almost out of sight with three brand new best-mutt friends. A mile or so across the rippling blue water planes were coming and going from SeaTac airport. A shout or a laugh came here or there, but Jo mostly heard only the steady wind, the shush of the waves, the chatting gulls, and underneath it all, the quiet.

She winced as she eased into her cleaned-up pea coat. Her chest was sore. The biopsy site was still angry at being so thoughtlessly manhandled last week. She ignored all the fear and the what-ifs as they surfaced, and instead turned her attention to the golden glittering Sound. What-if wasn't now.

She smiled as she helped Laura into her indestructible red parka and wound her scarf tight, tucking her long black hair underneath to keep it from blowing everywhere. It would tease out in a while, but right now it was good.

Her phone buzzed in her pocket. She almost ignored it. But Jo didn't think there'd come a day when she didn't give in to curiosity. It was Valerie.

"Hey it's Jo."

"Hi – are you out with Laura? I just stopped by your place with a blackberry pie. I made two, and I know your week could have gone better. I'll leave you one on the porch. If you're not going to be out too long, it should be safe from the raccoons."

"That's sweet, Valerie. Thank you." Jo squeezed Laura's hand. She'd come around a little to Vi's way of thinking. If she were going to lose the thing that meant the most to her today, it wasn't going to be because she'd left the mudroom unlocked. "But you can just go ahead and leave it in the kitchen. The door's open."

The End.

BECAUSE IT TAKES A VILLAGE

Thank you to all the beta readers of this book and the training-wheel works that came before it: Susan Denaro, Amy Kolquist, Katie Wire, Cindy Powell, Bill Henderson, Shana Kelly, and Craig Sanders. Thanks to Jan Dorn for enthusiastically reading everything early and being kind when it wasn't warranted, and Julie Jaffee who taught me to love journalism.

Thank you to Conor Plunkett, Patsy Atwell, and Claire L .Fishback
for donating your time and talent.

Thank you to Bill Henderson at Lighthouse Writers Workshop and my indomitable cohort for your loving support and insightful critique: Britnie Kane, Jenn Green, Laurel Kallenbach, the Phillips Huffeldt and Van Hoevenberg, and Sue Gelber.

A huge thank you Rocky Mountain Fiction Writers and Sisters in Crime, two fantastic, volunteer-run writer's organizations that light the fires and provide the spirit and the know-how to so many. Thanks particularly to Shawn, Joe, Michael, and Craig in south Denver who read my stuff …
and were kind when it wasn't warranted.

Thank you to all my Scripps sisters for instilling me with the confidence, courage, and hope to undertake and follow-through on such
an audacious endeavor.

And finally, this one's for anyone who has ever been knocked down but not out.
Still with her.

A SNEAK PEEK AT
TETHER

THE SECOND BOOK IN THE JO FORD MAKAH MYSTERIES

Learn more about upcoming books and the world of Makah Island at
www.MakahIslandMysteries.com

THE SET UP

The half-moon split the rural landscape in black and white. Pin lights of stars offered their weak glow as he neared the barn. In the thin moonlight, a shining white X crossed the face of it.

It was just past midnight and the rest of Makah slept easy. The capitalists, the laborers, the artists and their slaves. There were so many small farms just like this on the Island, so many prisons for the wild things these people claimed to love. Hours ago, he'd seen their owner bring the dogs inside the unlit house. That did not mean the domesticated brutes were sleeping.

The wet night-air would be thick if it weren't so cold, but still, he had waited until the time was right. He proceeded with deliberate footsteps through the knee-high grass. Green with spring rains, it shushed against his pant leg, gentler than his own breathing, the only sound in his ears. Not a cluck from the chickens nor a bump from the rabbit cages. He slipped through the side door of the barn. It was pleasant inside. The horses' heat and gentle breath filled the darkness with warm, and sweet smell. He listened to them shift in their stalls. Down toward the end, he heard one struggle to her feet. Her hooves slipped, then crunched on the brittle straw. She whinnied, soft. He clicked on a tiny pocket light and made his way to the end of the aisle littered with hay.

He met her with a treat. A lovely, tart apple. She nodded vigorously. He reached up for a good scratch behind her ears as her big lips slipped over his offering before she took it gentle with her teeth to nibble it down. He waited until she finished, shone the light in the stall. Couldn't leave even a seed behind.

Now, hurry. No time to delay, to spend with these magnificent creatures. There was more business to attend. He touched foreheads with the beautiful blaze of white marking her ebony body, and he mourned the dead horse. It was how he thought of all the animals he was sacrificing, as already dead.

He took off a glove to feel her velvet as he stroked her nose. He rubbed her powerful shoulder. She chuffed, nudged his chest. He rested his head against hers. "You'll be free soon, Aggie."

BITCH OF A HANGOVER

Vi Mitchell stuffed Paula-cat under her coat and slammed the door on her creaking Datsun pickup. She looked left, she looked right, and crossed the quiet two-lane road. The cool morning air smelled like new-cut cedar and bitter, fresh-roasted coffee beans. It helped ease the quease of her stomach. Dark blend at the Roastery and a warm hello from a friend would go as far to help the dry, tight, ache in her head as the aspirin she'd already taken.

Last night had finished pleasant at Jo Ford's. Bit of a back-road buzz to escort her home, but she could drive these old roads in the blind-dark and that wasn't a lie. She'd cajoled Connie into the car with her years ago to help her test the theory out. A little laughing, a little girlish screaming later, they'd made it from Connie's to her place safe and sound.

She was woman enough to admit that she'd be just fine right now, if she hadn't decided after returning home that a tumbler of brown liquor to ease her sleep would be just the ticket. Well, tell the truth, the *real* mistake had been getting out that worn cigar box. Pulling out that old black and white photo of Henry. One tumbler had turned to two, and somehow Johnnie Walker had walked himself right into the recycle bin.

The light-gray quality to the world around her told her it'd be a partly sunny one. She rubbed a fist in her eyes and squinted around. Yep. Leaves on the rhodies lining the roadside had green to them. She'd see that yellow orb for sure this morning. But the rusty halo on the half-moon last night and the red-sky sunrise also told her that wouldn't last long.

She set Paula down on the gravel at the bottom of the stairs leading up to the long front porch running the length of the Roastery. The noisy Siamese yowled and wound her way through her ankles. Vi groused, then smiled. Good to have her back. Couldn't stand those weeks she'd been missing this winter. Never felt so lonely. Except maybe these days. She was ghost-lonely again, Paula or no.

Sunny days seemed fewer by number and the dwindling of them pushed the lonely to the fore. But nothing to be done. She'd cast her die and she'd live with her choices. Had all these years, after all.

The few steps up to the wooden porch winded her. She fished in her pocket for a handful of quarters. They clinked in the honor jar brightly. She stuck her mug under the spigot on the air pot and pulled the lever. Happiness, coming right up.

Nothing. Course it was empty. She snapped at Paula. "Be right back."

The rattling hum of the bean grinder greeted her sensitive ears as she stepped through the swinging door, mouth still watering for a little Makah Orca Blend. But the familiar sound was all that met her. A group of gray-bearded old-farts sat on a red wooden bench under the narrow display shelf that featured every style of every coffee bag the place had put out for the last thirty years. Vi had a collection just like it. Each of them cast down his eyes as she surveyed her silent friends.

"Who died?" She stepped up to the counter and considered she was being dramatic. She would of heard hours ago if they really had lost someone.

"No one. Damn *Geoduck's* out again." Garrett Zellerhoff made a nice job of missing her gaze and re-arranging the pastries as he answered.

"Son of whore." *The Geoduck.* "We dig deep," was their motto, and what they dredged up and dished out was as poisonous as their moniker at red tide. Spilling secrets and telling lies. Two sins Vi Mitchell would never engage in at her paper, *The Quartermaster*. Particularly in a small town, the mixture was pernicious. When sprinkled with a little truth, the lies took on a air of reality, and folks swallowed them down whole.

A new edition of the anonymous rag might explain the pall in the air. But not the peculiar aversion folks seemed to have picked up for her. The oil slick in her stomach turned a big slosh and came half-way up her windpipe.

"Something about me in there, son?"

"No ma'am."

"Then what gives?"

Garret turned his back. He filled her cup, then retrieved a copy of the paper from the recycle bin. "Coffee's on the house."

"Thanks." Vi glared at him and snatched the paper.

She ignored the people ignoring her and let the door slam on her way out, hinges and bell declaring her consternation. She set her coffee on the porch rail and got to searching. Vi whipped through the paper to get to the point of the whole ridiculous exercise. She skimmed the filler, parody articles, "Dangerous on-Island shortage of rusting Subarus announced by the Makah Town Council." "Area man refuses to compost coffee grounds despite tripled fines."

She paused her search right at the centerfold. "Will Moody get slapped with ABC fine for un-permitted septic system?" That one started with the truth but wasn't nearly mean enough – even if the County decided to follow up.

Next down. "Connie Wilcox caught pocketing what isn't hers at Aunt Ida's." Not true at all and damn hurtful. Vi almost dropped the thing then and there to call and comfort her friend, surely moaning into her coffee already.

But before she did, her eye caught the big story. The intended mark. "Valerie Larsen – Makah's favorite veterinarian and her nasty past."

The bench behind her rushed up to meet her generous posterior. At her feet, Paula yowled and swatted Vi's leg claws-in, then settled. Vi began reading, though she did not want to.

"Two decades ago, a strung-out junkie made her way to Makah Island. Kicked out of UW Medical and flooding local drug dealers' dens with her family's plentiful cash, Valerie Larsen, addict and adulterer, isn't anything like the girl next door she wants you to think she is…."

Twenty-some column inches of truth, lies, and innuendo followed. Valerie would certainly lose work over it. Worse, the girl would lose a lot of dignity she'd fought for tooth and nail over twenty years here. Damn.

Well, it wasn't the *whole* story. She was the only one who knew all those secret little ins and outs, and Vi could at least count her chickens over that. But it was enough. Fat tears dropped onto the paper resting on her lap. A couple folks paused to rest a hand on her shoulder on their way in or out. Not one of them stupid enough to say a word. Garrett brought her one of the vegan bran muffins he made special for the Roastery, and that was nice of him. She fed most of it to Paula.

She cried for a minute, then took another minute to think before she got in the truck to get over to Valerie's. More than her gut and her heart aching over a girl she cared about very much, who hadn't done much to invite this shit storm, Vi had more than a passing anxiety that her own indiscretions would come out before this was all over. And that would hurt others far more than it would her. She also had more than a worry to spare over the fact that she knew many of these secrets shared by *The Geoduck* to be some of Mr. Brian Stewart's closely held prize possessions. Either he was spending his capital just for the fun of watching the resulting chaos, or someone was spending it for him. Either way – well – the time had come for Jo Ford to put a stop to it.

She'd proved she was up to the investigative task. They didn't hand out Pulitzers like goldfish at the carnival, and there was a murderer already in jail since she'd moved to Makah. But that girl had troubles of her own these days. She was up further in them than she'd been last time Vi put her on the hunt. Fact was, right now Jo needed Makah's help a lot more than it needed hers.

ABOUT THE AUTHOR

Amy Drayer grew up a free-range kid on a small, rural island in the Pacific Northwest, then migrated south to attend Scripps College in California. After earning her degree in Women's Studies, she moved to Washington, D.C. where she worked in politics for more than six years. Now living in Denver, Colorado with her wife, she's a graduate of the inimitable Lighthouse Writers Workshop Book Project and an active member of Rocky Mountain Fiction Writers and Sisters in Crime. She writes mystery novels, short stories, and essays (humorous and otherwise), and is currently world-building for a spec fiction novel.

Read more of Amy's work at www.MakahIslandMysteries.com

253